LOVE WAS A DANGEROUS GAME—
ESPECIALLY WHEN YOU PLAYED FOR KEEPS

"Doe, you are a delight I can't live without. Not any longer." Rogue's piercing blue eyes seemed to sear right through her flimsy rose-colored chemise, kindling an answering flame of passion deep within her.

Slowly, deliberately, she stepped toward him until she was close enough to feel the heat of his body on her almost-bare skin. "Aren't you afraid of the distraction?" she murmured teasingly, as her arms slipped around his neck.

For answer, he pulled her against him, his lips crushing hers in a kiss that spoke of tenderness, but also of a deep, driving need to be joined with her in the full fury of his passion. "I don't care who sees, or what happens," Rogue whispered harshly, "not as long as you're playing straight with me." And their lips met again in an explosion of passion and tension that promised a night of unforgettable ecstasy. . . .

SATIN AND SILVER

SATIN AND SILVER

JANE ARCHER

A SIGNET BOOK

NEW AMERICAN LIBRARY

PUBLISHER'S NOTE

This novel is a work of fiction. Names, characters, places, and incidents either are the product of the author's imagination or are used fictitiously, and any resemblance to actual persons, living or dead, events, or locales is entirely coincidental.

NAL BOOKS ARE AVAILABLE AT QUANTITY DISCOUNTS WHEN USED TO PROMOTE PRODUCTS OR SERVICES. FOR INFORMATION PLEASE WRITE TO PREMIUM MARKETING DIVISION, NEW AMERICAN LIBRARY, 1633 BROADWAY, NEW YORK, NEW YORK 10019.

SIGNET TRADEMARK REG. U.S. PAT. OFF. AND FOREIGN COUNTRIES
REGISTERED TRADEMARK—MARCA REGISTRADA
HECHO EN CHICAGO, U.S.A.

SIGNET, SIGNET CLASSIC, MENTOR, PLUME, MERIDIAN AND NAL BOOKS are published by New American Library, 1633 Broadway, New York, New York 10019

First Printing, February, 1986

1 2 3 4 5 6 7 8 9

PRINTED IN THE UNITED STATES OF AMERICA

for Lady Luck

I

Spring 1883
HOT DESERT SANDS

1

Smoke spiraled upward, cloaking the You Bet gambling hall in Tombstone, Arizona, in thick clouds of tobacco fumes. Players sat hunched over cards held tightly in rough, dirty hands. Some leaned over faro tables, their eyes flicking between the dealer's box and the brightly painted faro board. The room was silent except for the loud exclamation from a winner or loser now and then. Several men stood at the bar, the low murmur of their voices mixing with the steady clink of bottles and glasses.

At a round table in the back of the room, Shenandoah Davis absentmindedly pushed a stray hair back from her face. Her thick auburn hair was unruly at best and seemed to draw all the color from her pale, smooth skin. Her slanted green eyes gave her the look of a cat. A small straight nose and full rosy lips were set in a face of prominent cheekbones, square jaws, and a pointed chin. She was dressed in satin, its emerald green a foil to her eyes, its sheath design a complement to her figure. There was absolutely no expression on her face or in her body as she carefully watched the players at her poker table.

The man across from her suddenly reached out. He started drawing the pile of chips in the middle of the table toward him, gloating that he had won the hand.

"Not so fast, Jack," Shenandoah said firmly, stopping his movement with her words.

He looked up, frowning.

"I'll see you and raise you five."

Tension raced around the table, Shenandoah casually dropped her right hand out of sight below the table. Slowly drawing up the fabric of her skirt, she gripped the butt of the derringer strapped to her right thigh. Her uncle had taught her never to trust a man, especially if he were losing. Although she had never shot a man, she was ready. She had to be.

"Now, Shenandoah," Jack Shannon said, his voice rough as he carefully kept his hands above the table. "I'm calling you on this one."

Relief flooded Shenandoah. There would be no quick gunplay, like she had seen so many times. Not yet anyway. Jack was backing off. She relaxed, but only slightly. He was going to lose and he wasn't going to like it, especially since he would lose to a woman. But none of Shenandoah's thoughts crossed the calm, cool features of her face. In the six years since she had left the East, she had learned to stifle her emotions. It hadn't been easy at first, but her life and livelihood depended on that ability. Now it was second nature.

"Hey, Shenandoah, you going to fold, or what?"

Shenandoah mentally shook her head, trying to bring her thoughts back to the present. This wasn't like her. She absolutely couldn't afford to let her mind wander. "Sure, Jack, that's what I always do, isn't it?" she replied jokingly.

There was a murmur of laughter from the players who had already folded. Shenandoah Davis was known to have a steadier hand and head than anyone else in Tombstone, now that her uncle, Fast Ed Davis, had left.

Pushing several chips to the center of the table with her long, slender fingers, she said, "I'm meeting your call, Jack. Let's see what you've got."

The beefy Irishman smiled through a full beard as he slowly, deftly laid out an impressive straight, five consecutively numbered cards. "Let's see you beat that."

Shenandoah did not blink an eye, nor let a smile reach her lips as she laid down her own hand. A flush, five cards of one suit.

Jack Shannon jerked out of his chair, fury snarling his features. His chair hit the floor with a crash. All noise in the gambling hall ceased. "A flush," he growled. "That's the last time you beat me, sharper, or any other miner." He pulled out the forty-five he'd had hidden under his vest.

Shenandoah jerked on her own gun, but it caught in her garter. As she tugged on her derringer, she watched Jack cock the hammer of the Colt. She knew that in less than a second she would be dead. Just as she expected to feel the slug from Jack's pistol hit her breast, the loud retort of another forty-five sounded in her left ear.

Jack Shannon looked surprised. Blood suddenly spurted from his chest. Still glaring at Shenandoah, he aimed his gun to shoot her, but his strength had left him. He shot, and the bullet lodged in the wooden floor. Then he collapsed. Loud voices suddenly filled the room as men rushed over to Jack Shannon and somebody yelled for the sheriff.

Shenandoah slumped against the gambling table, scattering the flush that had ended a man's life. She felt sick. The shouts of the miners gathering around Jack rang in her ears. Another man was dead. Life and death were so closely intermingled in the West that no one thought anything of adding another body to Boot Hill. But she did. She felt responsible. Yet, she was still alive, and grateful for that.

She suddenly remembered that the shot which had killed Jack had come from her left. Slowly she turned in that direction.

A tall, broad-shouldered stranger stood there. His feet were planted firmly apart as he snapped a large Colt .45 back into the black leather holster that hung low on his right hip. He was wearing Levi's, a black shirt, a black leather vest, and black boots that reached to his knees. He had a mane of thick blond hair, and he was staring directly at Shenandoah. She could not miss the clear blue eyes, deeply tanned skin, angular face, and broken nose. In a clean-shaven face, his lips were full and sensual. He was obviously a dangerous man, as well as a quick draw.

Shenandoah licked her dry lips, cleared her throat, and started to thank the stranger.

"You need a drink," he said before she could speak. A large, strong hand drew her to her feet. She was a tall woman, but he was much taller. In a few strides he led her to the bar.

Tim the bartender looked at Shenandoah in concern.

"Two whiskeys," the stranger ordered.

Tim glanced at Shenandoah for confirmation. It was well known that she didn't drink, in order to maintain a clear head when gambling.

"I don't—" she began, but was interrupted.

"Two whiskeys," the stranger repeated, this time more firmly.

"Yes, sir," Tim said, reacting to the authority in the man's voice, and set two glasses on the bar.

"But I—" Shenandoah tried again.

"Drink up," the stranger said, pushing the full shot glass toward Shenandoah. "You're white as a sheet." He threw his own drink back in one gulp, then looked at Shenandoah again.

Still feeling unsteady, Shenandoah decided that a drink might help. She took a sip. The liquid burned all the way down. She felt a little warmer. She took a bigger sip, choked, coughed. Her eyes burned. She inhaled deeply. Embarrassed, she glanced over at the stranger. There was no expression on his face.

"Finish it," he ordered.

Obediently, feeling quite unlike her usual self, Shenandoah obeyed him and downed the drink. She did feel a little better. She shouldn't have let the death affect her so much. She had seen plenty of men die in six years, but never one directly connected with her.

"You look better," the stranger said.

Turning to glance up into his piercing blue eyes, Shenandoah answered, "Thank you for saving my life and for suggesting the drink. I don't know what came over me. I usually—"

"Staring death in the face can shake the best of us." Glancing at her leg, he continued with a slight smile on his lips. "Damn fool business."

"What?"

"Wearing that derringer on your leg."

Shenandoah blushed, then felt like a bigger fool, realizing the man had been staring at her leg earlier. While he had probably seen lots of women's legs, it was an intimate point which embarrassed her. She suddenly wanted to get away from him. He had seen too much of her, physically and emotionally. Besides, he was right. Her uncle had warned her that her thigh wasn't a practical spot to carry a gun, but she had never really expected to need it.

"You should find a better place for that derringer, or change professions."

She inhaled deeply, felt more like herself, and said, "You're right. I will. Let me thank you again. You were quick."

He nodded, his eyes roaming over her face, then lower to the wide expanse of creamy skin exposed by her low cut gown. When he looked back, she saw the heat burning there.

She turned from him, saying, "I'll be all right now, Mr. . . ."

"Call me Rogue."

She didn't want to call him anything, nor did she care to know his name. She just wanted to get away from him. "I'm fine now, Mr. Rogue."

"Rogue Rogan."

She inhaled deeply again, trying not to simply run out of the gambling hall and to the safety of her room in the boardinghouse. She didn't feel as if she could take much more this day. But the man had saved her life. She must at least be polite.

"Mr. Rogan. Thank you. I'm much better. I think I'll simply go home and lie down for a while. You will excuse me?"

"I'll walk you."

Becoming quickly exasperated, she said, "Really—"

"Excuse me, Shenandoah, but is this man a friend of yours?" Sheriff Walker asked, stopping beside them after he had inspected the body.

Of course, she would have to explain what had happened. She should have thought of that. "Sheriff Walker, this is Rogue Rogan. I had not met him before Jack . . . Jack . . ."

"Jack always was a hothead. But it's been worse of late. The miners are getting mean. The silver's playing out. Water's filling the mines. They know their time here is limited. They're going to shoot quick, and to kill. I don't want to see you buried up on Boot Hill, Shenandoah."

"I don't either, Sheriff Walker."

"I got the story from the gamblers around your table. If what they say is true, you were damned lucky this guy was there."

"Yes, I'm lucky to be alive. I have a derringer which I wear strapped to my . . . my leg. But it caught in my . . . my garter, and I couldn't . . ."

The sheriff tried not to grin, but amusement was plainly written on his face.

"Really, Sheriff. It may not seem smart now, but I never thought I'd have to use it. Miners are hot-headed, but I should have been more cautious. I honestly hate what happened to Jack. I'll pay for his burial."

"Right decent of you, Shenandoah. Officially, I have to remind you that guns aren't allowed in Tombstone, but unofficially you and I both know that everyone just hides them and wears them anyway. Damn lot of good the law does, but you know the ordinance."

"Thank you for reminding me, Sheriff Walker, but you know a gambler has to be prepared."

"I know, Shenandoah." The sheriff turned to Rogue Rogan and said, "You're mighty quick with a gun. Don't suppose you were hired to come to town?"

"I'm just a stranger here on business. Sorry if I disturbed the peace of your city."

Sheriff Walker snorted. "Peace! Well, I'd appreciate it if you walked a little more cautiously around here. And put that Colt away. I'm just warning you this time, but next time I'll have to do something about it. I wouldn't want to hear you'd shot anybody else."

"I'll remember that, Sheriff."

"Good. And, Shenandoah, I don't want any more trouble from you, either."

"There won't be any. I'm going home right now."

"Want one of my men to walk you back?"

"I'll see her home," Rogue Rogan interrupted, his voice low and firm.

Surprised, Sheriff Walked looked at the stranger, then back at Shenandoah. "That right?"

Shenandoah quickly turned from the bar. "I can take care of myself. Thank you, Mr. Rogan . . . Sheriff Walker." She walked swiftly away from them and headed for the front doors, but not before she had seen the raised eyebrows on the stranger's face. Well, she amended to herself, I can usually take care of myself.

Outside, the sun was just beginning to rise in the east as she hurried down Allen Street away from the You Bet. Allen was the main street through Tombstone, and its north side sported most of the dance halls, saloons, and gambling houses in town, while the south side boasted the best shops and restaurants anywhere. The miners who frequented the south side of Allen rarely crossed over to the shops on the north side. As a gambler, Shenandoah spent most of her time on the south side, too, and like other gamblers she was a night person, sleeping during the day and waking in the afternoon to work all night.

It was cool now, but when the sun rose it would be

a typically warm, sunny day in the southern Arizona desert. Allen Street no longer teemed with miners drinking and gambling on a Friday night. There was no doubt the citizens of Tombstone were moving off to find more fertile fields. Even her uncle, Fast Ed Davis, had left, after he won part interest in a silver mine in Leadville, Colorado. He was there investigating the mine and gambling situation, and if all looked good, he planned to send for her.

Alone for the first time in twenty-one years, Shenandoah grew lonelier with each day, making her realize just how important her uncle was to her. Not only did she miss him, but she worried about him, too. He was not a young man anymore, and his health had not been good since he had fought for the South in the War Between the States.

If not for the letter she had received the day before, she would probably have been even more lonely and worried, especially after the terrible shoot-out in the You Bet earlier. The letter was from her eighteen-year-old half-sister, Arabella White. Arabella was coming West to join her, and would be arriving any day.

Shenandoah was glad she and Arabella were finally going to be reunited. After their parents' death in a tragic carriage accident six years before, they had been separated. Their mother had been a gentle Southern woman who had lost her first husband, Shenandoah's father, in the War Between the States, then had married a Northerner and moved to Philadelphia, Pennsylvania. Arabella had been born shortly thereafter. She and Shenandoah had been inseparable until the accident.

Shenandoah's uncle had come from the West to claim her, determined that she would not be raised in the North. He vowed to teach her his trade—gambling—so that she would always be able to take care of herself. Arabella's aunt was determined to raise her younger niece as a well-educated young lady of Philadelphia. Neither relative could afford to raise both of the children, and since there were no other living family members, they were separated despite their protests. They agreed to write to each other until Arabella could come West.

As Shenandoah mounted the steps to the small, neat boardinghouse where she lived, she suddenly realized that she would have no warm, cozy house in which to welcome her sister. Shenandoah and her uncle had been constantly on the move for six years, traveling from mining town to mining town. There had been no place for a permanent home in their lives, or the possessions that went with one. They traveled quickly and lightly, taking clothing and little more, and lived in boardinghouses or hotels.

After her uncle had lost everything in the war, he had never wanted the attachment of home and land again. However, Shenandoah remembered the happy years with her mother, stepfather, and Arabella in Philadelphia. She had never told her uncle, but she missed that settled family life.

Arabella had spent the past six years in Philadelphia, living with her aunt in a small house. She might not like boardinghouses. Nevertheless, it was possibly better that Shenandoah was inviting her into a small bedroom, with meals served in the dining room below. Shenandoah hadn't cooked a meal in six years, nor cleaned a room, nor sewn very much. In fact, all that her mother had been teaching her had been pushed to the back of her mind so that she could concentrate on learning to gamble from her uncle's lessons. She had caught on quickly, but she was suddenly concerned about all she had left behind.

Arabella had spent that time learning to be a proper young lady. She would know how to entertain and how to take care of a house. As she compared her knowledge to her sister's, Shenandoah became acutely aware of how different she was from other young women. She realized how much she had missed, and yet how much she had gained, too. She could only hope that she and Arabella had not grown too far apart.

She quietly slipped into her upstairs bedroom, shutting the door firmly behind her. As she took the pins from her thick auburn hair, she watched herself in the oval mirror above the washstand, and wondered if she were lonely for more than her uncle and her sister.

Shaking out her hair until it hung heavily about her waist, she thought about the fact that she was twenty-one and had never had a steady beau. Men were attracted to her, but she and her uncle had moved so frequently there had never been time for building friendships. Or perhaps she had just never met the right man. Whatever the case, she felt something stir deep within her.

She had been alone for a month. Her sister was finally coming to join her. A man had just died at her poker table, and a stranger had saved her life. If she were feeling a little unusual, it was no small wonder.

She must think of happy things, like her sister's letter. She sat down on the side of the bed, pulled Arabella's letter off the table next to it, and began to read.

March 28, 1883

Dear Shenandoah,

Aunt Edna's long illness is finally over. It was a blessing that she could pass on and be out of pain. However, I'll miss her, even though I'm finally free to come West.

After all the debts were settled, there was not much left. I have enough to buy my tickets to Tombstone, a few clothes, and presents for you and Uncle Ed.

I hope I won't be a burden on you two, but I can help out. I am educated, can sew well, and keep house. You know, all the usual things.

I should be arriving around the fifteenth of April, so look for me then. I can hardly wait to be with you.

Your loving sister,
Arabella

Shenandoah put the letter away, still hardly able to believe her sister was really scheduled to arrive anytime. She had already made plans for Arabella's arrival. Her uncle would really be surprised and pleased when they joined him in Leadville, which she hoped would be soon.

Taking off her satin gown, Shenandoah lay down on the bed. As she pulled the soft quilt over her, she determinedly shut her eyes. She had to get some sleep before the long night of gambling ahead. She did not expect a hard night, nor unusually long hours, but she and her uncle had been known to stay in a game for more than thirty-six hours straight, and she wanted to be prepared.

Sleep did not come, for she couldn't shake the visions of a stranger with piercing blue eyes and golden blond hair which flooded her mind.

2

Rogue Rogan walked with a light, easy gait toward the Blue Miner saloon. Under his vest, a gunbelt was slung over his right shoulder, tightly notched so that his holstered pistol hung under his left armpit. The weight of his Colt .45 reminded him of the man he had shot earlier that day at the You Bet gambling hall. He always tried to avoid killing, but when it was his life or someone else's, he preferred to live. And he considered Shenandoah Davis part of his life until he got her to Leadville, Colorado.

He thrust open the double swinging doors of the Blue Miner and entered. Shenandoah Davis was going to be very surprised to learn that the man who had saved her life had also been assigned to take her safely to her uncle in Leadville. After meeting her, he had the impression she wasn't going to like those plans. He hadn't been too fond of them either until he had met the lady in question. Now, if he could keep them out of trouble, he might enjoy the trip.

The saloon was thick with smoke, and the smell of

cheap whiskey permeated the long, narrow room. Rogue shouldered his way to the bar and ordered a whiskey. He towered over most of the other men leaning against the smooth surface of the long bar. With a full shot glass in his hand, Rogue surveyed the room, looking for a large dark-haired miner.

Tom Burton, a well-known Welsh miner, had agreed to meet him there. Supposedly, there wasn't any better expert than the Welshman. Burton had grown up working in the Welsh mines in Britain and was much sought after in the West, and Rogue wanted the Welshman to manage his silver mine in Leadville. All he had to do was persuade him to move to Colorado.

Rogue walked deep into the room and took a seat with his back to the wall at a small round table. Burton had said he might be late when Rogue had met him that morning at the silver mine he managed. Things were not going well in Tombstone. The water table in the mines was rising and pumps were being installed in the mines, though the water still poured in. Rogue didn't think Tombstone would be around much longer.

He swallowed half the contents of the shot glass with one quick motion of his left hand. He set the glass down, then grimaced. The stuff was worse than usual. If a man's gut wasn't rotted out by the time he was twenty-five, he was lucky. Rogue had made it to twenty-eight with his stomach intact, but probably only because he usually bought good whiskey. That type of liquor wouldn't even be available in a place like the Blue Miner.

Rogue grimaced a second time, then downed the rest of his drink. The burning in his stomach didn't stop the action in his mind. Neither did the inactivity of waiting. He reluctantly took out several telegrams, folded and refolded, from his inside vest pocket. Carefully spreading them out on the table, he read them again.

February 11, 1883
   Your father and uncle dead. Blackie moving on mines. Come immediately.

Cougar Kane

March 4, 1883
   Getting worse, Blackie mining. Come soon or lose silver.

Cougar Kane

April 1, 1883
   Time running out.

Cougar Kane

Rogue refolded the telegrams and replaced them in his pocket. He sighed, eyed his empty glass, then decided to wait for another whiskey, though a drink was all he could think of that might help his problems.

He knew Cougar was right. He needed to get back to New Mexico before Blackie finished. Left alone long enough, Blackie would mine all the silver out and leave nothing but empty shafts. Rogue was not going to let his cousin steal what was rightfully his, not while he had a chance to get back to New Mexico and stop him.

But he had to have money to stop Blackie. He needed money to hire men to work for him, money to buy equipment, and money to feed and house them all. He didn't have that kind of cash and he needed time to get it. But he was as short of time as he was money, because until he could get back to New Mexico, Blackie would continue to mine.

Cougar Kane was a good friend, an old friend, but Rogue was not going to try to borrow from him. Cougar hadn't seen Rogue in ten years, though Rogue had let this friend know where he was over the years. Cougar knew nothing more about him, and Rogue was determined not to return home after ten years empty-handed.

His silver mine in Leadville, Colorado, was therefore important to him and he needed Tom Burton to work for him. With an experienced man like Burton helping, the silver could be brought out in probably half the normally allotted time.

Not that Rogue was inexperienced. He had been all over the West in ten years, striking gold or silver in the camps. But he had never hit it big, or not big enough to come out ahead. Besides, when he was younger, whatever he'd had was lost to fast-talkers, tricksters, gamblers, and women. But he didn't regret those years. He'd had a good time. He had learned a lot. But now was the time to become serious.

Getting the silver out in Leadville was tricky, not just picking the shiny nuggets out of a stream, or sluicing to separate the gold dust from the sand. The silver in Colorado was mixed with lead and had to be smelted. That was why the place was called Leadville. Burton had experience in this type of mining and Rogue needed him. If Rogue could start bringing the silver out of what he believed to be a very rich mine, he could then sell the bulk to smelters, or pay them to melt it down. Either way, he could start bringing in the cash needed to go home to New Mexico and stop Blackie.

It all depended on time. He had never been so short of it. That was why he had come to Tombstone. He had to hire Tom Burton, and soon. In person, he thought he could persuade the miner to work for him, then escort him back to Leadville. Time would be saved, and that was what mattered most, especially since Cougar's telegrams were becoming more urgent.

That brought him back to Shenandoah Davis. Suddenly he wished he had bought a whole bottle of the rotgut. The woman was nothing but trouble. Her uncle had failed to mention that she was breathtakingly beautiful, icy and fiery at the same time. She was also a brilliant gambler. That was a dangerous combination for any man, or men, associated with her. She was a woman to covet, and he had not been immune to her charms.

But she was still trouble. He hadn't wanted to be saddled with her at all. But his damn fool of a partner had lost his eighth share of the mine to Fast Ed Davis in a poker game. He had only taken on the partner to provide him with mining funds. Now he was reaping the rewards of that decision. Fast Ed had thought his niece would like Leadville, especially the gambling, and since Fast Ed had decided to stay there to help with the mine, he had wanted his niece with him. Rogue had agreed, pressured by Fast Ed, who had insisted that it would not be out of Rogue's way to escort his niece back with him to Leadville.

Although it was not out of his way, he wondered how many more men he would have to kill to get her safely to Leadville. He realized he was being hard on her. But he was pressed for time, and she was a beautiful distraction he simply didn't need. Still, he had hoped she would be grateful when he saved her life. Grateful, and perhaps anxious to thank him. She hadn't been any of those things, and he had a feeling it was going to be a long, cold trip back to Leadville.

Suddenly a shadow fell over Rogue's face. "Hey, Rogan, you've got a face longer than a cat's tail," Tom Burton said, plunking down two shot glasses and a bottle of whiskey on the table.

As the big, burly man sat down, Rogue said, "Just thinking of mining, Burton."

"That'll make any man's face long," Tom agreed, then twisted the cap off the bottle and poured two drinks.

"By the way, speaking of cats, did you find your cat?"

"Damned miners!" Tom exploded. "I tell you, if I ever find out who stole my cat, I'm going to—"

Rogue laughed. "You going to give the cat back to the miner you stole it from?"

Tom looked sheepish a moment, then said, "Well, anyway, if I'd had all the cats I could sell to miners, I'd have made my fortune and gone home long ago."

Rogue nodded. "Rodents back in your shack now that the cat's gone?"

"Back? I'm going to have to move out, it's so crowded. In fact, think I'll drink to the rodents. Nothing beats them—not miners, not Indians, not water, nothing. Here" —and he raised his glass to Rogue—"here's to our furry little friends."

Both men downed their whiskey, then grimaced as they set the glasses down.

"Worst damned liquor I ever drank. I think the stuff could melt silver. By the way, did you hear the Brayton brothers hit the stage again this afternoon?"

"Yes. But I'm new in town. Who are these Braytons?"

Tom poured them both another drink and said, "Three brothers who rob the mine-payroll stage just often enough to keep themselves in whiskey and women."

"Can't the sheriff catch them?"

"No. They've got a Mexican hideout. He chases them to the border, then has to stop." Tom swallowed his drink in one gulp, frowned at the empty glass, then added, "But this time there's an added twist to the robbery."

"You mean the woman?" Rogue asked, downing his whiskey.

"Yes. Kidnapped. From what I hear, she was beautiful, young, and fought them like a wildcat. But Tad Brayton is as lusty as they come and has a notorious appetite for women. I just hope the young lady has a rich, powerful family. It'll take that to get her back from the Braytons."

"Suppose you're right. Say, Burton," Rogue added, changing the subject to get down to business, "Tombstone's days are numbered. You know that. Leadville is going strong. I've got a mine there that is sure to deliver. Look." Rogue took a leather bag out of his pants pocket, opened it, then dumped a large solid rock onto the table.

Tom Burton picked it up, rolled it around in his hand, sniffed it, then laid it back down. "Looks good, but how does the assay report read?"

Rogue pulled a folded piece of paper from his vest pocket and handed it to Burton.

After reading it, Tom whistled softly. He picked up the piece of ore again, weighed it in his hand, then glanced back at Rogue. "I'd say you got a real winner there."

"I'd say so too. I've worked in mines all over the West. But the process is different in Leadville and I want your expertise in getting the silver out."

Burton was quiet as he silently examined the sample, his mind obviously working over the possibilities of Rogue's offer.

"I'll pay you top dollar," Rogue added, his voice quiet yet forceful.

Tom looked up at him, set the ore down, then shoved it and the assay report toward Rogue. He poured two more drinks. Finally he said, "I'd be a fool to pass up such an offer. Let's drink to Leadville."

Rogue nodded, smiled, and upended his whiskey.

Burton did the same, then asked, "How soon do you need me?"

"Yesterday."

"In a hurry?"

"In a devil of a hurry. I've got another problem hanging over me that forces me to push this deal through as soon as possible. When can you come to Leadville?"

"Well," Tom said, running a hand over his full black beard, "I'll have to finish up a few matters, tell my boss. You know, the usual things. It'll be several days to a week."

"Make it a few days and we'll travel together," Rogue said firmly.

"I'll sure try. I was getting the itch to move on, anyway. I hear Leadville is the place to go."

"It's got silver, all right. By the way, there'll be another person traveling with us."

"You hired another miner?"

"No, not exactly. I have a partner in Leadville. He wants me to escort his niece there."

"Oh no," Burton groaned. "Some pasty-faced, tight-stayed missy, no doubt."

"Not quite," Rogue said dryly. "You may know her. She gambles in Tombstone."

"Shenandoah Davis!" Tom Burton sat bolt upright. "You mean Fast Ed Davis' niece?"

Rogue nodded.

"You mean the coldest, most beautiful woman in Tombstone?"

Rogue nodded again.

"You mean the best damned gambler I ever played with?"

Rogue nodded once more.

Burton poured another drink, downed it fast, then said, "I won't have a dime left by the time we get to Leadville, and I'll be so much in love I'll be sick. I don't know if I can take it, Rogan. Cave-ins, Indians, fights, robbers—I can handle. But a woman like that? I don't know if I'll be in heaven or hell."

Rogue couldn't keep from chuckling. "She's not that powerful, Burton. If necessary, we can sit separately from her."

"Wouldn't think of it. I'd defend that woman with my life. Damn, I'm beginning to look forward to this trip." He stood up suddenly. "Here, you finish off the bottle. I've got to get ready to go. As far as I'm concerned, the sooner the better." He took several steps away, then turned back. "I'm even going to take a bath."

Rogue watched the big Welshman stride purposefully from the room, then poured another drink. Shenandoah Davis was going to be a bigger problem than he had originally thought, irresistible as she was. Maybe on the journey *he* could warm her cold heart, for he sure wasn't going to leave that pleasure to Tom Burton.

3

Shenandoah could feel Rogue Rogan's piercing blue gaze on her from across the room. It was close to midnight. All evening long Rogue had paced the floor of the You Bet gambling hall, pausing from time to time at the bar or at the faro table, though his main interest had obviously been her. She didn't understand his actions, nor did she understand her unaccountable interest in him.

For the first time since she had begun gambling, she was truly distracted from her cards. She frequently found herself looking for his tall form among the miners crowded into the Yet Bet. Her game suffered, but she postponed the break that might have helped her regain her poise. Somehow she felt that if she left the poker table, Rogue would seek her out, and she didn't want that. She didn't want to have another personal confrontation with him. He was very dangerous to her, dangerous in a way she had not thought possible.

Perhaps she was distracted because she was worried about her sister. Arabella had not arrived on the afternoon's stage, and she knew the coach had been robbed and a young woman kidnapped. There was no reason to believe the young lady was her sister, for lots of women were drawn to Tombstone by the quick money to be made in a mining town.

Nevertheless, her sister was due to arrive any day and Shenandoah was anxious to talk with Sheriff Walker. Once she knew that her sister hadn't been involved, she would relax.

The sheriff, his deputies, and a posse had ridden after the Brayton brothers, and Shenandoah awaited their return.

Even as Shenandoah thought about her sister, her eyes still followed Rogue, noting how his thick blond hair glinted in the light of the oil lamps hanging from the ceiling. Although clean-shaven, he wore his hair long, so that it brushed the collar of his black shirt. As Shenandoah watched him, she thought of running her hands through that mane of golden hair. Her eyes traveled lower, imagining her hands on the thick muscles of his arms and chest. His legs were long and hard-muscled, and he walked with the natural grace of a wild animal. She suddenly wanted to smell his scent, feel his warm flesh next to hers, hear his voice calling her name.

Shenandoah was shocked at her own thoughts. She had never had such fantasies about a man before. As far as actually touching a man in such a way, she was a complete innocent. Of course, she knew what went on between men and women. She had seen too much around gambling halls and saloons not to, but she had no experience herself. It was a completely unaccustomed train of thought and she didn't quite know how to deal with it.

She started to look away, but Rogue had caught her stare and the message he was returning went well beyond the propriety of the public gambling hall. Shenandoah blushed, something she did not often do. She felt as if he had read her thoughts, and she was embarrassed and furious with herself. Tearing her gaze from him, she discovered that she had lost at poker again.

She was professional enough to know when there was no hope. She threw in her cards, finally taking a break. Rogue Rogan was ruining her ability to concentrate. If she didn't compose herself, she was going to lose her gambling reputation in one night.

Standing, she smoothed out the skirt of her burgundy satin gown. Trailing her fingers along the decorative fringe, she checked to make sure the bow was still tied in back over the small bustle. Deciding that all was in order, although wishing on this one occasion she had worn a gown with a little less revealing bodice, she walked toward the swinging doors. She planned to get a cup of coffee at a small café nearby, but mainly she was determined to try to forget the man who disturbed her tranquillity.

But Rogue Rogan had other plans. He caught up with Shenandoah halfway to the doors and steered her out into the cool desert night air. Against her protests, he escorted her to the side of the gambling hall, into an alley, and out of the light of the streetlamps. There he stopped. Still without speaking, Rogue pulled her close, so close the heat of their bodies mingled.

Stunned by Rogue's quick and decisive action, Shenandoah stared up at him, automatically masking her expressions. With his hard strong hands holding her shoulders, she seemed to forget that she had decided to stay far away from him. Now all she could think of was the overpowering maleness of him as he towered over her.

Rogue looked at Shenandoah's upturned face for a long while in the moonlight, then slowly lowered his head, giving her time to refuse him. The scent of lavender filled his nostrils. She trembled slightly but did not move away as his warm lips softly brushed hers. He kissed her again. This time his lips lingered longer and his warm hands caressed her shoulders. He raised his head to look at her face again. Her eyes were large and luminous, but no expression touched her features.

Shenandoah opened her lips to say his name, but Rogue took them, this time pushing past into the warm sweet depths of her mouth. He pulled her body against his, molding her soft curves to his hard frame, as if he could not get close enough. His kiss beckoned her with fire, urging the spark within her to ignite and burn with him.

But Rogue did not feel her give or soften against him. She did not return the kiss with a passion of her own. She did not respond to him. For her, they might as well have been sharing a game of poker, and Rogue thought he had just lost the first hand.

He slowly released her. The touch of her had affected him more than he had expected. She had fired him, tantalized him in a way he had never felt before. He wanted her badly, but he needed her to want him, too. He wanted her to be all fire for him, but she was all ice. Yet he sensed that dormant fires lay deep within her, waiting for the right man to ignite them.

Rogue felt her tremble again as he let his hands slide down the smooth, soft skin of her arms to her hands. When he enclosed them in his large strong ones, he said, forcing a touch of humor to his voice, "Was that: 'No, Rogue Rogan, I don't want to go outside with you, and no, I don't want you to kiss me'?"

Shenandoah took a deep, shaky breath and replied, "That's right."

"You didn't try to stop me."

"You were going to kiss me, Rogue, one way or another. Now that it's over, you can go on your way."

"You think one kiss is enough?"

"For us it is. There are other women around for you."

"There are other women, but only one Shenandoah."

"I'd like to go back in now, Rogue."

"Not yet. I have several things to tell you."

Suddenly loud, raucous laughter interrupted their

conversation, as several miners stumbled drunkenly down the street. When they had moved on, Rogue pulled Shenandoah deeper into the shadows of the alley.

"I think we should go, Rogue."

Rogue's voice was very husky and his breath was warm on her face when he said, "Shenandoah, I want you." He pulled her closer, wrapping his strong arms around her small waist. "I really mean that. I want you and I can be very, very gentle." As if to prove his point, he dropped soft kisses along her temple to an earlobe, which he teased between his teeth for a moment before saying, as he felt her tremble against him, "I know you like me, Shenandoah. I can see it in your eyes when you forget to guard them."

Shenandoah took a deep breath to steady herself, then carefully said, "My likes and dislikes have nothing to do with this. I'm a gambler. I don't—"

"You're a woman, too. A woman I want very much. Come back with me to my hotel room tonight."

Shenandoah put her hands against the broad expanse of his chest and tried to push him away, resisting the urge to do just the opposite. Never had she been affected by a man this way, never had she simply wanted to forget all else and follow his lead, and never would she have guessed she had the emotions that were threatening to overwhelm her.

"Doe," he said softly, using the diminutive of her name for the first time. "I wouldn't ever hurt you. Come back with me right now."

"No." Her voice was little more than a whisper and her hands were suddenly stealing up around his neck with a will of their own.

He groaned and crushed her against him, feeling her breasts flatten against his chest, enticing him, making him long for more of her, all of her. He quickly found her lips, smothering her with short, quick kisses before delving deeply into her mouth with his searching tongue. She moaned and clung to him, beginning to respond to the deepest inner core of her body. Her skin flushed. Her coldness was suddenly enveloped in fire as his kisses blazed a path that she hurried to follow.

Then Rogue's mouth left hers. He nibbled along her jawline, tracing her throat with kisses. Her breath caught as he supported her with one arm, leaving the other hand free to find the outline of her breasts through the satin of her bodice. His mouth soon followed his hand, and the heat of his kisses singed the pale rounded skin of her breasts exposed by her low-cut gown.

"Doe," Rogue groaned thickly, covering her with small fierce kisses as he made his way back to her soft, yielding lips. "Shenandoah, I must have you." Then he began to lead her from the alley, an arm possessively wrapped around her waist, keeping her close to him.

For a moment Shenandoah was too caught up in her budding emotions to think at all, content to feel the heat of Rogue's body warming hers, content with the languor that had stolen over her.

Then she said, "Where are we going, Rogue?"

He was walking very determinedly, and answered softly, "Back to my hotel room. Isn't that what you want?"

Shenandoah's heat turned to cold. Everything froze inside of her. This was too fast. Rogue Rogan was a stranger. "No! Stop!"

What?" Rogue slowed down, obviously confused.

"I'm not going back to your hotel. You didn't really think that I would, surely."

Rogue stopped walking. They had reached the end of the alley and stood near a streetlight. His voice was heavy when he said, "I thought you'd go because you wanted me. Shenandoah, I—"

"Hey, Rogue?" a large, burly man called from across the street. "Is that you?"

"Oh no," Rogue said under his breath as the large man quickly crossed the street and joined them.

"Tom Burton," Shenandoah said, smiling slightly at the man who had lost to her many times at poker.

"Say, Miss Shenandoah, I'm about ready to go. Even had a bath today." He beamed from Rogue to Shenandoah, then back again. If he noticed Shenandoah's flushed face or the arm Rogue quickly dropped from her waist, he didn't say so.

"How nice. Are you leaving Tombstone?" Shenandoah asked politely, trying to still her racing heart.

"Am I leaving Tombstone?" Tom guffawed several times, clapped Rogue on the back, then said, "That's real good, Miss Shenandoah. Real good. Huh, Rogue?"

"Sure is. Well, we've got to—"

"Miss Shenandoah, I'll make sure you get the best seats all the way."

"The best seats?"

"Sure. You deserve the best. And will we ever play cards. It's a long way to Leadville, you know."

"Leadville?" Shenandoah was turning from confused to wary. She looked from Rogue back to Tom. "Just who is going to Leadville?"

Tom Burton suddenly got very quiet, then said softly, "Didn't Rogue tell you yet?"

Shenandoah looked at Rogue. "No, he didn't. He had other things on his mind."

Rogue looked uncomfortable, scowled at Tom, then said, "I was waiting for an appropriate time."

"Would that have been tomorrow morning?" Shenandoah asked, her voice cold.

Tom looked very confused and said, "Well, didn't mean to let the cat out of the bag, but I'm looking forward to our trip, Miss Shenandoah. See you both later." He quickly strode away, whistling a happy tune.

Shenandoah looked back at Rogue. "Perhaps you should start at the first."

"Now, Shenandoah, what I have to tell you has absolutely nothing to do with what happened earlier. I swear it. Two separate matters."

"Go on."

"Your uncle asked me to escort you to Leadville."

"So you were planning to use this little arrangement tonight to get me to go all the way to Leadville.

Everyone knows my uncle is in Leadville. It was an easy ploy, or were you planning to take me somewhere else? And what does Tom Burton have to do with it?''

"Damn, you're making this a lot more complicated than it is, Shenandoah. It's just like this. Your uncle is my new partner. Since I was going to be in Tombstone anyway, he asked me to escort you back."

"And you came to Tombstone to . . ."

"Hire Tom Burton to manage my silver mine in Leadville. That's it."

"Thank you for the explanation. You'll understand if I don't believe you. Good-bye, Mr. Rogan." Shenandoah turned and started away.

Rogue stopped her, pulling her back toward him. He handed her a letter and said, "Your uncle thought you might not believe me. He sent this. Tom and I are leaving in a few days. I want you to be packed and ready to go."

After Shenandoah had read the letter, she said, "So, my uncle *is* your partner and he thinks I would be safer traveling to Leadville with you. I wonder just how safe he would consider me if he knew—"

"I made a promise. I always keep my promises, Shenandoah. I will take you safely to Leadville. Whatever you choose to think now, I wanted you. I thought you wanted me, too. It was that simple. But you're not going to cause me to break a promise. We'll be leaving in a few days, and you'll be going with us."

Taking a deep pleasure in thwarting him, Shenandoah smiled sweetly up at Rogue and said, "Well, this is one promise you won't be keeping. I'll be happy to join my uncle, but I won't be traveling with you. I don't need or want your escort. And that begins right now." She turned and started walking toward the You Bet.

Rogue didn't stop her this time. Instead he fell in step with her. "You're damn bullheaded. Well, I knew you were going to be trouble the moment I saw you."

Shenandoah glared at him, then looked away.

"Nevertheless, you're going with me to Leadville."

Just as Shenandoah started to push in the swinging doors at the You Bet, she heard some commotion down Allen Street. Looking in the direction of the noise, she saw Sheriff Walker and the posse returning. Suddenly all she could think of was Arabella. Her argument with Rogue no longer mattered. She pushed past him and hurried to see if a young woman was riding with them.

Surprised, Rogue walked to her side and said, "I guess you're as anxious as everybody else in town to know if the sheriff caught the Braytons."

Shenandoah didn't answer him, hardly hearing him as she watched the posse begin to disband as it progressed down the street. There seemed to be no young lady with them. When the sheriff was abreast of them, Shenandoah called out, "Sheriff, did you find the young woman?"

Sheriff Walker, tired and dusty, stopped his horse

near Shenandoah and said, "Sorry, but the Braytons got away again. They took the girl with them."

"Oh no! Do you know who she is?" Shenandoah asked, appearing calm, but feeling her heart begin to race.

"Yes, got it from the stage company. Arabella White. I'm going to try to locate her family."

Shenandoah felt faint a moment, but didn't realize she had swayed until she felt Rogue's strong arms supporting her. "Sheriff Walker," she said, her voice hardly more than a whisper, "you have just notified Arabella White's family."

"What?"

Rogue's arms tightened around Shenandoah.

"I'm her half-sister. I was expecting her. But . . . but I never dreamed anything like this could happen to so innocent a young woman. What are you going to do about it, Sheriff?" Shenandoah asked, her voice growing stronger as she determinedly held all her building emotions in check.

"Nothing I can do. I'm sorry. It's out of my jurisdiction. They're in Mexico. As far as I know, nobody even knows where the Braytons have their hideout."

"Sheriff, surely you can help, or someone in town can. I'll pay anything."

"I can't help you, Shenandoah, other than giving you what little information I have. And as far as hiring someone in Tombstone to go into Mexico and fight the Braytons, if they could find them, I don't know of a solitary soul who would take that on. You might be able to hire someone from out of town, but—"

"There isn't time, Sheriff. Someone must go after her right away. The longer she's with them, the worse it will be."

"You can ask around town, but the Braytons have a mean reputation here. Come on down to the jail later and I'll give you all the information I have. You can get her baggage from the stage company. I'm sorry, but that's all I can do." The sheriff tipped his hat, nodded regretfully, then rode on down the street.

Shenandoah slumped against Rogue's hard strong body for a moment, then determinedly pushed her emotions down and pulled her strength together. There had to be a way she could save her sister. Suddenly she knew what to do.

She stepped back from Rogue, looked him over, then said, "You're good with a gun, aren't you, Rogue Rogan?"

Rogue frowned. "If what you're thinking—"

"Help me, Rogue. You heard the sheriff. No one else will. I can't leave my sister down there all alone with those men. She's so young, so innocent."

"Shenandoah, I've just hired Tom Burton and we're going back to Leadville in a day or two. I'm on a real tight schedule."

"Nothing could be more important than saving a young woman."

"You don't know what you're asking of me."

"Yes I do. I'll pay you. Whatever you want. I

don't have much money, but I can earn more. Please help me, Rogue.''

"I don't want your damned money."

"Rogue, *please*. I can't leave my sister down there. If you don't go with me, I'll have to go alone.''

"You can't do that, Shenandoah. Not a woman like you."

"I won't simply go off and leave her. Help me." She stepped closer to Rogue, her eyes large, luminous green orbs. "Rogue, whatever you want of me you can have if you'll just help me get my sister back.''

"Damn, Shenandoah, don't look at me that way and don't say that. I'm not made of stone.''

She put her hands on his arms, feeling the muscles straining there. "Rogue, I mean it. I'll pay you, whatever you want.''

"Hell!" He shook off her arms, paced several steps away, stood with his back to her a moment, then walked back, his face set. "I must be out of my mind, but all right.''

Shenandoah threw her arms around his neck and hugged him close. "Oh, Rogue," she murmured, "thank you, thank you.''

He set her from him, looked sternly at her, and said, "I'll take you to Mexico, but it'll be a bargain. I'll be losing a lot of valuable time.''

"What bargain?"

"I won't take your money, but I'll take it out in trade. Your services, whatever I decide I need from you, for going with you and bringing back your sister.''

"My services?"

"Yes."

Shenandoah hesitated. "But, Rogue? Is there a time limit? What kind of services?"

"This isn't a game, Shenandoah. I'm not bargaining with you. That's my offer. Take it or leave it. And there's no time limit. I'll decide when you've repaid me."

She didn't hesitate this time. "All right. I told you anything. I mean it. You have a deal. Let's just get my sister back quickly."

"I'm in as big a hurry as you are. Let's go down to the Blue Miner and talk this over. We've got a lot of plans to make."

"Thanks, Rogue. And I'll keep my end of the bargain, you can be sure of that."

Rogue nodded, his eyes thoughtful as he looked her over, then gently took her arm. As they hurried down the sidewalk, he tried not to think of Blackie stealing his silver, or of an innocent young woman at the mercy of unscrupulous men.

4

Sun glinted off the cool waters of the San Pedro River. For three days Rogue and Shenandoah had followed its winding path across southern Arizona into Mexico. They rode mustangs, small hardy geldings bought for their strength and stamina. Beef jerky and corn tortillas were packed in their saddlebags. And they both wore wide-brimmed hats to protect them from the sun.

Shenandoah could do nothing to stop the ache in her lower back. She was not accustomed to long hours in the saddle and her body was painfully complaining, especially since the sidesaddles women used had many drawbacks. She was also not used to being out in the daytime and couldn't seem to get accustomed to the heat or the intense glare of the sun.

No matter how she felt, she had no intention of asking Rogue to stop for a break. She was in just as much hurry as he was to find her sister, although his hurry had as much to do with his own plans as with saving Arabella. Not that he was immune to Arabella's need, but Rogue was driven by some inner demon that he had no wish to share with her.

In fact, once Rogue had agreed to help her rescue Arabella, he seemed to have no desire to share anything else with her except their basic plans and necessities for travel. Naturally, that was all they should be sharing, but she couldn't seem to forget the kisses that had once forged them, nor stop her eyes from wandering to his body. She chided herself for the unexpected interest, but there seemed to be nothing she could do to stop it. She was convinced that once they reached their destination, she would cease to think about Rogue Rogan.

However, she was beginning to wonder if they ever would reach their destination. They had sent Tom Burton on to Leadville to start mining and to tell her uncle what had happened. Then they had learned that the Brayton brothers frequented a small cantina in a village near the San Pedro River in Mexico. The cantina was called El Toro Rojo and their directions to find it had been rather vague. She was depending on Rogue to get her there and back, and she didn't like relying on anyone.

The plan they had formed to rescue Arabella was risky, dangerous, and depended on so many things out of their control that Shenandoah was not in the least convinced it would work. If it had been a game of poker or faro, she would have known the odds, but this was entirely different from anything she was prepared to handle. Relatively safe in the confines of a gambling hall in some town or city, she had civilization and her gambler's training on her side, but out in the open desert of another country, she felt almost helplessly lost and vulnerable. Nevertheless, she wouldn't let her emotions overcome her, and continued to push them down, along with the sensations Rogue stirred in her.

Arabella was depending on her to be strong, to be unafraid, to be the older sister she had always counted on when she was a child. But Shenandoah did not feel like any of those things, and she moved her mustang closer to Rogue's, needing his warmth and strength and wisdom.

"Rogue, are you sure we're still on the right trail? It would be easy to get lost out here and eventually starve."

Rogue looked over at Shenandoah in surprise. "We're following the San Pedro. That's the best we can do."

"But, Rogue, we've been traveling for so long with no sign of human life that I wonder if we might not have missed . . ."

Rogue stopped his mustang, concern beginning to transform his features. "You're worried, aren't you?"

"Well, perhaps not exactly worried, but I always try to think of all the possibilities."

"Come here," he said, and reached out to capture her horse's reins. He pulled the mustang close to his, then took her gloved hands. As he slowly began to strip the leather from her fingers, he said, "Shenandoah, contrary to what you may believe, life is not a poker game. Sometimes it's better not to think of all the possibilities. If I started doing that, I'd turn around right now and head straight for Leadville.''

"You would?'' He had her glove off by now and was gently caressing each long, slender finger in turn. It made her feel strangely warm and excited inside.

"Of course. We don't know for sure that our plan will work. First we have to find the village, then we have to convince everyone there that we're outlaws, as well as . . . lovers.''

Shenandoah shivered, even though the sun was warm on her back. "I'm not sure I can—''

"Sure you can, Shenandoah. You're a warm, sensitive woman underneath that cold exterior. Just look at the way you're responding to me now.''

Shenandoah snatched her hand back, then turned her horse away from Rogue. She was a gambler, and that was the only role she could play. When she looked back at Rogue, he was watching her with a strange light in his eyes, drawing the glove back and forth across the palm of his left hand. She couldn't look away from that slow, fascinating movement.

"Or we might be captured by Apache.''

"Rogue! We will not. Anyway, they're all on—''

"They're not all on reservations. And remember, this was their land first.''

"Well, we're not going to harm anything. We're just riding through.''

"I'm afraid they wouldn't see it that way. But it's like I said, Shenandoah. If you go keeping track of all the numbers of the deck, where they are, when they might appear, what you might do if you get what you want, you can lose at life before you ever have a chance to live.''

''I don't know what you're talking about, and give me back my glove. I'll burn out here in moments without protection.''

Rogue nodded and edged his horse closer to hers. ''You may not know what I mean now, but I think you will one day.''

He handed her the glove and as she quickly jerked it back on, he looked over her apparel. She was right: with her pale, delicate skin, she wouldn't last a day without protection. But he had known that, and she was wearing a comfortable riding skirt, a long-sleeved shirt that was buttoned to her throat, leather boots to her knees, long gloves, and a wide-brimmed hat. Even completely covered, she was beautiful. She had a natural, unconscious grace that made him want to watch her all the time. He'd had to force himself to keep his distance, or he'd go so far that he would never be able to stop. That kind of distraction was dangerous in open country, and especially dangerous on their type of mission.

''But you do think our plan will work, don't you, Rogue?''

''Yes, but we'd better get moving if we want to find El Toro Rojo.'' As they urged their mustangs forward, he added, ''You know it's going to be dangerous for both of us, but if we can convince the Braytons that we're outlaws and want to join their gang, then I think they'll accept us and take us to their hideout. Without that, I don't know if we could ever find it.''

"But why will they want outsiders to join their group?''

"I already told you, Shenandoah. They might not. But with you as bait, I don't think we can miss. From what we heard, Tad Brayton will not pass up any beautiful woman he wants. And any red-blooded man is going to want you.''

They rode through the country which had a stark beauty that could not help but impress Shenandoah. Tall, jagged mountains loomed all around them, turning to intense shades of purple in the distance. Varieties of cacti sprouted from the desert sands, and in the spring many were beginning to bloom, their delicate blossoms impossibly bright against the muted colors of the desert. Even the giant saguaro cactus had bloomed, white blossoms covering its three tips that reached for the sun. The air was so dry that Shenandoah felt it pulled the moisture from her skin, and her throat felt raw from breathing it.

But she said nothing to Rogue about the grandeur around them, or of her many discomforts. She was probably much more comfortable than her sister. She must remember why she was on this journey. Arabella must be saved from those terrible Brayton men.

They rode on through the long, hot day. Shenandoah had no need for any timekeeper except the sun itself, for as it made its way across the sky, she felt the angle of its movement from its intense rays of heat as they hit her body at different angles. Finally, as the sun began its descent in the west and the chill of night began to grow, Rogue halted his horse.

Shenandoah gratefully stopped beside him.

"We should reach El Toro Rojo tomorrow some-time, Shenandoah, if what we were told is right."

"It won't be any too soon for me, Rogue. I hate to think of what Arabella may have been enduring while we're out here."

"Don't think about it. We'll get to her as soon as we can. We'll camp down by the river again tonight. You go ahead and pick out a good place. I'll see if I can find something we can eat. I've had about enough beef jerky."

"Eat? Rogue, there's nothing out there."

"You'd be surprised how much life there is in the desert, Shenandoah. A rattler might be good." And he turned his mustang away.

"A rattler?" she said aloud, then shook her head and started for the river alone. He had better not bring back a rattlesnake. She had no intention of eating one. Even beef jerky was preferable to that idea.

Shadows began to loom around her as she urged her mustang among the cottonwood trees and small scrubs that grew in abundance along the banks of the river. In the desert the sun set fast because the land was so flat. There was light and heat; then suddenly there was dark and cold. Shenandoah wanted to get settled before night descended on them.

In a cleared area, she got off her mustang, then let the horse drink from the river. While the animal gulped huge drafts of water, she relaxed in the cool shade of a cottonwood. Taking off her hat, she felt the perspiration quickly drying. She liked the evenings best. The cool quiet of the desert surrounded her and she could almost forget all the problems and the dangers ahead.

As her mustang continued to drink, she watched the water, and began to think how wonderful it would feel against her skin. After four days she was hopelessly hot and dirty. Rogue was gone. If he were looking for food, he could be gone a long time. If they were going to arrive at El Toro Rojo the next day, she wanted to be at least fairly clean. Suddenly determined to wash, she looked around to make sure she was concealed by brush and trees. When her horse was through, she led it to a tree, tied it there, then took a bar of lavender soap from her saddlebag.

She would not take off all her clothing, but she could get rid of the boots, skirt, and shirt. She hurriedly removed them, then threw her gloves on top of the pile of clothes. She wore only a rose chemise, made of fine silk and trimmed with pink lace, with matching drawers. She was not wearing a corset on the journey, and had been enjoying the freedom from its confinement.

Feeling the coolest she had in days, Shenandoah waded out into the water. The riverbed was composed of smooth pebbles that felt good under her feet. Rubbing the lavender-scented soap between her hands in the water, she soon had suds to wash away the grime of four days. She washed her face, arms, and legs, then waded a little farther out into the water to rinse. It was not a deep river, nor did it have a strong current, so she felt safe.

But it was still not enough. She wanted to feel clean all over. She tossed the soap onto the bank, then waded to the center of the stream and knelt down. The water felt wonderful as it cascaded over her skin. She had never enjoyed a bath so much. She stood up, and suddenly felt chilled. She looked west and noticed that the sun had set. Night was quickly descending. Rogue would be back soon.

She began hurrying to the bank, realizing belatedly that the wet fabric clung to her, outlining her curves and making her uncomfortably aware of her exposed body. She wanted to be dry and dressed before Rogue returned. As she reached the bank, she looked up and in the shadows saw movement.

Stifling a cry, she stepped back into the river. All she could think of were Apache, or the Braytons, or Comancheros, so when Rogue stepped into the clearing she was relieved. But that relief vanished when she saw the anger on his face.

"Damn, Shenandoah, what the hell do you think you're doing?"

She stepped father back into the river, putting her hands around her upper arms, trying to stop the shivering and conceal her near-nudity. She was suddenly very cold. Rogue's face was set in hard, angry planes. Then she became angry too. She had a right to do what she wanted. She dropped her arms and boldly stepped from the stream, saying, "I'm taking a bath. You could probably use one too."

"A bath!" He grabbed her by the shoulders, pulling her close.

She could smell him, a combination of horse and leather and his own male scent. As he looked at her the anger turned to something stronger. He pulled her closer, so that her cool wet body was against his hot dry one.

"Shenandoah," he said, his voice husky and low, "it's not safe for you to do this alone. What if someone had seen you?"

"Someone did."

"Yes, someone did." He pulled her still closer, his lips curved in a smile of pleasure as his hands began to roam over her back, the sheer wet silk smooth against his rough hands. "Doe," he said, "you shouldn't do this to any man, especially me."

Then his lips captured hers. His kiss was not soft, but hard, determined, as if he could no longer endure the agony of being separated from her. And Shenandoah responded, feeling emotions well up in her that she had tried to ignore but Rogue was too much for her and soon ignited her with his own desire and passion.

She opened her lips to him, feeling his tongue invade and conquer the soft inner depths of her mouth. She responded further by following his lead, wanting more of him as he taught her by example what he wanted from her.

"Shenandoah," Rogue said as he jerked his mouth

from hers. "I didn't mean to touch you on the trip. It's not safe for us when I'm this distracted. But how could a man not hold you, want you, when he sees you like this? Doe." His breath was hot against her temples as he covered her face with soft, warm kisses. He didn't stop with her face, but continued kissing her, down her long neck, pausing to feel the fast beating of her heart at the base of her throat. Then he moved lower, unable to stay away from the fullness of her soft breasts, separated from him by only the sheerest of silk. He cupped them in his hands, then lowered his head to kiss each taut nipple.

"Doe," he groaned, dropping to his knees and pulling her with him. He reached up to tug the chemise down, slowly exposing more and more of her round breasts until the chemise lay softly around her hips and pale moonlight glinted on her smooth white skin. Rogue abruptly pulled her against him, covering her face with hot hard kisses until he reached her mouth again. He quickly delved inside, straining against her, wanting more and more.

Shenandoah ran her hands over the hard muscles of Rogue's back, feeling the tension in his body, the need, the desire. He was igniting something in her that she was fighting, but she could tell she was losing the battle. Something about this man made her want him in a way she had never wanted a man before. She began to return his kiss, not wanting the moment to stop, and when his mouth left her lips to explore, she pressed soft kisses against his temple, his neck, and held onto his strong arms as if only he could save her.

Rogue thrust his hands deep into Shenandoah's thick auburn hair, forcing the pins to fall, leaving it free. When it fell, curling softly around her hips, he grabbed it in two fists, smelled its soft lavender scent, then wound it around a hand, binding her to him. "I'm not ever going to let you go, Shenandoah Davis," he murmured, then once more sought her warm, fragrant breasts. This time nothing separated him from their smooth, silken skin and he kissed them, trailing fire from peak to peak.

Shenandoah moaned in response, surprised that she was letting a man touch her this way and yet unable to give up the feelings he was causing to flow through her. She ran her hands through his thick blond hair, reveling in being so close to him, so excited by him. As he continued to kiss her breasts, she pulled him closer, kissing his hair, running her hands over his shoulders, now wanting to be able to touch his flesh as he was touching hers.

Rogue abruptly stopped. He set Shanandoah away from him and began slowly drawing up her chemise, as if forcing himself to do so against his will. Surprised, and feeling suddenly bereft, Shenandoah looked at him in bewilderment until she thought she understood what he was telling her through his actions.

"I suppose you were just showing me what could happen if someone had come along. You could have told me in words, Rogue."

The chemise in place, Rogue looked up at her face

in surprise. "Shenandoah, that's what *I* would do if I saw you looking like that. I think I might kill another man who saw you undressed. And, for sure, I'd kill him if he touched you."

Amazed at the intensity of Rogue's words, Shenandoah could only stare at him in astonishment.

"I told you I wanted you in Tombstone. Nothing has happened to change that. It's too dangerous out here for me to want you. But you can't expect me to keep my hands off you if you go around looking like that."

"I thought I'd be dressed by the time you returned."

"It's not safe for you to take a bath like that alone, anyway. Next time you want one, let me know. I'll stand guard."

"All right, Rogue," she agreed reluctantly, then added, "Did you find anything for dinner?"

"No. At least nothing you'd eat. You go ahead and have what we brought. The best thing for me to do now is take a long cold swim. Call if you need me." Rogue began heading for the river, pulling off his shirt as he went.

When he had walked out of sight in the trees, Shenandoah thought about the way his hard-muscled back had looked in the moonlight. She also thought about the way he had made her feel earlier. She hadn't wanted him to stop. If he hadn't pulled away from her, would she have been able to stop? She didn't know. She was finding it harder and harder to keep her emotions under control.

Her silk underwear had dried, so she hurriedly put

on her other clothing and was glad for the warmth against the cool night air. Besides the green plaid shirt of soft cotton and the dark green skirt she was wearing, she had been able to bring only one other piece of clothing. Rogue had insisted there was not room for more, so she had brought a ruffled blouse made of emerald green satin to wear with the green skirt when she gambled. It was much less than she was used to having available, but she could wash and wear it often.

She unrolled their blankets, laid them on the ground, then set out beef jerky, tortillas, and a canteen of water. Coffee would have been good, or just any hot food. But Rogue didn't want them to build a fire on the trip, for then they could easily be spotted.

When Shenandoah had finished eating, she left some of the food on Rogue's blanket. Neither of them had eaten very much on the trip, partly because there wasn't much to eat and partly because there was so much else to think about. Once they reached the cantina and they put their plan in action, she would feel more relaxed. She was always that way before a game of cards.

Shenandoah thought of poker and got out a deck of cards. She began to cut, shuffle, and deal, recalling all the gambler's tricks her uncle had taught her. Although she and Fast Ed Davis didn't cheat, they had to know how to spot a cheater. There were a lot of clever tricks, as well as advantage tools, and any game could be rigged. Shenandoah had learned to play straight, and she was good enough to win that way. She was even good enough to be called a high roller.

"Dealing cards again?" Rogue asked, suddenly emerging from the shadows of the trees.

Shenandoah jumped. "Rogue! Don't scare me like that."

"Sorry," he said, stopping beside her to look down at the cards. Several drops of water fell on her blanket. Rogue stepped back.

She looked up at him. His hair was wet, curly with water and his torso gleamed sleek and wet in the moonlight. He had on nothing but his Levi's, holding his shirt, boots, and holstered pistol in one hand. Sitting down near her on his blanket, he began to pull on his boots.

Shenandoah lost interest in her cards. As she idly shuffled them, she watched Rogue. The muscles of his back rippled as he pulled on his boots. Checking to make sure his knife was still in place, he pulled a long dirk with a staghorn handle from an inner sheath in his right boot. Most people in the West wore hidden weapons, so Shenandoah was not surprised to see Rogue's knife. She also noticed several scars on his back and wondered how he had gotten them, but decided not to ask.

Finally Rogue pulled on his shirt, carefully placed his Colt .45 within easy reach, then turned toward Shenandoah and said, "Winning?"

She smiled. "I always try to win, Rogue. Want to play?"

"No. I'm not that big a fool. I'd probably lose my

silver mine to you, and then you'd have to take care of me.''

"I might do that.''

Picking up a piece of beef jerky and wrapping a tortilla around it, Rogue asked, "Win my silver mine or take care of me?''

Shenandoah put down the cards. "Both.''

Rogue smiled, then leaned forward and caught a strand of her hair. "I'm glad you didn't put it up. You've got the most beautiful hair I've ever seen.''

"I forgot. I'd better plait it. Otherwise I'll never get it untangled in the morning.''

"I could help.''

"You don't know what you're offering. We might never get to El Toro Rojo.''

Rogue looked serious suddenly. "I almost wish we didn't have that hanging over us, or what I've got to do in Leadville. If it were just the two of us, no problems, no place to go—''

"You'd be bored in no time, and who would gamble with me?''

"Believe me, I wouldn't be bored and you wouldn't need to gamble.'' His eyes smoldered as he said those words, and Shenandoah could not help but understand the underlying meaning. She looked away from the intensity of his gaze when he said, "But it isn't that way, is it? So, let's get some sleep. It'll be another long hot ride tomorrow.''

"All right,'' she said, putting her cards away.

When she glanced back, Rogue was watching her intently. "It'll be a cold night, Shenandoah. The least you can do is lie close to me and keep me warm.'' With those words he pulled her close, then threw her blanket on top of them. ''Now, this is just what I had in mind,'' he said as he wrapped his arms around her.

⤳ 5 ⤳

El Toro Rojo was a two-storied adobe building looming over small adobe homes in a quiet, dusty Mexican village. Several horses were tied to a split-rail hitching post in front of the cantina. The village was primarily the color of sand, with the only spots of bright color coming from the *rebozos* worn by women who were drawing water from the well in the center of the plaza.

As Rogue and Shenandoah rode quietly into the square, heads turned in their direction but no one spoke to them. They were guided to El Toro Rojo by the painting of a red bull on a sign which creaked back and forth on rusty hinges above the cantina's front door. Looking cautiously around them, Rogue motioned for Shenandoah to get off her horse. Then, after tying their mustangs to the hitching post, they took their saddlebags and headed for the front door.

The cantina was dark inside, yet cool compared to the desert heat outside, for its earthen adobe walls insulated it from the intense afternoon sun. After their eyes had adjusted to the dim interior, Rogue and Shenandoah had a chance to look around.

The cantina had a long bar, a number of solid wooden chairs and tables, and several occupants drinking and gambling. There were also two other small rooms, separated from the main one by hanging strands of glass beads. Behind the bar stood a large, portly American who was eyeing Rogue and Shenandoah closely, obviously sizing them up.

Rogue walked over to him, Shenandoah following, and both knew everyone in the room was watching and listening. They couldn't make one mistake from now until they rescued Arabella; they needed to play their parts well or find themselves dead and left in the desert for buzzards.

"Just got into town," Rogue said in English. "We're looking for a room and a place to relax for a spell."

"Haven't seen you around here before," the bartender replied in English, carefully wiping the bar with a dingy white cloth.

"That's 'cause we haven't been here before. We just finished a job on the other side of the border and heard this was a good place to rest."

"Could be. What kind of job were you doing?"

Rogue looked at Shenandoah and smiled slightly. She smiled back, feeling calm for the first time since they had started their trip. The game had begun. "We've just been helping relieve people of the extra weight they carry. Isn't that right, Baby Doe?"

"That's right, honey," Shenandoah agreed, then looked at the bartender. "We've been doing good, helping people with all their excess baggage." Then she laughed low in her throat. "We're always glad to help people, aren't we, Dirk?"

"You bet. But we're kind of tired from all that helping out. You got a place for us here, Mr. . . . ?"

Although looking at them suspiciously, the bartender seemed a little more relaxed. "Call me Red."

For the first time Shenandoah noticed the man had a graying red mustache and a fringe of red hair around the back of his head. For the most part, his head was quite smooth and round, like his stomach.

The bartender nodded at Shenandoah, then added, "I've got red hair. That's why I named this place The Red Bull."

Shenandoah smiled, saying, "Good choice."

"Don't get many lookers like you around here, unless they're Mexican, of course. What's a lady like you doing mixed up with a man like Dirk here?"

Rogue bristled at her side and put a proprietary hand on Shenandoah's shoulder. She leaned against Rogue and smiled with what she hoped was a seductive look in her eyes.

"This is my man," she said, looking back at Red. "I'd follow him anywhere."

Red snorted. "Girls always go for the good-looking types. It's not fair. Sometimes good loving comes in less attractive packages."

"Oh, don't worry about me," Shenandoah said, snuggling against Rogue. "I've got good loving."

"That's what they always say," Red complained, then went back to polishing his bar. "Got a clean room upstairs. Mexican woman comes in every few days to clean. She cooks, too. I want to see some gold first, though, and I don't want no trouble."

Rogue tossed a gold U.S. cartwheel on the bar. "We're not looking for trouble."

"Good," Red said, picking up the gold piece and biting down hard on it. Impressed with the genuine gold, he nodded more companionably at them. "Don't suppose you two gamble?"

"Baby Doe here likes to play a little poker. I imagine she'd like to win that cartwheel back for me. Right, Baby?"

Shenandoah smiled at Red. "When we're all settled in, maybe we can play together. Would you like that, Red?"

"I'll be waiting, Baby Doe. I'm sure these other guys in here would like a chance to gamble with you too."

"I'll be happy to give them that chance . . . later."

"Right now we'd like to get some of this trail dust off us," Rogue said, slapping his sleeve so that dust billowed out.

"Sure. First room at the top of the stairs on the right. All yours."

"Thanks." Rogue nodded to Red, then steered Shenandoah across the room, returning the stares of the other men before disappearing up the stairs.

Once in their room, Shenandoah let out a deep breath. "Do you think they believed us, Rogue?"

"I think so, but call me Dirk. We don't want any mistakes, and anyone could be listening at the door."

"You're right. We won't really have any privacy, will we?"

"No. We've got to be on guard all the time."

"Not a bad room," she said, walking slowly around it. There was a large, comfortable-looking double bed, a straight chair, a small dresser, and a washstand. Just as Red had said, the place was clean.

"Better than I expected," Rogue agreed, and sat down on the bed to test it.

"I'll be glad to sleep on a feather mattress rather than the hard earth."

"You going to share it with me, Shenandoah?" Rogue asked, his eyes suddenly dark pools of intense blue.

Shenandoah hesitated. She didn't want to sleep on the floor, but sharing the bed was an intimacy she didn't know if she could handle.

Rogue stood up and took several strides to her side. "I'm beginning to think you don't like me nearly as much as you made Red think."

"Rogue . . . Dirk, that was just for their benefit. I've told you I'm a gambler, and—"

"I don't want to hear it, Doe." Rogue lowered his head, his eyes on her lips.

Shenandoah knew it was time to move away from him. She should make him understand that she didn't share the same feelings. She was completely independent. A gambler. But she felt mesmerized by his nearness and she remembered the feel of his warm body cradling hers the night before. She didn't move.

Rogue touched her lips gently, his own warm and sensual. "I think we'd better sleep together, Doe, in case someone should decide to check up on us. There's no lock on the door." He kissed her again, longer this time. "I want you, Shenandoah, but you know I'd never force anything on you. Trust me."

This time she returned his kiss, unable to resist the fire in his lips or the heat in his body. "I trust you, Rogue," she said, her voice husky. "Otherwise, how could I have come with you this far?"

Rogue smiled, then kissed her lips again. "I don't know if you really trust me or if you just didn't have any other choice."

"Well," she said, tilting her head back to look deep into his eyes, "if you'd tell me why you're in such a big hurry to get back to Leadville, then I could trust you more."

"That's none of your concern, Shenandoah. I've got things I have to do. Things that began a long time before I met you. I'm short of time and that's all there is to it."

"Rogue, I—"

"I've got to see to the horses. Red probably has some kind of stable in back. You can freshen up and rest if you like. It'll be a long night tonight. But stay in here where it's safe."

"All right. But, Rogue . . . Dirk, see about some hot food, will you?"

"That's where I'm headed. Put a chair under the doorknob when I leave, okay?"

"Yes. And, Dirk?"

Rogue turned back.

"Be careful."

He smiled at her, then left the room.

Shenandoah went to the washstand and as she washed her face and hands, she thought of Rogue. There were probably a lot of reasons why he was anxious to get back to Leadville, but she hoped they didn't have to do with another woman. Whatever his past and whatever his hurry, he wasn't willing to share it with her. She wished that didn't make any difference, but for some reason it did. He trusted her much less than she trusted him. Nevertheless, in order for them to rescue Arabella, they would probably have to trust each other more than they had ever trusted anyone before.

She sat down on the bed, thinking she would need to have all her wits about her tonight. She not only planned to gamble and win, but she *had* to make everyone believe that she and Rogue were outlaws and lovers. Tonight she would no longer be a virgin, but an experienced, sensual woman. She only hoped she could make everyone believe it.

Night enclosed El Toro Rojo in a cocoon of darkness, and the silence of the sleepy Mexican village was broken only by revelers in the cantina. The villagers did not complain at the sudden outbursts of laughter, or anger, or occasional gunfire. The *norte-americanos* had guns and gold on their side, were quick-tempered and quick-triggered.

Shenandoah was learning just how quick-tempered the men who frequented El Toro Rojo were as she cut, shuffled, and dealt cards in one of the two private rooms in the cantina. She had been gambling for hours, serving a steady group of men. Rogue had rarely left her side, and the grim set of his jaw told her more than she wanted to know about the cantina's patrons.

She was surprised at the number of Americans who entered El Toro Rojo that night. There was little doubt in her mind that most of them were outlaws, for there was a deadly glint in their eyes and an air about them of living only for the moment, for the next drink, for the next turn of a card. They were dangerous men who lived south of the border and fed off the men and women of their country to the north.

The desperadoes were very appreciative of beautiful women, and they were thrilled to find an American woman in their midst. Most took a turn gambling with her. Even though many of them lost, they did not feel like losers; it had been a pleasure to play with her.

They were men who were bored much of the time, with too little to do between forays across the border. Shenandoah was a pleasant surprise, and she would have been even more exciting to them if not for the big blond stranger who seldom left her side. They all wished they could be so lucky as to receive the languid, searing looks she occasionally gave him, but they didn't trespass on what was obviously his property. They contented themselves with gambling with her and with speculating on what they might have done if she had been available.

Shenandoah carefully learned each man's name or alias as he sat down to play at her table. She was anxiously watching for a Brayton, but so far that night none of the brothers had played at her table. She was confident that word would spread about the woman gambler at El Toro Rojo and would hopefully draw the Braytons to her game. She and Rogue would simply have to be patient, although that was growing increasingly hard.

Not all of the men at the cantina were American. Some were Mexican or Spanish, mingling with little concern for their different nationalities. Red had obviously established a haven for outlaws and it paid him well. Although the proprietor of El Toro Rojo had played at her table a few times, he had spent most of his time behind the bar, making sure the patrons had plenty of drinks. He was glad to have Shenandoah in his cantina because she was drawing customers, as a good gambler always did.

As the night wore on, Shenandoah became more and more concerned about the gambler across from her. He was a professional, just like her. She usually liked to play with a professional gambler because the game was more intense, but this night she was beginning to think the slim, pale-skinned, dark-haired Spanish gentleman named Alfredo who sat across from her was cheating. He hadn't been at first, but she had won too many times. His stakes were getting low. She suspected him of a holdout, a device for secreting a card or cards on the body or under the table until just the right moment, when a low card could be exchanged for a high card to win a game.

Cheating was dangerous in the West. If caught, the cheater was frequently killed on the spot. Even so, cheating flourished and mail-order houses such as Grandine's in New York or Will and Finck Company in San Francisco supplied the West with advantage tools.

These companies and others sold table holdouts and sleeve, cuff, ring, and vest holdouts. Cards could be punched, trimmed, marked, or faded, in addition to the use of reflectors such as shiny gold watches, cufflinks, and mirrors to show the gambler the face of a card as it was dealt. Of course, that didn't count stacked decks, false shuffles, false cuts, or dealing seconds. There were as many ways to cheat as there were gamblers.

Yet, even if a gambler might suspect someone of cheating, it was often hard to prove. Shenandoah was fairly sure the man across from her was using a holdout. In time, if she didn't lose too much, she would discover just what kind and then she would have to settle with him. That was something she didn't like to do, but if she let this man continue to cheat, she could be taken for all she and Rogue had.

They played another round. Shenandoah won. Alfredo was clever enough not to cheat every time, and he was good, a real sharper. Shenandoah glanced over at Rogue, wondering if he had noticed what was going on at her table.

He nodded, encouraging her.

She smiled back, giving him what she hoped was a seductive look.

"Want something to drink, Baby Doe?" Rogue asked, caressing her bare shoulder with a warm hand.

"Coffee, if you can get it."

"Be back in a moment."

With Rogue gone, Shenandoah felt more vulnerable. She needed Rogue, more than she cared to admit.

"Gentlemen," she said, looking around the table, "another game?" She used the term "gentleman" loosely when referring to these outlaws, but it was a standard term used by gamblers, no matter who the players were.

"Why don't you get rid of the big man, then we could play some real games," one of the men said, his eyes exploring the soft pale flesh exposed by the décolletage of Shenandoah's emerald satin blouse.

"That's right," another agreed. "A woman like you could be real popular around here."

"I'm a gambler, gentlemen," Shenandoah said, trying not to be too cold, since word about her must be passed to the Braytons.

"Sure, but you're more than that. Any man here can see that."

Shenandoah smiled seductively, then said, "I don't think any of you would want to discuss this with Dirk, now, would you?"

They hesitated, then mumbled under their breath.

Finally Alfredo said, "Let's play poker, *amigos*. The *señorita* has obviously chosen her companion."

"Or maybe he chose her," one of the players said, followed by a nod of approval from the other man at the table.

Shenandoah cut the deck, glanced around, then smiled. "Poker, anyone?"

Rogue pushed his way through the delicate strands of hanging glass beads with a cup of coffee and a shot glass of whiskey. He glanced suspiciously around the room, feeling the tension that had not been there before he left. He set the cup of coffee near her hand, then looked hard at each man before stepping back from the table.

No further words were spoken as Shenandoah shuffled, then dealt the cards.

She had dealt herself a good hand. If luck were with her, she might turn it into a unbeatable hand. She had two kings and an ace. That meant no one else could get the unbeatable four-ace hand, since she already had one of the aces. She needed two more kings to win the game, but she knew that was extremely unlikely. Even though she was excited by her cards, she let no expression cross her face.

"Who wants another card?" she asked.

The first player stood pat, satisfied with his hand.

Alfredo indicated that he wanted one more, exchanging one from the five he held for the new card. As he put his new hand together, Shenandoah turned to the next player, but she was still watching the man she thought was cheating. As she dealt out three cards, she saw the slight forward motion of Alfredo's body, then a move of his hands toward his chest. A vest holdout. She had him.

She gave herself two new cards. Two kings. Excitement coursed through her. Just what she wanted. She had an unbeatable hand.

The bidding began and quickly escalated. Shenandoah was sure the cheater had to be holding four aces, one of them a holdout card. He was betting high, probably planning to make this the last game. The other gamblers had good hands too, for they continued to stay in the game. Shenandoah kept on pushing her chips forward. She was going to win, one way or another.

Finally the bidding stopped. The player on Shenandoah's left laid out his hand, three jacks. Good, but not good enough. Alfredo laid down four aces and a small card. The other man groaned, knowing he had lost. Shenandoah made no sound, but watched as the next player laid out a straight. At last her time came. She laid down four kings and an ace.

"Where have you got your aces stashed?" Alfredo quickly accused her, drawing a derringer from under his coat.

The other players drew guns too, furious that Shenandoah had been cheating them all evening.

Rogue stepped closer, drawing his gun and aiming it at Alfredo.

Shenandoah did not move, knowing her life hung by a thread. "Gentlemen," she said softly. "there is no place I can hide cards on myself. Look at my clothing."

"There are other ways," one of them muttered.

"Someone *is* cheating at this table. Check him," Shenandoah said, nodding at Alfredo, "for a vest holdout."

The other two players looked suspiciously at Alfredo, but he stood up suddenly and with one hand began raking in the chips. "Since you're a woman I'll let you off easy this time, but you should be more careful in the future."

"Wait a minute," Rogue interrupted, stepping closer, his Colt trained on Alfredo.

"I'm not waiting. You try to shoot me and she'll be dead before you ever get off a shot." Alfredo began sliding the chips into a bag, his gun still on Shenandoah.

"Now, wait a minute," one of the other players said. "Why don't you just open up your vest and show us how clean you are."

"Are you accusing me of cheating?"

"Not yet, but the little lady seemed honest to me."

"The way she looks, she could have been using cold decks all evening and no one would have noticed. Now, I've won and I'm taking—"

"That'll be about enough, Alfredo," Red said.

The bartender had suddenly entered the room and stuck the point of his pistol in the man's back. "Drop your gun on the table."

Alfredo did as he was ordered.

"Put the chips back, too."

He did that.

"Now, open your vest."

Alfredo hesitated.

Red pushed his pistol against Alfredo's back.

Alfredo slowly opened his vest. Inside the left side was a single strip of elastic sewn onto it. Several cards and a miniature pencil used to mark cards were held against the vest by the elastic.

"Damn!" one of the other players exclaimed, sliding his forty-five back into its holster. "You've been cheating us for a long time."

The other gambler holstered his gun too, then looked at Shenandoah and said, "Sorry, Baby Doe, but you never can tell."

"I know. It can be a dangerous game."

"I've suspected you of cheating for some time, Alfredo," Red said. "I run an honest place here. I doesn't pay me to do otherwise. Get out of here and stay out. News of this will spread fast."

Alfredo's dark eyes glittered with menace as he tossed the last of the chips on the table. He gave Shenandoah and Rogue a hard stare, then left the room.

Red watched him, making sure he left the cantina, then looked back. "Made yourselves an enemy. Al-

fredo's not a man to cross. He's got friends. Glad
you exposed him, though. Thanks. Drinks on the
house.''

Red left, followed by the other two men angrily
discussing Alfredo.

Rogue sat down beside Shenandoah and took her
hands. They were cold. He rubbed them, warming
them with his own heat.

"I knew he was cheating, too, but I didn't know
how you were going to handle it. Anybody else
would probably have just shot him. That'd have been
the safest thing to do. Damn dangerous letting him
get the bead on you. Don't do it again, Shenandoah.
I was damn near helpless.''

Shenandoah looked into Rogue's eyes and saw the
concern, anger, and frustration there. For some reason, his worry made her feel good deep inside. "Sorry,
Dirk, but I didn't mean for it to go that way. Thanks
for backing me up.''

"Wasn't much I could do once he'd drawn that
peashooter and had it aimed at you.''

"I know, but you still made the difference. I've
about had enough tonight. Do you suppose we could
go to bed?''

Rogue's eyes suddenly darkened. "I'd like that.
I'd like that a lot.''

Shenandoah looked away. She had forgotten what
"going to bed'' meant here, yet she knew that with
him close to her, she would feel safe, a lot safer than
she felt just now. "Let's go upstairs, Dirk.''

They were gone by the time Red brought their

drinks, and the bartender only chuckled, knowing how fear, excitement, and winning big like Baby Doe had just done could make bed games even better. Those two were good for business and he would be glad to have them at El Toro Rojo as long as they wanted to stay.

6

Shenandoah sat on the edge of the bed, wishing she had something more enveloping to wear while she slept than her silk chemise and drawers. Unfortunately, there hadn't been room in her saddlebags to bring more than a fancy gambling blouse. While Rogue's back was turned to her, she slipped out of her blouse, skirt, petticoat, and boots, then quickly got into bed and drew the covers up to her chin.

She watched Rogue. Soft light from the lamp by the bed illuminated his back as he stood in front of the washstand washing his face and hands. His shirt was slung over the chair. Once more she noticed the strong, powerful muscles of his back and wanted to feel them against the soft palms of her hands.

But she stopped her thoughts there. It was going to be difficult enough sleeping with Rogue in the same bed without thinking of him like that. He would help her find her sister and that was all. She should be thinking of Arabella's plight, not of Rogue's body.

Rogue finished washing and turned toward Shenandoah. He smiled at her. "Do you think you need all those covers?"

"It gets cold at night."

"Not with me to warm you."

Shenandoah could not keep the crimson flush from spreading up her neck to her face. She looked away. "Rogue, we—"

"No. Let's not talk." He unbuckled his gunbelt, then carefully pulled the chair to his side of the bed and laid his Colt on it, making sure he could reach the pistol quickly should the need arise.

"What about the door?"

"I'm here now, and I don't want anyone to think we have anything to hide should they decide to try the door."

Shenandoah looked suspiciously at the unlocked door across from the foot of their bed. If Rogue hadn't been with her, she would have felt extremely vulnerable sleeping with an unlocked door.

"I don't think there'll be any problem, Shenandoah. Those men downstairs will all be leaving soon. This place should be empty after a while."

"All right, but I'm trusting you to protect us," she said, then turned out the lamp.

Rogue smiled. "We'll be all right. Let's just forget about what's going on out there and get a good night's sleep."

Soft moonlight shone in through the small open window, bathing their bed in silver and shadows. Shenandoah felt Rogue's weight on the bed as he sat on his side, then lay down, putting his arms behind his head on a pillow.

She couldn't sleep. She could sense Rogue's nearness, the heat of his body, and his care not to lie too close to her. When she couldn't lie still any longer she turned on her side, only to discover that she was lying nearer Rogue. She could see his strong profile outlined by moonlight.

"Rogue?" she said softly, not wanting to wake him if he slept.

"Yes?" he answered just as softly.

"I wondered if you were asleep."

"No. I told you I'd watch over you."

"But Rogue, aren't you going to sleep?"

"It'll be dawn soon, then I might."

"That doesn't seem fair."

He turned his head to look at her. The covers had slipped down, exposing the soft curve of her breasts revealed by the chemise. He smiled, a reluctant movement of his sensual lips. "I'd find it hard to sleep anyway, Doe."

"Why?" she asked, her voice suddenly breathless.

"I think you know why."

"No. No, I don't."

Rogue closed his eyelids a moment, then opened them and said, "Pull the covers up, Shenandoah. You're making this even more difficult."

"You don't have any covers on you."

Rogue looked at her in surprise, then glanced down at his naked torso. He still wore his pants and boots, always prepared for trouble. "That's not the same thing," he responded, looking back at her.

Her lips curved in a smile. "Why not?"

Rogue frowned. "Damn, Shenandoah. Pull up the covers and go to sleep."

"No." She tugged the covers down a little farther and the chemise slipped, revealing one round white shoulder.

Rogue's body tensed. His eyes didn't leave her exposed flesh as he said, "I made you a promise, Shenandoah. I said you'd be safe in bed with me, and you will be unless you taunt me too far. I'm not made of—"

"Neither am I."

"What are you saying?"

"Hold me, Rogue. I need you."

Rogue swallowed hard, looked away, then pulled her close. Shenandoah smiled as the covers slipped down to her waist. She could hear the strong beat of his heart as she nestled her face against his bare chest. Golden blond hairs tickled her nose and she rubbed it against him, stopping the itch.

"Damn, Shenandoah. Don't do that."

She leaned her head back to look at his face. He was determinedly looking across the room, his mouth set in a straight line. "Does that bother you?" she asked, beginning to enjoy the reaction she was getting from him. She'd had no idea she could have this kind of power over a man. It made her feel less worried about her own reactions to Rogue.

"You know damn well it does. If you aren't good, I'm going to put you back across the bed."

"Don't do that," she said, rubbing her face against his chest, enjoying the multiple feelings it aroused in her. His heart beat faster and his hands clenched on her arms. She kissed the curly hair on his chest, unable to stop herself.

Rogue sat up and pushed her away. "What the hell are you trying to do?"

Contrite, Shenandoah simply shook her head. "I don't know, Rogue. I just wanted to touch you. I'm sorry. You must not want me to do that."

Rogue's frown suddenly left his face. He pulled her back into his arms and began stroking her head. "Sometimes I forget how innocent you are, Doe. I mean, to look at you and to think of the places you've worked, a man forgets . . ."

"Yes?" She didn't really care what he was saying. She was just glad to be back in his arms, feeling the heat of his body, smelling his scent, and listening to his heartbeat.

"What I'm trying to say is that of course I want you to touch me. I want it so bad it's making me crazy. I thought you were teasing me."

"Why would I do that?" she asked, raising her head to look at him.

Rogue glanced into her wide green eyes and said with a touch of exasperation, "For such a damned good gambler, you are almost unbelievably innocent."

Shenandoah bristled. "I am not completely innocent."

"Oh no?"

"I've been around sporting emporiums enough to know what goes on between men and women."

"All right. Prove it to me."

Shenandoah raised her head and looked deep into his eyes. There was humor there, but also a hungry look, and a dare. As a gambler, she had never turned down a dare, a gamble, and she didn't want to now, especially when it was exactly what she wanted. But, she didn't want to make a fool of herself.

Shenandoah had never initiated a kiss with a man before, but in the past few days Rogue had taught her a great deal. Now she didn't hesitate. She ran her hands through his thick hair, reveling in its feel. She smiled into eyes that intently watched her. Then she leaned forward, letting the tips of her breasts touch his chest as her lips softly met his mouth.

Rogue groaned. She lowered her hands to his shoulders, slowly letting her hands trail down the hard muscles of his arms. She felt his body stiffen under her touch. Encouraged by his obvious response, she kissed his eyes, the lids soft under her feathery touch. She kissed the tip of his nose, then around his mouth, lightly putting the tip of her tongue to each corner.

Rogue groaned again. "You're teasing me, Shenandoah."

"No. I'm touching you. We didn't specify how or what."

Rogue exhaled loudly, but didn't move. "I can see I should have been more specific."

"No," she laughed. "These are my rules."

Rogue shut his eyes, as if in exasperation, but Shenandoah knew it was more than that for she could feel the tension in his body as her hands explored even more. She leaned back to look as she moved her long, sensitive fingers over his broad, muscular chest. She let one palm caress the spot over his heart, feeling the hard rhythmic beating there. Then she moved her hands lower, finding the deep indentation of his navel. His stomach muscles tightened against her hands, but she didn't go lower, even though it was obvious in the moonlight that Rogue's Levi's were stretched to their limit. Again, she felt an incredible power and yearning sweep through her.

She quickly wound her arms around his neck, pressing her warm mouth to his. She wanted more, needed more. Rogue opened his lips to let her enter and she explored his inner depths as he had once explored hers. As she kissed him, she pressed her breasts against his bare chest, wanting more and more, yet knowing not quite what. Rogue was right, she really didn't know all that went on between a man and a woman.

After the long kiss, she raised her head and looked into Rogue's passion-clouded eyes. "Rogue, I . . ."

"Do you want me to teach you what comes next?" Rogue's voice was husky and low.

Shenandoah hesitated only a moment, then nodded slowly and said, "Yes."

Rogue pulled her roughly against him, rolling them over so that she was on her back and he was pressing her into the soft bed. He covered her face in hard, desperate kisses, returning to her mouth over and over again, as if he could not get enough of the taste of her.

Finally he raised his head and said, "I couldn't

have stood much more of that, Shenandoah. A man shouldn't have to endure that kind of torture.''

Shenandoah smiled and ran her fingers through his hair. "That wasn't torture, Rogue."

"Let's see if you think so now that it's your turn." He quickly grabbed her wrists and pulled her hands behind her back, effectively pinning her against the bed. Then, his eyes never leaving her startled face, he slowly pulled the cover off her legs and began spreading them with his own, never looking away from her eyes. When he finally lay between her legs, he pushed hard against her.

Shenandoah moaned, suddenly realizing just how far she had come. She felt captured, bound, and at Rogue's mercy. She struggled against the hand that held her arms behind her back. She struggled against the hardness that pushed against the most sensitive part of her body. Then she moaned again as Rogue began to move against her, his hips creating a rhythm that echoed throughout her body.

She stopped struggling and began wanting more. As Rogue's lips found the tips of her breasts and as his tongue toyed with her nipples through the sheer fabric of her chemise, she writhed up against him, her body responding to him in a way that she could never have imagined.

"Rogue, Rogue," she whispered, his name a chant that repeated over and over in her mind.

"Doe," he answered, his voice husky and tense as he spread hot kisses from her breasts to her mouth. He entered between soft lips, spreading his fire inside her honeyed mouth. He pushed against her with his lips, the movement echoing the thrust of his tongue, burying into her depths.

Suddenly their door creaked open. Rogue went stiff. Shenandoah stopped breathing. Rogue was a hot, heavy weight on top of her. Reality returned to her like a douse of cold water. Rogue's body was now tense with danger rather than passion.

The door creaked again, and soft footsteps sounded in the room. Rogue quietly rolled over, putting a hand on Shenandoah's mouth, warning her not to speak. When he removed his hand, she lay perfectly still, waiting for Rogue to make the first move.

A shadowy form crept forward, checked to make sure Shenandoah and Rogue were asleep, then went to their saddlebags. Shenandoah's winnings from gambling that night were in a bag tossed on top. The man pocketed those, drew a knife. It gleamed silver in the moonlight.

As the dark form neared their bed, Rogue slowly slid his dirk from his boot, unable to reach his Colt from Shenandoah's side of the bed. As the figure raised the blade and leaned over Shenandoah, Rogue threw his knife. It struck the figure's raised arm and sank deep. The assailant gave a surprised yelp and dropped his knife on the bed. The shadowy figure jerked Rogue's knife from his arm as he started to run from the room.

Rogue leapt from the bed and tackled the man. They went down in a heap on the floor. As they fought, Shenandoah lit the lamp with shaking hands.

What she saw terrified her. The attacker was brandishing Rogue's dirk and Rogue had no weapon. With the light filling the room, she saw that their assailant was Alfredo, back to get what he had lost and kill them in the process. Red had been right. They had made an enemy.

Even with his bleeding arm, Alfredo was a powerful fighter, and he had the dirk. He and Rogue fought each other until Rogue knocked the knife from Alfredo's hand, then Alfredo pulled a derringer from his vest. Holding that, he motioned Rogue to back away. Rogue obeyed, maneuvering Alfredo so that his back was to Shenandoah.

She suddenly realized that Rogue wanted her to help. Looking wildly about her, she saw the knife that Alfredo had dropped on the bed. She picked it up, then took several quick steps on bare feet toward Alfredo. A floorboard creaked beneath her. Alfredo glanced to the side and saw her. She hit his arm and the one-shot derringer went off, propelling its bullet into the floor. She quickly tossed the knife to Rogue.

Rogue jumped Alfredo, putting the knife to his throat. Shenandoah picked up the dirk and went to Rogue's side, holding the knife as a weapon.

"Check the hall, Baby Doe," Rogue said brusquely.

Shenandoah carried the lamp to the door, then flung it open. Holding the light high, she looked down the hall, but saw no one lurking there. Satisfied, she stepped back into the room and shut the door. She set the lamp back in place, then went to Rogue.

"Check him for other weapons."

Shenandoah ran her hands over Alfredo, trying to avoid the blood that was running down his sleeve into his hand. She found a bowie knife and another derringer. She tossed these on the bed. "That's all."

Rogue let the man go. "You really think you were going to sneak in here and take what you wanted?"

Alfredo scowled. "Nobody's ever beat me like that before."

"No reason to murder the lady," Rogue said.

Alfredo spat in Shenandoah's direction.

Rogue grabbed the man and shook him hard. "Treat her that way again and the buzzards will have you for breakfast."

When Rogue let him go, Alfredo straightened his coat, took out a white handkerchief, and tied it around his wound. "If you're going to kill me, go ahead."

"I'm not killing you this time, but only because I want you alive."

Surprised, Alfredo looked up.

"As a warning. You let the rest of these *hombres* around here know that Dirk won't stand anyone messing with his woman or trying to steal from him. *¿Comprende?*"

Alfredo scowled, then said, "Sure, I understand."

"Now, apologize to the lady."

"What?"

"You heard me. You've caused Baby Doe a lot of trouble tonight. Apologize."

Alfredo turned toward Shenandoah. Tensing his jaws, he said, "My apologies, *señorita*."

"All right," Rogue growled. "Now get the hell out of here and stay away from us."

Alfredo walked to the door, but turned back. "This is not over, *señor*." Then he was gone into the blackness of the night.

"Rogue!" Shenandoah exclaimed. "Are you all right?" She hurried to his side and looked him up and down. "Come with me. You've got blood all over you."

Rogue let her lead him to the washstand.

As she began gently rubbing at the blood with a wet cloth, she said, "I don't know if this is his blood or yours."

"His, probably."

"You're going to be sore tomorrow."

"Doesn't matter. This is just the break we needed."

"What do you mean?" She continued to wash the blood away and found only a few scratches.

"You can be damn sure he knows the Braytons. This will just prove we're the quality of outlaw the Braytons might be interested in having join their gang. They'll also hear about you. If I'm not mistaken, Tad Brayton won't be able to resist taking you away from me. He'll have to try. Alfredo played right into our hands."

"Well, I'm glad you see it that way. Frankly, I don't know when I've been so scared. He could have killed you."

Rogue took the cloth from Shenandoah and pulled her close. "Would you have cared?"

Shenandoah's breath suddenly caught in her throat.

Rogue's eyes were a deep, intense blue trying to see into her very soul. "Of course I would have cared."

Rogue smiled.

Shenandoah smiled back, then looked mischievous. "After all, who would have helped me rescue my sister?"

"Damn! Woman, you're really in trouble now," Rogue growled.

Shenandoah laughed out loud, then ran, circling around the bed. Rogue hurried after her, but she scrambled to the center of the bed away from his outstretched arms.

"You can't get away from me that easily," he said, throwing himself forward and bringing her down with him into the middle of the soft bed.

"Oh, no," she said, breathless, squirming against him.

"Yes. Oh yes," he said, pinning her beneath him. He jerked her hands up over her head with one hand. "Now, tell me why you're glad Alfredo didn't kill me."

Out of breath, she panted, "I need you to get me to—"

"Wrong! Try again."

"I need you to protect me and get me to—"

"Try again."

"I need you—"

"Right. You need me," he stated, then covered her mouth with his so that she couldn't give him any other reasons.

After he had kissed her thoroughly and she was

quiet under him, he raised his head and looked deep into her eyes. "You're more dangerous to me than any Alfredo, or Brayton, or outlaw. If we're going to make it safely out of Mexico, I'm going to have to keep my hands off you."

"I don't know, Rogue," she said, smiling teasingly up at him. "You quite turn my head."

"I'd like to turn it . . . over to your pillow." And he pushed her to her side of the bed. "Now, go to sleep. I'm going to sit in the chair for a while."

"No, Rogue. Stay in bed. That chair looks horribly uncomfortable. I'm going to sleep. Really I am. I'm exhausted."

"Good. Go to sleep. We'll have plenty to do when the Braytons get here."

"But, Rogue . . . ?"

"Go on to sleep. I'll be fine." He got up, picked up his Colt, and sat down. The small chair creaked under his weight.

Shenandoah watched him a moment, then her eyelids grew heavy. Soon sleep overtook her. She never knew when Rogue came to bed and pulled her close to him. The sun was just rising when they both finally slept, their arms entwined and their bodies melded.

7

A week had passed at El Toro Rojo, but the Braytons had not made an appearance. Shenandoah and Rogue seemed no closer to reaching Arabella than they had before leaving Tombstone. Frustration was evident in their movements as they got ready for another night of gambling.

Shenandoah finished putting up her hair and glanced at Rogue in the mirror. He was checking his gun. The longer they were at El Toro Rojo, the more often he checked the forty-five, as if knowing that when the time came he would need it, and need it fast. She felt the stress, too. It was all she could do to sit down and calmly play cards for another long night. Jerking at the ruffles of her blouse, she turned toward Rogue.

"I'm sick of this blouse. When we leave Mexico, I'm going to throw it away."

Rogue looked at her and nodded. He understood her feelings, but it was not the blouse that she wanted to get rid of. It was the situation. They were both tense, waiting for the Braytons, and their constant companionship increased their own personal tension. Rogue hadn't slept in the bed again, for if he were that close to Shenandoah he couldn't count on hearing someone sneak into their room. And he couldn't take that kind of chance with their lives, although it was almost killing him to stay away from her.

"I don't care if that woman did a good job of laundering this blouse or not, Rogue. I just can't stand to look at the color anymore. Maybe I'll never wear green again."

"It's not the blouse, Doe," Rogue said quietly.

Shenandoah frowned at him, dropped her hands to her skirt, crumpled the fabric, then walked to the window. Nothing new there to see, only the lengthening shadows. She turned back. Her voice was very soft when she said, "Rogue, what if the Braytons don't come?"

Rogue holstered his Colt with a quick, sharp snap of metal against leather. He took several long strides to her side. He turned her around, leaving a large, strong hand on each shoulder. "Don't think that, Shenandoah. They'll come. I can't believe Tad Brayton won't come, for you at least."

"But what if they don't, Rogue? We can't stay here forever, just waiting. We'll have to—"

Rogue pulled her close, and she buried her head against his shoulder. "Don't talk that way, Shenandoah. We wait. If they don't come soon, then we'll make other plans. But for now, don't think that far ahead."

In Rogue's arms, Shenandoah quieted, calmed and

reassured by his strength. After a time she began to feel other emotions, feelings that she had been trying to hold down for a week. Slowly her hands moved up Rogue's chest, feeling the hard muscles ripple in response to her touch. When her hands were around his neck, she tilted her head back and looked up into his eyes. They were dark with desire.

"Rogue," she said, the word more breath than sound.

"Doe," he returned, an expression of pain crossing his features. "I don't—"

"Kiss me, Rogue."

He hesitated.

"I need you."

He lowered his head slowly, his eyes burning with an intensity that could almost have consumed her. When his lips met hers, they were hot and eager, and when her mouth opened to receive him, tendrils of fire leapt between them. Shenandoah moaned as she felt Rogue's tongue pursue hers, then search the inside of her mouth as if he had to reassure himself that all was as it had been and that her honeyed depths were still his to explore.

After a long moment Rogue gently raised his head, then caressed her with his eyes. "It's not safe for us to do that here, Shenandoah. We both know it. I don't know how much longer I can go without touching you. I want you more than I did in Tombstone, although at the time I wouldn't have thought that possible. I have a present for you," he said, suddenly grinning, and distracting them both.

"A present?"

He nodded. "Stay right there. Shut your eyes."

"But I don't know if I can accept—"

"Damn, Shenandoah, don't say anything like that. I'm not going to listen to it. Just shut your eyes."

"Well, all right, but—"

"Shut your mouth, as well, and then I'll give you your present."

Finally she did as he bid and heard him rustling around in his saddlebags. He had gone out in the afternoons, looking around the village, but she couldn't imagine where he could have found a present for her. In a moment she felt something of gossamer settle around her shoulders.

"Open your eyes," Rogue said, pleasure in his voice.

Shenandoah quickly looked down and saw a shawl of purest white cotton. She ran her hands up and down its soft length. Finally she looked at Rogue, happiness in her eyes. "Oh, Rogue. It's beautiful. Thank you so much."

Rogue smiled, moved closer to adjust the shawl, then stepped back to look at the effect. "You're beautiful," he said simply.

Shenandoah ran her hands over the light, filmy fabric again. She smiled mischieviously at him. "Now I won't have to look at this blouse so much. The shawl will cover it nicely."

She hurried to the small mirror over the washstand and looked at herself. The shawl was hand-woven on a loom, and into the weave had been threaded the images of magnificent birds. It was one of the most beautiful shawls she had ever seen, and it was even more special because Rogue had given it to her.

She looked back at him and said, "I love it, Rogue, but where did you find this? It couldn't have been easy."

"Not so hard. One of the village women weaves."

"And just what did this village woman look like?" Shenandoah asked sharply, surprised at the sudden flare of jealousy that stung her.

Rogue chuckled. "You have nothing to fear, my dear. She can't hold a candle to you, being all of eighty summers, I'd say."

"I wasn't—"

Rogue stepped closer and, grasping the shawl, pulled her toward him. "I like to see that fire in your eyes at the thought of another woman. That's what I feel like all the time inside with all those outlaws gambling with you but wishing they were doing something else with you."

Shenandoah blushed. "They aren't doing that."

"Oh yes they are. And I don't know what I'm going to do when Tad Brayton lays his claim to you."

"Break his arms?" Shenandoah asked sweetly, mischievousness in her voice.

"Yes, and both legs, perhaps. Then he'd be unable to do anything about his desire for you."

"Rogue, you really won't try to stop him, will you?" she asked, suddenly concerned that he might ruin their plans.

Rogue grimaced, let go of the shawl, then paced away from her. He stopped, and looked back. "No, I won't ruin our plans. But it's going to be damned hard to play along with any man wanting you. I'm warning you now that I'll only play so far, Shenandoah."

"That's all we need, Rogue. Downstairs, just remember that I'm your woman. Tad will simply be trying to take me away from you, and I'll not be too reluctant."

"Okay, so long as you remember that it's all just a game. I've heard that Tad Brayton has the devil's own way with women."

"Really? You hadn't told me that, Rogue. Perhaps this won't be so bad after all," she teased.

Rogue frowned. "That's not funny. You go too far and you'll find out how little I'll take where you're concerned."

"I'm sorry, Rogue. It's just this waiting and worrying about poor Arabella. What must she be suffering at the hands of those men?"

"Don't think about it, Shenandoah. We'll get to her soon. Now, it's time to go downstairs. Maybe we'll be lucky tonight."

Shenandoah nodded, pulled her new shawl more closely around her, then walked with Rogue from the room.

Downstairs, El Toro Rojo held no surprises for Rogue and Shenandoah. Red was glad to see them as always because they brought in business, and the Baby Doe room was waiting for them to enter so that the outlaws could start gambling with Baby Doe herself.

Shenandoah had been surprised, and a little touched, that the room where she played poker night after night had quickly, and with unspoken agreement between Red and his patrons, become Baby Doe's room. No one else gambled there when she was upstairs. When she left El Toro Rojo, the room would probably continue to be called that until, finally, no one would remember why, unless Red stayed with the cantina.

After she entered the Baby Doe room, she soon had a full table. She nodded at the players around her, cut the cards, and began the game. No one watching would have realized the tension she was concealing, or her unwavering concern about her sister.

The night had not gone on too long before Shenandoah suddenly felt an intense gaze on her. Glancing up, she saw two tall men standing on the other side of the glass-bead curtain. Their presence was compelling, and they had eyes for no one but her. Her chest suddenly felt tight, her heart beat faster, her palms grew moist; then she forced her gaze away. They were the most powerful men she had seen since entering El Toro Rojo, and there was something basically frightening about them. But she forced her fear down and continued to calmly play poker.

After a long moment, they entered the small room, their size and presence overpowering all the other occupants, except Rogue. Shenandoah felt him stiffen behind her, and she tensed in response. Whoever these men were, they were not to be taken lightly.

Without a word being spoken, the three men at Shenandoah's table quickly finished their game and left the room. The two strangers took two of the chairs. The bigger of the two motioned for Rogue to take the third chair. After a moment, Rogue did. Shenandoah didn't know why Rogue had suddenly decided to play at her table, but she thought it must be important if he did. Probably he thought he could better protect her.

Swallowing hard, she shuffled the cards and said, "I'm Baby Doe. Don't think I've seen you two around here before."

Heavy silence followed her words. She persisted, determined to find out their names. She had been doing that for a week and still hadn't found a Brayton. "I like to know the names of the men who play at my table," she continued, then nodded toward Rogue. "That's Dirk."

After a long pause, the slimmer, younger of the two men said, his voice soft and smooth, "Just deal the cards, lady. You'll know our names soon enough."

For some reason the man's voice made a shiver run up Shenandoah's spine, and for the first time since she had begun playing poker, she had trouble keeping her hands steady.

The two men were handsome. They had thick, dark wavy hair, worn long. Their eyes were large and dark, surrounded by long curly lashes. Both had long straight noses and strong angular faces; both were tall, long-legged, and well-muscled. However, there were differences between the two. One was larger, about Rogue's size, had sharper features, and sported a thick black mustache. The other was a few inches shorter, less heavily muscled, and clean-shaven.

The two men were enough alike to be brothers. Shenandoah suddenly caught her breath. Could these men be the Braytons? Overwhelmed with the possibility, she glanced at Rogue. He nodded slightly at her. So, he'd had the same idea. At last, the game was really being played. Shenandoah became calm. She smiled at both men, not knowing which would be Tad, if either. She dealt as she never had before. She dealt to win at all costs.

The men were good poker players, playing easily and yet intently. But Shenandoah and Rogue were good too. The games evened out between them, all of them winning equally at first, but then Shenandoah began to win a little more often. It had an immediate effect on the two brothers. The older, larger one threw in his cards and told the younger to go get them a bottle and four glasses.

Then he turned his attention on Shenandoah. "Name's Tad. Tad Brayton. Maybe you've heard of me." He grinned, showing large white teeth, amazingly straight. His eyes undressed Shenandoah while he leaned back casually in his chair.

She nodded. "Yes. Seems like I may have."

"Something around Tombstone," Rogue added, drawing Tad's attention away from Shenandoah.

Tad kept his eyes on Shenandoah as he answered, "Tombstone. Mighty rich place."

"So I've heard," Rogue agreed.

The younger brother entered silently, bearing the bottle and glasses. He slid into a chair, then poured four drinks.

"I never drink when gambling," Shenandoah said, noticing that Rogue didn't take his drink either.

"I suppose you never drink with strangers," the younger brother added, nodding at Rogue.

"That's right."

"Name's Tobe. Tobe Brayton."

Rogue picked up his drink and downed it.

Shenandoah shuffled cards. "You want to play poker, gentlemen?"

Tad said, "I'd like to play, lady, but not poker."

Shenandoah forced herself not to show any emotion, but instead smiled slyly and glanced toward Rogue. This was going to be much harder than she had imagined.

"The lady belongs to me," Rogue said, breaking into the conversation.

Tad looked at Rogue, put his hands on the two guns he wore low on his hips, and said, "Tobe, who do you think the lady belongs to?"

Tobe chuckled low in his throat, then said, "Never knew a woman yet who didn't go for you, Tad."

Shenandoah forced a laugh from her throat. "And, gentlemen, I haven't known a man yet who didn't go for me. That sometimes leads to a problem. Wouldn't you say?"

"Not a problem for long," Tad muttered, his eyes smoldering as he looked at Shenandoah.

"Perhaps," Shenandoah responded, "but I never leave one of my men in the lurch, so to speak. I mean, I always see that they have—"

"I've got a real beauty out at the hacienda," Tad interrupted quickly.

"He's right," Tobe agreed. "She used to be a real hellcat, but we tamed her good."

"Too good, maybe," Tad said, looking at Shenandoah with barely concealed lust.

"Tad likes them feisty," Tobe added.

"And what do you like, Tobe?" Shenandoah asked, her voice low and seductive.

"Whatever Tad likes. He gets all the women, and then lets me and T.J. have them when he's done. Breaks them in, you might say."

"Don't they have any choice?"

Tobe laughed. "They all want Tad, and when he gets done, they're happy to have us . . . happy to get us because by then they've got to have a man, any man."

Tad nodded in agreement. "A woman needs more than one man anyway, especially a woman like you, Baby Doe. Dirk may be all right, but we can show you a real good time out at our place."

"I told you she's *my* woman," Rogue growled.

Tad nodded at the bottle and Tobe poured three more drinks. Tad pointedly drank Shenandoah's drink, then upended his other with Tobe and Rogue. "I'm not saying she's not your woman. I hear you're good with a gun and that you and Baby Doe have had a little experience in our line of work on the other side of the border."

"Could be," Rogue said.

"We're planning some big jobs. Could use some outside help, especially a woman's help."

"What about the one out at your hacienda?" Shenandoah asked, anxious for news about Arabella.

Tad frowned. "She's not cut out for that kind of work."

"Thinks she's too good," Tobe agreed, drawing a long, thin dagger from his boot and running the cool, smooth, flat side of the blade down his cheek. "I've taught her some manners, but she has more to learn."

"You like to teach women manners, Tobe?" Shenandoah asked sweetly, feeling her stomach churn in disgust.

"Don't necessarily like to, but have to now and then. For instance, she wouldn't give us her name at first. But when I showed her what my sweet little blade here could do, she told us quick enough."

"What is her name?" Shenandoah asked breathlessly.

"No need to know it, unless you two plan to join us out at the hacienda," Tad said firmly, his eyes darting from Rogue to Shenandoah and back again.

"Bella," Tobe replied, as if he hadn't heard his brother. "Pretty name. Pretty lady."

Shenandoah felt sick, but sure now that they were on the right track. Bella had been a childhood name for Arabella. She glanced over at Rogue. He put a hand out and grasped hers, then turned toward Tad.

"Baby Doe and I here are always interested in a good job."

Tad nodded, glanced at Tobe, then looked hard at Shenandoah. "Come on out to the hacienda, Baby Doe, and I'll give you all the time you want to decide you want me, not this fellow you've outgrown."

"Your offer sounds interesting, Tad. I've got to admit you appeal to a woman, but so does Dirk here."

Rogue nodded, crushed Shenandoah's hand in his, then leaned back in his chair. "If you want, Doe, we might go on out to their place. Have a look around. Maybe we'll stay, maybe we won't."

Shenandoah looked at Rogue, smiled, then glanced over at Tad. "All right," she said slowly. "Why don't you show us your place, and we'll see if we like what you've got."

A grin slowly spread over Tad's face. "I can guarantee you'll like what I've got, ma'am."

Shenandoah nodded, set the cards down decisively, and stood up. "When shall we leave?"

"The sooner the better," Tad said. "The dark won't make any difference to you. You'll both be blindfolded."

"Now wait a minute," Rogue interrupted. "We're not—"

"Can't take any chances," Tad stopped him. "It's a full-moon night, and almost as bright as day out there. If you go to the hacienda and plan to come out alive, you're going in blindfolded."

Shenandoah looked urgently at Rogue.

He shrugged. "All right."

"Good," Tad said, standing up, his Spanish spurs

jingling. "We'll get the horses ready. They won't be any too happy starting back this soon, but when we take the only reason to be in El Toro Rojo with us, there won't be any reason to stay."

As they maneuvered their way out of the small room, Tad made it a point to pull Shenandoah to his side. His body heat radiated over her as he fingered the fine fabric of her shawl, smiling down at her. "You won't regret this decision," he said softly. "You want pretty gowns and shawls like this, just say so. I'll see you have all you want at the hacienda. I'll make you real happy, just as soon as we get rid of Dirk."

She smiled up at him, leaning close, so that her breasts almost touched his shirt. "Not so fast, Tad Brayton. I'll make up my mind later, and don't go branding me before I decide."

He grinned, his teeth sharp and white in the light. "I like a woman with spunk, and I sure like a woman who can play hell out of cards. We're going to get along fine."

"Baby Doe," Rogue called from the bottom of the stairs.

Shenandoah gave Tad a long, considering look, then went to Rogue.

Once in the shadows of their room, Rogue pulled Shenandoah roughly against him, crushing her to his chest. "I thought I'd kill him on the spot, and that pandering brother along with him. Hell, Shenandoah, I don't know if I can go along with all this. That man's practically eating you alive, and I'm not supposed to stop him."

Shenandoah shivered against Rogue, putting her hands around his neck and drawing his mouth down to hers. Their lips met in a fiery explosion of passion, fear, and tension. They radiated their frustrations to each other through their bodies, each reaching out to the other. Finally they broke apart, more frustrated, more tense than ever.

"Rogue, please help me in this. Tad is not going to touch me, but I have to let him think he might. I have to feed his ego if he is to take us to Arabella. And you heard. They have her, and who knows what they've done. Please help me."

Rogue ran a hand through his hair, took a deep breath, and said, "I'm sorry. Of course we're going after Arabella. It's just that I want to smash in his face every time I see it. And I hate the way he looks at you."

"He means nothing to me, Rogue. And when I think of what he has done to Arabella, I can hardly stand to be near him, much less be nice to him."

"Is that right?" Rogue asked softly. "He's a good-looking devil."

"Not to me he isn't. Hold me tight for a moment, Rogue. I'm scared. Those men play for keeps."

Rogue held her against him and stroked her hair. "I'll take care of you, Doe. Don't worry. And we'll get your sister out of there."

Suddenly she jerked her head up. "Rogue, how will we get out? We're going in blindfolded."

"Don't worry about that. We'll get out of there, one way or another. Now, we'd better get our things together and get downstairs. They're waiting, and impatiently, if I know Tad Brayton.''

"Red will be sorry to see us go, but he always knew we'd be moving on.''

"I doubt if anyone stays here long.''

Shenandoah looked into Rogue's eyes, her own expression becoming more serious. "In case I don't get to tell you later, I really appreciate your helping me out on this.''

"I wouldn't have let you come alone, Shenandoah.''

"Well, I wanted to thank you and tell you again that if we all come through this, I plan to keep my end of the bargain.''

"We'll talk about that once Arabella is free. Now, let's get ready. It may be a long ride to the Brayton's hideout. And, Shenandoah, we *will* come out of this alive.''

Not long after, four riders—two who were blind-folded—were seen leaving the sleepy Mexican village, traveling southeast as moonlight sparkled off the San Pedro River. Making their way to its banks, they followed its winding path south.

8

After traveling through the night and past noon the next day, the four riders turned to follow a steep, narrow trail up the side of a mountain. Still blindfolded, Rogue and Shenandoah could not see, but their mustangs went single file, carefully picking their way over stony ground and through scrub brush and twisted, gnarled trees. As they rose in elevation, the temperature cooled and the scent of evergreen filled the air.

When at last they stopped, Shenandoah felt as if she might never walk again. The long ride across the flat desert had been bad enough, but clinging to her horse in a sidesaddle as it found its way up a sharp incline had been almost more than she could endure. Her limbs felt permanently locked in place.

Large warm hands suddenly removed her blindfold, but even though the sun was low, the unaccustomed light made her eyes tear and she quickly shut them against the pain. The strong hands encircled her waist and lifted her from the mustang, then pulled her to a hard body and let her slide down its length until her feet reached the ground.

As her legs regained their strength, the hands held her close and she could smell the scent of a man, but the scent was not Rogue's. She wanted to move away, wanted to call out to Rogue, for she was suddenly aware of just how vulnerable she could be in the Braytons' hideout. But she didn't move, or say anything, and when her eyes adjusted, she opened them to see Tad Brayton smiling triumphantly down at her.

"Take a look around, Baby Doe. You're home. We're proud of the place we've got here."

Shenandoah took the opportunity to step out of Tad's embrace and put distance between them. However, she was careful not to let it seem like rejection. She looked for Rogue first. He stood near his mustang, not far from her. There was strain in his face, and anger too. He had not missed Tad's hands on her. This was not going to be easy for either of them. She smiled encouragingly at Rogue, and when he nodded back, she finally looked around.

She was surprised to see they were in some type of a ghost town, or what looked to have been an abandoned mining town. The Braytons had obviously revived it. The small adobe and wood buildings hung precariously to the side of a steep, rocky mountain. Behind them loomed the open faces of abandoned mines. Dust billowed around them as a sudden gust of wind swirled down the short street that made up the town. At one end, a large, imposing hacienda stood looming over the small, squat structures that ranged down from it.

She looked around further, but as far as she could see there was no trail or road leading out of the place. She suddenly felt trapped. But there had to be at least one trail that could take them out, because they had just come up one. It was obviously well hidden, for the Braytons were taking no chances on anyone accidentally finding their hideout or on anyone leaving without their permission.

Shenandoah shivered in the late-afternoon sun, and turned toward Rogue. He did no more than raise one craggy brow at her, but suddenly she felt less alone. With Rogue near her, she didn't need to be worried. They would find her sister and then leave. Nothing could keep them in this place once they had Arabella. She smiled slightly at Rogue, then turned to look at Tad Brayton.

"Security's good, too," Tad said, motioning toward several armed guards walking the perimeter of the town. "Easy place to secure. Mountain behind, steep ledge on the other side. We could hold an army off from here, with enough supplies. So, little lady," Tad added, putting a strong, thick arm around Shenandoah's shoulders and beginning to lead her in the direction of the largest building, "there's no need for you to be worried. You'll be the safest here you've ever been."

"Safe from whom?" she asked, glancing at Tad sideways. She felt Rogue's eyes boring into her back as he and Tobe fell into step behind them.

Tad laughed, pulled her against his side, and said in a low tone, "Nothing to fear from me, ma'am. All I want to do is worship you." His eyes were dark and hot as he ran a hand up and down her arm.

Shenandoah wanted to push him away from her, but she couldn't. She would have to endure his attentions until they could free Arabella. She was glad that as a gambler she was used to concealing her emotions, or the anger that she was holding deep inside might have boiled over and ruined all their plans. Finally, in response to Tad's words, she laughed lightly, trying to play an experienced woman, and said, "You talk fine, Tad Brayton, but is that all you do well?"

Tad's hand tensed on her shoulder. "I do everything well, Baby. And I'll be happy to prove that just as soon as you give the word."

Shenandoah smiled seductively at him. "I never like to rush into anything, Tad. Besides, there's Dirk to think about. He's quite a man."

"Give me the chance and I can make you forget all about him."

"That's the way I like to hear a man talk. I just may like this place."

"Better that you like me," Tad responded, his voice low and intimate.

Shenandoah smiled at him again, but said nothing, preferring to let him think she was considering his offer. Secretly she wondered how long he would play her game before he grew bored with the chase and decided to end it. With as many men as he had here,

Rogue couldn't stand against them all. One man and two women wouldn't be able to hold off the Braytons and their gang. They would have to get Arabella out of here fast. There was no other answer.

A few dark-haired, dark-eyed Mexicans silently watched them from adobe buildings as they covered the short distance to the hacienda. Tad noticed her interest in them and said, "Brought a few locals up here to help out. They'll take care of our horses. Got some women to take care of the hacienda. You don't have to worry about anything, Baby . . . except pleasing me."

"Think I could do that?" she asked, glancing down his long form in mock interest.

Tad growled, "No doubt about that, Baby Doe. No doubt at all."

She laughed lightly, and heard Rogue curse behind them. She didn't know why, but Rogue seemed to think she had some kind of personal interest in Tad Brayton. Rogue knew this was a game. He knew she was the lure to get Arabella out. But could he still be jealous?

Tad was a good-looking man. Although Rogue knew they were playing roles in a very dangerous game, he had been acting jealous since they had first met Tad. Maybe he was overacting, or maybe he was concerned about their precarious position, or maybe he was feeling pressure to get back to Leadville. Whatever the case, he couldn't really believe she would be interested in the man who had kidnapped her sister, no matter how much personal charm and looks Tad Brayton had. Still, there was a tiny lingering doubt about Rogue's jealousy in her mind as she turned her attention on the coming reunion with her little sister.

The hacienda was a large two-story building made of stone, with a red-tiled roof and elaborate black wrought-iron grilles over the windows. It was an imposing structure, more stronghold than house. Shenandoah suddenly wondered how Arabella had survived at all, coming from her warm, safe home in Philadelphia to be faced with the horror and terror of the Brayton brothers, their gunmen, and their fortress-hideout in Mexico. Once here, Arabella would surely have believed that no one, not even a loving sister and uncle, could reach her. But Shenandoah knew her sister had survived, somehow, because Tad and Tobe had mentioned her.

Tad steered Shenandoah through tall wrought-iron gates into a derelict courtyard. A small, forgotten fountain gurgled sluggishly in the background. The interior was cool and dim. Shenandoah shivered, feeling the oppressive atmosphere of the place affect her. Several gunmen, wearing faded Levi's, frayed plaid shirts, and Colt .45's displayed prominently on their hips, leaned against the walls of the courtyard. They chewed tobacco and spat at will. Seeing Shenandoah, they straightened up, then followed her with their eyes.

Tad nodded curtly toward the gunmen as they walked by, and said to one, "T.J. in his office?"

An affirmative nod was his reply.

They crossed dirty, broken tiles, then Tad abruptly stopped outside an intricately carved heavy wooden door. He knocked once, then twice, swung the door inward, and motioned for Shenandoah to enter.

Heavy, faded burgundy draperies covered the outside window, shutting out most of the natural light. A kerosene lamp lit the top of a scarred large desk and cast eerie shadows on the face of the man sitting behind it. Open books, maps, and papers were scattered over the top of the desk, and a sawed-off shotgun lay within easy reach. The man glanced up as they entered, then quickly stood and opened the draperies.

Light flooded the area around the desk, leaving the rest of the room in shadow and revealing the toll time had taken on the once elegant interior. Where there had been expensive imported carpet there was now only cold bare stone. And of furniture, only the desk remained, too heavy to have been worth moving down the mountainside. Wooden crates served as chairs.

The man behind the desk looked remarkably like Tad and Tobe, only he was older by at least ten years. A silver streak ran from his right temple through his long dark hair. A silver-tinged full beard and mustache covered the lower half of his face. His eyes were cold and hard, calculating, clever. Standing, he was tall and lean. He looked Shenandoah over carefully, then motioned for her to sit down. As she eased onto a hard crate, Rogue became the center of the man's attention.

Finally Tad said, "T.J., these are the two Alfredo told us about. Knew we wouldn't have any difficulty getting them to join up with us."

Shenandoah glanced at Rogue. He had been right that Alfredo would make a good messenger. Rogue did not see her glance. His face was stern. His right hand hovered near the gun he wore on his hip. And his eyes were hard slits fastened on the man standing behind the desk.

Tad continued, "This is Dirk, and that's Baby Doe."

"We know their names," T.J. Brayton said quietly, his voice low and firm. "Montaña Diablo. Devil Mountain. That's the name of this place. As I'm sure you've already noticed, this used to be a mining community. Silver. Too many deaths, too many cave-ins. No one will work it anymore. The natives think devils reside here. Maybe they're right."

Tad laughed softly. "Now that we're here, they're right."

Tobe pulled his dagger from his boot and gently ran the flat of the blade down his cheek. "At least the natives that work here think we're devils."

Tad smiled at his brother. "And we've only just arrived. Give us some time and maybe they'll think of some other names for us."

"Remember, brothers, we're not here to impress the Mexicans. We're here to enlarge our operation," T.J. said firmly, then turned his attention to Rogue. "Dirk, I've heard you're a good man with a fast gun.

We've need of that. And we've need of a woman who can handle a gun, and handle men.''

Shenandoah forced herself to laugh a low, seductive sound, remembering the role she must play to rescue Arabella. ''Well, I know which end of a gun to hold, but I'd rather handle a man any day.''

Tad laughed, and T.J. smiled.

Rogue stiffened and looked at Shenandoah through slitted eyes, his jaw clenched.

''Well, you may like to handle men, but you'd better leave mine alone,'' a soft, cultured voice said from the back of the room.

Shenandoah and Rogue jerked their heads toward a dark corner. Out of the shadows walked a young woman, long blond hair falling in a riotous mass of curls to her hips. She was of medium height, slim, small-boned, with full breasts and hips. She glided toward them, her wide-spaced large blue eyes throwing angry darts around the room. She wore a simple gown of dark blue cotton, but what once had been a demure gown had been changed to sensual because most of the front buttons had been left undone, exposing the deep cleft of her breasts.

Shenandoah could only stare as the woman walked toward her, for this had to be her sister, Arabella. All grown up she looked almost exactly like their dead mother.

The young woman stopped in front of Shenandoah, placed her hands on her hips, and said, ''If you think you're going to take Tad away from me, you can forget it. He's my man.''

Up close, Shenandoah could see dark circles under the blue eyes, the blond hair was matted, and the dress was stained. There were dark marks on the pale white skin that looked like old bruises. Still, Arabella was a beautiful woman, and Shenandoah hurt inside for what had been done to her.

Whatever torment the Braytons had put Arabella through must have affected her mind, for she seemed not to recognize Shenandoah at all and she was jealously guarding Tad, the man who had kidnapped her. But then, perhaps Tad was the only one who could keep the other men from Arabella, protecting her somewhat. Shenandoah was probably the last person Arabella expected to see walk into the hacienda, especially playing the role of Baby Doe, a wanton outlaw, so it was not too surprising if she didn't recognize her own half-sister after six years. Still, Shenandoah had somehow expected to be recognized.

"Damn, Bella," Tad said angrily, and jerked the young woman away from Shenandoah. "You stay out of my business." He cuffed her lightly against the head, and sent her sprawling toward Rogue.

Rogue caught her, steadied her, then dropped his hands to his sides. Bella looked up at him thoughtfully, then walked back to Tad.

"Is that some new man you're throwing me to?"

"I'll do whatever I want with you, Bella. Now, be nice to the man. His name is Dirk. Make him happy, or"—he pulled her long hair hard before continuing— "you know what I'll do if you don't keep me happy."

Arabella winced. Her anger and defiance suddenly

crumpled. She hung her head. "Yes, Tad, but you know it's only you I want." She pressed her soft, voluptuous body against Tad's muscular one and ran a hand up his chest to begin unbuttoning the front of his shirt so that she could reach the matted black hair underneath.

Tad watched Shenandoah as Bella touched him, wanting to see Baby Doe's reaction.

Knowing he was watching her, Shenandoah raised an eyebrow and said, "Trying to hobble a lusty bull can sure make him mean."

Tad snorted, then laughed.

Arabella whirled around, her anger quickly returning. "He's mine and I'm not going to share him."

"You don't own *anything* around here, Bella. Get out," T.J. said quietly, sternly.

Arabella took one look at him, hesitated, then turned to go.

Tobe stopped her, a hand on her arm. She looked suspiciously up at him, then shuddered as he ran the long, cool blade of his dagger down her throat to the deep cleft of her breasts. "I'll be down to see you later, girl," he said softly, then removed his knife.

Arabella hurried from the room.

"Don't pay no never-mind to the boys," T.J. said to Shenandoah. "They'll have their fun. She's just a little something Tad picked up on one of our jobs."

Shenandoah forced herself to smile, while feeling sick and angry inside. "I don't care how you treat anyone but me, and I'll telling all of you right now that nobody messes with Baby Doe unless she wants it."

T.J. smiled. "I think you're just the kind of woman we're looking for, Baby Doe. We're planning something big. Expanding our business, you might say. We're adding on some new people."

"Will it be worth our time?" Rogue asked, playing the part of a greedy small-time robber perfectly.

"I can guarantee it. But we'll get down to the plans later. Know you had a long, hard ride here. Settle in. We'll talk later. Tad, find them some rooms. Tobe, stay here. I want to talk to you."

"All right," Rogue agreed, then added, "but I'll want to hear those plans soon."

T.J. nodded, and Tobe joined him by the desk.

Outside, Tad said, "You sure you want your own room, Baby Doe?"

"No," she replied, "I'll share a room with Dirk, like I've been doing."

Tad frowned. "No. If you don't bunk with me, you'll have your own room. There's lots of them."

"The lady stays with me," Rogue said firmly.

Tad glanced at Rogue. "Everyone has separate rooms here. T.J.'s orders. You want something different, ask him. He's the boss."

Rogue nodded. "All right. I'll take it up with him later. Right now, let's get settled in. Baby Doe's tired."

Tad looked with concern at Shenandoah. "Sorry, honey. Sure you're tired, and hot, I bet. Dusty, too. Look, there's a great pool for bathing not far from here. Real private, too. Nobody'll bother you. I'll see to that."

Suspicious, Shenandoah started to refuse the offer, then remembered the role she was playing. As they started upstairs, she said, "Sounds good, Tad. Maybe I'm beginning to like the place."

Tad looked back at her, his eyes dark and gleaming. "I knew you would, Baby."

Behind them, Rogue clenched his teeth, his eyes hard bits of blue fire.

9

Shenandoah stepped from a rocky mountain path into a small secluded glade. The place was just as wonderful as Tad had described it. Sunlight filtered through scrub oaks and piñon trees to glimmer off the still dark waters of a deep pool, leaving its banks in shadow. A stream of water gurgled as it cascaded over rocks to join the silent pool below. The scent of evergreen filled the air, and birds chirped from the tops of the tallest trees.

Although it seemed a perfect place for a bath, Shenandoah didn't know how safe she was. Tad had given her directions to find the pool, then left on business. Rogue had gone to scout around the Braytons' hideout. She had been left alone to bathe and relax, as the sensual Baby Doe would surely have wanted to do. But Shenandoah didn't trust Tad, or his brothers, or their hired men. In fact, there was little she trusted about the Braytons or their town.

Even her sister seemed a stranger to her, for she had not expected the Arabella she had found. She was anxious to speak with her sister alone, but there had not yet been an opportunity. If she appeared too interested in Bella, it might make someone suspicious. However, she felt sure her sister would be anxious to leave as soon as she learned that Shenandoah had come to rescue her, no matter the way Arabella had acted about Tad Brayton earlier.

But in order to rescue her sister, Shenandoah had to play the role of Baby Doe, and that included a bath in the deep pool. Even though she wanted a bath, she had not forgotten Rogue's warning when she had bathed in the San Pedro River. Although she felt vulnerable, she determinedly set the bar of lavender soap she had brought with her near the pool, then began to unbutton her shirt.

Suddenly she heard a spur jingle behind her. She whirled. Tad Brayton stepped into the glade, a look of triumph in his eyes, a smile of pleasure on his lips.

"You didn't have to wait long, did you, Baby Doe?" he said as he stalked toward her.

"Wait?" She didn't know what to do. Her worst fear had come true. She was completely alone with Tad Brayton, and there was no one near to help. She couldn't even try to escape. She had to play the part of Baby Doe, a woman who was interested in Tad Brayton and who was well acquainted with the ways of women and men. She would simply have to talk her way around Tad, if that were possible.

"For me. You knew I'd be joining you."

"I thought you had business, so—"

"You're the only business I have, Baby Doe."

"You do know how to flatter a woman, Tad."

The big brawny man smiled. "A man doesn't have to flatter you, honey. You've got all a woman needs, and more besides."

Shenandoah forced herself to smile. She held her ground as Tad stopped close beside her. She could feel the heat of his body surrounding her, closing out the cool, clean air of the glade. "Well, I was going to bathe," she said, hoping to discourage him.

He grinned, showing big strong teeth. He looked hungry as he said, "Good. I'll join you." He unbuckled his gunbelt and carefully laid it nearby. When he turned back to Shenandoah, he said, "I never mix guns with women."

Shenandoah nodded, trying desperately to figure a way out of the situation without offending Tad.

"I'll just finish what you started," he said, reaching for the front of her shirt. He began unbuttoning where Shenandoah had left off. His hands were hot and sure as they moved quickly against her, exposing more and more of her pale flesh.

Shenandoah held her breath, fighting down the fury and fear that were threatening to overwhelm her. She had to remain calm and somehow stop Tad from going any further. When he started pulling the shirt out of her waistband, she laughed low in her throat, and said, putting her hands on his shoulders, "You know, you never did ask me if I'd made my choice."

Tad didn't stop his movements. He simply pulled the shirt out, unbuttoned the last buttons, then jerked it open. He exhaled loudly as he eagerly looked at Shenandoah's full breasts covered only by the sheer silk of her rose-colored chemise. "Baby, you didn't have to give me your answer, just like I don't have to tell you what you do to me."

"But, Tad . . ." she protested, stepping back from him as she dropped her hands from his shoulders.

"Never wanted a woman as bad as I want you, Baby Doe. Nothing in heaven or hell is going to stop me from having you." He pulled Shenandoah close to him, one arm wrapped around her waist, the huge hand hot on her hip. With the other, he quickly covered one breast, massaging it hard as his breath began to come quickly.

"Tad," she protested again, pushing against his shoulders with her hands. "You must wait. I . . . well, I . . ."

"I didn't figure you for a woman who needed all the sweet talk, Baby. Be still a minute and you'll forget all about talking." His hand left one breast to capture the other, stroking it, toying with the tip, then kneading it hard.

"Tad," she gasped. "You must—"

"I know, Baby. In a minute. I want to see all of you first. We've got plenty of time."

He suddenly pulled her hard against him, flattening her breasts against his broad chest. "Baby," he murmured, his hands stroking down her back to her hips. Grabbing them, he pushed her into him, grinding his hardness against her. When she tried to push him away, he didn't seem to notice. Instead, he moved one hand to the back of her head and held her firmly as he sought her lips with his mouth.

Horrified and repulsed, unable to move her head, Shenandoah opened her mouth to protest. But Tad quickly caught her lips with his own, scratching her with his mustache as he pressed hard against her mouth and brutally pushed inside with his tongue. She struggled within his grasp, but he was too big, too strong to stop. Belatedly she realized just how powerless she was against a big man who was determined to have her. Rogue had been gentle and considerate. She had thought all men would be like him. Now she knew different, but the knowledge might have come to late.

Suddenly a voice broke the quiet of the glade. "Take your hands off her, Brayton."

Tad jerked away from Shenandoah, his hands going for his guns. But he had left them by the pool. Cursing, he started for them.

Rogue Rogan stepped into the glade, his right hand hovering near the Colt .45 on his right hip. "Don't move, Brayton," Rogue commanded, his voice hard with menace.

Tad didn't move. He knew a man didn't like to lose at cards or women. It could make them deadly. And Tad didn't intend to die, just yet.

"Ro . . . Dirk," Shenandoah said, trying to keep the relief from her voice.

"Stay out of this," he responded, his eyes still on Tad.

Surprised, Shenandoah stepped away from Tad,

tasting blood where he had cut her lips with his teeth. Her hands were shaking. Tad had frightened her. He had repulsed her. She had been helpless against him. Still, all their lives depended on him wanting her. She could not reject him, and Rogue must not kill him. They had to continue their charade if they were to rescue her sister and get out alive.

As she shakily buttoned her shirt, Shenandoah forced sweetness into her voice and said, "Dirk, honey, you're a jealous man, I know. But remember, you were interested in what Tad had here. That Bella's real fine if you'd clean her up a little. Besides, we're all going to be working together and we have to get to know each other better."

Rogue frowned. "You and Tad know each other too well already. I'll make up my mind about Bella later. Why don't you go keep her company, Tad? And stay away from Baby Doe. She's mine till I say different."

"Now, Dirk, honey," Shenandoah began, "I—"

"Don't push me, Baby. I'm feeling mean," Rogue said, his blue eyes hot. "And you, Brayton, keep your hands off what belongs to me. Your honey's waiting for you back at the hacienda."

"You're pushing hard, Dirk. Better remember where you are before you go and do something foolish," Tad replied.

"I know only too well where I am. Doe, bring me his guns."

Tad stiffened but didn't move. It would be easy for

the man before him to pump him full of lead before he could reach his own pistols.

Shenandoah felt as if everything were spiraling out of control as she carefully picked up Tad's heavy guns and carried them to Rogue.

"Empty the chambers." Rogue's right hand flinched over his forty-five, as if he had to force it to keep from drawing and killing Tad Brayton.

Fumbling, then making her hands stay calm, Shenandoah did as Rogue bid. When the pistols were harmless, she holstered them, set them on the ground near Rogue, then turned toward Tad.

Tad was glowering, hating for another person to touch his Colts. But when he saw Baby Doe's concerned face, he nodded, saying, "That's all right, Baby. We'll take care of him later. All in good time."

"You stay away from my property and there won't be any problems," Rogue said, taking hold of Shenandoah's arm and backing away from Tad's pistols as he drew her with him. "Now, take your guns and go."

"You must be looking to die, mister," Tad said, glaring at Rogue. He quickly picked up his Colt .45's, buckled them on his hips, then nodded at Shenandoah before stalking from the glade.

Shenandoah let out a sigh of relief and slumped against Rogue, hardly able to believe he had faced down Tad Brayton without getting any of them killed.

Rogue stepped away from Shenandoah and said,

his voice low and tense, "If you want that bath, you'd better take it."

"Rogue, thanks. I don't know what I would have done if you hadn't shown up when you did. Tad—"

"Don't play games with me, Shenandoah," he interrupted coldly. "I saw you with Brayton. Now, bathe. It'll be dark soon and I want to get back to the hacienda." He turned and walked away from her.

For a moment Shenandoah could only stare in confusion at Rogue's broad back. He seemed to be studying the pool, but she knew all his thoughts were centered on her. What did he mean? Did he actually think she had wanted Tad's attentions? "Rogue, I don't understand. I was frightened until you—"

"Shenandoah." Rogue's voice was strained, anger near the surface. "Either take the bath or let's go. I don't want to discuss Tad Brayton."

She took the few steps to Rogue's side. "Rogue, I'm playing a part. I can't reject Tad Brayton outright, or we won't be able to get Arabella—"

"Tad Brayton seems to have a strong appeal for both you sisters. I wonder if—"

"Rogue! He does not. How can you say such a thing? Arabella is confused, distraught, trying to stay alive. I'm trying to rescue her. So are you, or I thought you were."

"I'm willing to rescue her, if she's willing to leave."

"Of course she wants to leave."

"I'm not so sure after seeing—"

"She must be playing some kind of role too. Rogue—"

"Okay. We're all playing a game. Now, take the bath. Shenandoah, I said—"

"Rogue, will you listen to me?" She put a hand on Rogue's muscled arm.

He jerked his arm away and walked away from her. When he turned back, his eyes were hooded. He stood with his legs wide apart, hand near his Colt when he said, "Go ahead and take your clothes off, Shenandoah. Take your bath. I have as much right to see you as Tad does."

Shocked, Shenandoah could only stare at him. "What do you mean?" she asked, her voice hardly more than a whisper, her eyes deep green pools.

"You know what I mean. Just how far would you have gone with Tad if I hadn't show up?"

"I told you—"

"I know what you told me, but I also know what I saw."

"Rogue, I—"

"Take your clothes off, Shenandoah."

She had never seen him this way before. Suddenly she was frightened of Rogue. All her plans for Arabella were tied up with him. What if he demanded a price she did not want to pay? At El Toro Rojo, she had wanted him, but now when he looked so aloof, like a stranger judging her for imagined wrongs, she wanted to be far away from him. He was wrong, so totally wrong. She didn't want Tad Brayton. She would have found some way to stop him. But how did she stop Rogue from hurting her?

"Go ahead," Rogue repeated. "I'm included in this game, aren't I? Anyway, it's all just been a game with you from the start, hasn't it? I wonder how far I can believe anything you've ever said. After all, you're a gambler and you're good at winning, no matter the odds."

"Rogue, you've got this all wrong. I don't understand you. I just want to rescue Arabella."

"What about what I want?"

She looked away from him and said quietly, "What do you want, Rogue?"

"You know what I want."

She heard him move toward her. She looked up. He was close. His eyes were hard blue chips of stone. "Is that the payment you demand?"

"Take your clothes off and take a bath, Shenandoah. We'll talk about my payment later."

She took a deep breath. She wasn't reaching him. She didn't know if she could, not right now. She wanted to scream out at him, force him to see the truth, but most of all she wanted him to hold her . . . gently. She needed his strength wrapped around her, comforting her. Instead he was frightening her, accusing her of something that wasn't true. Once more, she forced her emotions down. She must not let him push her out of control. She must remain calm if she were to free her sister and get them all out alive. Perhaps it was just the pressure getting to Rogue.

She smiled slightly. "All right, Rogue. I'll take a bath. Here, you hold my clothes."

His eyes narrowed and she suddenly took perverse pleasure in slowly undressing before him. She unbuttoned her shirt again, slipped it from her body, watching Rogue watching her. His eyes never left her. His face never changed expression. When she held the shirt out for him, he slowly took it as if mesmerized. It was still warm with her body heat and his large hand curled involuntarily around its softness, crushing it in a hard grip.

Next, she undid her long skirt and let it slide down her legs to the ground, followed by a white cotton petticoat. She picked up these, too, and placed them in his arms. The scent of lavender suddenly floated around them. His nostrils flared. He gripped her clothing harder.

"Help me with my boots, Rogue," she said.

He grimaced, but set the clothes aside.

She sat down on the pine-cushioned ground. He knelt before her, then quickly jerked off each boot. He set them aside, then held out a hand for her. She took it, feeling his heat sear up her arm. He slowly helped her stand, then stepped back, as if wanting to get away from her.

Completely nude except for her sheer chemise and drawers, she stood very still, letting Rogue look at her in long, slow detail. Then she calmly walked by him toward the pool. Just as she was about to step into it, he stopped her.

"All your clothes, Shenandoah."

Her breath caught. She glanced back at him. His blue eyes were hooded, his face implacable. "Rogue, I—"

"You were ready to do this for Tad."

She started to protest, then stopped. He wouldn't believe her, not then, not now. She must pacify him for Arabella's sake. Later, she would have this out with him. Taking a deep breath, she said nothing but slowly drew the chemise from her body. Her flesh gleamed white in the shadows of the glade. Rogue inhaled suddenly. His muscles grew taut. She hesitated, then continued, slowly removing her drawers. When she held the last of her clothing in her hands, she walked quietly toward Rogue, determined not to show her fear, uncertainty, and deep shock at being nude before a man. She had to appear strong and unafraid for Arabella's sake.

Holding out the silken underclothes to him, she said, "I'm going to take my bath now, Rogue."

A nerve jumped in his cheek as he took the still-warm clothing from her.

She walked away from Rogue, entered the water, then took her lavender bar of soap from the bank. His eyes were on her. She could feel his hot, searing gaze even when she moved away from him, deliberately turning her back to him.

In the water she suddenly felt chilled, and shivered. She didn't know how much more she could stand, caught between Rogue and the Braytons. Then she thought of her sister again. Arabella had probably endured more, much more. Shenandoah must be strong and brave, the kind of older sister Arabella expected her to be.

Determined to enjoy the bath as much as possible,

Shenandoah moved to the other side of the pool, away from Rogue, and lavished soap all over her. It felt good to be clean again, and she tried to wash away all her worries, fears, and the touch of Tad Brayton. It didn't completely work, of course, but she felt better for being clean. She moved into deeper water, rinsed off, then faced Rogue again.

He hadn't moved. He still stood with legs widespread, holding her silk underwear, his eyes hooded. She moved slowly through the water toward him, dreading any further confrontation, but determined to keep them on their path until Arabella could be rescued.

She stepped out of the pool, water cascading from her. She shivered. The air was chill. Night would soon be upon them. Rogue did not move. His eyes feasted hungrily on her. To distract him, she said, "Rogue, I'll dress, then we can go back."

"Is that what you and Tad planned to do?"

"We hadn't planned anything!" she snapped, her control beginning to break. She grabbed for her underclothes.

He held them away from her. "Come here, Shenandoah," he said softly.

"Keep the clothes," she hissed, heading for her other clothing. But she didn't get far. Rogue suddenly grabbed her arm and spun her back to him. Before she quite knew what had happened, she was in his arms, her cool body pressed against his hot, rough clothes.

"Shenandoah," he said through gritted teeth as his

mouth descended on hers. For the second time that day, a man forced entry into her mouth.

Furious, Shenandoah struggled against Rogue. He held her tighter. She kicked against him, but she was barefoot and only hurt herself. She beat her fists against his shoulders, but he seemed not to notice as he tasted the sweetness of her mouth. As she fought him, Rogue became rougher, his hands moving hard over her bare flesh. His tongue plunged forcefully into her mouth, taking what he wanted. His clothes scratched her soft skin.

Frightened and furious, Shenandoah felt her control slipping further. As Rogue ended the kiss, she suddenly bit his lip and tasted blood. Rogue jerked up his head, tasting his own blood, then smiled wickedly.

"You want to play rough, Shenandoah?"

"I want you to leave me alone!"

"We've gone too far now."

She tried to jerk away. He let her go, holding her by only one wrist. She tried to break that grip, but he was too strong, too determined. "Rogue, stop this."

"You wouldn't have said that to Tad. In fact, you'd have been so eager you'd have undressed him. Isn't that right?"

She didn't answer. She continued to struggle, glaring at him, trying to keep in control. He had to come to his senses soon, unless he really believed she preferred Tad Brayton.

He shook her. "Answer me!"

"No! You're wrong. Leave me alone."

"Unbutton my shirt, like you'd have done for him."

"I will not."

He shook her again. Her hair finally came undone and tumbled down around her hips. Rogue's eyes widened for a moment, then he said, "You were willing to do whatever it took to rescue your sister, Shenandoah. Tad could get what he wanted. What about me?"

"It's not the same, Rogue." She suddenly felt like crying. She was so frustrated, so helpless. And she didn't want to see Rogue like this. But she pushed those feelings down.

"My shirt, Baby Doe, or I can leave the mountain right now."

"You'd go?"

His eyes narrowed.

"But you promised."

His face didn't change.

If he left, she could never rescue her sister alone, and then she, too, would be at the mercy of the Braytons. But would Rogue really leave, really break his promise? She couldn't afford to call his bluff, if it were one. This game was too important. Defeated. she stopped struggling and slowly began to unbutton his shirt, exposing curly blond hair.

Rogue stood very still as she carefully unbuttoned his shirt down to his pants. She tried not to notice, but his Levi's were once more giving testimony to what she aroused in him. She was afraid of him and yet at the same time the feel of his skin as she had touched him ever so lightly to unbutton the shirt had brought back the memory of lying in bed with him, wanting to touch him, wanting to be touched by him. She shook her head to get rid of the memory. This had nothing to do with that.

"Take it off, Shenandoah."

She jerked the shirt out of his Levi's, very aware of the hard, tanned flesh exposed to her. Without his prompting, she moved closer to him, pulling the shirt down his back, off his arms, exposing his complete torso. She let it drop to the ground. Suddenly she wanted to bury her fingers in the thick blond hair on his chest, feel the hardness of his muscles, press her breasts against his hot skin. Confused at her reaction, she shook her head again, puzzled at her own feelings.

"Now what would you have done to Tad?"

"Nothing," she mumbled, unable to take her eyes away from him, noticing once again the scars on his body.

"Nothing! I don't believe you. Come closer. Press yourself against me."

"Rogue, I—"

He pulled her to him, flattening her full breasts against his chest. He shuddered, his muscles straining as if against great internal stress. He grabbed her hair in his fists, binding her to him, pulling her head back so he could look into her eyes. "It's amazing how innocent you can look and act, but I know different. You weren't innocent with Brayton. Unbuckle my pants."

She swallowed, now fighting a growing languor, a

growing desire for him, no matter what he thought or said. "Your gun. I—"

"Unbuckle it, too."

With a will of their own, her hands did as he bid. When the gunbelt lay nearby, she unbuckled his belt, then began to unbutton his Levi's slowly, carefully, vitally aware of what she was about to expose. When the buttons were undone, she hesitated, looked back into his hard, implacable face, and said, "Rogue, I don't—"

"You wanted this, Doe. One man's as good as another, isn't he?"

"No. I—"

"I can satisfy you, Shenandoah. Don't worry—"

"Rogue, no!" she said suddenly, her voice cutting sharply through the gathering shadows. Her emotions were breaking through, threatening to overwhelm her. She had to get away. Surprising them both, she pushed back, then ran for her clothing. She grabbed it and started for the path. But Rogue caught her, whirled her around, and pulled her against him. She fought. They went down in a heap, clothes scattering around them.

"No, Rogue. No!" she cried again. "Not like this, please." She struggled against him, fighting his weight, fighting her own self as their bodies came together. She must not give in to him. Not this way. She must make him understand.

Rogue held her down, his body gleaming with sweat, his eyes blue fire. "I want you, Shenandoah. I don't care if you'd rather have Brayton."

"No."

"I've waited long enough."

"Rogue, I don't want Tad." His body was hot and hard against her. "I want *you*."

He suddenly went very still, his muscles taut. "What?" His voice was quiet.

"I want you, Rogue, even though you're treating me this way. I want *you*. Do you hear?"

"What about Brayton?"

"I've told you. He's nothing to me. I want you. I don't know why or how, but having you near me is more exciting than any game I ever dealt."

Rogue suddenly chuckled low in his throat. His body relaxed. He rolled over onto his back, keeping Shenandoah pulled close to his side. "Leave it to you to compare me to a game of poker."

Stunned by his sudden change, she sat up and looked at him. "Rogue?"

"Prove you want me."

She shook her head, wondering if she had heard him correctly. She felt completely off balance.

"Touch me, Shenandoah. Complete what you started. I ache all over for your touch."

She felt color rise in her cheeks. Her heart began to beat a heavy, drugging pattern. Although the light in the glade had grown dim, she could see Rogue very well. Once more, her hands moved on their own, seeking out the muscles of his chest, the thick blond hair, then following that hair lower and lower. She parted the front of his Levi's and released the vital symbol of his manhood.

Her breath caught in her throat. She had never seen a man like this before.

"Touch me, Doe." Rogue's voice was strained.

Carefully, afraid to hurt him, she reached out and took hold, stroking the smooth hard skin.

Rogue groaned. "I'm going to go crazy with wanting you if we don't do something about it soon."

"Oh," she said, "Rogue, you're beautiful."

Rogue coughed. "No. You're beautiful." His hands explored her nude body.

"You're beautiful too," she insisted, moving her hands more boldly on him.

Rogue gasped. "I can't take much more of that, Doe."

"You wanted me to touch you." She suddenly felt powerful, knowing the reaction she could invoke in him, and light-headed with the way he made her feel.

"I know what I wanted, but now I want more. Come here, Shenandoah." He drew her down to him, letting his hot hands glide over her, searching out the most intimate parts of her body. His hands moved between her thighs, igniting a fiery passion which spread from that center outward to consume her entire body.

This time, it was Shenandoah who gasped.

Rogue smothered her face with kisses as his hands continued to work their magic on her body.

As his mouth moved down her neck, she panted, "*Rogue*. Rogue, I had no idea I could feel this way."

"It gets better."

"Oh, Rogue."

His lips traced an intricate pattern over her breasts, stopping at each peak to arouse them with his hot, searing tongue. Shenandoah writhed against him, moaning, her hands clutching at his arms, his shoulders, trying to find support in the torrent of emotion that was flooding through her. But Rogue gave her no chance to find a safe haven; instead he pushed her feelings further, drawing her into a whirlpool of sensual delight.

"Shenandoah," Rogue finally said, his voice husky and low. "I don't want to hurt you."

She clutched him to her, unable to respond. How could he hurt her? All she could feel was bliss.

He shook her shoulders slightly. "Shenandoah, are you sure this is what you want? I can stop . . . I think."

"Rogue, please. I want you."

She could almost feel the relief that flooded through him.

"You won't regret this," he mumbled against the wild tangle of her hair, and kissed her tenderly, bringing sweet torment to her lips.

She clutched him, drawing him closer, and whispered, "Rogue. I've never wanted anything as much as I want you. Now, please."

Rogue reached for her, then remembered his Levi's, his boots. "Damn," he muttered.

"Rogue?"

He didn't take time to answer, but sat up and jerked off his boots, then his pants. She hardly knew he was gone before he was back with her, nuzzling her face, her neck, her aching breasts. Then he was over her, his hands slipping under her hips, raising her to meet him. There was a moment's hesitation, then she felt him probing for entry. All her feelings were centered there, around the deep, throbbing tension that Rogue had created within her.

"Rogue. Oh, Rogue," she murmured, wanting him desperately.

He pressed against her, finding entry, slipping inside, then was stopped by the barrier that he had hoped to find but had not actually expected. "Shenandoah," he said, his voice almost reverent. "I don't know. You're a—"

"Please, Rogue," she groaned. "Now."

Once more a tension went out of him. He gripped her more firmly, then pushed . . . hard. He broke through. Entry was no longer denied him, and he slipped inside. Embedded deep within Shenandoah, he fought for control. He had waited so long, wanted her so much, that now he could hardly stem the flood of his desire. But for her sake, he didn't want to hurry. He began to move, furthering the tension that had existed between them from the first moment they had met.

Shenandoah moaned, and clutched at his shoulders. She could not believe the sensations that were flooding her. She could only hold on to Rogue, knowing that he was giving her the ultimate pleasure. Better than any game she had ever played. She moaned his name, and pulled his face toward her, wanting to kiss him, wanting to be joined with him as completely as possible.

Rogue kissed her, delving into the depths of her mouth as he moved deep inside her. The scent of lavender filled his nostrils and the air was cool on his sweat-beaded body. He moved faster, harder, now unable to restrain himself, not wanting to, wanting only to reach the pinnacle of his desire with Shenandoah.

Then he gasped, felt her shudder against him, and let the wave of sheer agonizing pleasure wash over him, so intense that he almost couldn't believe it. He felt Shenandoah strain against him, holding him as if she would never let him go. She moaned his name, her nails raking his back as her pleasure swept through her, making her one with him. Then they both slowly floated back, breathing hard, their bodies hot, their sweat mingling.

After a long moment, Rogue gently eased from her, then drew her to his side, feeling as if she were so fragile he might break her with too hard a touch.

She snuggled against him and said, "Rogue, I didn't know."

Rogue kissed her forehead. "I didn't know it could be so good either."

She opened her eyes wide, looked at him, and said, "But, Rogue, I thought—"

He kissed her eyes shut. "No. There have been women, but nothing compared to you, Doe. I'm not sure just what the difference is, but with you it's dynamite."

Shenandoah was quiet, wishing irrationally that there hadn't been any other women for him.

"I guess I knew it would be good since the first time I saw you."

Shenandoah looked at him again. "Is that what you were thinking when we first met?"

Rogue chuckled. "That's what I was thinking the first time I laid eyes on you, playing cards at the You Bet. I wasn't supposed to be thinking that. I was there to find Fast Ed's niece. That was all. After I saw you, though, there was no turning back."

"You were patient."

He laughed. "No. I was desperate. I didn't want to scare you off, like I almost did the first night. Besides that, you were so cold I thought maybe you hated men."

It was her turn to laugh. "I guess I just never met the right man."

"I'm glad you think I'm the right man for you."

"You are." She snuggled closer to him, then ran a hand down his damp chest. "Rogue, do you think we could—"

"Keep that up and we can, but . . ."

"Yes?"

"Damn!" He sat up suddenly. "Where's my gun?"

"By the pool. You had me take it off you earlier."

"Hell! The Braytons could have crept in and we'd never have known. We'd have been completely helpless."

"But, Rogue—"

"I knew I was going to forget, one of these times.

Shenandoah, you make me go out of my mind. We're in the middle of an enemy camp. Your sister's in trouble. And all we can think of is—''

She grasped his arm, feeling the muscles straining against her. "Rogue, it's all right. We're safe. Nothing has happened. And it's my fault as much as yours. I wanted this, and I wanted it now. So did you."

"But I'm supposed to protect you. Fine job I'm doing."

She chuckled. "You're doing a good job. Come back. There's no hurry. We're safe."

Rogue looked back down at her. Night had descended and a full moon shone brilliantly down on Shenandoah, turning the full curves of her satiny white body into silver, beckoning him to take what he wanted. He reached for her, then shook his head. He got up, his own hard-muscled body gleaming silver in the moonlight. He looked down at Shenandoah. She held out her hands to him.

"You don't know how much I want you again," he said, "but we've got to go back, Doe. They'll be expecting us, and they'll be sending someone looking for us soon. Tad Brayton's not going to leave us alone long."

She dropped her hands. "I suppose you're right, Rogue. And there's Arabella to think about. Still, I wish we could stay here all night. Now that we've been together, I want more, much more."

"Believe me, so do I." He dropped to his knees

beside her, pulled her against his chest. "There'll be time for us later, Shenandoah. Believe me."

She looked up at him. His blue eyes were warm and intense. She nodded.

"But we've got to get out of here alive. Otherwise, there won't be any more time for us."

She nodded again. "You're right."

"Do you want me to help you dress?"

She hesitated, then said, "Rogue, let's bathe together before we get dressed. You can use my soap."

Rogue laughed dryly. "If I go back smelling like lavender, Tad Brayton will shoot me dead on the spot."

Shenandoah laughed too. "You're probably right."

"But let's cool off anyway. I could sure use that."

He led her to the water. Moonlight glinted off its surface. They swam together, laughed softly, splashed water, wanting all the while to be joined again like they had been on the soft, fragrant bed of pine needles.

After a while, Rogue reluctantly said, "We'd better go back."

Shenandoah followed him from the pool. When they were once more dressed, Rogue took her hand and said, "Doe, I'm sorry about earlier, but I can hardly stand to see Tad Brayton touching you, much less kissing you."

"I know. I'm sorry. too, but for Arabella's sake—"

"It's all right. My temper just got out of control."

"He doesn't interest me, Rogue."

"Good. See that he doesn't."

She stood on tiptoe and kissed him lightly, then

stroked his crooked nose. "Only you interest me, Rogue."

"Nevertheless, if he tries to go too far, I'll kill him, no matter the consequences."

"I'll keep him under control, Rogue, and soon we'll be gone."

"Won't be too soon for me."

"Me either."

Rogue suddenly smiled, touched her cheek, then said, "Time to resume our roles, Baby Doe. Your sister awaits."

She returned his smile. "Let's go, Dirk."

Holding hands, they left the glade, but they didn't leave their memories behind. They took with them the smell of evergreen, a pool lit by moonlight, and the union of two bodies.

～⌾ 10 ⌾～

Lights blazed from the hacienda as Rogue and Shenandoah approached it, still holding hands. Voices, occasional laughter, then a brief burst of a bawdy song broke the stillness of the night. Cooking smells wafted on the cool air, and the mournful sound of a harmonica resounded through the town. There was no sound or light from any of the Mexican houses. All activity centered on the hacienda.

Shenandoah and Rogue gave each other one last hungry look, then unclasped hands. They stepped past the hacienda's open wrought-iron gates, then followed the light and sound to a large room, its wide doors open to the courtyard. They hesitated just outside the room, allowing their eyes to adjust to the light. When they entered, Rogue's right hand hovered near his gun and Shenandoah smiled seductively.

"There you are," Tad exclaimed, quickly coming toward Shenandoah. He glared at Rogue, then led Shenandoah toward the assembled group.

"I think you know everybody here, including Alfredo.'' Tad chuckled, glancing from Shenandoah to Alfredo, then back again.

Alfredo stood, his manner stiff, but his words were smooth when he said, "*Buenas tardes, señorita.* We meet again."

"Good evening, Alfredo," she replied formally, wondering what the gambler was doing there.

Rogue stopped close beside Shenandoah, glared at Alfredo, then looked around. The room must once have been intended for large gatherings, such as a fancy ball. Now it was lit by several dented lanterns, and its center was filled with packing crates which served as tables and chairs. Its corners were left in shadow, as was its high ceiling.

T.J. Brayton sat on one of those crates, what was left of a meal of beans, beef, and tortillas set aside. He held a tin cup of coffee in his left hand, and in his right hand he held Arabella, who perched on his knee. Tobe sat nearby, a bottle of tequila on a crate next to him and his dagger in his left hand.

When Rogue glanced back, Alfredo still watched him, slowly turning a deck of cards over and over with his long, deft fingers. "Hear you're thinking of joining up with the Braytons," Alfredo said.

Rogue nodded. "Want to hear the plan first."

"All in good time," T.J. said, interrupting them. "You two must be hungry. Bella, get them something."

Arabella quickly left the room, and T.J. motioned for Shenandoah and Rogue to join him. When they were all seated around T.J., he said, "Now, I don't want you boys squabbling, not over women, not over cards.'' He looked pointedly at Tad, Rogue, and Alfredo. ''We work together as a team and we share everything.''

''Wait a minute—'' Rogue began.

''Dirk, we consider Baby Doe part of the team. She does what she wants, and with whatever man she wants. I—''

''Baby Doe's mine,'' Rogue insisted.

''Now, just a minute, Dirk,'' Shenandoah interrupted. ''I've told you and everybody else. I'm my own woman. You're my man right now, but that could change.'' She glanced sidelong at Tad.

Rogue bristled. ''Baby Doe, you keep that up and we'll leave right now.''

''Hold on,'' T.J. interrupted. ''Dirk, you're a smart man. You're not going to let a good job get away because of some woman.''

Rogue hesitated. ''Well—''

''Long as Baby wants you, fine. Don't forget Bella. And we'll get some others. The main thing here is that we work as a team. Right, Alfredo?''

Alfredo hesitated.

''I don't want you carrying grudges,'' T.J. insisted. ''You and Baby Doe can play cards all you want, but no grudges. And play fair.''

''I always play fair,'' Alfredo defended himself.

Shenandoah simply looked at him and raised a brow.

He glared at her.

"Okay, now that's settled, we can get on with the plans," T.J. said, starting to unroll a map.

But Arabella interrupted him, bringing back two full plates of food. The plates were made of tin, and bean juice dripped from their sides, falling to the floor and staining the front of Arabella's dress. She seemed not to notice, or didn't care. She quickly slapped the plates on a crate near Shenandoah, then went to Tad's side and snuggled up to him. He pushed her away. She glared at Shenandoah, then started to walk away, but Tobe caught her and pulled her to his side.

"Go ahead and eat," T.J. said, taking a gulp of his coffee.

Tobe took a draw on his bottle of tequila, then forced some on Arabella.

Tad picked up the plate and handed it to Shenandoah, smiled at her, and said, "Got to keep up your strength, honey."

Shenandoah reluctantly dug a fork out of the beans and began eating. It was surprisingly good, well spiced, and she was especially hungry. That reminded her of Rogue. She started to blush, remembering what they had shared in the glade, then determinedly stopped the telltale sign. She must not let Tad suspect, or the consequences could be terrible. Still, she knew that her lips were rosy, her color heightened, and she could hardly stop looking at Rogue. But she must be calm. She must not give them away. Her sister depended on her.

She ate quickly, wanting to be done, and noticed

that Rogue had the same ravenous hunger that she did. Their eyes met and darkened. Each remembered the glade. They quickly looked away, hoping no one had noticed.

"You always this hungry?" Tad asked, still watching Shenandoah.

"No. It must be the mountain air."

Rogue choked, coughed, then continued eating.

Tad glared at Rogue, then turned back to Shenandoah, a puzzled expression beginning to form on his face.

Shenandoah saw it, and quickly finished her meal, set the plate aside, and took Tad's hand. "Why don't you move closer to me, Tad?" She gave him what she thought was a seductive smile. When he eagerly edged close to her, she gave a small sigh of relief. She must keep her mind off Rogue. But when she looked up, she found Arabella's wide blue eyes narrowed and focused on her, hate pouring out with every breath her sister took. Shenandoah started to push Tad away, then stopped. She would explain everything to Arabella later, then all would be fine.

Rogue finished his meal, set the plate aside, and sat down on the other side of Shenandoah.

"All right," T.J. said. "As you know, the money's in mining, whether you're a gambler, a fancy lady, a miner, or a robber."

Tad and Tobe nodded enthusiastically.

"We've been doing well around Tombstone, but the mines are filling with water. That's going to be a ghost town in no time at all."

Everyone agreed with that, except Arabella, who was not part of the gang and didn't care about the plans. Her eyes were on Tad and Shenandoah.

"Besides, we weren't making enough around Tombstone. We all want to be rich, agreed?"

Everyone agreed to that, with the exception of Arabella, who was becoming more agitated by the moment as she watched Tad run a hand up and down Shenandoah's arm.

"If we want to be rich, and stay rich, we've got to do more than just hit a payroll stage now and again."

"Back me on a faro game and we'll be rich in no time," Alfredo exclaimed, his eyes gleaming. "I never heard of a straight faro game, and the miners love to play it."

T.J. glowered at Alfredo. "Problem with you, Alfredo, is that you think small. One faro game may make you money, but I'm talking *big* money. Money like those Eastern bankers have. So much money you can't even count it."

Alfredo nodded. "But I still say—"

"You gamblers," T.J. said in disgust. "All you can think about is—"

"Gambling," Shenandoah finished for him.

T.J. looked at her. "You the same?"

"You're a gambling man too, T.J., or you wouldn't be setting up this deal. Life's a gamble," she continued, trying to sound experienced. "It all depends on how you play it."

T.J. nodded. "You're right, Baby. Got a good head on your shoulders. We can use that."

Tad grinned. "Told you we could use her." He squeezed Shenandoah's arm and nuzzled her neck.

Arabella suddenly stood up, walked toward Shenandoah and Tad, but stopped before she reached them. Her eyes on Tad, she leaned up against Rogue, letting her full breasts press up against his chest.

Rogue tried not to appear surprised. He didn't move when she sat down close to him. He had a role to play too.

Arabella put a small white hand up to his face, turned it so that he was looking down at her, and said, "You're not bad, honey. A girl can get lonely."

Rogue stiffened, then relaxed. All the Braytons were watching him closely. He pushed her hand away. "You've already got enough men to keep you busy. I'll let you know if I want to be added to the list."

Tobe laughed out loud. "Come here, Bella. I told you your charms weren't that impressive."

Tad said, "You ought to get cleaned up, Bella. No man will want you the way you are."

Crimson stained Arabella's cheeks as she stiffly got up from Rogue's side.

But he stopped her, hating to see her demeaned. "Nothing wrong with you, Bella. My mind's on somebody else."

She flung his hand away and started out of the room.

T.J. stopped her. "Come back here, Bella. Don't want you wandering around."

Arabella flounced toward the group. Tobe caught

her, swung her down on his lap, then began to run the blade of his dagger between her breasts.

Shenandoah shuddered as she watched Tobe, horrified at what was happening to her sister. The humiliation was unthinkable, but Rogue had done the right thing. Tobe and T.J. were probably not nearly as willing to share Arabella as they seemed. She didn't want any of them endangered more than they already were. She felt Tad's hand on her and wanted to run away, but she relaxed, knowing she must endure his touch until Arabella was free.

"Damn woman," T.J. muttered. "Always distracting us. Now, far as I can tell, Leadville, Colorado, is one of the richest towns around, plus there's a lot of smaller places around there, too."

Rogue and Shenandoah stiffened at the sound of Leadville, glanced at each other, then waited for what T.J. would propose.

"What we've been doing is too dangerous. We're bound to get caught, sooner or later."

"I don't know," Tad objected. "We're good and we can always get across the border."

T.J. glared at him, then continued. "We can always get across the border as long as Tombstone is thriving, but it's not going to be much longer. So I'm looking north."

"I've heard Leadville is rich, too," Rogue agreed.

T.J. nodded. "I want to work a deal that looks legal. We can buy up some land with the money we've got, dig some mines, salt them good, then sell them at fancy prices to Eastern financiers. By the time they've discovered that the chunks of high-assayed ore we've salted in the ground are all there is, we'll be gone. They'll be left holding a few chunks of silver ore and a plot of worthless ground. So, what do you think?''

"Good idea," Rogue said quickly, for it was an excellent plan used by a lot of smart swindlers.

"Great," Shenandoah agreed.

"Doesn't sound like much fun," Tad complained.

"Won't need many weapons," Tobe reproached, eyeing his dagger.

"Land's getting settled," T.J. responded. "Things are changing. We've got to change too. I'm too old to be strung up by my neck now."

"Tell us some more about your plan," Shenandoah encouraged T.J., then smiled up at Tad.

"Want to send in some scouts, gamblers like you and Alfredo. The two of you can find out over your tables and in your beds who's got money, who's coming in from back East, and who'll go along with us. Baby, you can take the men. Alfredo, you can find out anything from the women."

Alfredo smiled slyly, then nodded.

"The rest of us will come in separately. Dirk here will buy land, just as I will. Tad and Tobe will salt the mines, stay in the background, keep their ears to the ground, and handle anyone who wants to cause trouble."

"Sounds good," Rogue agreed.

"Then, when we've made our money there, we move on, say, to South Dakota or Nevada. We'll go wherever the mines are and the money's flowing. After a time, we'll have all we need, nice and legal. We can go our separate ways, or come back here. I'd kind of like to see this hacienda fixed up. Might even get these silver mines to working again. I may become nice and respectable in my old age. In any case, that's on down the line. What I want to know is, are you all going to throw in with me?''

There was a moment of silence; then Rogue said, "The plan's good. Besides, I never did like to stay in one spot too long." He glanced at Shenandoah.

She nodded. "I agree. You've got a good plan, T.J. I like your kind of thinking." She looked around, then added, "I like this old place, too."

"You can count me in," Alfredo agreed. "I'll be gambling, just the same as always. This'll give it all an added spice and an extra percentage."

"You're always right, T.J.," Tad said, "but I'd rather continue what we're doing."

"Tombstone won't have money much longer," T.J. insisted.

"So you say. Well, I'm in too," Tad agreed. "We're brothers and that's that. Anyway, if Baby is going, so am I."

Shenandoah smiled at Tad.

"I'm in," Tobe said, "so long as we take Bella with us. You know I like to have a woman around."

"She goes," T.J. agreed. "Then we're all in on it. There'll be a few more details to clear up. I've got to finalize the plans. We'll hang around here a little longer, then we can start for Leadville. Let's drink to being rich and to the poor suckers who are about to lose their money.''

Tobe took a drink from his tequila bottle, then passed it around. After the bottle had made its way around the group and returned to Tobe, he held it up to Arabella's lips. Making a face, she took a sip, then drank deeply.

Watching her, Shenandoah wondered how her sister could stay sober drinking so much, for she knew Arabella had to be unaccustomed to it. But then, Tobe was giving her sister little choice, and maybe it helped Arabella to get through her terrible ordeal.

T.J. stood up. "Okay, the meeting's over. Go on and get some sleep. I'll let each of you know what I want from you later." He glanced at his map, rolled it back up, then said, "It's a big country. There's lots of pickings for us."

As they began to go their separate ways, Rogue took Shenandoah's arm. Tad took the other. She had to do something and said, "Now, boys, I'm going *alone* to my room tonight. It's been a long, hard day. A woman needs her sleep. Okay?"

"I'll walk you," Tad said quickly.

"So will I," Rogue agreed.

Shenandoah forced herself to laugh a soft, seductive sound. "One of these days soon I just might take on both you boys." She put a hand on Tad's arm, then put her other hand in Rogue's. She let them lead her from the room, the men glaring at each other. However, she did not fail to notice Tobe leading a swaying Arabella from the room.

Upstairs, Shenandoah pushed both men from her, said good night, and entered her room. There was no lock on the door. There was no furniture in the room. Other than dust and cobwebs, there was nothing in the bedroom except her saddlebags, her blanket, and herself. She wished that Rogue were with her, but was satisfied knowing he was only a few doors away. Of course, Tad was nearby too. However, she pushed thoughts of Tad from her mind as she rolled out her blanket, then let down her hair. She would sleep fully dressed this night, and hope that in the morning she could catch Arabella alone and tell her of their plans for escape.

After making herself as comfortable as possible on the hard floor, Shenandoah determinedly shut her eyes, letting thoughts of Rogue wash over her.

Just as she was drifting off to sleep, she heard her door creak open. Heavy, tattered draperies kept out most of the moonlight, but where they didn't meet, a sliver of light entered the room. Shenandoah strained to see who crept into her room, shutting the door quietly behind, but she could make out only a dark shape. She guessed it must be Rogue, so waited for him to come to her.

Suddenly a knife glinted in the sliver of light, posed to strike her. She screamed. As the blade came down, she rolled away.

"You'll not take my man away. I'll kill you first," Arabella growled, brandishing the knife. She swayed, then followed Shenandoah's shadowy form. "Tad Brayton wants me, not you. He's mine. I've nothing else." The blade parted the air, coming close to Shenandoah as she dodged her sister.

"Bella, stop," Shenandoah shouted, trying to reach her sister's liquor-clouded brain.

"Never! Tad's mine!" Arabella sliced through the air again.

The bedroom door was kicked open. Light filled the room. As Shenandoah stopped to look, Arabella took advantage, lunged, caught Shenandoah, and both went down in a heap. The smell of tequila filled Shenandoah's nostrils as Arabella panted over her, trying to plunge the knife into her sister's heart. But Shenandoah was stronger, sober, and pushed Arabella aside.

"Damn!" Tobe shouted, grabbing Arabella and twisting his dagger out of her hands. "You stole my knife. I told you never to touch it." He backhanded her. She fell against a wall, then slowly crumpled.

Shenandoah wanted to go to her sister, but Tad rushed to her side and held her tight.

"Damn stupid Bella," Tad said harshly. "You keep this up, woman, and we'll leave you for the Mexicans." He stroked Shenandoah's back, determined to comfort her.

She looked past him. Rogue was standing in the doorway with T.J. She wanted desperately to go to Rogue, but knew she must not. He nodded, knowing she couldn't.

"Bella'll go with me," T.J. said, his voice low and firm. "I'll keep her downstairs."

Arabella paled at those words.

Shenandoah noticed for the first time that her sister was wearing a dirty nightgown. Its modest bodice had been torn or cut to expose most of her full young breasts and in several places her soft flesh had been pricked by a knife. Shenandoah shuddered, thinking of Tobe's dagger, and was even further horrified for her sister. It was no wonder if her sister were drunk and half-mad from torment.

"Come here, Bella," T.J. said.

Bella cringed back. "You won't punish me, will you?" she asked, a frightened, plaintive note creeping into her slurred voice. "I did what was right. We don't need her. I'm enough for all of you."

"Come, Bella," T.J. repeated, more forcefully this time.

Arabella slowly got to her feet. She walked unsteadily toward T.J. until she neared Shenandoah, then stopped. "It's all your fault. I hate you!" she hissed at Shenandoah.

"Bella, come here," T.J. said, his patience obviously at an end.

Arabella gave Shenandoah one long, hate-filled look, then went to T.J.

Horrified at her sister's vehemence, Shenandoah could only stare in silence as T.J. took Arabella's hand, then led her away. Upset, Shenandoah looked at Rogue. He shook his head, trying to comfort her in some way. But there was no comfort. There was only horror. They had to get Arabella away, and soon.

"Sorry, Baby," Tad said, caressing her shoulder with a large warm hand. "Women have a way of—"

"They never want to let Tad go," Tobe interrupted, running the flat side of his dagger up and down his cheek. There was accusation in his voice, but acceptance, too. "T.J. and me, we're just second best." He walked quickly from the room.

"You want me to stay with you, honey?" Tad asked solicitously.

Rogue still hovered in the doorway.

Shenandoah glanced at him, then at Tad. "No, that's all right. Just keep that woman away from me, all right?"

"Sure, Baby. I'm damned sorry. Won't happen again. T.J.'ll see to that. He's good at teaching people their place."

Shenandoah cringed. She wanted to stop whatever kind of punishment T.J. had in mind, but she couldn't. As Baby Doe she would want revenge. "Good," she said, making her voice hard. "I don't want that woman coming at me with a knife again."

"She won't. You call if you need me, okay?"

"Sure. You men go on. I want to get some sleep."

When Tad and Rogue had left, Shenandoah opened the draperies, letting moonlight enter her room. She lay down, but could not sleep. Her chest hurt. She felt a terrible pain deep inside. What had they done to her little sister? Arabella was almost unrecognizable.

It wasn't fair. An innocent young lady like Arabella should never have come into contact with men like the Braytons. Shenandoah felt responsible. She had invited her sister to come West. But she could never have dreamed anything like this would happen. She felt so helpless. Yet she must be strong. She must rescue Arabella at all costs, then help her sister heal.

Turning over on her side, Shenandoah looked out the window. She couldn't sleep. Her eyes were dry. Her throat hurt. She would not cry. She must not give way to her emotions. They would not help. She must stay in control no matter what. Arabella would be all right. Once they got her away from this terrible place, her sister would heal and be just the same as before. Everything would be fine. It just had to be.

She strained to hear some sound of Arabella, but the hacienda was still. No sounds reached her ears, and after a time she drifted into an uneasy sleep.

11

Rogue burst into Shenandoah's room. "They're gone. Get up. Hurry."

Startled, sleep still misting her mind, Shenandoah rolled over. At the sight of Rogue, she smiled, then remembered their situation, and frowned.

"Arabella's in the kitchen. Alone."

Shenandoah threw off her blanket, took Rogue's offered hand, and got up. Her hair was a wild disorder, framing her tired face.

Touched, Rogue gently swept back her hair and said, "How did you sleep?"

"Terribly. You?"

"Not at all. Don't take time to do your hair or anything. I don't know how long they'll be gone."

"Are we all alone?"

"As far as I know we are. At least, in the hacienda."

Shenandoah brushed at the wrinkles in her clothes as Rogue hurried her from the room. She had slept fully dressed, ready for anything in the Brayton stronghold, but now her shirt and skirt were sadly wrinkled. But she pushed that thought quickly from her mind. Only one thing counted now, freeing Arabella.

In the large, almost empty kitchen, Arabella sat on a crate picking uninterestedly at a plate of food. At their step, she looked up anxiously, but on seeing them, her look changed to a glower. "What do you want?" she muttered.

"Arabella," Shenandoah said happily, rushing to her sister. She sat down close beside Arabella, while Rogue took a watchful stance nearby.

"I said, what do you want?" Arabella repeated, more belligerently. There were dark circles under her eyes and her lower lip had been cut.

Shenandoah hurt inside at this evidence of her sister's bad treatment, but she hurried on, saying, "Arabella, don't you recognize me?"

"Sure. I've heard enough about you to—"

"I'm not who you think I am."

Arabella frowned, put a forkful of beans in her mouth, glanced at Rogue, then stared stonily at the floor while she ate.

Shenandoah didn't know how best to approach her sister. Arabella had already had enough shocks. "I know you were coming from Philadelphia to be with your sister, Shenandoah, and your uncle, Fast Ed Davis."

Arabella dropped her fork, turning wide eyes on Shenandoah.

"I know your name is Arabella White."

Arabella set down the plate of food, got up, and backed away from Shenandoah, horror on her face.

"Arabella, say something."

"Go away."

"Don't you recognize me? I know it's been six years, but I've waited for you."

Arabella turned around, her shoulders hunched as she hid her face in her hands.

Shenandoah looked at Rogue, but was afraid to go closer to her sister. Arabella was still rejecting her. "Arabella, I'm your sister, Shenandoah."

Silence echoed throughout the room, broken finally by a sob from Arabella, who didn't move except now her shoulders shook in silent sobs.

Shenandoah stood up, glanced in concern at Rogue. He nodded encouragingly, but still kept watch for the Braytons. She walked to her sister's side and put a hand on Arabella's shoulder.

Arabella shrugged off her hand.

"Didn't you hear me? I'm your sister. I—"

"I heard you," Arabella hissed, whirling around. Her eyes were dry, but her mouth trembled when she said, "I thought you were a gambler, not an outlaw. What do you want with Tad anyway? You've got *him*." Arabella motioned at Rogue with her head.

Surprised, Shenandoah quickly said, "Nothing's as it seems, Arabella. We aren't outlaws and I *am* a gambler."

"Where's Uncle Ed?"

"He's in Leadville, Colorado."

Arabella looked even more suspicious.

"Arabella," Shenandoah said in exasperation, "we came to rescue you. I was waiting for you in Tombstone. When I got your letter, Uncle Ed had already gone to Leadville. He's waiting for us there. We can go anytime you want.''

Arabella looked at her for a long moment, then flung out a hand as if to push Shenandoah away. Then she hung her head. "I can't go with you.''

"What?" Shenandoah glanced in desperation at Rogue. But he merely shook his head. "I don't understand. Of course you'll go with us. Uncle Ed is waiting."

This time a sob escaped Arabella and she walked away from Shenandoah. "Why did you come after me? Why didn't you just leave me alone? Now you've seen me. It was the one thing that kept me going, knowing my sister and uncle would never see what I'd become.''

"But, Arabella, you're the same person you always were.''

Arabella looked hard at Shenandoah, then laughed harshly. "You're not that big a fool. Look at me. I'm a whore. Worse, I'm not even paid.''

"That's not true. You are the same young lady you were when you left Philadelphia. You've simply had an unfortunate . . . an unfortunate . . .''

"Unfortunate? Yes, I'd say so. But I'm not the same. I'll never be again. How could I possibly face Uncle Ed? How could I ever go back to *polite* society? I'm just glad Aunt Edna isn't alive to see me.''

"Arabella," Shenandoah said firmly, walking to her sister and taking her arms. "You are not a whore. You are a young lady. You are my sister. There is nothing wrong with you. You've had a terrible experience, but you will get over it. As far as polite society, who cares? I don't travel in those circles myself, and neither does Uncle Ed.''

Arabella shook off Shenandoah's hands, then stalked over to Rogue. "He'll tell you I'm a whore. I can see it in his eyes. Tell her."

Rogue shook his head in denial. "We came to rescue you, Arabella. Shenandoah went through a lot to find you."

"I'll bet! Well, I wish she hadn't. I didn't want her to find me. I wanted her to remember me as I was. This just makes it all that much worse."

"We know it's been terrible for you, but we've got to leave soon. They'll be back anytime," Rogue said gently.

Arabella turned from him. She walked back to Shenandoah. "If you go, Tad will forget you. I can handle him then. He's not really a bad man, not like his brothers. And he'll protect me. Besides, he's taught me a lot."

"Arabella! Tad Brayton kidnapped you. He also . . ."

"Can't you say it? He raped me. Well, that seems like a long time ago. Tad is not so bad. He's good-looking. I could do much worse. Besides, T.J. has big plans. We'll be rich soon, then none of this will matter so much."

"You don't know what you're saying. You can't stay here, not with the Braytons."

"Why not? It's better than going back, having to

see your face and Uncle Ed's every day, knowing what you're thinking when you look at me. I'm a soiled woman. I can never marry. No one would ever want me. I'm a whore.''

Shenandoah felt weak. She had never considered that her sister would think these terrible things about herself. She had only thought of rescuing Arabella. She must somehow make her see the truth. ''You're distraught, and it's no wonder. Once away from here, you'll be all right.''

Arabella laughed a short, dry sound that held no mirth. ''I will never be all right again, at least not what you think is all right. But I will make it. My mother made it through the war. She was a strong woman. I'm strong too. And I've made it through the worst. Perhaps if you had come sooner, I might have—''

''It's not too late.''

''I am a whore now. Nothing can ever change that.''

''Shenandoah,'' Rogue interrupted. ''We're running out of time. We can't wait much longer. I don't know when they might come back.''

''Soon,'' Arabella said. ''Go ahead. Look, I appreciate your coming for me. I never expected that. But it would have been better if you hadn't. Tad's my man now, and once you're gone, he'll come back to me.''

''Arabella,'' Shenandoah said desperately, ''you're confused. They've turned your mind around. These men are dangerous outlaws. They rob and kill. You don't belong here.''

"Yes, I do. After what's happened, how can I go back?"

Shenandoah suddenly realized that Arabella was not going to listen to her, not here, not now. The Braytons had made her believe she was a whore by the way they had treated her. Maybe it was the only way she had survived them. But it wasn't true, no matter what her sister now thought. They had to get her away, then she would be able to heal and realize her true worth, not something the Braytons had imposed on her.

"Leave, quickly," Arabella urged, seeing Shenandoah falter.

"Rogue," Shenandoah said, "would you get our saddlebags so we can leave?"

He looked surprised, then nodded in agreement.

When he was gone, Shenandoah turned back toward Arabella. "I want you to come with us, Arabella. You are no less in my eyes because of what the Braytons have done to you. I hate them for doing this to my sister. Uncle Ed will feel the same. Once out of here, you can begin a new life in Leadville. No one will know about this."

"You will know. My uncle will know. Dirk will know."

"It doesn't matter to us. You matter, not what the Braytons forced on you."

"I wish you'd never come. I simply can't face you anymore, or my uncle, or anything else in my former life. I'm Bella now, Bella the whore, who wants nothing more than a soft bed and a warm man. Can't you understand?"

"I understand why you think this, but I don't believe it. The Braytons are to blame."

"I want Tad Brayton. He was my first man. I'm going to keep him. I belong to him now. It's best. You and Dirk go on. Leave me here. Forget I ever existed."

Rogue quietly entered, carrying the saddlebags, a worried frown on his face. "I think we can walk down to the stables without causing too much interest. We're accepted now. I don't know if we'll be able to ride out, though."

"We'll try," Shenandoah said determinedly. "Rogue, I'm a little chilly. I'd like to wear my shawl."

Rogue looked surprised, but as she walked toward him, he pulled it out of her saddlebags.

As she took the white shawl from his hands. she said in a low voice, "Rogue, we're going to have to take her. She won't come on her own."

Rogue's brows came together. "You sure?"

"Yes. Don't you agree?"

He hesitated. "She could be right."

"No! She's my sister."

"What are you two whispering about?" Arabella called suspiciously from across the room.

Shenandoah turned toward her sister. "I was asking if he thought it a good idea to give you my new shawl."

Arabella looked at the gossamer gift Shenandoah held in her hands and smiled. "I'd certainly accept it."

Shenandoah smiled back, then said under her breath, "Can we tie her up with it, Rogue?"

"Yes. I'll come with you."

As they met in the center of the room, Arabella held her hands out for the shawl. She was unprepared when Rogue grabbed her wrists, took the shawl from Shenandoah's hands, then quickly tied Arabella's hands behind her.

Furious, Arabella struggled, kicking out at them. "What do you think you're doing?" she panted.

"We're taking you with us, one way or another," Shenandoah said firmly.

"No! Shenandoah, please. If you ever loved me, don't. Leave me here where I belong."

"I *do* love you, Arabella. That's why I'm doing this. Later, you'll be glad I did."

"No! Dirk, listen to reason. The Braytons will come after you. They'll see you dead before—"

Suddenly a horse whinnied outside.

Arabella jerked up her head. Her nostrils flared. She screamed as loud as she could.

Rogue clamped a hand over her mouth. She tried to bite him. "Damn! Shenandoah, see if you can tell who's out there."

As Shenandoah slipped to a front window. Rogue pulled a bandanna out of his back pocket and gagged Arabella, who struggled desperately against him. Pulling her with him, he picked up the saddlebags and made his way to Shenandoah in a front room. "What do you see?"

"They're back," she said tensely. "I see four horses. No riders. They must have heard her and rushed inside."

"Hell!"

"What are we—"

Suddenly a knife was flung deep into the wood near Rogue's face. He whirled, his hand going for his gun. Tobe was already drawing his pistol, fury contorting his features. He shot first, but the bullet missed and lodged in the wall behind Rogue. As Tobe pumped the trigger again, Rogue aimed carefully and hit Tobe in the chest. The man slumped, blood bubbling to his lips. "Bella," he said as he slumped to the floor.

Forgotten by Rogue, Arabella hurried to Tobe and knelt by his side. Shenandoah went after her, while Rogue quickly reloaded. Shenandoah pulled her sister away from Tobe and said, "He's dead." Arabella shook her head, tried to twist away, but Shenandoah pushed her back toward Rogue.

"Keep her still," Rogue said. "I don't know where the others are. He found us first. Maybe he wanted Arabella the most. Anyway, they'll be gunning to avenge Tobe now. We've got to get out of here."

"How?" Shenandoah asked, holding tightly to her sister.

"Their horses are out there. I can try to keep them busy while you and Arabella get to the horses. The trail is just this side of the third building on the right."

"What about you?"

"I'll stay and try to hold them while you get away."

"Rogue," Shenandoah said, her heart beating fast, "they'll kill you."

"Maybe not. I want you safely out of here."

"I won't leave you."

"Damn! Doe, save yourself, at least."

"There has to be another way."

"Okay, Dirk," T.J. Brayton shouted from another room, "throw out your gun. You haven't got a chance."

"Be quiet," Rogue hissed. "We might still make it. Take Arabella and—"

"How am I going to get her on a horse, then get her away? Rogue, she'll fight me."

As if to prove Shenandoah right, Arabella struggled against her captor.

Rogue grimaced. "There are two Braytons left, plus Alfredo and whatever gunmen heard the shots and rushed up here. However, we have surprise on our side. They'll be in here in a minute."

"I won't leave you, Rogue."

He smiled grimly at her. "All right, we'll go out together."

She nodded.

"Go through the window. I'll shove Arabella out after you. Head straight for the horses. Once your sister's mounted, lead her animal from yours. If they think you're getting away, they'll probably shoot to kill both of you, too. They can't let their secret out. So be careful. I'll be right behind you."

"Rogue, I'm scared."

"Be scared later. You don't have time for it now. And, Shenandoah, don't run straight. That way you'll stand a good chance of being missed, especially if they're using pistols."

Shenandoah jumped through the window, then caught Arabella as Rogue pushed her through, along with their saddlebags. "Arabella," she hissed, "don't fight me and run, or you're going to get us all killed."

Arabella flashed angry blue eyes at her but did not move from the ground. Shenandoah took her sister's hand and tried to pull her up, but her sister resisted. She knew she couldn't carry Arabella and run. Furious, she held on to her sister and looked back.

Just as Rogue came through the window, several shots rang out. Blood spurted from his shoulder. He glanced down at Arabella, picked her up, threw her over his good shoulder, and shouted, "Run, Doe. Get the horses."

Shenandoah snatched up the saddlebags and ran as Rogue shot behind them, protecting their back. She got through the wrought-iron gates, grabbed the reins of three horses, then held one steady as Rogue threw Arabella into the saddle. Shenandoah mounted, threw the saddlebags across her lap, then looked back. Tad and T.J. were coming through the front door, Alfredo and several gunmen right behind them. Rogue hit the rump of Arabella's horse and they took off down the road, bullets whizzing around them.

From the back of his mount, Rogue returned fire. Tad went down. T.J. grabbed the other horse, mounted it, then came after them. Rogue cursed as T.J. pulled a rifle from the horse's saddle. Bullets zipped close around their ears.

Shenandoah felt something sting her arm, but she

didn't look. Her eyes were searching for the path leading down. Finally she saw it and turned her horse, pulling Arabella along behind her. But just as she started onto the trail, she heard a shout and looked back.

T.J. was bearing down on Rogue, his rifle aimed and ready. "You can't escape now, Dirk," T.J. shouted as he pulled the trigger. But nothing happened. He had spent all his bullets. He grabbed his forty-five and fired. He missed.

That was all the chance Rogue needed. He aimed his pistol carefully and fired. Blood spurted from T.J.'s chest. Rogue turned back to Shenandoah. "Quick, the other gunmen are on foot, but they'll catch up any minute, or get horses."

Arabella moaned and tried to slide off her moving horse. Rogue stopped her. Shenandoah urged her mount down the trail, pulling Arabella single file behind her.

"Go faster, Shenandoah," Rogue shouted, following them.

She reined her horse through thick brush, feeling sharp twigs tear through the fabric of her skirt to scratch the soft skin underneath. She ignored the pain, urging her mount faster and faster, while clinging desperately to the reins of Arabella's horse.

After a moment, Rogue called in a tight voice, "No matter what you hear, just keep going, Shenandoah. It's the only way out. I'm going to reload and head back. I've got to know if we're being followed."

"Rogue, no. Please don't."

"Go on, Doe. And keep going. If I don't come back, when you get off the mountain, turn north. You'll come to the San Pedro River soon. Follow it to Tombstone, like we did before. All right?"

"Rogue, I'm afraid for you."

"Remember, life's a gamble. You dealt this hand and now you're going to have to see it through."

"Rogue."

"I've got to do it."

"Rogue?"

She heard him turn his horse around and start back. There was suddenly a heavy weight in the pit of her stomach. But Rogue was right. She had dealt the hand. They had to play it to the end. She took a firmer grip on the reins of Arabella's mount and grimly pushed her own horse to its limit. Rogue would be back. He was her holdout. And a good holdout always won.

∽ 12 ∽

Shenandoah had almost reached the San Pedro River when she looked back and saw dust billowing into the wind from a rider or riders. They must be following her. She urged her tired horse into a lope, pulling Arabella behind her. Her sister groaned, as tired and sore from riding as Shenandoah, but Shenandoah could not be sure if the person following were friend or foe. She desperately wanted it to be Rogue, but she could not take any chances.

They would be safer among the cottonwood trees along the banks of the San Pedro and she planned to get there before the rider following them. There was a rifle holstered on her saddle and she would use it if necessary to save them. She was not going to let the Braytons or their men take Arabella back. They wouldn't get her, either.

Determined, she pushed the horses to their limit once again. By nightfall she was near the river and the dust kicked up by whoever was following them had remained at a constant distance, not falling back.

She only hoped it was Rogue. If it were not Rogue, she would wait for him by the San Pedro. She wouldn't go on to Tombstone, not until she knew about him, one way or another.

She urged the horses deep into the cool shade of the cottonwood trees. The animals could go no farther. She would have to make her stand there. Trying not to feel frightened, she pulled Arabella off her horse, then led their mounts to water, taking the rifle out of its sheath, then checking to make sure it was loaded.

Finally she looked at her sister and said, "I'm putting you behind that tree. Someone's following us. Until I know who it is, I'm taking no chances on you giving us away. Now, sit down and be still."

Arabella glared at her, but sat down and didn't move, obviously exhausted.

When the horses had finished drinking their fill, Shenandoah tied them near Arabella, positioned herself behind a stump, then waited.

After a time she heard a horse enter the cottonwood trees. She could make out only one animal. Her heart raced. One rider would surely mean Rogue. Twigs snapped as the sound grew louder. Finally she could stand it no longer and called, "You're covered. Come out and keep your hands away from your gun."

There was a rustling in the brush, then slowly a figure came out, hands in the air.

"Rogue!" Shenandoah cried out in relief.

He smiled tiredly at her, then dropped his hands.

"Rogue, I didn't mean for—"

"You sounded mean, woman. Thought I'd better—"

"Oh, Rogue." She threw herself into his arms. "You're safe."

He clasped her to him. "So are you," he murmured into her long disheveled hair. "Didn't know if I'd ever see you again. How come you didn't wait up when you saw my dust?"

"I couldn't be sure it was you. I was taking no chances. If it were the Braytons or their men, I was going to shoot them, then start back after you."

"You were?"

"Yes."

"Didn't know I meant so much."

"You're my holdout. Couldn't let anything happen to you."

"Holdout? I've been called better, but then, I've been called a lot worse. Well, since this holdout has worked so hard, do I get fed, bathed, and . . ." Rogue trailed off, glancing over at Arabella, who was peering around a tree. "How is she?"

"Alive."

He nodded. "You can untie her. She has no place to go."

Shenandoah walked over to her sister, then quickly unbound her and removed the gag. "I'm sorry, Arabella, but it was for the best." She gave Rogue back his bandanna, then carefully folded her wrinkled shawl. She didn't know if she could ever wear it again.

Arabella stood up, then glared at Shenandoah and Rogue. "You killed them. You killed Tad. I'm all alone now. You murdered all I had."

"Arabella, you have me and your uncle. Those men were outlaws, killers," Shenandoah said.

"You forget, I was a Brayton too. You just killed my family. I have no other." She walked away from Rogue and Shenandoah, her face set.

While Arabella drank at the river, Shenandoah turned to Rogue. "I don't know what to say. I don't know how to reach her. What happened, Rogue, are they all dead?"

"I went back, tied my horse down the trail, then scouted the perimeter on foot. Far as I know, Tobe and T.J. will never move again. I'm not so sure about Tad. I shot him, but he'd been carried inside so I didn't see him. Anyway, the gunmen didn't follow us. They decided to save their leader, if they could. Besides, none of them wanted to die, and we'd put up a good fight."

"I'm glad they didn't come after us. Did you see Alfredo?"

"No. I suppose he helped carry Tad inside."

"And Tad?"

"I don't know. Even if he did make it, he and Alfredo would have a hard time tracking us. I think we've seen the last of the Braytons. I'm sorry it ended in so much bloodshed, though."

"So am I. But I don't know how we could have done it differently."

"We did what we had to do. Arabella's safe now."

"Yes. And so are you. No one saw you when you went back?"

"No. They'd never have dreamed I'd come back."

"Rogue, I'm sorry I got you involved in—"

"It's all right. We're all safe now. Anyway, someone was going to get the Braytons sooner or later."

She nodded. "We'll take Arabella back to Tombstone where she can begin to recouperate. I think once she's in Leadville she'll see things differently."

"I hope so."

"So do I." She ran her hands down his arms.

Rogue winced.

"Are you hurt?"

"Caught a couple of bullets."

"Oh, Rogue." She set her shawl aside, then hurried him down to the river and carefully removed his shirt. A bullet had gone through the thick muscle of one shoulder but had left no fragments. It was a clean wound. Another bullet had nicked his right arm. He had lost blood, but he would be all right. Shenandoah tore strips of cloth from her petticoat, washed Rogue's wounds, then bound them with the soft cotton fabric.

Arabella watched silently, then said, "At least you still have a man to help." She walked away from them and sat down near a cottonwood tree.

Shenandoah watched her a moment, then turned back to Rogue. "There's nothing I can do," she said. "At least not yet."

"Give her time," Rogue replied, taking Shenandoah's arm and examining a tear in the sleeve of her shirt. He probed the area with a finger. She winced. "You were hit too." After Rogue had cleaned her wound and bound it with a strip from her petticoat, he said, "I think it's safe to spend the night here, but we should be on our way tomorrow. I want to be back across the border as soon as possible."

"All right. I think there's still some beef jerky left in our saddlebags. I've got them all on my horse."

"Glad you were able to bring them."

"So am I. Rogue, I—"

"Later. Let's get some food in everybody first, then we'll settle down. We all need some rest."

Fortunately, the horses they had stolen were good mounts. Although there were no sidesaddles, Shenandoah had not even given it a thought as they had ridden out of the Braytons' hideout. Now it didn't seem to matter. As far as their own mustangs, no doubt the outlaws or Mexicans would find a use for them. There were blankets tied behind each saddle, a rifle holstered to one, but no canteens of water. However, they would travel the rest of the way near the San Pedro River, so there would be no need of canteens.

Shenandoah picked up her shawl, put it carefully in her saddlebag, then gave everyone a blanket and strips of beef jerky. Arabella ate what was given her, but then she sat stonily silent, glaring out across the river. Shenandoah and Rogue ate hungrily since they hadn't eaten all day, then drank deeply of the cool water and washed their faces and hands in the river.

As night settled over them, Arabella wrapped herself in her blanket and settled quietly down on the hard earth, ignoring her companions and maintaining her stony silence. Across the clearing near the river, Rogue and Shenandoah watched her in concern, then turned to each other, sharing their blankets as they had by the San Pedro once before.

When they had snuggled close, Shenandoah said, "Rogue, I don't want Arabella to feel rejected or lonely, but I don't know how to reach her."

"You can't, not now. Give her time. She'll come around. She's been through a lot. She's just had another bad shock. Give her time to heal."

"You're right. Rogue, I was terrified you weren't going to return."

"I wanted you safe, and I thought I could pick them off if they followed. There was no other way, Shenandoah, even though I hated to leave you."

"Thank you, Rogue. I don't know if I can ever repay you."

"I'll think of something," he said, letting his hands run down her arms, then back again, before pulling her closer.

She laughed softly, then moved further into the circle of his warmth. "I haven't forgotten our bargain. You've done what I asked, so now I owe you."

He lightly kissed her hair. "It may take a long time for you to pay me off, Shenandoah."

"I'm in no hurry," she said breathlessly.

"Good. I'll remember that."

She kissed his lips, feeling a warmth begin to course through her. "Rogue, I—"

He groaned, moved her hand down his chest to the front of his Levi's. He was hard, ready for her.

"Rogue," she whispered, moving her hand against him, "how can you at a time like this?"

"Time and place don't matter when I'm around you, Shenandoah. If I wasn't so tired, I think I'd—"

"You're tired?"

He groaned. "Remind me not to take on any of your problems again. This one damned near killed us both."

"I know," she said, suddenly serious. "Rogue, I mean it. I owe you. You can collect your debt anytime you want."

"Good. I'll remember that. But for now, you'd better get some sleep."

"What about you?"

"No. I'll guard."

"Rogue, you didn't sleep last night."

"Can't take a chance, Shenandoah."

"You sleep. I'll watch and wake you later."

Rogue hesitated.

"Go ahead. I'm not sleepy anyway."

Rogue hesitated once more, then said, "All right. But don't let me sleep long."

He fell quickly into a deep, exhausted sleep. She smiled at his tired face, then lay awake listening to the night sounds around them. She tried to think back to their escape but her mind slipped around it, wanting to forget the fear, the death. Instead, she remembered the glade where Rogue had made her a woman.

She stroked his arm, watching him sleep. Her mother would probably have been shocked at what her daughter had done so freely, so willingly with a man, almost a stranger. Her uncle would probably also have disapproved, if he had known. But life could be short in the West. She was a grown woman and she had never met a man like Rogue before. If she had thrown her chance with him away, another might not have come along. Cards were fickle; so was life. When Rogue had been dealt her, she had taken what she wanted and needed. She was glad she had.

She didn't expect it to last, of course. She was a gambler. She couldn't allow herself the emotions that had surfaced while on this trip. When she got to Leadville she would have to get herself back under control. That was the only way to win, and win she must if she were to survive as a gambler. Besides, Rogue had his own life. He had a mine that was waiting for him. They would go their separate ways, remembering the good times.

The moonlight turned the hard angles of his face soft and she kissed him lightly, trying to ignore the sudden pain that had stabbed her. She was a gambler. That was all. Rogue was a mining man. They weren't the kind of people who came together and stayed together. Neither of them wanted that. It would involve too many things she didn't want to think about. When the pain came again, she pushed it away. She was a gambler, and she didn't need emotions. In fact, strong feelings could be her downfall. Rogue was just a pleasant interlude. That was all.

She kissed him lightly again and he said, "Damn, Shenandoah, how can a man sleep when you keep waking him that way?" He pulled her close, pressing her breasts to his chest. When their mouths met, fire leapt between them and Rogue pushed inside with his tongue, hunting deep into his territory, staking his claim once more.

Shenandoah moaned, feeling herself respond, feeling her body begin to ache for his touch, feeling the need for him grow all over again.

Rogue suddenly broke away from her lips, saying, "I've got to stop this or we're never going to get back to Tombstone. Besides, Arabella—"

"You make me forget everything else."

"Damn. I want you so bad I hurt all over, but we've got to think of the future. Arabella needs to be back in a town, safe from any threats. And—"

"You've got your mine."

"Yes, but I wish I didn't have that hanging over me. If I didn't, we could go somewhere together."

"I can't leave Arabella, and don't forget I've also got a job."

"I know you're a gambler. You never let me forget. But Arabella has your uncle, too."

"He's not really her uncle. He's my father's brother. Although he thinks of her as his niece, she still needs me, her only living kin. Anyway, what we're really saying, Rogue, is that we have our own lives, our own *separate* lives. Isn't that right?"

Rogue hesitated. "You're not thinking about backing out on our deal, are you?"

"I owe you. I pay my debts."

He let out a sigh of relief, then said, "I'd prefer if you just wanted to be with me, but I'll take payment."

"Rogue, I—"

"No, don't explain. I don't want to hear what you have to say. We'll get back to Tombstone, tell the sheriff what happened, then head out for Leadville. There's lots waiting for us there."

"I hope Arabella will like Leadville."

"It's a fancy town. She should. But, Shenandoah, don't forget. Once we get there, nothing's going to change. I still want you, and you still owe me."

She hesitated. He almost sounded like he didn't think she wanted him too. "Like I said, I pay my debts, Rogue, but also, I want you. You know that."

"No. I don't know what you want. I don't know if you do, either. But I'll settle for what I can get now. Later, well, we'll see then."

"Rogue, I—"

"Kiss me. Consider it part of the debt, if you must."

His lips covered hers and soon she had forgotten

everything except the warmth of Rogue's lips, the hardness of his body, and her consuming need to be close to him. Leadville was a long way away. She would think about it when she got there.

II

Summer 1883

WILD MOUNTAIN WINDS

‿❧ 13 ❧‿

Passengers on the Denver and Rio Grande Railway got a spectacular view of the rushing Arkansas River far below as their train pulled up the steep grade of the Royal Gorge, the only pass through the Rocky Mountains to the two-mile-high city of Leadville, Colorado.

The hustling, bustling city of 35,000 people and 667 businesses was in stark contrast to the majestic mountains around it, but it was the city, not the countryside, which had brought the passengers to Colorado. They quickly turned their attention to the town as the train pulled into its depot.

Standing to one side under the overhanging roof of the train station was a slim man of medium height. He wore the black frock coat, black trousers, and frilled white shirt of a gambling man. His auburn hair, streaked with silver, was neatly trimmed, as was his mustache. Beside him was a big tall miner with wild black hair and beard.

The two men stepped forward as the train stopped and passengers began to debark.

Soon a voice cried out, "Uncle Ed! We made it."

The gambler threw wide his arms to catch the young woman with auburn hair who threw herself at him. They hugged each other, then he set her back to quickly look her over.

"You've been in the sun. There's some tan on your face, Shenandoah," Fast Ed Davis said.

She nodded. "I see you haven't been run out of town for a sharper yet."

"Shame on you. I'm as honest a gambler as they come."

She chuckled. "It's good to see you, Uncle Ed."

"I was afraid—"

"No, everything's fine. Arbella's with us, but—"

"Tom Burton's here too. He wanted to meet your train."

Shenandoah turned to look at the tall miner. "Tom, thanks for coming."

"Wouldn't have missed it, Miss Shenandoah. Your sister all right?"

"Please, don't either of you mention her . . . her ordeal. I'll tell you about it later, when we're alone. All right?"

Both men looked puzzled, but quickly nodded agreement.

"Rogan make it okay?" Tom asked, glancing at the train.

"Yes, Arabella became . . . well, I told her I'd see if you were here and let the other people go their way before she got off."

Fast Ed nodded, then took out a black silk handkerchief and coughed into it.

"Right now, let's get Arabella off the train and safely to . . . where are we staying?"

"I've been looking for a house to rent, but haven't found anything suitable," Fast Ed said as they moved toward the train. "I've rented two rooms for you and Arabella at Colorado Kate's boardinghouse. It's a nice clean place. Kate will take good care of you there."

"Thank you." Shenandoah looked up at the train, wondering if her sister would be happy here, then stopped her thoughts as Arabella suddenly appeared and stepped down, Rogue Rogan right behind her.

"Arabella," Shenandoah said, taking her sister's cold hand. "You remember Uncle Ed. This is Tom Burton. He works for Rogue at his mine."

Arabella glanced at the two men, then looked hurriedly away. Her hand crept up to the high neckline of her bodice. "Hello," she said softly, looking around the depot.

Fast Ed glanced at Shenandoah in concern, then at his other niece. "You remind me a great deal of your mother, Arabella. My brother was lucky to marry her, and I'm lucky to have you here with Shenandoah. Please consider this your home and us your family."

"Thank you," Arabella said politely. She smiled faintly.

"Rogan," Tom Burton said, slapping Rogue on the back. "It's good to see you. Got a lot of news for you."

"How's the Silver Star?"

"The mine looks good, but there's been trouble."

"Trouble?" Rogue's brows drew together. "What kind?"

"Let's get the young ladies situated first," Fast Ed said quickly. "I've already left word that their baggage is to be delivered to Colorado Kate's boardinghouse. By the way, thanks for seeing Shenandoah and Arabella here."

"My pleasure."

"By the way, there's a telegram for you at the telegraph office. We can pick it up on the way," Tom added.

Shenandoah watched Rogue carefully. Just as she had anticipated, they would be going their separate ways. Rogue would have too much on his mind now to think of her, and she would likewise begin her work again. She pushed down the strange pain that flickered through her. She had her sister to think about, her job, and her uncle. She had no time to think about Rogue Rogan.

"Afternoon, Fast Ed."

Shenandoah looked up to see a tall, slim man with a long dark mustache, silver-streaked dark hair, and intense gray eyes. He was staring hard at Arabella. Suddenly feeling alarmed, she moved closer to her sister. The man wore the black dress clothes of a gambler, with the heavy gold jewelry that branded him as successful.

Fast Ed stiffened as he turned to face the man who had quietly joined their group. "Spike Cameron. 'Afternoon. What brings you to the train station?"

"Had a little item arriving. Wanted to make sure it got here safe and sound. Friends of yours?"

Reluctantly Fast Ed made the introductions. "These are my nieces, Shenandoah Davis and Arabella White. Ladies, this is Spike Cameron. He owns the Postmortem."

"Delighted to meet you. Leadville can always use more lovely gentlewomen." He deftly bent over Arabella's hand, then kissed it, all the while keeping his eyes on her face.

In a show of unaccustomed bad manners, Shenandoah turned away and said, "Rogue, do you know Mr. Cameron?" She stepped closer to Rogue.

"We've met," Rogue replied, showing no pleasure.

"What's the Postmortem?" Arabella asked, her clear young voice cutting through the strain of the introductions.

"A silver exchange, and one of the best in Leadville," Spike Cameron answered.

"Silver exchange?" Arabella asked breathlessly, fingering the top buttons of her bodice and leaving a few undone as Spike's eyes focused on her.

Shenandoah inhaled deeply as she recognized the look Arabella had once given Tad Brayton. She could hardly believe her sister was interested in this man, especially so soon after her ordeal with the Brayton brothers. She had better get her safely to the boardinghouse and keep her there until she had time to adjust.

But Fast Ed was ahead of her. "Well, Cameron, we'd best be on our way. The young ladies are anxious to get settled in."

"But surely not without a tour of Leadville, or the best part of Leadville—the Postmortem. All of you come on over to my place. Drinks on the house. And I'll show the little lady just what a silver exchange is."

"A silver exchange, " Shenandoah said tersely, "is a combination gambling house, saloon, and dance hall."

"Really?" Arabella replied, her blue eyes large. "I'd like to see that."

"I'll be glad to show you the Postmortem and a lot of other things in Leadville. But, say, you must not be from around here. Where—"

"My sister's from back East. She's just arrived."

"Glad she's here," Spike said, taking Arabella's arm and beginning to lead her from the depot. "First stop is the Postmortem, then everything about Leadville will look good." He laughed, a short, dry sound.

As Arabella and Spike stepped away, Shenandoah looked in concern at Rogue, then at Fast Ed and Tom Burton. "What are we going to do?"

"Follow them," Fast Ed said, then coughed into his handkerchief. "Spike Cameron is not the sort of man my niece should be alone with."

As they hurried to catch up with Spike and Arabella, Shenandoah had her first good look at the town. It was more than she could have imagined. There were businesses of all kinds, boardwalks crowded with people, and a rumbling sound that echoed across the city from the constant noise and activity of businesses, mines, and smelters. There were gas streetlights, and even telephone wires strung to connect the mines with the heart of town. But the streets were a chaos of dust, racing wagons, runaway teams, and stampeding horse riders.

Before crossing the first street, Spike picked up Arabella in his arms and ran across, dodging wagons, horses, and people. Shenandoah could only stand in horror as her sister was suddenly separated from her. She turned to Rogue for help but he was striding down the boardwalk, a curt "Be right back" flung over his shoulder.

She glanced at her uncle. "What about Arabella?"

Fast Ed shook his head. "These streets are nothing but dust in the summer, mud in the spring and fall, and ice in the winter. They're about the most dangerous part of Leadville. It would be best if Rogue or Tom carried you across."

"That's all right. I can walk."

"Don't do it, Miss Shenandoah," Tom insisted. "You'd never get the dust and dirt out of your clothes. Don't matter on mine, but yours are real fine."

"Well, I don't know," she began.

"He's right," Fast Ed agreed. "Rogue'll be back in a minute and we can all cross together."

"Where did he go?" Shenandoah asked, then saw Rogue coming toward them, a telegram in his hands.

When he had read it, he folded it and thrust it into his vest pocket. His eyes were hard when he glanced up and saw them waiting. "Where's Arabella?" he asked as he joined them.

"Spike carried her across the street," Shenandoah explained.

"Hell! That's trouble we don't need," he said, and quickly scooped up Shenandoah and started across the street.

The dust that billowed up around them was unbelievable. Shenandoah was glad Rogue was carrying her, but for more than that reason. They'd had little time together since Arabella joined them and she missed his strong arms around her. In fact, she missed much more than that.

When they got to the other side, Rogue said, his breath warm on her ear, "Looks like I need an excuse to hold you. I'm not going to put up with it much longer, Shenandoah. I want you to come out to the mine soon."

Her heart beat faster. He hadn't forgotten her after all. Still, she hesitated. She didn't know if she could leave the city; Arabella might need her.

"Hear me? I want you out at the mine soon. Do I have to remind you that you owe me?"

"No, Rogue. It's just that—"

"Now that we're back in town and you're with your family, you don't want—"

"I'll come as soon as I can."

"Tomorrow."

"I don't know if—"

"Be there."

"Cussing cats!" Tom exclaimed as he and Fast Ed made it across the street. "I'm glad I don't have to fight that all the time."

"Quieter at the mine?" Fast Ed asked, then coughed hard into his handkerchief.

"In some ways," Tom replied, glancing hastily at Rogue.

Rogue set Shenandoah down, but did not miss Tom's glance. "I just hope it's trouble we can handle, Tom."

"Come on, we'd better get to the Postmortem," Fast Ed said. "The sooner we get there, the sooner we can get Arabella out of that place, and the sooner—"

"You can let me in on the news," Rogue finished as they all began to walk quickly down the boardwalk.

The Postmortem was on State Street, which boasted twenty-one saloons, plus numerous gambling houses, dance halls, variety theaters, restaurants, brothels, and lodging houses. Spike Cameron's silver exchange was as famous and popular as the Board of Trade, Pap Wyman's, the Texas House, and St. Anne's Rest because of its lavish furnishings, excellent gamblers, and beautiful dance-hall women.

The Postmortem had a high ceiling from which hung brilliantly lit cut-glass chandeliers to illuminate the huge room that sported red velvet draperies, a thick crimson carpet, numerous round tables covered with dark green cloths, and a polished wooden dance floor. A long mahogany bar stretched across one end of the room, and rows of bottles and glasses were reflected in the mirror behind it. Original oil paintings were hung all around the room on gold-flecked red-velvet wallpaper. A winding staircase led to other rooms where patrons could gamble, dine, or meet in private.

Shenandoah scarcely noticed any of this. The only thing she saw was Arabella sitting on a plush red velvet settee, a crystal glass filled with red liquid in one hand, the other hand gesturing at Spike Cameron, who was sitting close on her right. She was laughing, her blue eyes sparkling, and she looked amazingly at home. In fact, Shenandoah thought, it was the first time she had seen her sister happy since finding her in Mexico.

She walked over to her. "I think we should be going, Arabella. It's been a long trip and—"

"But I've just arrived, Shenandoah. This place is beautiful, and Spike has promised to show me the upstairs soon."

"I bet he has," Fast Ed said under his breath as he stopped beside them, his face stern.

Spike stood and motioned to another settee by his table. "Please sit down," he said, then turned toward the bar. "Harry, drinks all around. My special stock."

"Shenandoah, this is wonderful," Arabella said. "You didn't tell me how fine the West could be, and to think you've been working in places like this for years."

Shenandoah glanced around. "I don't always work in places this fancy."

"But you should," Spike insisted. "I'd be happy to have you gamble here. Fast Ed, you know you always have an open invitation too."

Fast Ed nodded as he reluctantly sat down.

Spike positioned Arabella to one side of him and Shenandoah to the other, but Rogue determinedly took the vacant seat next to Shenandoah, his brows drawn together, his right hand near the Colt he had concealed beneath his vest. He didn't like the situation, but he knew Shenandoah didn't want to upset Arabella by forcing her out of the Postmortem. Spike Cameron was taking advantage of the situation, but he wouldn't for long. They would play along with him, then get Arabella out and keep her out.

"Beautiful women deserve beautiful surroundings. The women who work here are very happy," Spike continued, looking from one woman to the other. "Either of you want to work here, just say the word."

"Shenandoah will be working the tables with me down at the Board of Trade," Fast Ed said firmly as the bartender set a bottle of whiskey and several glasses down on the table.

"Do you woo the fickle goddess over the green cloth too, Arabella?" Spike asked.

Arabella hesitated a moment, then said as she tossed her blond head, "Call me Bella. I prefer that. No, I never learned, but I'm sure I could find something that I could do well in a silver exchange."

"I'm sure you dance very well, Bella."

She smiled at him. "Yes, as a matter of fact I do."

"You know, the miners pay fifty cents for one dance with a woman, but only five cents for a glass of beer. A woman can do real well out here. Why don't you come to work for me? I could—"

"Arabella doesn't need to work," Fast Ed interrupted. "Her family can take good care of her. Besides, she's just arrived and needs a chance to get settled in."

"Well, perhaps my uncle's right, but I'll keep your offer in mind," Arabella said.

"Do that," Spike replied, "and don't forget you have friends here." He glanced at Shenandoah. "That goes for you too."

"Both my nieces have friends here, Cameron," Fast Ed said, "although I'm sure we all appreciate your interest."

"Just trying to be neighborly," Spike responded, then looked at Rogue. "Hear you're having a little trouble at your mine."

Rogue shrugged.

" 'Course you've been out of town. Maybe you don't know—"

"Rogan knows all he needs to know, Cameron," Tom growled.

"Sure. Just thought—"

"Don't. Mining's my specialty," Tom said firmly.

"In Leadville, mining is everybody's specialty. It pays to know what's going on out in the hills," Spike said, as if he knew more than he should.

"That's right," Fast Ed agreed, "but how come you're so interested in Rogue's—"

"No special interest. Just wondered how the mining was going. Neighborly question."

"You're mighty neighborly today," Rogue muttered.

Cameron shrugged and smiled, but there was a cold hardness in his eyes.

Fast Ed then got to his feet, "We must leave now. Arabella, you'll have time to see the sights of Leadville later. Let's go."

Reluctantly she rose, her eyes steady on Spike Cameron.

Everyone else stood too, leaving their untouched drinks behind as they began moving toward the front doors. Spike carefully kept Arabella by his side, and at the doors he said, "Now, don't forget my offer, Bella. There's always a place for you at the Postmortem."

"Thank you," Arabella said earnestly. "You have a beautiful silver exchange, Spike. I'll try to stop by again soon so you can finish the tour."

"Do that, and make it real soon."

⟪ 14 ⟫

Colorado Kate's place was not too far from State Street. Her two-story lodging house was Victorian in style, built of local lumber, and painted a soft yellow with dark brown accents.

Fast Ed motioned them into a small, cozy parlor where muted sunlight entered through white lace curtains. They sat down on dark gold velvet-cushioned furniture. There were several small tables of dark wood and two hand-painted china lamps set on lace-covered tables. Several small oil paintings of flowers adorned the walls.

"Make yourselves comfortable," Fast Ed said. "I'll go find Kate."

Soon a woman burst into the room. She was of indeterminate age. Her face was smooth and tanned, her hair and eyes were a medium brown, and her firm, stocky body was encased in men's trousers and a workshirt. Heavy boots were on her feet and she stepped into the room with a long, sure stride. Fast Ed was right behind her.

"Glad to see you folks. I'm Colorado Kate. Welcome to my place. You two my girls?"

While Arabella looked on in stunned surprise, hardly able to equate the woman before her with the Victorian house, Shenandoah stood up and shook Kate's hand. "I'm Shenandoah Davis. Thanks for saving rooms for us. This is a lovely home."

Kate glanced around her. "Like it? A bit fancy for my taste, but I won it in a poker game. By the way, heard you're a real sharp. Plan to try my hand at your table. Going to be playing with Fast Ed at the Board of Trade?"

"Yes, I plan to—"

"Good. Nice place. Hey, that your sister? Pretty little thing. Yankee?"

Arabella remained seated. "Philadelphia."

"That's my niece Arabella White," Fast Ed said.

"Nice family, Fast, Who's the big guy with the mud on his boots?"

Since Tom and Rogue were equally tall, they both looked down at their feet. Tom's boots had mud from the mine. "Sorry," he said. "I was at the mine earlier, and never planned on being in—"

"Don't make no never-mind. Got a girl comes in and cleans up. Besides, you miners are all alike. I should know. Ran a string of pack jacks from the mines to the smelters day in, day out until I won this place. Afraid I'm getting soft. What do you think?"

Tom Burton stood, his large frame dwarfing the room. "You look mighty fine just the way you are, Miss Kate."

Colorado Kate beamed. "Call me Kate. All my friends do."

"Kate, this is Tom Burton. He manages Rogue Rogan's mine," Fast Ed inserted quickly.

"Good to meet you, Tom," she said, then tilted her head to one side as if thinking. "Rogan? Do I know him?"

"You do now," Fast Ed continued, gesturing at Rogue.

"So you're Rogan. Glad to meet you." Kate pumped Rogue's hand, then stood back, her hands on her hips. "Well, I've got some fancy sandwiches and tea, or you can have beer. What do you say?"

"Beer any day," Tom answered, his eyes never leaving Colorado Kate as he sat back down.

"I'll have the same," Rogue agreed. "You too, Fast Ed?"

Fast Ed nodded in agreement. "But I think Arabella and Shenandoah may want to see their rooms and freshen up some."

"Sure thing," Colorado Kate agreed. "I'll show them up myself. You'll like your rooms. I've got one in back and one in front. Choice is yours."

"I'll take the front one," Arabella said quickly.

"That's fine," Shenandoah agreed. "I'll appreciate the seclusion of the back room."

Colorado Kate snorted. "Not much seclusion in this town, but it's a nice room."

Upstairs, Arabella looked very pleased with the small front room. There was a narrow bed covered in a lace spread, a small rocking chair, an armoire, and a washstand with pitcher and bowl.

"I'll have your baggage sent up soon as it arrives," Colorado Kate stated.

"I'd like to lie down if it's all right," Arabella said to her sister.

"Of course. I'll tell Uncle Ed."

Shenandoah walked with Kate down the hall to the room in back. "Try to be real quiet during the day. That's when the other working girls usually sleep," Kate said.

"I understand. I'll be sleeping then too."

Colorado Kate chuckled. "Gambler. Good for you, girl. I've always done a man's work myself. Grew up strong. Besides, I always had an independent streak and liked to make my own way. Heard that suffragist, Susan B. Anthony, speak over at Billy Nye's saloon back in seventy-seven. That woman made a lot of sense, but then, I figure if you work hard you'll be all right."

"If your luck holds," Shenandoah added.

Colorado Kate grinned. "A gambler would say that. But you're right. Luck's important. Well, what do you think of the place?"

"It's a beautiful room. I'll enjoy it." Shenandoah glanced around at a bedroom almost identical to Arabella's.

"There's water in the basin if you want to rinse your face and hands," Kate added.

Shenandoah nodded and quickly poured water from

the pitcher into the bowl. As she rinsed, Colorado Kate continued to talk.

"That Tom Burton's a fine-looking man. Don't suppose he has a family, does he?"

"As far as I know, he's all alone. He's Welsh and a good manager."

"I like a good, solid man."

Shenandoah dried her face and hands, then turned back toward Kate. "You want me to help you with the beer?"

Colorado Kate beamed. "Good! Didn't figure you for the tea-and-cake kind."

Shenandoah followed Kate down the back stairs to the kitchen, which was a large, spotless, airy room. When Kate had five bottles of beer on a tray, they returned to the parlor. The men stood up and Kate passed around the beer.

As they all sat down, Kate managed to maneuver herself onto the settee beside Tom, then set the empty tray down on a low table. Kate and Tom filled the small couch, but didn't seem to notice that their bulk was threatening the piece of furniture as they raised their beers in a salute, then downed them in one long swallow.

"That was good," Tom said, setting his empty bottle on the tray. "I had a thirst as long as a cat's tail."

"Cats!" Kate exclaimed, setting her bottle beside his. "They're stealing my cats."

"Who is?" Tom asked, outraged.

"If I knew, I'd stop them, wouldn't I?"

Tom nodded. "They stole my cat in Tombstone."

"You've just about got to have a cat here, or the rodents will run you out. Besides, I like cats."

"So do I. Tell you what. I've got one out at the mine that's about to have kittens. I'll give you one."

"Boy or girl?"

"Depends on what she has. If there's more than one girl, I'll give you a female. Otherwise, you'll have to settle for a male."

"Agreed. You're a good man, Tom Burton."

"Thanks," he said, then added, "I like your kind of spirit, Kate."

Fast Ed cleared his throat, sure that the two on the settee had completely forgotten everyone else in the room. "I hate to bring this up, but we did have a lot to discuss with Rogue, Tom."

"Damn! Excuse me, Kate."

"Go right ahead. My mules used to hear a lot worse."

"I forgot all about our problems. If you don't mind, Kate, I've got a lot to tell Rogan and—"

"Say no more. A man's got a right to his own business. Let me know if I can help out, though."

"Sure will. And thanks for the beer."

"Anytime."

When Colorado Kate had left the room, Tom Burton turned a serious face to Rogue. "That woman made me forget all about our problems, but we've got some, Rogue. That's for sure."

Rogue leaned back in his chair. "Tell me about them."

"Someone's trying to run us out!" Tom stated angrily.

"What's happened?"

"Well, everything was going according to plan," Tom began. "We'd begun digging deep when we started having small problems. You know, a rope would break, a beam would give way. Nothing big, nothing obvious, but it took up time. We kept going, but it was making the miners uneasy. You know how they are about a jinxed mine."

"The miners still think they see ghosts and hear strange sounds in the Mikado mine, and they'll rarely work there long," Fast Ed said.

"Is that what you're both worried about?" Rogue asked.

"Yes," Tom said. "I'm worried about losing miners. They put their lives on the line every time they go down. That makes a man careful, and it can make him superstitious. If this keeps up, we may not be able to get skilled workers. So far, we haven't lost any miners, but it could happen . . . and soon."

"I don't like it either." Rogue agreed. "Did the trouble just start all at once?"

"Yes," Fast Ed replied. "Right after Tom got here. I guess someone figured with his kind of help on the mine, you'd have it paying off soon."

"Well, we're not going to be run out," Rogue said decisively.

Fast Ed glanced at Shenandoah, who was listening intently. "We've got to find out who's behind this and stop them, Rogue. I thought maybe Shenandoah and I could help out there. A lot of men pass by our tables, and they'll have information.''

Rogue looked at Shenandoah, then said, "I don't want to put either of you into any kind of danger. This is my problem more than yours.''

"I'm your partner," Fast Ed reminded him. "That makes it just as much my problem.''

"I'll be glad to help any way I can," Shenandoah added quickly. "We did it at El Toro Rojo, Rogue. You know I can take care of myself.''

"That was different.''

"No. I—''

"I don't want you hurt," Rogue said intently, then stopped, not wanting to reveal their relationship just yet.

"We'll be careful," Tom said, "but we've got to get this stopped before someone does get hurt down in that mine.''

"How's the time? Are we going to be producing good ore soon?" Rogue asked.

"Barring any more freak problems, we'll be striking rich ore soon. It looks like a solid mine, Rogue, but it takes time.''

"I know," Rogue replied, then stood up and crossed to the window. "But time is one thing I don't have.''

"If you have a problem, Rogue, share it with us," Fast Ed said. "Four heads are better than one.''

Rogue shook his head, then turned back. "Thanks for the offer, but you can't help on this one. Now, the best thing for all of us is to get that mine running smoothly. Fast Ed, you and Shenandoah take to the tables. I've got some old friends I can look up and see if they've heard anything. Tom, you'd best get back to the mine.''

Tom nodded. ''You going to stay in town tonight?''

Rogue looked at Shenandoah, then said, ''Yes, but I'll be going out to the mine tomorrow. Shenandoah, you want to come with me and see the Silver Star?''

She hesitated briefly, saw his eyes darken, and said, ''Yes, I'd like that. Uncle Ed, do you think it will be all right for me to leave Arabella alone?''

''You'll be leaving her alone all night anyway, so tomorrow won't make much difference. Besides, I'll be in town and Kate will watch out for her.''

''Good, then I'll ride out to the mine with you, Rogue.''

He nodded, then moved to the front door. ''Let's go, Tom, we've got work to do.'' He looked over at Shenandoah. ''I'll see you tomorrow morning.''

When the two men were gone, Fast Ed took a drink of his beer and commented, ''Rogue's a good man, Shenandoah. I like him. He's got a problem, but he'll work it out.''

''I hope so. You know, I don't think I could have rescued Arabella without his help.''

''I'm glad he was there for you. It's hard to be alone in this world, but sometimes it's just as hard to share your life. I know I missed out on a lot by letting the women I've loved slip away from me. Don't make the same mistakes I've made.''

''What do you mean?''

''Life can get lonely, even when you're surrounded

by people. Just remember, when you find the right person—and you'll know it—don't let him get away.''

''Well, I—''

''You don't have to say anything. Just remember my words. While you're looking the other way, life can come and go. You mustn't feel you're tied to me forever.''

''But, Uncle Ed—''

''Just listen. You're a grown woman. There may come a time when you'll want a different life, settle down somewhere.''

''I'm a gambler, Uncle Ed, and a good one.''

''Yes, you are. I wanted to make sure you had a profession so that you could take care of yourself. After the war, there wasn't much left anyone could do. No jobs. And the brutal destruction. There seemed no way to rebuild. All the money was Confederate paper and that was worthless. What I'm saying is, you can choose the type of life you want, Shenandoah, but you don't have to feel you must gamble forever.''

''I understand, Uncle Ed, but you never talked this way before.''

''Maybe I'm feeling my mortality. Maybe I'm just seeing you all grown-up. What I'm saying is that you can make the choice of how you want to live your life. Follow your heart, Shenandoah, and you won't have any regrets in life.''

''I'll try.''

''Enough of an old man's ramblings! Tell me about Arabella. She doesn't look well,'' he said, then set his beer aside and took out his black handkerchief. He coughed hard into the square of silk.

"Are you all right, Uncle Ed?"

He coughed again, put away the handkerchief, and said, "This altitude isn't good for me."

"I'd notice that I have more trouble breathing since we arrived."

"You'll get used to it in a few weeks, but my lungs haven't been good since the war and they won't take much more of this. When they start bringing good ore out of the Silver Star, I'm going to have to move on, maybe south to Silver City, New Mexico. Somewhere hotter and drier."

"Should you wait?"

"Rogue's my partner, and he needs our help. I've been here this long and I'm not leaving now. I'm okay, just a little short of breath sometimes. Maybe I'm getting too old for this kind of life."

"I don't want to hear you talk that way. You aren't old. We're just too high in the mountains."

Fast Ed nodded. "I'll be all right. Now, tell me about Arabella. I'm concerned about her."

"She isn't well, and I don't know what to do for her. We rescued her, but she blames me for bringing her here and killing the men who kidnapped her."

"The Braytons?"

"Yes. We didn't have a choice. They weren't going to let any of us out alive."

"You did what you had to do. You got your sister back."

Shenandoah fought down the emotions that rose

every time she thought of the Braytons. "They kidnapped her, then raped her . . . all three of them."

Fast Ed shook his head and groaned. "How terrible for her. Criminals." He slammed one fist hard into the palm of his other hand. "At least she's safe now."

"Yes, but it's not out of her mind. She thinks she's a whore, Uncle Ed. She thinks she's worthless, that she doesn't belong with respectable people. She wanted to stay with the Braytons. I forced her to leave, and now she blames me for making her unhappy."

"Give her time, Shenandoah. She'll come around. We just have to be patient and understanding. And keep her away from men like Spike Cameron. She's vulnerable, easy prey to men who would use her. We'll watch over her and do what we can, although I'm afraid it's precious little now."

"I know. Every time I think of Tad Brayton, I want to—"

"He's dead now, and his brothers too. We have to go on, and so does Arabella. Rogue needs our help. Let's think about gambling tonight."

"All right. I'll find out all I can."

"So will I. Now, we'd better get some sleep. I'll come back for you after sundown and take you over to the Board of Trade and introduce you around. It's a good place. I think you'll like it."

"I'm sure I will, if you do."

Fast Ed stood up, smiled at his niece, then walked to the door. "I'll see you later, then."

Shenandoah followed him to the front door and gave him a quick hug. "I'm sure glad to be back with you, Uncle Ed."

He touched her face gently. "I've missed you too, and I'm glad to have you with me again."

Shenandoah watched him go and noticed for the first time that his shoulders seemed slightly stooped. He again pulled out his silk handkerchief and coughed into it, long and hard. When he was out of sight, she shut the door, her eyes clouded with concern for her uncle. She must not let anything happen to him. He and Arabella were all the family she had. If Leadville wasn't good for him, then they had to leave, and as soon as possible—even if it meant never seeing Rogue Rogan again.

∾ 15 ∾

The Board of Trade was luxurious. The gamblers were treated with great respect. Spirits were high and money flowed freely. But for some reason, Shenandoah had trouble concentrating on her game. Disgusted with her inability to control her thoughts, she finished a game and threw in her cards. It was late and time for a break anyway. The men at her table wandered away, seeking the fast game of faro or the suspense of chuck-a-luck.

Shenandoah felt her feet sink into the deep pile of the imported carpet, noticed the soft light from expensive chandeliers, and smiled at the bright colors of the dresses on the dance-hall women. The Board of Trade was an exciting place to be, the noise of laughter, conversation, and gambling rising and falling with the excitement of the revelers.

She stopped by the bar and got a glass of water, then wandered through the crowd, turning down offers to dance, offers to drink, and offers that led far from the silver exchange. She stopped to watch the dancers awhile, listening to the ragged, tinny music of the band, and wondered if Arabella might really be considering working in a dance hall.

She was glad her sister was sleeping safely at Colorado Kate's. Arabella didn't need to worry about working yet. In time she would be able to think clearly and make her own decisions, but for now she should stay far away from men like Spike Cameron. Shenandoah had seen men like him before, and they were quick to use anyone they could. She didn't like him, or his kind, especially when they were trying to take advantage of her own sister.

She looked around the crowded room, and her eyes widened with surprise as she saw Rogue Rogan coming toward her. He was wearing Levi's, a black cotton shirt, a black leather vest, and knee-high black leather boots. A warm feeling flooded her. Tomorrow she would be going with him to his mine. Perhaps they would be alone together. She stopped her thoughts there. A mine would be a very busy place. They probably couldn't be alone. Nevertheless, they would be together, and she wanted that, more than she could have thought possible.

She waited for him to reach her, but instead, he stopped and smiled at someone. Shenandoah was shocked to see a petite woman clinging to his arm in a way that spoke of long, intimate acquaintance. The woman had pale blond hair arranged in a multitude of curls. She wore rouge, lipstick, and powder to enhance her natural beauty. Her voluptuous body was squeezed into a gold satin gown, displaying a deep cleavage.

Shenandoah felt a fiery flame of jealousy rush through her. Her chest burned and her need to separate Rogue from this other woman was overwhelming. Furious, she could only stand and dig her nails into her palms, waiting for rational thought to prevail.

She was still seething when Rogue began steering the beautiful woman toward Shenandoah. She couldn't decide if she wanted to hurt them both, or run, hiding her own pain in solitude. But she was given no chance to do either.

"Shenandoah, I want you to meet Topaz," Rogue said, bringing the two women face to face.

"Topaz, how nice," Shenandoah muttered coldly, feeling her face stiffen. She noticed that the woman wore a huge topaz stone on a heavy gold chain around her neck, and it rested in the soft place between her breasts.

"Nice to meet you," Topaz said, her eyes quickly appraising Shenandoah. "Rogue told me he had a little business in Arizona. I suppose you were it."

Rogue chuckled. "No, Topaz. Regardless of what you may think, I was there on mining business. Shenandoah is Fast Ed's niece."

Topaz nodded, still watching Shenandoah suspiciously. "You dance here?"

"She's a gambler," Rogue answered. "Damn near as good as her uncle."

Topaz looked even more suspicious. "I imagine

it's easy for you to win, looking the way you do. The miners probably don't see anything but your—''

''I win because I'm good,'' Shenandoah interrupted, her green eyes beginning to sparkle dangerously. She cast a cold glance at Rogue, then said. ''Well, it's been nice, but I have work to do.''

As she started to move away, Rogue said, ''Don't go, Shenandoah. I came over because—''

''Anything you have to say can be said to my uncle.'' She turned another cold look on him, then swept on by.

''Now, what did you do to make her so unfriendly?'' Topaz asked, laughter in her voice, then added, ''Finish your business, honey, then let's go on back to my place.''

Shenandoah's back stiffened as she walked away, knowing Topaz had deliberately spoken loud enough so that she would hear. Whatever Rogue replied, she didn't know, because she had moved far enough away that his words were swallowed up by the noise of the crowd.

Shenandoah had been caught off guard. She hadn't expected to see Rogue with another woman, especially after what they had shared. Of course, she told herself, it was logical that he would have someone in Leadville, and a woman like Topaz would be experienced company, a woman not to be forgotten. But still, she hadn't thought . . . not after . . .

Suddenly a hand grabbed her arm and she was whirled around.

"Shenandoah," Rogue said, his voice low and clipped, "let's go outside."

"No!" She tried to shrug his hand off, but he was holding her tight, almost hurting her.

"We're going to talk. Get this straightened out."

"Leave me alone," she insisted, pushing at his chest.

"I think we've played out this little scene before, round about Tombstone, but if you want to do it again—"

"Go away," she hissed, her green eyes flashing.

"If you want me to embarrass you, Shenandoah, I will. I'll pick you up and carry you out. Nobody'll stop me."

"You wouldn't."

He bent as if to carry out his threat.

"All right."

He dropped his hand and followed her through the crowded, noisy room until they were outside in the cool summer air.

There Shenandoah stopped abruptly. "I don't appreciate your highhanded manners. Now, whatever you have to say, say it quickly. I have work to do."

"Never give an inch, do you?" Suddenly he picked her up, then stepped quickly into an alley, walking away from the gas lights into the darkness. There he set her down, but kept a good grip on her arms.

"Rogue, really, I don't understand. Topaz must be waiting for you, and—"

Rogue grinned, his teeth white in the darkness. "If she is, she'll be waiting a long time."

"What do you mean?"

"Much as I like to see you jealous, I—"

"I am not jealous."

"Sure you are."

She pushed at his chest, feeling his hard muscles tighten. "Rogue, you have a right to see whatever women you want."

"Do I?" His voice grew low, more intimate, and his hands began to caress her arms, moving up her bare shoulders.

She trembled under his touch. "Yes, of course you do."

"Then why did you run out on me?"

"I didn't run out. I just had things . . . to do." His strong fingers were weaving a pattern along her collarbones, making small shivers run up and down her spine.

"What could be more important than us?"

She jerked away from him. "Everything! And don't tease me."

He slowly, carefully turned her back to him. "I'm not teasing you, Shenandoah. You *are* important to me. I'd hoped that—"

"What about your mine?"

"That has nothing to do with you, with us. It has to do with something that started long ago. I'm just finishing up what I have to do. Shenandoah, I—"

"Tell me about it, Rogue."

"No! There's no point. It doesn't concern you."

"It's a woman, isn't it? I bet it has to do with that Topaz."

"No, Shenandoah. Topaz and I have been friends for some time, but she has nothing to do with my mine or my past."

"You were with her tonight."

Rogue ran his hands up Shenandoah's arms, to her neck, then let their warmth encircle her throat. "I told you I was going to talk to some friends, find out anything I could. Topaz happens—"

"To hear a lot that goes on in this town," Shenandoah finished for him.

Rogue chuckled. "Yes, that's true. Men are eager to talk to Topaz. You can probably see why."

Shenandoah squirmed under his touch. "Yes, I can see why you were with her, too."

"I want to be with you, Doe. Believe me. There's no need to be jealous."

"I'm not."

Rogue chuckled again, then lowered his head, briefly brushing her warm lips with his own. "You smell like lavender. I'm jealous of every man who looks at you, Shenandoah, and the thought of you playing cards with men all night doesn't do me any good at all."

"But, Rogue, I'm only playing a game with them."

"Yes, but you can meet a lot of men that way."

"I hardly notice them. Anyway, I have to concentrate on my game." Her voice was suddenly breathless as his hands moved again, over her shoulders, down her back, pulling her closer to him. The heat of his body radiated outward, drawing her to him, making her remember how his heat had consumed her in Mexico.

"That's good, Shenandoah, because I'm not going to let any other man have you."

She shivered at the intensity of his words. "But, Rogue, I—"

"Don't talk," he murmured, taking her lips with his, feeding off her soft warmth, then plunging into her depths as she melted against him, feeling his strength and desire wash over her.

Once more he staked out his claim, reminding her of all they had experienced in Mexico, reminding her of what only he could make her feel, reminding her that she needed him, wanted him beyond anything she had ever wanted or needed before. When the kiss ended, she leaned breathless and tingling against his chest, aware how easily her body became pliant and hot at his touch.

"Now, what did you want to protest?"

"Oh, Rogue, I've missed having your arms around me, feeling your kisses on my lips, being so close to you that there is only us. I couldn't stand the sight of you with that other woman!"

Rogue kissed her lips lightly. "I know. That's how I felt about Tad Brayton. I thought I'd go out of my mind when he put his hands on you. I just hope I got that bastard through the heart."

"That's all behind us now, Rogue. We don't have to worry about the Braytons ever again."

"You're right. It's just that I like to see a man

dead for myself. Sometimes supposed corpses have a way of turning up all too alive and well.''

"In any case, we're far from Mexico.''

"That's true. But I don't want to talk about the Braytons or Topaz. I want to talk about us. You're still coming out to the Silver Star with me tomorrow, aren't you?''

She hesitated a moment, moved a little away from him, then smiled mischievously up at him. "Well, let's see if—''

He shook her. "That's not funny, Shenandoah. I don't want you turning cold on me again. If necessary, I'll remind you of our bargain.''

"You don't have to remind me of our bargain, Rogue. I want to see the Silver Star, and I want to be with you.''

He pulled her close, ran his hands up and down her arms briefly, then, exercising great restraint, dropped his hands and stepped away from her.

"All I want to do is take you to bed, Shenandoah. It's been so long I'm starting to hurt every time I see you.''

"Rogue,'' she said gently, feeling her heart grow warm.

"I don't know if it's better holding you or staying away from you.''

She touched his hand, caressed it with her long supple fingers, then raised it to her lips and kissed each finger gently, slowly moving down to the palm, which she quickly touched with her tongue.

Rogue groaned and jerked his hand away as if he

had been burned. "Damn! Don't do that to me, Shenandoah, or I may just haul you down to my hotel room. I won't be pushed far, I warn you."

She smiled and moved closer, putting her hands around his neck, drawing his face down to hers. "Rogue, I want you, too. I need you."

She didn't have to say more. His lips were hot and ready when he kissed her, pressing his hard body against hers, letting his large hands roam over her back, forcing her against him. As he held her close, her hips firmly clasped in his hands, he pushed deep into her mouth, wanting to unite them completely, but unable to do more than kiss her with a hunger that turned both their bodies to fire.

When he finally set her from him, she was gasping. "Rogue, Rogue, I don't know what you do to me. I lose all control. I want you more than I've ever wanted an ace to complete a hand of four kings."

Rogue chuckled, then said, "Good. As long as you think I'm ace quality."

"You're ace quality all right, and you're the best holdout a woman ever had."

"Let's keep it that way," he replied, putting an arm around her shoulders. "But we'd better go back before I bust my Levi's and have to take the back streets home."

She laughed. "At least we'll be together tomorrow."

"Right. And if I have to send every miner I've got into town, we're going to find a way to be alone. I can't wait any longer, Shenandoah."

She took his hand, squeezed his fingers, and said, "We'll find a way, Rogue. Tomorrow will be ours."

As they started to leave, Rogue suddenly stopped. "Did you hear something?"

Shenandoah listened, but heard nothing beyond the usual sounds of a city at night. "No, did—"

He shook his head. "I don't hear anything now either. Must have been my imagination."

"What was it?"

"Sounded close. Like a spur jingling. Miners don't wear spurs."

"Probably just some passing stranger."

"Guess so. Come on. We've still got work to do."

He took her hand, and they walked out of the alley and back into the Board of Trade. No one seemed to notice that Shenandoah's eyes glittered more brightly or that her lips were redder than when she had left, or that a fierce determination burned in Rogue Rogan's eyes as he watched Fast Ed's niece make her way back to a table and sit down.

When Shenandoah said, "Anyone for poker, gentlemen?" Rogue turned away and again left the silver exchange, his stride sure and determined. Someone in Leadville was trying to stop him from getting the cash and heading for New Mexico. The latest telegram from Cougar Kane had told him to get home on the double. Blackie's reach was long; somehow it had even stretched into Leadville.

But Rogue would not be stopped. One way or another he was going to get money out of the Silver Star and stop his cousin Blackie from stealing his half of the silver mines their fathers had left them in New Mexico.

That thought fixed firmly in mind, he made his way down State Street, the lights of Leadville brightening the street but not his mood.

$\backsim$ 16 $\backsim$

The road out of Leadville was dusty, throwing a cloud of fine dirt into the air as Rogue and Shenandoah rode to the Silver Star the next morning. They were in a freight wagon piled high with supplies for the mine.

Shenandoah had dressed for the high country, wearing a rose plaid cotton shirt with a mauve-colored cotton skirt. She also wore brown leather boots and gloves, plus a wide-brimmed hat to protect her fair skin. Rogue was wearing Levi's and a dark blue shirt. Shenandoah could not help noticing how his hard muscles strained against the fabric of his clothes as he drove the team of mules. Now that he was out of the city, he also wore his pistol strapped to his thigh.

As they moved farther from Leadville, they traveled through land that had been denuded of trees, leaving stumps, rocks, and gullies where once had been rich forest. The mines were in the hills around

California Gulch, where Leadville had been founded as the Carbonate Camp. Rogue pointed out Long and Derry Hill, Rock Hill, Iron Hill, and Carbonate Hill, all important mineral belts of the Leadville region.

Wooden buildings covered these hills, but most of the activity took place far below the surface. Few miners were to be seen as Shenandoah looked out over the rich mining area, although freight wagons and pack jacks were being loaded with the ore brought out from deep within the earth. The carbonate ore would be hauled into Leadville to the smelters, where it would be separated in the fiery furnaces, producing silver as well as large amounts of iron and lead.

As Rogue and Shenandoah traveled north, they passed Stray Horse Gulch, then Fryer Hill, where Rogue pointed out the famous Matchless mine, the Little Pittsburgh, and the Robert E. Lee, all million-dollar producers. On Breece Hill, the Highland Chief Consolidated mines were well known for their rich ore.

Most of the big mines were now owned by investors back East, but Rogue planned to bring in the Silver Star on his own. It might never be as large as the Robert E. Lee, but if everything went well it would provide him with the money he needed to get back to New Mexico and save his half of the rich silver mines he had inherited there.

That is, he would do that if he could solve the problems at the Silver Star.

Rogue glanced over at Shenandoah, noticing the swell of her breasts, the shape of her thighs under the skirt. He felt the familiar tension that would build in him whenever he was near her, or when he thought of her. Shenandoah had gotten into his blood in a way he wouldn't have thought possible. She was like a fire in him that couldn't be quenched. Not that he wanted to put out the fire, but he would damned well like to bank it for a while.

He looked away from her, staring hard at the strong backs of the mules. He had known all along that the extra time he would lose in Mexico might cost him heavily in Leadville. He had been right. With him gone, someone had felt safe enough to sabotage the Silver Star. He didn't think whoever it was would be quite so free now that he was back. Still, it had cost time and money, and Blackie had gained.

His eyes drifted back to Shenandoah. He would do the same thing if he had it all to do over again. Shenandoah was not a woman you let get away. He wished it all had been different, especially for Arabella's sake, but in the West you took the good with the bad and made the most of it when your luck was running.

Shenandoah was good luck. So was the Silver Star. And he wasn't going to let his cousin turn them to bad. He would do whatever he had to do. He was going back and claim his inheritance with enough money to make it stick, and he was not going to give up Shenandoah to do it. She was a part of him, a fire in his blood.

He reached over and took her hand. She smiled at

him, her green eyes lighting up. Yes, she was a woman to fight for, a woman to be treasured.

"How soon do we reach the Silver Star?" she asked.

"Not much farther. It's near Half-Moon Gulch."

"Half-Moon Gulch? That sounds interesting."

"It is. It's one of the most beautiful places around here, and not too many people know where it is."

"Really?"

"They used to think it hid a fortune in gold, but no gold has ever been found there. They also said it was a wild spot, full of mountain lions and bears."

"Is it?"

"It's wild, all right, but the wild beauty of the mountains. I've never seen a lion or bear there."

"Then you've been to Half-Moon Gulch?"

"Yes. An old miner took me to the canyon. Like I said, not a lot of people know its exact location because the gulch is hard to find if you haven't been taken there. And those of us who have been don't tell many others its location. We want to keep it all to ourselves."

"And the gold?"

"I've looked. No gold, and I'm almost glad. That way there won't be any reason to tear up its natural beauty."

"Perhaps I can see it sometime."

Rogue squeezed her hand, then let it go as he took up the reins in both hands. "I'd be more than happy to show it to you. Hey, there's the Silver Star up ahead."

Shenandoah turned to look in the direction Rogue was pointing. She was surprised that there was so little to see. A tunnel had been dug into the side of a hill and several wooden buildings had been built nearby. The buildings were unpainted and weathering fast.

"The Silver Star may not look like much now, but the mine will grow," Rogue said. "Those million-dollar producers started out like this, and look at them now. In fact, the mining in this area began down in the riverbeds where the miners sluiced for gold. After they'd gotten the golden nuggets from the streams, their sluice boxes started getting jammed with heavy black mud and rock. Disgusted, a lot of the miners left, thinking they'd gotten all there was. Later, they were proved wrong, for the major wealth turned out to be in that heavy black rock which when smelted produced fortunes in silver and lead."

As Rogue drove the mules up to the largest building, there was suddenly a loud rumble from within the tunnel and dust began to billow out from it. Men started shouting as the earth shook around them. The mules brayed loudly, pulling against the reins.

"Damn! What now?" Rogue exclaimed as he fought the mules for control, then set the brake and wrapped the reins tightly around the long brake handle. He jumped from the wagon, then helped Shenandoah down.

As they rushed to the entrance of the Silver Star, several men began to run outside, coughing, covered in dust, blinking against the brightness of the sunlight.

"What happened?" Rogue shouted.

The men were too busy coughing, knocking dirt from themselves, as others continued to emerge from the mouth of the mine, to answer. Rogue started toward the entrance, but Shenandoah held him back.

"Is everyone all right?" Rogue asked the group of miners. "Is anyone left inside?"

"Got two men trapped down there," one of them answered. "Burton stayed behind to help."

"I'm going in," Rogue said without hesitation. "Will one of you go with me to show me the place?"

"Name's Lefty. Guess I'll go. Better get some rope and more candles. Don't know what it's like in there now."

Rogue shucked off his leather vest, handed it to Shenandoah, then unbuckled his gunbelt.

"Rogue," she began, feeling helpless and terrified for him, as well as for Tom.

Rogue turned to her, grasped her shoulders hard, and said, "I've got to go, Shenandoah. It's my mine. We'll get them out or—"

"I understand. Just be careful, please."

The miner returned with the rope and candles. Rogue and Lefty each took a handful of candles and a length of rope.

"If we're not back soon, better notify the authorities in town and see if you can get some help," Rogue told Shenandoah, then disappeared into the darkness and swirling dust of the mine.

Shenandoah felt the strength drain from her. Rogue's vest and gun were suddenly too heavy, but she pulled them close to her body, smelling his scent on them, needing their warmth. Rogue would rescue the miners and return to her. He had to.

She stepped closer to the entrance, her eyes straining to see into the darkness. The miners clustered around her, but just like Shenandoah, they could do nothing now but wait.

After what seemed a long time, another rumble shook the mine. Dust billowed out again.

Shenandoah and the miners stepped back, their eyes trained on the entrance, fear clutching at them. They could see nothing but the dust for a moment; then they heard coughs coming from the mine. Finally the sound of feet scuffing over ground came to them. And at last men emerged from the Silver Star.

For a moment Shenandoah could only stand still as relief flooded her; then she stepped forward ready to throw herself into Rogue's arms. But she stopped abruptly. He was supporting another man, his arm around the miner's shoulders. Tom was right behind him, supporting a man too. Lefty followed them, carrying the candles and rope.

A loud hurrah came from the men as the two trapped miners were helped to stand on their own feet. They glanced around the group, then grinned broadly, glad to be alive and well. Rogue quickly took his vest and pistol from Shenandoah, and squeezed her hand in silent thanks.

"Men, I'm sorry about this, but we're all out safe," he said to the group. "I know you've been having trouble, but I'm going to put a stop to that."

There was mumbling among the miners, then quiet.

"We've had one guard here at night. We're going to have three. This is going to be a safe mine to work."

"I don't know," Lefty spoke up. "We've had a lot of trouble here, but nothing this bad. This keeps up, we're going to have some dead or hurt miners."

The group sounded its agreement.

"Listen, men," Rogue broke in. "I know there have been problems, but they're going to stop. I'm back and I'm not going to leave until things are okay here."

"In that case, I'll go down again, but at the first sign of trouble I'm leaving," Lefty, the apparent leader of the miners, stated, then turned to the others. "What do the rest of you say?"

The other miners mumbled cautious agreement.

"Good," Rogue said. "Now, take the rest of the day off on the Silver Star. You need the rest."

The miners whooped out their pleasure at the paid day off, and there was a stampede for the buildings as the miners hurried to get cleaned up and start for Leadville.

Rogue turned to Tom. "Somebody's getting serious about stopping the Silver Star."

"I'll say they are," Tom agreed. "We damn near had two dead men, Rogan."

"Not to mention a mine manager."

"I was all right," Tom said, "but I'd never have gotten those men out without you and Lefty."

"What happened?" Shenandoah asked.

"Somebody's getting into the mine," Tom replied. "At night, I guess. The guard probably falls asleep, although he swears he doesn't."

"Three guards can take shifts," Rogue said. "Nobody should get past them. The mine ought to be safe after this."

"The men are beginning to think it's jinxed."

"No wonder," Rogue said.

"The fact of the matter is," Tom began, then stopped and glanced at Shenandoah.

"Go ahead," Rogue urged him. "She's one of us."

"Hit some good ore. Heavy, black carbonate. Sent it in to be assayed yesterday."

"Get the report?"

"Was going in today."

"But somebody found out ahead of you."

Tom nodded. "Could be. The cave-in came right at the breast of the new drift. The timbers gave way, and they were solid beams. They shouldn't have caved in, but they did when the men started digging in that drift today."

"So we've hit the rich vein, then," Rogue said eagerly.

Tom rubbed his thick black beard. "From what we took out of that vein, and from the extent of this cave-in, I'd say you've hit one of the richest veins I've seen in a while. But somebody is watching our every move. I don't like it."

"I don't either."

"You know who's behind this, Rogan?"

"Maybe. But with me here and three guards on duty, I think we'll be all right."

"Hope so," Tom said.

"Let it go for now. I'll pick up the assay report when I take Shenandoah back to town. You get some rest."

Suddenly a man came riding furiously up to the camp. He threw himself off his horse, looked hurriedly about the place, then asked Rogue, "Had any trouble?"

"Some. What brings you out of your assay office, Slim?"

"Damn thieves broke into my office last night. I've been sorting it out all morning. Left the place a mess, but only thing they stole was a copy of your assay report."

Rogue stiffened.

"That's why I came rushing out as soon as I could. Thought it might mean trouble."

"Sure did. Had a cave-in this morning."

"Accident?"

"I don't think so."

"Anybody hurt?"

"No. We were lucky."

"Well, here's your report. I'd say your accident may have been caused by this."

Rogue took the piece of paper, then held it so Tom and Shenandoah could read with him. The assay showed a high silver content in the ore. Just what he had hoped for. Grinning, he hugged Shenandoah to him, then clasped Tom's hand.

Tom hollered at the other miners, and in a moment they were all outside, tossing their hats into the air. It was great news for everyone. Now the Silver Star would become a major producer and provide jobs for the miners and money for Rogue. There was plenty of reason to celebrate.

"I'm going into town," Tom said. "Wait'll Kate hears this. We'll tie one on."

"I'll ride in with you," Slim said, then added, "Hope I didn't cause you any trouble over the assay report, Rogue."

"Nothing you could have helped," Rogue replied. "We'll be posting a double watch from now on."

After the miners headed into town to celebrate, Rogue took Shenandoah by the hand and led her to a couple of horses hitched nearby. "Let's get that lunch I had the hotel pack for us," he said, "then get on over to Half-Moon Gulch. I want to celebrate and I don't know a better place, or a better person to celebrate with."

∿ 17 ∿

Half-Moon Gulch was more beautiful than Shenandoah could have believed possible. A waterfall cascaded down from the mountains above to run in a stream through the canyon. Mist swirled up from the waterfall, shrouding the canyon in mystery. Tall trees enveloped the gulch and wildflowers and tall grasses covered the canyon bed. Birds could be heard singing in the trees and insects buzzed as they flitted from flower to flower. The scent of evergreen permeated the breezes.

Once inside the canyon, the outside world was left far behind. Only the beauty and peace of nature existed. Shenandoah and Rogue tied their mounts to trees, then walked into the wild, rustic land. Rogue carried a blanket and picnic basket in one hand, while the other firmly clasped Shenandoah's long, slim fingers.

Near the running stream, Shenandoah stooped to thrust a hand into the cool water, letting it ripple over her fingers. She could see rocks rounded by the constant rush of water, and small fish flitting through the clear, clean depths. She touched wet fingertips to her lips and smiled.

"Drink it," Rogue said. "It's the best water you'll ever taste."

She cupped her hands and brought the sparkling water to her mouth. When her thirst was quenched, she patted her hands dry on her skirt and looked at Rogue with eyes as sparkling as the mountain stream.

They walked along the stream, picking their way over rocks, twigs, and clumps of grass. Shenandoah felt free, as if she could forget the outside world for a while, forget her troubles. Here, there was only the two of them.

Rogue kicked a few stones and twigs from an area of ground, then shook out the blanket he carried. Shenandoah helped him spread it flat on the earth.

"This looks like a good spot," Rogue said, setting down the picnic basket.

Shenandoah sat down and stretched out her legs.

Rogue sat close to her. "I've almost wished several times lately that we were back in Mexico, alone."

She gazed at his hard, tanned face. His blue eyes were intense.

"With so many people around," he continued, "I haven't had much of a chance to be alone with you. I don't like it."

She smiled and stroked his clean-shaven jawline. "I don't either. I've missed you."

"And that accident at the Silver Star this morning. Not what I'd planned for us," he said ruefully.

"I was terrified. For you. For the men. Whatever is going on, Rogue, please be careful. I don't want you hurt."

He took her hand and kissed its palm. His lips were warm and firm, coaxing a feeling of pleasure deep within her.

"I'll be careful, Shenandoah. I have a lot to live for now, and a lot to do."

"Can I help?"

"No. I'll get this worked out on my own."

"Rogue, I—"

"Don't say anything. Just let me look at you."

Rogue's eyes burned brightly as they roamed over her face, noticing how her rich auburn hair had strayed, strands coming loose from the chignon at the back of her neck. Her eyes were a deep, expectant green, sparkling and clear.

He reached out, touched the tip of her nose, the full, passionate lips, her pointed chin, then moved on, letting his fingers delve into her thick, fragrant hair. The scent of lavender came to him as he freed her hair of its confinement, letting it fall in a riotous mass down her back.

"Shenandoah," he said, his breath coming more quickly. "You are so beautiful . . . a delight I cannot do without."

She could see the desire in his eyes. The muscles in his jaws tensed. His hair gleamed golden in the sunlight. His finely chiseled lips beckoned her. She touched his broken nose gently, lovingly.

"You sure you still like men with broken noses?"

"More sure than ever . . . as long as the nose is yours."

"That's what I wanted to hear." He took her hand and kissed each fingertip lightly, then spread out her hand. As he examined it closely, he said, "You have beautiful hands. They're so long and slender. Extremely sensitive fingertips, just like a gambler."

She smiled. "Mine aren't as sensitive as some gamblers' hands I've seen. They keep the skin rubbed off their fingertips until they're almost bleeding all the time. Of course, I rarely play with a gambler like that. Sure sign they're using cards marked with little raised dots."

"I'm almost sorry I mentioned gambling," Rogue said, humor in his voice.

"Oh. Well, I do get carried away sometimes."

"Get carried away with me instead."

Shenandoah smiled slowly; then Rogue thrust a hand into the wild tresses of her hair, pulling her close. His eyes were like molten lava as his mouth neared hers.

She waited, hardly breathing, for the first touch of his lips to hers. When it came, so light and feathery as almost to be nonexistent, her body shuddered in deep response. He pulled her hard against him, his lips crushing hers in a kiss that spoke of tenderness but also of a deep, driving need to be joined with her in the full fury of his passion.

His lips moved quickly down her neck, causing pinpoints of pleasure to pierce her. He bit her lightly, then moved back to her ear, where he traced its intricacies with his tongue.

She felt him stealing her strength, and a languor grew within her, heat rising with it, drawing her to him in a way that could not be denied. She sought out the curling blond hairs exposed by his open-necked shirt, and began caressing his chest.

"Doe," Rogue said, his voice lost in the depths of her hair. "Do you want me?"

"Oh, Rogue, is there any doubt?"

He trailed fiery kisses back to her lips, then made a mockery of all the kisses that had ever gone before. She melted in his arms, seeing, hearing, feeling, tasting nothing but Rogue Rogan.

When she lay pliant in his arms, he raised his face, his eyes dark with desire as he looked tenderly over her flushed face. "I could kiss you all day, but I'd rather—"

She reached up and began unbuttoning his shirt.

Rogue grinned and helped her. When he shrugged out of the dark blue shirt, his naked torso gleamed with a golden tan, the chest hair a gilded mat that spread across the hard muscles, then tapered downward into his Levi's.

"I'd rather you undressed us both. I don't think I have the strength."

"You need food?" he teased.

"No. I need you."

Rogue nodded, his eyes suddenly intense as he

unbuckled his gunbelt. He laid the Colt .45 aside, but within easy reach. Then he reached for her.

His hands were steady and gentle as he swiftly undid her cotton shirt, then pulled it off. He hesitated a moment to look at her full, rounded breasts covered only by a sheer lavender chemise, then said, "Stand up. I'll have you out of those clothes in no time."

Her skirt and petticoat settled around her feet, then Rogue pulled the chemise off in one swift movement. The mountain air was cool on Shenandoah's bare flesh. She felt her nipples harden in response.

Rogue's eyes darkened as he moved his hands downward to encircle her breasts, letting his thumbs gently rub her taut peaks. Their eyes met in a hot, knowing exchange. Without speaking, she removed the rest of her clothing and her boots, and she stood nude in the bright mountain sunlight.

Rogue took a deep, ragged breath, his eyes devouring her. "You're like an ancient Goddess. I could worship you forever."

She didn't answer but watched with unmistakable longing as Rogue removed the rest of his clothes. His finely sculptured body glowed golden brown, the blond hair a soft accent over the hard muscles. He was beautifully shaped, with long, well-muscled legs, hard, narrow hips, a full, deep chest, broad, muscled shoulders, and long, strong arms. Shenandoah wanted him. She wanted to run her hands all over his body, feel him deep inside her. He was all that she could ever have wanted, and more.

She held out a hand to him, and he took it.

Their bodies met, and they sank to the ground, their arms around each other, searching, finding, joining.

The scent of lavender filled Rogue's nostrils as he kissed Shenandoah's neck. He cupped her breasts, kissed them gently, then nuzzled them. His nibbles sent shooting sparks of ecstasy through her and she moaned, writhing up against his hard body.

He moved farther down, letting his hands roam over her soft, creamy flesh, letting his tongue settle deep within her navel, causing the muscles of her thighs to clench against him, exciting her still further. "Shenandoah," he murmured, his breath hot against her bare skin. His hands found the soft skin of her inner thighs.

Shenandoah gasped as his strong fingers taught her new pleasures. "Rogue," she groaned, panting now, "oh, Rogue . . . please."

Rogue continued to ply her sensitive flesh, pushing her ever closer to the point of ecstasy. Then he covered her body with his, whispering into her ear, "There is so much we can share, Shenandoah. You have no idea . . . not yet."

She groaned as he filled her with his fire. He grabbed her hips, lifted her toward him, and began to move in hard, fast motions. His tension and passion were flooding over her. He could not wait. Neither could she. As Rogue brought them both toward the final culmination of their desire, Shenandoah clutched at his shoulders, digging her long fingers into the hard muscles straining with exertion. For a long moment they were one.

Slowly they began to return to reality, to their separate bodies. They dozed, their arms and legs entwined.

When Shenandoah woke later, she yawned, stretched, snuggled closer to Rogue, then finally opened her eyes and smiled. He still held her close, his eyes a warm, tantalizing blue as they swept over her.

"Rogue," she murmured, running long fingers down his bronzed chest, "I don't know why I fell asleep."

"I dozed too. You've had a rough time lately. You can use the rest."

"But I don't want to sleep. I want to enjoy every moment of this day with you."

Rogue smiled, stroked her tousled hair, and said, "I feel the same. Are you hungry?"

She toyed with the hair on his chest a moment, then said, "Now that you mention it, I'm starved."

Rogue chuckled. "Well, you'd better take your hands off me or the food will have to wait."

"In that case—"

"We'll eat first. I need my strength. So do you," Rogue stopped her, reaching for the picnic basket.

Shenandoah sat up, moving reluctantly away from the warmth of his naked body. She glanced around Half-Moon Gulch. "Do you think we should dress?"

Rogue opened the basket and began taking out food. "Few people know of this place, Shenandoah, and they'll all be working, if they're still in the area. Besides, I don't want you covered up.''

She couldn't help the slight blush that rose from her breasts, staining her face a light pink. She didn't think she had ever eaten a meal undressed, but she didn't want to put on her tight, confining clothing again. She wanted to feel the cool mountain breezes against her skin, watch Rogue's eyes darken when he looked at her. She would throw propriety to the winds and forget everything beyond the canyon.

Smiling, she looked at the food Rogue had spread out on their blanket. The hotel had packed fried chicken, fried okra, biscuits, fried pies, and beer. The food looked delicious and she didn't know when she had been so hungry.

She found herself thinking how shocked some people might be at their actions. But she didn't care what anyone thought. She and Rogue were happy together, happy to share themselves. She smiled at his ravenous eating. He had finished a chicken leg, was putting the last bit of a biscuit into his mouth, and was reaching for more okra.

He noticed her look and smiled. "With you around, I've got to keep up my strength."

She blushed noticeably, and looked away.

Rogue touched her cheek gently. "I wouldn't have you any other way, Shenandoah. Believe me."

She nodded, still a little surprised and embarrassed by her wanton behavior. With Rogue, though, she couldn't help herself. He brought out a side of her that she had never even known existed.

When they were down to the pies and Rogue looked mildly sated, he said, "I don't know when food has tasted so good."

A few moments later they were standing in the cold mountain stream. "Beautiful, isn't it?" Rogue asked, gesturing at the waterfall.

Shenandoah nodded, shivered, and moved closer to him.

He grinned. "Cold?"

"I'm trying not to be."

"You just need to get used to it." He reached down and splashed water on her.

Chilled further, she retaliated.

Rogue laughed, splashed more water on her, then turned to run into the waterfall.

Shenandoah followed, only to find herself sputtering as the cold water of the mountain wet her completely. But suddenly she was pulled from the fall into Rogue's warm arms. As he pushed her wet hair back from her face, she looked around.

They were behind the waterfall. The water that lapped around their ankles was cool and calm. The rocks under their feet were smooth and sleek with moss. It was almost like being in a cave, for it was suddenly hushed, everything muffled by the rushing rapids, and they were enclosed in the dim interior formed by the waterfall.

"I know how to make you warm," Rogue said, his hot hands running up and down her arms. "Doe, I want you now . . . here."

Later, they walked back through the waterfall.

Holding hands, they glanced almost shyly at each other. They had both been exposed to more of their true feelings than they had even known existed, and they would never be the same. The beauty of Half-Moon Gulch had touched them, opened them up to each other, drawn them into pleasure that would always be remembered.

And they knew that Half-Moon Gulch's treasures were not of gold or silver, but of love and passion.

18

Shenandoah stepped from the Board of Trade into the cool night air. She shivered slightly, her lavender satin gown providing little warmth, then wished she had brought the shawl Rogue had given her in Mexico. But she hadn't worn the shawl since they had returned. It held too many unpleasant memories that she didn't want to recall.

A strolling musician walked up to her, smiled, then played a fast, lilting melody of love in mining camps on his banjo. Shenandoah thought of Rogue, remembering their exquisite day in Half-Moon Gulch. But that had been a week ago and she had not seen Rogue since. He was busy with the Silver Star, and she was still trying to reestablish the closeness she and Arabella had once shared. But Arabella was not the same. In the last few days she had brightened up considerably, but it was a forced cheerfulness that worried Shenandoah more than her sullen silence.

Shenandoah's thoughts were interrupted when the

musician finished his tune and stepped closer to her. "Hear about the robberies?"

She nodded.

"The masked stranger struck again today."

"I thought Leadville had its robbers under control."

"They did until this lone man started hitting the stages. He hasn't gone for the trains yet, but he will."

"The sheriff going to catch the robber soon?"

The musician picked a chord, then said, "Seems the man's hard to catch, and he's masked. Could be anybody."

"Yes, I suppose," Shenandoah agreed, then smiled as the musician tipped his hat and wandered on down the street. As she watched him go, she noticed her uncle rushing toward her, bumping into people as he made his way in her direction.

As Fast Ed walked rapidly toward his niece, he coughed hard into his black silk handkerchief. He had left for a break a little before Shenandoah. She had thought he had just gone for a leisurely stroll, but his intensity now made her wonder.

"Shenandoah," Fast Ed gasped, coming to a stop beside her, his face flushed.

"Uncle Ed, please don't hurry. You know better than to—"

"Niece, your sister is working at the Postmortem."

"What?"

"Yes. I've just been there."

"Is she dancing?"

"Yes, and who knows what else."

Shenandoah took her uncle's arm and guided him toward a chair outside a storefront. "Sit down, Uncle Ed. Rest."

"I can't."

Shenandoah took a deep breath. So Spike Cameron had managed to reach Arabella, even though they had been so careful. But they hadn't been able to be with her all the time. She felt as if she had failed Arabella again. "I'm so sorry. I don't—"

"We must remove her from there immediately. Perhaps no harm has been done yet."

"The harm was done in Mexico," Shenandoah said dully. "I don't think you realized the extent of the damage. She thinks there's nothing for her except to be a whore, and Spike Cameron has played on those beliefs. The Braytons started this, and Cameron's taking advantage of it."

"Nevertheless," Fast Ed insisted, "your sister does not belong there."

"No, she doesn't. I tried to talk to her in Mexico, and I've repeated those efforts every day since then, Uncle Ed."

"Spike Cameron has influenced her mind. He will have to be stopped."

"Stopped?"

"Yes, of course. This is a matter of family honor. This is a matter of an innocent child being corrupted. We will save her."

Shenandoah could see battle fire gleaming in her uncle's eyes. She had never seen him like this before. There was a deadly, concentrated force in him.

This must have been what the Yankees saw when the Southerners came at them. She would not have been surprised to hear a Rebel yell tear through the night. Yes, her uncle and his Southern Rebels must have been powerful enemies.

"Come, Shenandoah," Fast Ed said, taking her hand firmly. "We will free your sister."

Shenandoah was afraid her uncle would be disappointed, but she said nothing as they headed for the Postmortem.

Lights blazed in Spike Cameron's silver exchange. People were crowded into the Postmortem, drinking, dancing, and gambling.

The young lady from Philadelphia was sitting on the lap of a miner, laughing gaily as she toasted him with a full shot glass of whiskey. She downed the drink in one swallow, then held out her glass for more. Her blue eyes were bright, her hair was in wild disarray, and her cheeks were painted pink. One hand toyed with the fringe that dangled from the very low bodice of her red satin gown.

As she finished the new drink, the miner nuzzled her neck. She laughed, then ran a hand up his sleeve to clasp his strong shoulder, drawing him toward her. Emboldened, the miner moved work-roughened hands over her soft bare arms. She snuggled closer, pursing red lips as she flirted with him. The miner suddenly stood, pulled her to him, and headed for the dance floor.

Shenandoah and Fast Ed stopped them. Surprised, the miner started to become loud and nasty. But Fast

Ed discouraged him with the promise of money and drinks. As the miner concentrated on her uncle, Shenandoah pulled Arabella away.

Finding a quiet corner, Shenandoah rounded on her sister. "How can you possibly work here?"

Arabella shrugged, then tried to edge away.

But Shenandoah was growing more angry by the moment. She jerked Arabella back. "Do you know what this is doing to Uncle Ed? He's already sick. I know you were hurt, but—"

"You don't know anything. I want to work here. Spike says I can make lots of money. He's been good to me."

"You don't need the money. And you can't trust Spike. Besides, how can you do this to yourself?"

"Do what? Take a job? You have one. Get a man? You have one."

"What?"

"Rogue Rogan. I'm not a fool. And I'm no innocent, not since the Braytons. I'm not going to stay penned up in some boardinghouse for the rest of my life, or let you and Uncle Ed dictate to me."

"We're not dictating to you. We're trying to help you." Shenandoah was having trouble controlling her anger.

"Just leave me alone. This is the only life that's right for me now, and—"

"Arabella," Fast Ed interrupted, having gotten rid of the miner, "let's step outside and discuss this."

"I'm staying here," Arabella insisted. "Spike says I can, and I like it here. So there's nothing to discuss."

"That's right," Spike Cameron said, suddenly appearing and putting an arm possessively around Arabella's shoulders.

"That's for her family to decide," Fast Ed replied, his eyes never leaving Arabella's face.

"You might say Bella's found a new family." Spike smirked. "Isn't that right, honey?" His right hand moved down Arabella's arm to wrap tightly and suggestively around the young woman's waist.

"What do you mean?" Shenandoah asked, beginning to realize that Spike was more dangerous than she had at first thought.

"I'm living with Spike," Arabella stated, glaring defiantly at Shenandoah and her uncle.

Shenandoah felt Fast Ed stiffen beside her. "Arabella, your uncle and I are—"

"I want to have a good time. Here I can work for my own money and have fun while I do it."

"Not that she has to work," Spike added. "I'm delighted to have her here just for myself."

"I'm sure you are," Fast Ed said coldly. "Whatever has happened to you, Arabella, you cannot forget your family, your roots. This man is taking advantage of you."

Arabella snuggled closer to Spike. "Maybe I'm taking advantage of him."

Spike chuckled. "The young lady is quite a woman. I'll do whatever I can to keep her happy."

"You're keeping me quite happy," Arabella said, smiling up at Spike.

"That is enough!" Fast Ed exploded. "You, sir,

have offended my family. We will meet at dawn. You may have your choice of weapons."

A small silence followed. The sounds of the silver exchange continued around the group, but the noise seemed muted, separated from them.

Spike Cameron laughed. "You aren't actually calling me out for a duel, are you?"

"I am. Name your weapon and your second."

Spike laughed again, then glanced around. "Mister, you're about a century too late."

"You're afraid. A coward," Fast Ed taunted.

"This is about the funniest thing I've ever heard," Spike replied. "Afraid? I don't have to be. Not only am I not going to join you at dawn, but I'm going to have you thrown out of here."

"Have you no honor?"

"As a matter of fact, I don't. Honor is damned expensive. You Southerners ought to know that better than anyone. I also happen to know that you're probably better than anyone around with a gun, probably even a rapier. That's not the way I fight. I like to win, so I always set the odds in my favor. Honor. You must be joking."

"I assure you, sir, I am not joking. I expect you to meet me at dawn."

Spike stroked Arabella's arm. "The lady wants to stay with me. And my bouncers say that she can. That's all there is to the matter." Spike looked away and called, "Hank! Dan!"

"Arabella," Shenandoah pleaded with her sister. "Come with us now. There's no need for this."

"No," she said stubbornly. "I told you back in Mexico. I have no family anymore. I'm living with Spike. You two go away. Forget this silly duel. I'm a grown woman."

The two bouncers then approached. "Boys, this man is not welcome in the Postmortem, or anywhere else near me or Bella. Now, throw him out," Spike instructed.

Shenandoah gasped as one of the huge men grabbed her uncle by his shirt collar and began to haul him from the room. Fast Ed struggled for a moment, then subsided. He would not give Spike Cameron the satisfaction of seeing him struggle when there was no hope of escape.

Shenandoah wheeled on Spike and her voice was low and intense when she spoke. "You've made a mistake this time. I'm going to personally see that you learn how to lose."

"Please, please, my dear. This is not between us. My offer still stands. I'd love to have you here with Bella and me."

With a hard look at her sister, Shenandoah said, "I know you've been hurt, Arabella, but you should leave this place at once."

"I'm staying. Spike can take care of me, and I can have a good time, too. What more could a woman want?"

"A lot more, Arabella. A lot more. I'll leave you for now, but I haven't given up."

"Good," Spike said. "Come back often, my dear. I never get tired of seeing lovely ladies."

Shenandoah turned on her heel and left. She hurried through the front doors and found her uncle dusting himself off in the street beyond. "Uncle Ed," she said, hurrying to his side.

He coughed hard into his handkerchief, then looked up at her with sad eyes. He seemed to have shrunk once more. There was no more fight in him. He had been defeated again. Shenandoah couldn't bear to see him this way, especially when a man like Spike Cameron had done it.

"He won't get away with this," she stated as she took her uncle's hand.

As they began to walk away, Fast Ed said, "He did, didn't he?"

"No. He had the advantage. He only won a battle, not the war," she said fiercely.

Fast Ed nodded. "Wouldn't duel. What is this world coming to?"

"He's a coward, hiding behind Arabella's skirts," Shenandoah said passionately.

"Some might consider him smart." Then Fast Ed chuckled, and the tension eased out of them both. "You remind me a great deal of my brother right now."

"He won't win. I swear to you. He's going to lose and we're going to get Arabella back."

Fast Ed squeezed Shenandoah's hand. "You've got the spirit, niece. That counts the most. All the others can fall by the wayside, but if the spirit endures, so will the person."

"You have spirit, Uncle Ed."

He coughed again. "I'm growing tired, Shenandoah. The world is changing, leaving me behind. Perhaps I shall leave it to the likes of you, with your fine spirit, your youth, and your courage. You don't know defeat yet. But I must warn you, the good and the right do not always win."

"We'll win, Uncle Ed. *We will*. And you'll be right by our side."

He coughed, a hard, racking sound that echoed around Shenandoah. "My blessings are with you."

"Now I think we should get back to work," Shenandoah said. "It'll take our minds off Spike and Arabella."

❦ 19 ❦

Shenandoah rode out to the Silver Star with her uncle the next morning. She didn't want him riding alone anymore, although she hadn't told him that. Between Spike Cameron's threats, the mysterious accidents at the mine, and his weak health, she was worried about her uncle. She had even strapped on her derringer again.

She also wanted to be out of Leadville today because she didn't want to be reminded that Arabella was now living with Spike Cameron at the Postmortem. Usually, she would get up late, have coffee with her sister, chat awhile, then get ready to go over to the Board of Trade. Now she wouldn't be sharing a part of her life with Arabella, and she would miss it. Not that she was going to give up on getting her sister away from Spike Cameron, but they didn't want to do anything that might cause Spike to hurt Arabella. They would wait. When it was time to leave Leadville, Arabella could go with them.

As they neared the Silver Star, Fast Ed smiled at her. "You know, Shenandoah, sometimes I think I'll get enough money ahead to start up a horse ranch out here in the West. The Silver Star could give us enough money to do that. A ranch would be a good place for Arabella to recover. She'd be safe there, and it'd probably be good for you too. You'd have a home of your own."

"That's a wonderful idea, Uncle Ed," she agreed, knowing that he could probably never invest that much of his spirit and emotion again. Everything he had been and had loved was lost with his horses. His prize stock had spilled their blood to the North. He had never really recovered from the loss of his horses, his land, or his family.

"But I don't know," he continued. "Maybe I'm too old, too tired. Horses require a lot of love and attention," he added, patting the dark mane of the animal he rode.

"We'll do whatever you want, Uncle Ed, as long as we move out of these mountains."

"Yes, we'll do that," he agreed, then pulled out his handkerchief and coughed. "You're a dear child. We could have raised Morgans, Starlands, Arabians, Barbs, and when I think of the breeding possibilities with mustangs . . ."

"Yes?"

"Well, back in the Shenandoah Valley, you would have grown up differently."

"Probably on horseback," she said, laughing.

"No doubt," he agreed, then continued musing

about their lost home. "Did you know your name meant 'Daughter of the Stars'? It's an Indian word. The Shenandoah Valley and its highlands are beautiful beyond belief. I suppose I'll always long for them."

Shenandoah smiled warmly at him. "Long ago Mother told me the meaning of 'Shenandoah.' I'm glad I was named for that beautiful place."

Fast Ed nodded. "You won't raise horses in the Shenandoah Valley, but you have a trade. We can teach your sister, too, just as soon as she sees that Spike Cameron is wrong for her."

"She will, Uncle Ed. Look, there's the Silver Star," Shenandoah exclaimed, pointing ahead.

"Maybe from now on our luck will all be good," Fast Ed said quietly, then pulled out his heavy gold watch. Already ten o'clock. He glanced upward. The sun was getting high in the sky. The men had been long at work deep in the Silver Star. There should have been no one around the mine, but he thought he had seen a shadow move through the trees nearby.

"Anything wrong, Uncle Ed?"

"No. Just thought I saw something."

"Must have been a deer."

"No doubt. Come on, let's tell them we're here."

As Fast Ed and Shenandoah tied their mounts to the hitching post in front of the main building, Rogue and Tom came out of the mine, hunks of ore in their hands. When they saw the newcomers, they set down the ore and hurried over to Shenandoah and Fast Ed.

"Shenandoah," Rogue greeted, smiling broadly. "Welcome back to the Silver Star."

"Is this the day I get my tour?"

"Sure is. And there shouldn't be any problems. We've got the debris cleaned out and the timbers back in place after that last accident."

"Nothing was hurt, then?"

"No, not really. We lost a lot of time, but we've already started digging in that drift again."

"Drift?" Shenandoah asked.

"The shafts that follow the ore through the earth," Tom explained. "We're back to the heavy black rock, and none too soon for me."

"Me either," Fast Ed agreed.

"The men have started picking and shoveling again. We should be bringing out that ore soon," Rogue said.

"By the way, Tom," Fast Ed inserted, "have you found your mother cat?"

"Oh, she eats the food I put out, and I catch a glimpse of her now and again, but I'll be danged if I can find her nest. I'd like to, because I think she's going to have her kittens soon and they'd be safer in one of the buildings than in the woods."

"But she thinks differently?" Fast Ed asked.

"Unfortunately, she's following the call of nature," Rogue added, "and there's nothing Tom can do about that."

"You need my help down in the drift today, Rogue?" Fast Ed asked, glancing around the clearing.

"No. I'd appreciate it if you'd check the supplies and get some samples ready to take into town."

"Glad to," Fast Ed said. "But before I start, I think I'll have a look around. I used to be pretty good with animals, especially skittish females ready to give birth. Bet I can find your cat's lair."

"Great," Tom agreed, enthused. "Find it and I'll treat you to all the beer you can drink this evening."

Fast Ed nodded. "I'll take you up on the offer. Now, Shenandoah, if you get tired of looking in the mine, just come on up to the big building. You can help me in there if you want."

"Okay, Uncle Ed." Impulsively she leaned over and gave him a quick kiss on his cheek.

He smiled warmly at her, then patted her face. "You're a good niece, Shenandoah. My brother would have been proud of you. I know your mother was."

"Well, let's take Shenandoah down into the Silver Star," Rogue said.

At the entrance, Tom handed them candles, then lit them, saying, "Ventilation's good, Miss Shenandoah, so we can use candles here. Miners just pack clay around them and stick them to the walls."

"Can't they use candles in all mines?" Shenandoah asked, stepping into the dark tunnel and noticing the sudden change in light and temperature.

"No," Rogue responded. "Less ventilation and they have to use lanterns."

"Look, Rogue," Tom said, "I'm going on down and join the miners. You two take your time. See you later." The tall Welshman quickly disappeared into the darkness of the Silver Star.

Suddenly alone, Shenandoah reached for Rogue's

arm, twining her long fingers around the thick muscles of his forearm. He pulled her close to him.

"You're safe with me, Shenandoah," he said as he led the way deeper into the mine.

The tunnel was lit only by the wavering flames of their candles, providing scant light in the total darkness surrounding them. Eerie shadows danced on the damp, gleaming walls. Shenandoah walked cautiously, feeling the chill, the dampness, the heaviness of the earth all around her. After a time, the tunnel slanted downward and she suddenly slid on the slick clay. Rogue stopped her fall.

"I've got you," Rogue murmured against her hair, his breath warm on her face. He held her tightly a long moment, then moved ahead.

They turned gradually to the right. Rogue stopped, then held his candle up to a wall. "See this dark stratum in the earth? That's lead-bearing silver, but not enough silver to make it worth following that vein and digging it out."

As Rogue led her on, Shenandoah watched the number and frequency of the heavy wooden timbers that held the earth above, below, and on the sides of the mine.

Noticing the direction of her interest, Rogue explained, "The beams are six feet high and twelve inches in diameter. They're supposed to last twenty years. They'll support this tunnel with no problem. In fact, in the larger mines, these same kinds of beams support many levels of shafts, just like a building built downward instead of upward."

"Are they really safe?"

"As safe as we can make them. The kinds of problems we've been having in the Silver Star aren't normal. Very few miners are lost or hurt in mines, but it does happen, so we're cautious."

They continued to walk downhill, their candles flickering on the dark, moist walls. Shenandoah now understood how miners could begin to see ghosts, hear voices, and have accidents in such a place. She thought she heard water dripping somewhere and wondered how deep into the earth they had gone.

They came to a fork in the tunnel. Rogue held his candle up in one direction and said, "There's the new drift. I don't want us going down into it, but that's where we'll start bringing out the rich silver deposits. It's one of the best ore beds I've ever seen."

"I'd like to see the ore when it's brought out," Shenandoah said as she peered into the blackness of the new drift.

As they started walking back out, she said, "Thanks for letting me see this. I'm really impressed with the amount of work that goes into producing silver."

"Well, the Earth doesn't give up her treasures easily, and sometimes not at all."

After a short time they were back in the sunlight. They glanced around for Fast Ed, but when they didn't see him they started for the main building. He wasn't there either. It looked as if he hadn't been there at all because no work had been done. The ore samples weren't ready to go into Leadville.

Rogue smiled at Shenandoah. "I bet he finds that cat's lair, what do you think?"

"Yes, but I hope he doesn't strain himself. He's been working so hard, and after yesterday—"

Suddenly the sound of a rifle shot cut through their conversation.

Shenandoah looked at Rogue in alarm.

Without hesitation, he started for the door, Shenandoah right behind him.

Outside, he stopped, then pushed her back. "No. I'm going alone."

"But what is it? Is someone hunting?"

Rogue's blue eyes were hard. "Maybe."

"Rogue, I'm not staying here alone."

He glanced around. "No, you shouldn't. Come on, then, but stay close."

Rogue set a quick pace, and Shenandoah kept up with him, wondering why he seemed so concerned. A lone gunshot was not that unusual. Perhaps her uncle had seen something and shot at it. Of course, he carried a derringer, not a rifle. But perhaps the sound of the shot had been distorted. Nevertheless, she became concerned too.

They made their way quickly to the tree line surrounding the mining area, then hurriedly stepped into denser brush. Rogue kept glancing around them, trying to pinpoint from which direction the sound had come, as they moved quietly forward. Shenandoah kept up with him, becoming more alarmed by the moment. Something was wrong. She felt it deep within her.

Rogue came to a sudden halt.

A dark shape could be seen on the ground ahead. Shenandoah tried to see it clearly but could not make out what it was.

"Stay here," Rogue hissed.

"No, I'm going with you," Shenandoah insisted, pushing past him and rushing to the dark shape on the forest floor. She knelt beside it. "Uncle Ed!" she cried out. "Oh, Rogue, it's Uncle Ed. He is hurt. Do something!" She turned the crumpled form over so that her uncle rested in her arms against her lap. "Uncle Ed, what happened?"

Fast Ed slowly opened his eyes. Blood oozed from a large hole in his chest. "Didn't watch my back. Bushwhacker. Don't think . . . we'll ever get that . . . horse ranch . . . now."

"Yes we will, Uncle Ed. Rogue's here. We'll take you into Leadville. You'll—"

"Take care of your sister, Shenandoah. She . . . needs you. I'm beyond . . . help."

"No! Uncle Ed, *please.*" Tears filled Shenandoah's eyes but she fought to hold them back. She had to be strong for her uncle.

"Found the mother . . . and her . . . kittens. Still had . . . my instincts."

"Tom will be pleased, Uncle Ed," Shenandoah said, her voice breaking. She pulled him closer, felt something wet and sticky against her skin. He was bleeding in back, too. She put a hand over the hole in his chest, trying to stop the blood. "Rogue, do something!"

Rogue shucked off his shirt and gave it to Shenandoah. She put it over the wound, but didn't dare move him again to try to stem the flow of blood from the back.

"Tell Tom," Fast Ed said, his face now a pale chalky white, "take the . . . kittens to safety."

"Yes, we will, Uncle Ed, but—"

"I loved you . . . like my own daughter." Then his head fell aside, his eyes staring into another world.

The sound of tiny mewing reached their ears. Rogue reached down and closed Fast Ed's eyes. The sound of insects buzzed loudly all around them.

"Rogue? Rogue, we must get him to a doctor quickly. We have to stop the flow of blood. Rogue?"

"He's dead, Shenandoah. He's finally at peace."

"No, he's just sleeping. He can't be dead. He can't be. Hurry, carry him back. We'll take him in to—"

"Stop it, Shenandoah. He's dead."

"*No!*"

The mewing of hungry kittens grew louder; then a small furry form fell from the hollow of a nearby tree. The calico kitten mewed even more loudly, its eyes still closed. Unable to see, it stumbled toward Shenandoah.

Soon the mother cat jumped out of the hollow, meowed at Shenandoah and Rogue, inspected Fast Ed, then picked up her baby in her mouth and disappeared back into the tree hollow.

"Oh, Uncle Ed," Shenandoah said softly, leaning down to hug him close. "I wanted so much for you to be happy." She noticed his black silk handkerchief lying on the ground. She picked it up and tucked it in his coat pocket. He couldn't be without his handkerchief.

"He is happy now, Shenandoah. He's gone to join all he lost so long ago."

"But he had plans. Just this morning . . ."

Rogue reached down to bring Shenandoah to her feet, but she clung to her uncle. "Shenandoah, let go."

"No, he's my uncle. He means nothing to you. I—"

"I'm going to take him back to the Silver Star. I'll send Tom for the kittens. Fast Ed wanted them to live."

"The mine!" Shenandoah exclaimed, jumping to her feet. "The mine killed him. If he hadn't been here, he'd be all right now. He'd be safe playing cards in some other town. It's your fault, Rogue Rogan. If you didn't have this mine, he wouldn't have been here. Those accidents. They're your fault. Somebody killed my uncle because of this mine!"

Rogus face stiffened, and his eyes turned menacing. "I know you don't mean what you're saying about me. But if he was killed because of the mine, we'll find out about that."

"That's right! But *I'll* find out. Whoever did this is going to pay."

Rogue started back through the forest, carrying the limp form of Fast Ed in his arms. Shenandoah followed, pushing down all the terror and pain and helplessness that she felt. Her uncle would not want her to cry. He would want her to be strong. And he would want revenge.

When they reached the edge of the forest, Rogue stopped and turned to Shenandoah. "Your uncle was a good man, Shenandoah. I can't tell you how much I hate this. But we'll find out who did it."

"It's your mine," she insisted. "And *you*. You've hurt us from the first. We shouldn't have come to Leadville. You almost made me forget everything I learned from my uncle. But I remember now. I have my gambling. I have my sister. That's all I want. You—"

"Rogan?" Tom hollered as he emerged from the mine. "What are you two doing? What's happened to Fast Ed? Oh no! Cussing cats!" Tom rushed to their side. As he looked down at Fast Ed, he said, "That was one of the best men I ever met. Kate is going to have a fit over this."

"Tom," Shenandoah said dully, her anger a glowing red coal deep within her, "will you drive me and my uncle to Leadville? The freight wagon will do."

"I'll take you, Shenandoah," Rogue said.

"No!" She rounded on him. "You . . . you murderer. You stay away from me and my family. I've had enough of you forever."

The color drained from Rogue's face, then an angry glint came into his eyes. "Shenandoah, I—"

"Leave me alone, and take your hands off my . . . my . . ."

Tom quietly took Fast Ed from Rogue's arm, shook

his head in warning at Rogue, then said, "I'll drive you into town, Miss Shenandoah. Don't you worry about a thing. Kate and I'll take care of everything."

Tears welled up in Shenandoah's eyes, but she fought them down. "Thank you, Tom," she said quietly. "Uncle Ed wanted you to know . . . to know that he found your mother cat. She's had her kittens."

"Guess he won't get that beer now," Tom said, his voice filled with grief.

"No, I guess not," Shenandoah replied. "He . . . he wanted you to get the kittens to safety. He wanted them to . . . live."

"I'll do that," Tom said. "I'll even name them all after him. "Fast. Ed. Fast Ed. Eddy."

"He'd like that," Shenandoah said. "Would you get the kittens now? I'll wait in the wagon with Uncle Ed. That way he'll know they're safe." Tears stung her eyes again, but she held on to her anger, finding that hard, cold center a gambler needed to survive.

Tom carried Fast Ed to the wagon, then left for the kittens after Rogue told him where they were.

When he had gone, Rogue approached Shenandoah. "I'm sorry this had to happen, Shenandoah, but—"

"Go away," she said, and stepped into the wagon to sit beside her uncle. "I'll just hold his hand while we drive back into town. That way he won't feel alone."

"Shenandoah, listen to reason. Don't blame me. If

Fast Ed's death had to do with the mine, we'll find out.''

"I know this mine killed my uncle. Now, leave me alone!''

There was a long pause. "All right. If that's the way you want it." Rogue's voice was suddenly stiff. "I'll harness the mules, then go look around. Should be some prints or something. We'll get his killer, Shenandoah.''

"No, *I* will.''

Rogue scowled, then turned away.

Dimly she heard the jingling of harness, the sound of birds nearby, but none of it seemed real. Everything she thought or felt was centered on the still form by her side.

She glanced at Rogue. He was shirtless and his tanned skin gleamed moist and golden in the sunlight. She reached under the blanket covering her uncle and pulled out Rogue's shirt. She started to hand it to him, but it was stiff with blood. "I'll get you a new shirt," she said, thrusting the shirt out of sight.

"I don't care about the shirt, Shenandoah," Rogue replied, his eyes dark with anger and frustration. "I care about you. If you'd let me—''

"No. Kate and Tom will help me if I need it. Besides, I can take care of myself.''

"You shouldn't be alone at a time like this.''

"Seems like I've been alone for a long time and just didn't realize it," she said tonelessly. Then she took a deep breath and added, "I'm going back to

Leadville to bury my uncle and get my sister away from Spike Cameron. I'm also going to find out who killed Uncle Ed and avenge him. That's all that's left for me now, and all I want."

"There's a hell of a lot more than that left for you, and you know it. If you weren't so damn stubborn, you'd realize—"

"Found the kittens," Tom interrupted, stopping by the wagon. "Took them to the main building, where they'll be warm." He got into the wagon.

"When you stop blaming me for your uncle's death, let me know," Rogue said, his voice hard and controlled.

Shenandoah refused to look at him. "Let's go, Tom."

As the wagon pulled away from the Silver Star, Shenandoah took hold of her uncle's cold hand. She didn't look back. She never wanted to see or hear of the Silver Star again. It was a bad-luck place.

The drive back to Leadville was rough and long, but it gave Shenandoah a chance to think. She had been hard on Rogue, but she knew deep down that her uncle's death had to do with Rogue's mine. Someone was trying to stop Rogue, and Fast Ed's death had been a warning. But Rogue wouldn't be stopped. She knew him too well.

Rogue Rogan was a hot, blinding force that had entered her calm, stable life and torn it apart. He had made her gambling falter, made her almost forget that she was one of the best gamblers in the West, and now her uncle was dead because of his mine.

A little more time and she might not have been able to pull herself away from him. Now she realized that no matter how he made her feel, she must encase those feelings in ice. There was no place for a man like him in her life. She was a cool, composed gambler. She had only one relative, her sister, Arabella. Together they would go on as her uncle had taught her. Arabella could learn to gamble and they would take care of themselves.

She would be strong, the way her uncle had taught her. And she would take care of her sister, the way he had wanted. She must not forget her heritage or her family. She would yet win, and her uncle would be avenged.

∽ 20 ∾

Shenandoah left the Board of Trade about midnight. Outside, the summer night was cool and fragrant. Gas lights softly illuminated the darkness. The sound of laughter, conversation, and gambling came through the open doors and windows of the silver exchanges on Harrison Avenue. Music from bands playing in the open beer gardens drifted on the wind. All was as it had been two weeks before, except that tonight, as it had been for fourteen nights, Fast Ed Davis did not play cards.

Much of the town had turned out for his funeral. He was mourned as a friend and as one of the best card players ever. But time moved fast in Leadville. Thoughts were for the living, not the dead. Fast Ed's name soon became part of history, part of legend, part of the past.

But not so for Shenandoah. Her uncle was still a part of her. Her memories were still keen. His death was still to be avenged. And her sister was still to be freed from Spike Cameron.

None of that proved easy to do. Arabella was still enthralled with Spike and life in a silver exchange. The only information about her uncle's death had come indirectly from Rogue. Shenandoah had refused to talk to him when he had tried to visit her at Colorado Kate's. Tom had told her that Rogue had found the tracks of one man and one horse, plus one spent cartridge from a rifle. Even with Tom and Kate's help, Shenandoah had not been able to learn any more.

She was frustrated, angry, and lonely, but she would not give up. In time, Arabella was bound to heal and Shenandoah would be there to help her. In time, there had to be more news about her uncle's death. As far as Rogue, she tried not to think of him, but she could do nothing to stop the sharp pain of longing in her heart.

As Shenandoah turned onto State Street, she suddenly ran into Rogue and Topaz. Anger rushed through her. Jealousy pounded in her veins. Obviously Rogue had lost no time in turning to another woman. Shenandoah's eyes flashed green fire as she glared at them in passing.

But Rogue stopped her, grabbing her arm. "Shenandoah, I want to talk to you."

She tried to break his grip on her arm. "Take your hand off me."

"Damn! Shenandoah, there's no need for you to be so stubborn."

"Leave me alone!"

Rogue frowned, then dropped his hand. "You can't avoid me forever, Shenandoah."

Shenandoah simply looked at him coldly, let her glance slide to the beautiful, petite woman by his side, then hurried on down State Street.

As she walked away, she heard Topaz say, "You sure know how to turn that woman cold."

"Not all the time," Rogue muttered in reply.

Shenandoah felt her face grow warm. But he was right. She had to admit she still wanted him.

Outside the Postmortem, she stopped and looked in at its bright lights and laughing customers. She did not want to go inside. She wanted to see her sister, but she did not want to see Spike Cameron. The man was proving to be more of a problem than she would have thought possible. Arabella would not come out, however, so Shenandoah had no choice.

Hesitating, she glanced down, then smoothed the skirt of her new gown. She'd had it made recently to lift her spirits, but it hadn't helped much even though it was beautiful. The gown was made of pale green silk in the sheath fashion with a small bustle in back. The bodice and sleeves were trimmed in dark green satin accented with pale green lace. There was also green satin and lace entwined in the bustle.

She took a deep breath, then entered the silver exchange. Miners packed the place from wall to wall. Men grasping satin-clad women struggled around the dance floor, trying to dance in the crowded area. Shenandoah searched for her sister.

Arabella was sitting on a piano near the dance

floor. The skirt of her red satin gown, trimmed with black lace, was pulled up over her knees, showing black silk stockings. She was singing a naughty camp song in a clear, sweet voice. In between verses she leaned down to smile and laugh with several men grouped around her, and her full, rounded breasts spilled outward, barely contained by the low-cut bodice.

As the song became more ribald, miners flocked to her side, some humming or singing along with her. Even the dancers began to stop and join in the music. Soon the silver exchange rocked with voices raised in raucous song. Finally, when all the verses had been sung, Arabella reached for a drink. As she downed it, the revelers slowly melted away to get drinks for themselves and to find gaming tables.

Shenandoah made her way to join her sister. She was not shocked by Arabella's behavior. She had seen her this way every night for two weeks. But she was sure that behind her sister's bright eyes and beckoning smile was a frightened, innocent young woman, a young woman plunged too harshly and too quickly into a life not of her choosing. The Brayton brothers might be dead, but their legacy lived on in the popular Bella, dance-hall darling.

But Shenandoah was becoming impatient. Arabella was not responding to her. She simply continued to insist that she liked her present life with Spike Cameron. But Shenandoah knew better. And she felt responsible for her sister's well-being.

Joining Arabella at the piano, she said, "Come on, I want to talk with you."

Arabella frowned. "I'm tired of listening to you. Why don't you just leave me alone?"

"I can't. And you know it."

"I'm not your responsibility. I'm a grown woman."

"Arabella, come down and let's find a quiet place to talk."

Arabella groaned. "Oh, all right. But this is it. No more. Say what you've got to say, then go."

They walked to a quiet corner and sat down. Arabella took a long sip from her whiskey glass, her blue eyes rebellious.

"Arabella, you don't have to work here. I'll be happy to teach you poker or any of the other games. You can make a living that way. You don't need to stay with Spike, and I can support us both until you learn."

"Thanks, but I've already given you my answer. No. It would take me a long time to learn, and besides, I might not even be good at gambling. I've made a place for myself here, I'm earning good money, and Spike treats me fine. I don't know what you have against him."

Shenandoah was quickly becoming disgusted. "He's a user. I've seen a lot of men like him in the West. Maybe he's good to you now, but—"

"No. I have my own life, so why don't you go back to yours?"

"Arabella, we can have a life together. You know

Uncle Ed wanted that, and our parents would have thought it best, too.''

''It won't work. Why can't you just accept what happened to me in Mexico? I'll never be the same again.''

Suddenly Shenandoah's tight control on her emotions exploded. ''I haven't forgotten Mexico! Why do you think I've been so patient? You don't have to live like this. You're the same person you always were. I've offered you a way to make a good living and be independent. But you won't listen.''

Shenandoah stood up. ''Listen to me! You are my sister. You may have been hurt, but you can recover. You can go on with your life. You don't have to hide behind Spike Cameron or any other man. Stop feeling sorry for yourself and get on with your life.''

Arabella watched in astonishment as her sister suddenly whirled and stormed away. Spike had said there was a lot of fire under Shenandoah's cold exterior. He had been right.

As Shenandoah hurried toward the front doors of the Postmortem, Spike Cameron caught her arm.

''You're looking lovely tonight, Shenandoah.''

She shrugged his hand from her arm, too angry and frustrated to put up with anything from him. ''You always say that, Cameron.''

''Because it's always true. Why don't you come upstairs with me? I have some beautiful oil paintings in my bedroom.''

Shenandoah raised her brows and smiled knowingly. ''There are plenty of paintings for me to look at here in the main room, if that's what I had come to do.''

"But these are special. The subject matter should interest you greatly.''

"I doubt it.''

"Your sister finds them most . . . informative.'' Spike's breath was warm on her face as he leaned closer.

Shenandoah stepped back. "Arabella is not herself at present.''

Spike glanced over at Arabella, who was dancing with a miner. "Perhaps you're right. She is most truly herself in my wide bed upstairs. Wide enough for three.''

Shenandoah threw him a look of utter disgust and started to walk away.

"Not so soon,'' Spike rasped, taking her arm.

"Let me go.''

"No. I've waited for two weeks. You should be over your uncle's death by now.''

"I will never be over my uncle's death.''

Spike pulled her with him to the back of the room.

She tried to stop, but his strength was greater. She glanced around, looking for help, knowing there would be none because Spike's bouncers answered only to him. She got Arabella's attention, but her sister simply frowned at her. "I'm not going anywhere with you, Spike Cameron.''

Spike stopped. "You know, Shenandoah, your sister is quite happy with me. She will stay no matter

how I treat her. Now, I want you to come upstairs
and see my paintings—willingly.''

"No."

"*Tonight* all I'm asking is that you see the paintings. If you love your sister and don't want to see her
hurt, you'll come upstairs with me . . . *now*.''

Shenandoah hesitated. Was Cameron bluffing? Could
she take a chance that he wasn't? Her face stiff, her
green eyes cold, she nodded at him. "Lead the way.''

At the top of the stairs, Spike opened a heavy
wooden door with an intricately carved brass handle
and large lock. He gestured her in ahead of him.
Shenandoah did not hear the door shut and the lock
click into place as she glanced around in shock at the
decadent decor of the room.

A huge bed on a platform with a canopy took up a
large part of the room. The bed was hung with
burgundy velvet and white lace. A heavy wooden
desk with a large leather chair behind it dominated
the wall across from the bed. The windows were
completely covered by heavy burgundy draperies,
shutting out all light. Hand-painted china gas lights lit
the room with a soft yellow glow. A thick carpet of
rose design muffled sounds from below. But none of
that compared to the huge gold-framed paintings that
hung from every wall.

Spike flung out a hand toward each painting, then
smiled at Shenandoah as he watched her face.

She managed to keep her shock from showing as
she studied each painting in turn. They were all of
women and men in various sexual positions. Shenan-

doah had never seen anything like it and could not help thinking of her sister sleeping here, ready to do whatever Spike Cameron commanded.

"The paintings do hold a certain charm, don't they?"

"For you, perhaps," Shenandoah said stiffly. "Now I've seen your paintings. I'd like to go."

"But there is so much more I could show you, my dear. And so much you could show me." He ran long, cold hands down Shenandoah's bare shoulders, dragging the low-cut bodice of her silk gown downward.

She jerked away and carefully slipped the bodice back into place. "Keep your hands off me," she said between gritted teeth, then turned and walked to the door.

"It's locked," Spike smoothly informed her.

She tried the brass knob. He spoke the truth. "I suppose only you have the key."

"That's right. You can have it if you can find it."

"Where is it?"

"On my body."

She inhaled sharply. "Stop these foolish games. I want to leave."

"Find the key and you may."

She glared at him in disgust.

"I'll give you a hint. It's in my pocket . . . in one of the front pockets of my trousers."

Shenandoah did not look down. She held his eyes. "Give me the key."

He shook his head, his eyes filled with amusement

and desire. "Step closer, Shenandoah. I won't bite. Besides, I could show you a very good time if you were willing."

"The key."

"Frankly, I have the key to solve all your problems, but at the moment I'm only offering you the one that will unlock the door."

"Stop speaking in riddles. I'm leaving if I have to break down this door."

"Impossible. It's quite heavy, for special protection." He stepped closer to her, so that his scent and body heat enveloped her. When she started to move back, he grabbed her arms and held her tightly. "Play my little game, Shenandoah dear, and I'll be good to your sister. Don't, and . . ."

Shenandoah straightened her back. "All right," she said, her eyes throwing green daggers of light at him.

He smiled, let his hands fall to his sides, and waited.

Shenandoah gently began to slide one hand down into his right pants pocket. He moved slightly and her hand was thrown into contact with his hardness. She jerked back as if scorched.

He smiled. "Did you find the key?"

"You know I didn't. Now, stop this and give me the key."

"Try the other pocket."

"No."

"Do it!"

Shenandoah took a deep breath, then plunged her

hand into the left front pocket of his trousers. Delving deep, she touched metal. But suddenly Spike pulled her to him, wrapping his strong arms about her and rubbing his hard maleness against her hand. Thus trapped, she could not get free and had to endure his lewd movements.

"Let me go," she commanded.

He nibbled at her throat. "You have the key. Do you want more now? Go ahead, take me in your hand. You can feel what a good time I can give you."

Shenandoah kicked him in the shin as hard as she could. He dropped his arms and grabbed his shin. While he was groaning in pain, she unlocked the door, leaving the key in the lock, and escaped his room. She rushed down the stairs and raced out of the Postmortem. She didn't think she could ever go back. Spike Cameron was even more dangerous than she had thought, and more detestable.

She was hurrying toward the Board of Trade when someone suddenly grabbed her arm and called her name. Without thinking, Shenandoah knocked off the hand, then turned to look.

Topaz stood there, a smile on her painted lips.

"What do you want?" Shenandoah asked, anger beginning to build anew. This was the woman who had taken Rogue, who was no doubt entertaining him in her bed just like the people in the paintings on Spike Cameron's walls. Frustration seethed in her veins.

"I wanted to warn you, honey."

"Warn me?" Shenandoah raised a brow, her face dangerously impassive.

"About Rogue Rogan."

"What about him?"

"The man's mine. He was mine before he went to Tombstone and found you, and he's mine again. I'm warning you to leave Rogue Rogan to me. That way I'll be happy, he'll be happy, and your little sister will be happy."

Shenandoah took several deep breaths, trying to stay cool and calm, but she was fast losing control. "What does my sister have to do with this?"

"Spike's a friend of mine too. It'd be easy enough to get him to send his little Bella over to make some extra money in Tiger Alley," she stated, referring to the town's district of prostitutes.

"Now, just a minute," Shenandoah said, clenching her fists. "You do anything to hurt my sister and—"

"Oh, I won't do anything—as long as you stay away from Rogue."

Something snapped in Shenandoah. Did the whole town think they could just walk all over her and her family? Well, she would show them.

Without warning, Shenandoah brought one arm behind her, swung it forward, and punched Topaz hard in the nose. Topaz was knocked off her feet and blood spurted from her nostrils. She put a hand to her nose as Shenandoah looked on in complete astonishment at what she had just done. Seeing blood on her hand, Topaz screamed and launched herself at Shenandoah.

They went down in a heap of flailing fists and kicking legs. They rolled over and over until they fell off the boardwalk into the dust of an alley. Topaz pulled Shenandoah's hair from its coils and tried to bite off her earlobe. Shenandoah punched her again, then pulled Topaz's golden locks. They came loose, and she flung the false curls into the dirt.

Shenandoah fought with a burning desire to overcome all the insults and troubles she had endured for too long. Topaz called her names and screamed as she clawed at Shenandoah's face and breasts. But Shenandoah held her own, fighting with a wild fury that continued to surprise her.

Just when Shenandoah felt she was beginning to win, someone suddenly pulled her off Topaz. She struggled with the intruder, then was thrust behind a broad back.

"What the hell is going on?" Rogue asked, his voice gruff.

"That bitch," Topaz started, then realized that her beloved was watching her. She swooned toward him.

Rogue caught her, then looked back at Shenandoah. "What's going on here?"

Shenandoah pinched Topaz hard.

Topaz squealed, then turned large blue eyes on Rogue. "Help me, Rogue, that bitch is trying to kill me." Topaz made sure her torn bodice fell further, exposing rounded breasts covered by only sheer silk.

Rogue stood Topaz on her feet, looked Shenandoah over from head to foot. "What do you two think you're doing?"

Shenandoah brushed off her gown, vividly aware of the torn fabric, her scratched limbs, and her still-burning anger. "Topaz seemed to think—"

"That *woman* told me to stay away from you," Topaz said, glaring at Shenandoah. "Well, you know I couldn't agree to that."

"So you hit her?"

"No. She decided to scare me away from you."

"Shenandoah fought for me?" Rogue's voice was incredulous. He looked at Shenandoah.

She scowled at him. "That's not quite the way it happened."

"Take me to a doctor, Rogue, please?" Topaz said, touching her nose gingerly.

"Doctor?" Rogue said absentmindedly, still looking at Shenandoah in surprise.

"Yes, she may have broken my nose."

"Shenandoah?"

"She asked for it," Shenandoah said firmly, still eyeing Topaz with anger.

"You fought for me?" Rogue repeated, moving close to Shenandoah so that he could see into her eyes.

"Well, I'm not going to let her order me about. I didn't notice a sign saying 'Topaz' hanging around your neck."

"Rogue?" Topaz said, touching his arm. "I'm hurt, dearest. Please see about my wounds."

Rogue turned to glance at her. "You look all right to me, Topaz. The doctor's a block down, one flight up."

"What?"

"Go ahead, Rogue," Shenandoah urged, starting to turn away. "I'll go back to Kate's. Everything's fine."

"No," he said, abruptly swinging her up into his arms. "We can't be sure. I'll carry you back to my hotel room. I've got to check you all over to make sure you're fine."

"Rogue," she said sternly, "put me down."

"That's right," Topaz agreed. "Put her down. I need you, not her. Besides—"

"You'd better heed what Shenandoah says from now on, Topaz," Rogue said, humor in his voice as he held on to a struggling Shenandoah. "What this lady says goes, and if she fought for me—"

"You are not her man."

"Is that what she said?"

Shenandoah squirmed, anxious to get away.

"Well, if she says I'm her man, then I guess I am," Rogue agreed.

"You've chosen the wrong woman," Topaz said, then turned and walked quickly away.

"Now that you've won me, what are you going to do with me?" Rogue asked, showing strong white teeth.

"I didn't win you, and put me down."

Rogue started toward his hotel. "You were winning. I pulled you off Topaz so you wouldn't ruin her for all time. You know, her looks are important to her business."

"Well, she deserved it."

"Did she?" He took long, sure strides, Shenando-ah's warm body held tightly against him. "Whatever you say. I wouldn't want to question anyone with a right hook like yours."

~ 21 ~

Rogue laid Shenandoah down on the narrow bed in his hotel room. She tried to scramble away from him, but he held her there, his large strong hands weights that she could not throw off.

"Rogue Rogan, let me go," she demanded. "I told you I didn't want to come here."

"And I told you I wanted to talk with you . . . in private."

"There are other places."

"Be still a moment while I examine you."

"I will not. I'm fine. Really, Rogue—"

"Damn! I'm losing my patience, Shenandoah. I'm going to get rough in a minute."

Shenandoah struggled harder. Rogue finally turned her over, pinned her legs with his, and began to unbutton the back of her gown.

She squirmed, but could do little under his weight.

"There," Rogue said. "All done." He helped her to a sitting position; then his eyes slowly traveled downward.

Shenandoah followed his gaze. Her gown had fallen around her waist, revealing rounded breasts, pushed upward by a tight corset and covered by the sheerest of green silk. She started to pull up the gown, but Rogue stopped her, pulling her to her feet so that the gown fell in a heap around her ankles. Rogue began to undo her petticoats.

"Rogue," she protested, but stopped, feeling the pull of him, the heat he engendered in her, the languor that being near him induced. "Rogue, please. I don't think we should—"

"Have you stopped wanting me?" he asked softly.

She didn't answer. Her petticoats were on the floor. She wore little except silk underwear and a corset. The night suddenly felt cold around her.

"Have you?" he insisted, noticing the derringer she once more wore strapped to her thigh. "I thought I told you to put that somewhere else." He reached for it.

She stepped away. "Where else could I hide it? It's better there than nowhere at all, especially after . . . after Fast Ed was bushwhacked."

"I'm sorry about your uncle, Shenandoah. You don't know how much I would give to undo that."

She shook her head. "It's over, Rogue. There's nothing you can do now."

He grabbed her arms and shook her. "Don't talk that way. Of course there's something I can do. I've already done something, and we'll get his killer."

She eyed him warily. "What did you do?"

Rogue hesitated, then tugged off her chemise, leaving her breasts bare, supported only by the confining corset.

"Rogue, stop." She covered her breasts with her arms. "Tell me—"

He pulled off her drawers, leaving them around her ankles. She wore only the corset and silk stockings with fancy garters. And the derringer.

"Give me the gun, Shenandoah," he said quietly.

She stepped back, and dropped her hands. She could stop Rogue. She had the gun. Of course, he was wearing the Colt .45 and was probably faster than she. But Rogue wouldn't shoot her. Just as she wouldn't shoot him. She couldn't. It would be like shooting a part of herself. Why did he affect her this way? She had tried so hard to stay away from him, but he wouldn't leave her alone.

She unstrapped the gun, then handed it to him.

He put it in a nearby chair. "We've got a lot to talk about, Shenandoah, but I don't want to do that first. You don't know how much I've wanted you the past two weeks." Warm hands stroked her bare shoulders.

She looked away, trying to still her racing heart. She must remember that she had her own life, her own goals. She must not let Rogue make her forget.

"Don't turn away from me, Shenandoah. I need you. It's what you need too."

"I told you before, Rogue. I have my own plans. I have things to do."

Rogue's eyes hardened. "You could make this easy, but you won't, will you? All right." He hesitated, then said, his voice low, "You owe me, Shenandoah, and you owe me until I say different. That was our agreement back in Tombstone, remember?"

The cold in Shenandoah's eyes seemed to fill her entire body. Rogue was more ruthless than she had imagined. She had been right to stay away from him.

"Remember?" he repeated.

"Yes, but—"

"No buts. I want to collect. Now."

As if in a trance, Shenandoah moved toward him, drawn by his words, by the agreement she had made, but most of all by her own deepest desires. He removed his pistol and clothes quickly.

"I'm going to make it impossible for you to forget me, Shenandoah, and impossible for you to leave me again."

He picked her up, nestled her against his hard chest, then placed her carefully on the narrow bed. He bent over her and slowly began to peel the silk stocking from one leg, then the other.

"Rogue," she murmured, feeling the heat begin to rise in her at the sight of his naked flesh, the feel of his hands on her body.

He kissed her lightly, teasing the sensitive area around her lips with his tongue, then moved inside her mouth, his tongue questing. She moaned and shifted under his weight as her hands stole up around his neck, her long, sensitive fingers pushing into the thickness of his hair.

"Why did you make this so hard?" Rogue whispered as he nibbled along her jawline to the sensitive place under her ear.

"Oh, Rogue," she breathed, not wanting to think.

"Is this all just part of the bargain to you?"

She didn't answer, delighting in the feel of his mouth on her.

"Is it?"

"Please, Rogue, just kiss me. I don't want—"

Rogue shook her lightly, then let his fingers trail down to her corset. Touching the fabric, he said thoughtfully, "I should take this off you, but I can't wait." And those were his last words as his mouth found the taut, sensitive peaks of her breasts, his hands massaging what his mouth didn't cover, until Shenandoah moaned and shuddered beneath him.

He moved lower, nibbling her pale, sensitive skin as he went on, until he came to the center of both their desire. He parted her legs and urgently pressed his mouth to her hot, pulsing center.

"Rogue?" she questioned, half-rising, then dropped back as pleasure shot through her. She clutched his thick hair with her hands, her hips moving upward as his tongue darted into her, teasing and tormenting.

As her pleasure mounted, Rogue gripped her hips firmly, holding her steady as he continued to probe into her softness, bringing her closer and closer to complete ecstasy. "Rogue," she moaned, and he delved deeper. Sweat beaded her body. Her legs clutched at him. Her hands writhed in helpless tension. "Rogue, please," she gasped, "please. I need you."

But Rogue did not stop. He intensified his movements, glorying in the taste and feel of her, wanting her to know the agony of desire before it became pure pleasure. When he felt her body tense, he grasped her harder, feeling the tension build as he increased his movements until finally the release came. As the waves began to subside, he held her tight, feeling her pleasure almost as if it had been his own, and when she lay softly panting, he moved upward, covering her damp body with his hot flesh.

"Rogue."

He kissed her lips lightly, then lifted her hips and plunged deep inside her in one swift movement. She gasped with the surprise and intensity of the action. Rogue began moving immediately, long, hard thrusts that spoke of his own need and hunger. Shenandoah grasped him with her thighs, dug her nails into his shoulders, and moved with him, giving him even more pleasure as she responded so naturally to his rhythm.

He lunged harder and harder, ever swifter, carrying her with him, intensifying the splendor with every thrust of his powerful hips. Her body arched up into him, taut, expectant, challenging him to fulfill them both.

And he did. He struck swiftly and the movement vibrated throughout their bodies. Rogue groaned, his body shuddered as he clung to her, riding the wave of intensity that pushed them into the realm of rapture.

When their pleasure had abated, Rogue didn't move for a long moment; then he said, "When I leave, you're going with me, Shenandoah. We can't deny ourselves this again."

"Where?" she murmured.

"Silver City, New Mexico, for starters."

"Silver City? What are you talking about? Your mine is here."

"Not anymore. I sold it."

Shenandoah sat upright, all languor gone. "What?"

"I told you I did something about Fast Ed's death."

"But you're not going to let them run you out, are you?"

"Nobody's running me out. But I wasn't going to let anybody else get killed over that mine. It's not worth it."

"Then Uncle Ed's death will have been in vain."

"I got a good price for the mine, Shenandoah. The vein we uncovered proved its worth. Fast Ed helped us do that. He wanted you to have some money. Well, you do now. You can have your cut whenever you want it."

Shenandoah shook her head in confusion. "But I thought you wanted to work the Silver Star."

"I needed the money. The Silver Star was supposed to help me get it. Well, it has. I just couldn't wait around any longer. Now I can go."

"Go?"

"Like I said, I'm going to Silver City, New Mexico, and then to—"

"But who bought the Silver Star?"

Rogue grinned. "Kate and Tom. They got a good deal, too. That mine will make them rich."

Shenandoah nodded. "I'm glad they bought it, but I still don't understand. Why Silver City?"

"I already own half-interest in several silver mines in New Mexico," Rogue explained. "My father left them to me, but my cousin is back there mining them right now. If I'm gone much longer, there won't be anything left for me, but I had to have a chunk of cash to go back and hire men to work the mines, buy equipment, and all. I didn't have it. I was counting on the Silver Star—"

"That's why you didn't want to go after Arabella?"

"I was damned short of time then, and I'm even shorter now. I've got to get back there and stop my cousin Blackie, who owns the other half of the mines, which his father left him. If I don't get back there soon, everything my father worked for will be gone."

"I see," Shenandoah said quietly. "That explains a lot. Well, you could have told me before."

"There was no point. You weren't involved."

"And I am now?"

"Yes, or you're going to be. I want you to go with me."

She stiffened. "I can't leave Leadville to go with you. I couldn't think of leaving Arabella. Besides, the gambling is good here and I need the money."

"I told you. With the sale of the Silver Star, you've got enough to take care of yourself and Arabella for a while."

"I won't leave my sister. She needs me."

"I need you too."

"For what? Am I to wait in your bed while—"

"Damn! I want you in my bed, yes. But I also

need you for other things. There's a house that needs
. . . who knows what.''

"A housekeeper?''

"Yes, I suppose that's what I need.''

"You can hire one.''

Rogue flushed, his blue eyes darkening. "I don't
have to hire one. I own one.'' He glared at her.

"What do you mean?''

"Remember our bargain? Well, I need you and I
need you in New Mexico helping me.''

"I can't leave Arabella,'' Shenandoah insisted.

"Then bring her along.''

"I don't know if she'll leave Spike Cameron, and
we can't force her to. Oh, Rogue, this is all so
sudden, so unexpected,'' she added dolefully.

"If you'd been seeing me the past two weeks, we
could have made plans.''

"I don't want to leave Leadville.''

"I'm giving you no choice.''

She hesitated. "Rogue, I'm not backing out on our
deal, but I've got to have time to persuade Arabella
to go with us.''

Rogue stood up and crossed the room. "You don't
want to go,'' he stated.

"I won't leave Arabella, and you can't make me.''

"I could make you, all right, but I won't. You'd
be worried about her all the time, and I wouldn't
blame you. But I want you with me.''

"Surely you could wait a week or two.''

Rogue looked at her hard, then strode back to the
bed. "A week or two could be a long time, Shenan-

doah. Without you, time moves slowly. After the last two weeks, I should know.''

"But Arabella is so vulnerable right now. Besides, I need to try to find out more about Uncle Ed's murderer.''

"I understand all that. I want to catch the killer too, but I can't right now. When everything's settled with my mines, then we can take care of it, even come back here if necessary. Will you wait?''

She hesitated. "If you'll wait for me and Arabella.''

Rogue looked deep into her green eyes, then said, "One week, two at the most, and I want you in Silver City.''

"All right, Rogue. It's a deal.''

∿ 22 ∽

The sun was not yet up when Shenandoah slowly awoke from tantalizing dreams of Rogue. She smiled, stretched, then realized that she was alone in the narrow bed. She sat up, looked around, but Rogue was not in the room. Neither were his things. She threw the covers back and started to step out of bed, but noticed that one of her garters was missing. She didn't remember ever taking them off the night before. She looked in the bed, but there was no other garter.

Trying to find the garter had simply put off the inevitable realization that Rogue had left without saying good-bye. But perhaps he had said farewell all night as he joined their bodies again and again. She felt sore all over, but happy too. Except that Rogue was gone.

After dressing, she left the hotel, then started down the boardwalk. She was stopped by the street musician she recognized from the other night.

"Town's getting pretty upset about the robberies," he said. "Sheriff's going to have to do something soon, don't you think?"

Shenandoah had been so caught up in her own concerns that she really hadn't thought much about the stage robberies. "I suppose so," she replied.

"Thought they had Leadville cleaned up," he continued, "until this lone bandit arrived."

"Well, I'm sure they'll stop him soon."

"Hope so. Leadville doesn't need this kind of thing." Then he strummed a chord, smiled, and moved away.

She walked briskly down the street. She had decided not to go home to sleep yet. She wanted to see Arabella first. And Spike Cameron was not going to stop her or scare her away. Her sister had to be made to realize that there was another life for her, one with the last remaining member of her family. Fast Ed would not rest easy until Arabella was safe, and neither would Shenandoah.

She pushed open the swinging doors of the Postmortem and stepped inside. The place was deserted. A chill ran up her spine. Something about the place felt strange.

"Arabella?" she called out, stepping farther into the ornate room.

"Arabella?" she called louder. Where could everyone be? It was not that late in the day yet. There should be someone around.

Just as she started to call again, the bartender hurried out of the back room. "What can I do for you?"

"I'm looking for Arabella White . . . Bella."

"Bella's gone."

Shenandoah felt her heart thump hard. "Gone? Where?"

"She and Spike moved to Silver City."

Shenandoah slumped down in the nearest chair. "I don't understand."

"You know how it is in mining towns. Everybody's on the move. Hey, you sick?"

"When did they leave?" she asked, ignoring his question.

He gave her a hard stare. "I don't suppose there's any harm in telling you. They left on the first train out this morning. Didn't take much with them. Spike's having his special paintings and things packed up and sent later."

"Did someone buy the Postmortem?"

"Sure did. It'll be all over town soon. Topaz . . . you know, from Tiger Alley . . . bought the place. Won't mind working for her at all."

Shenandoah nodded. "Well, thanks." She got up, started to walk away, then turned back. "Did Bella leave any messages?"

The man thought a moment. "No. Can't think of any."

"Thank you."

Shenandoah left the Postmortem as quickly as she could. Her heart was beating fast. Her palms were damp. She felt betrayed. How could Arabella have done this to her? But she knew why. Shenandoah would have done everything in her power to stop Arabella, and her sister knew that.

Shenandoah hesitated on a street corner, suddenly realizing that nothing was keeping her from going to Rogue now. But she had one more stop to make before she could leave.

She rented a horse at the stables, then rode out of town. On a hill nearby, she tethered her mount to the fence that surrounded Leadville's cemetery. She could not leave without saying good-bye to the man who had meant so much to her.

She walked through the graveyard, then knelt beside her uncle's grave. "I'll never forget you, Uncle Ed," she said softly.

She glanced up. For a moment she thought she had heard something. But all was quiet. She looked back down. "Don't worry about us, Uncle Ed. We'll be all right. I'll look after Arabella. And I'll be with Rogue awhile longer. He'll be waiting for me in Silver City."

She jerked her head up. There. She thought she had heard it again. A groan. She stood up, looking all around her. A low moan drifted through the graves. She shivered, but knew she had to follow the sound.

Not far from Uncle Ed's grave, behind a large, ornate tombstone, lay a crumpled body. Horrified, Shenandoah rushed to it, knelt, and rolled the person over.

She screamed, then extended shaking hands to touch the cold white features of Rogue Rogan's face.

"Rogue?"

He moaned.

She touched his body, running her hands down his chest. In the area of his stomach, she found the bullet hole. Bushwhacked! She felt a terrible fear stab at her heart. Her uncle had died this same way.

She stood up, glanced around. She was completely alone, and to go for help and bring it back could waste the precious minutes that might mean Rogue's life or death. Without hesitation, she stripped off her petticoat and carefully wrapped it around his waist to help stem the flow of blood. Then she ran through the graveyard to her horse and brought it back to Rogue.

When she was back by Rogue's side, she said, stroking his forehead, "Rogue, I'm here. I'm going to take you to the doctor. You'll be all right. *Please,* be all right."

Rogue's eyes moved behind his lids, then opened slowly before finally focusing on Shenandoah. "Doe—"

"No, don't talk. Save your strength."

"Came to say . . . good-bye to . . . Fast Ed."

"Yes. Yes, I understand. Now, I'm going to lift you to that horse. Can you help?"

Rogue glanced up at the tall palomino, then back at her. "You'll . . . never do it."

"Yes, I will. But don't talk."

"Doe, if I don't get a chance to tell you, I—"

"No!" There were tears burning her eyes as she reached for him and began to lift him from the ground. He was heavy; normally she could not have moved him, but nothing could have stopped her from getting him into Leadville.

Rogue groaned, leaning heavily on Shenandoah as she got him to his feet. Her white petticoat turned red rapidly as the exertion caused more blood to flow out of his wound.

Horrified, Shenandoah tried to push the fabric in to hold the blood inside him.

"Won't help," Rogue said as he stumbled.

"Rogue, you've got to get on that horse."

She helped him, but it was his own determination that got him on the animal. As he sat there swaying, she pulled up her gown and straddled the horse, pulling Rogue against her. "Lean against me, Rogue. I'll have you in town in no time."

But he didn't answer. The loss of blood was making him too weak to talk. All he could do was try to stay in the saddle.

Shenandoah urged their mount through the graveyard, then back onto the road to Leadville. She didn't dare move the animal faster than a walk for fear of hurting Rogue. The ride back into town seemed to take forever.

When they reached Kate's house, Shenandoah shouted, "Kate! Kate, hurry. Come out here."

There was silence.

"Kate! Please, Kate!"

The front door was jerked open, and a disheveled Colorado Kate suddenly stood looking out. Tom was right behind her.

"Cussing cats!" Tom exploded. "What happened?"

"Tom, get the doctor over here. Rogue needs him bad."

Tom didn't hesitate. He started running down the street.

"I'll carry him," Kate said, putting her strong arms up and grasping Rogue.

Shenandoah was fighting back tears as she helped to ease Rogue's limp body down into Kate's arms.

"We'll take him to my room in back. You run ahead and start boiling water."

But Shenandoah couldn't leave Rogue and she stayed by Kate's side as her friend carried him into the house. When he was on the bed, Shenandoah began to take off his shirt.

"Leave him be, honey," Kate said. "The doctor will know what to do. You stay with him. I'll boil water."

Shenandoah pulled a chair to Rogue's side and sat down. She took his cold hand and said, "Rogue. Rogue, please, you can't leave me." She leaned over and lightly kissed his lips. "Please, live for me, Rogue."

Then suddenly the room was full of people as Tom rushed in with the doctor and Kate came back with clean cloths. Shenandoah moved back, knowing she could only wait now.

The doctor cut away the petticoat and Rogue's shirt, then got down to business. Shenandoah could not keep from pacing the room. Tom hovered by the bed. Kate worked with the doctor, getting him what he needed. After what seemed a very long time, the doctor looked up.

"I think he'll live, but he's very weak. Can't be moved. But he's young and strong, and if he has the will to go on, he'll be all right. He'll need some nursing."

"I won't leave his side," Shenandoah said, her green eyes large and bright with unshed tears.

"I'll be here too," Kate said grimly.

"We'll get him whatever he needs," Tom added.

The doctor nodded. "It's a gut wound. Far as I can tell, there's no metal left in him. That's good. Come for me if he gets any worse. I'll stop by again this evening." He smiled at Shenandoah. "He was lucky. Much longer and he wouldn't have moved again. He was losing blood fast."

Shenandoah swallowed hard.

"Whoever shot him left him for dead," the doctor concluded, packed his bag, then left.

"Who shot Rogue?" Kate exploded.

"I don't know," Shenandoah said. "Rogue was leaving town this morning. He wanted me to follow him to Silver City. I went to say good-bye to Uncle Ed. That's where I found Rogue. He'd done the same."

"Somebody wants to stop him from getting to New Mexico," Tom said heavily. "And they want to stop him bad. We'd better make sure someone's with him all the time."

Kate nodded. "He'll be all right here."

"I thought selling the mine would have put an end to all his trouble," Shenandoah said.

"So did we," Kate agreed.

"I don't think he's told us near everything," Tom added.

"But a man's got a right to his own business," Kate said. "Now, Shenandoah, I want you to go upstairs, clean up, change your clothes. You've got blood all over you."

Rogue's blood was on her hands, the exposed skin of her breasts, and her green silk gown was stained crimson down the front. She felt sick at the amount of blood Rogue had lost. But nothing mattered so long as he lived, and she would see to that. "I hate to leave him."

"Tom'll stay with him. You go upstairs, and I'm going to get some good hot food in us all. We've got to keep up our strength if we're going to help Rogue."

Shenandoah glanced at her two friends and said, "Thank you. I don't know what I would have done—"

Kate waved her toward the door. "You'd have done the same for us. Go along now. Rogue Rogan's not going anyplace for a while."

Shenandoah started toward the door, hesitated, then sat down in the chair beside Rogue. "I can't go now, Kate. Not until I know he's really going to be all right." She took his cold hand and tried to warm it with her own.

Kate nodded in understanding, then looked at Tom and motioned him out of the room.

When Shenandoah was alone with Rogue, she said softly, "I won't leave you, Rogue. I'll stay right here, and when you're well we can go to Silver City together. I'll help you there, too. Don't worry about anything. Don't even worry about Arabella. She'll just have to take care of herself for a while. You need me now. And I'll take care of you. Only, Rogue, please don't leave me.''

Rogue moaned softly, then slowly turned his head in Shenandoah's direction.

When she felt a light pressure on her fingers, she smiled, tears stinging her eyes. ''I'm right here, Rogue. If this is part of the debt, I'm glad to pay it. I couldn't bear to lose you . . . the best holdout a woman could ever have.''

She stroked his hand, then moved farther up his arm, trying to warm him, comfort him. She felt something under the sleeve. Carefully she unbuttoned the cuff, then pushed up the sleeve. There, wound around his arm, was her other garter.

''Oh, Rogue . . . Rogue,'' she said with a light laugh, ''Perhaps I do mean more to you than a debt to collect.''

With tears brimming, she settled into the chair to wait . . . and watch over Rogue Rogan.

III

Autumn 1883

SWEET SILVER SECRETS

~ 23 ~

Rogue helped Shenandoah down from the stagecoach.

She glanced at the flat-roofed wooden buildings connected by boardwalks. They were built on the incline of foothills stretching into mountains in the distance. The land was dry and dusty; tumbleweeds rolled down the wide street. Men lounged in chairs tilted back while mule teams pulled heavily laden wagons. Loud voices issued from barrooms. Although it did not have the luxury or size of Leadville, it was a thriving town.

"What do you think of Silver City?" Rogue asked.

"Reminds me of Tombstone and a lot of other mining towns I've seen."

Rogue nodded in agreement. "That's the Pinos Altos Range of the Mongollón Mountains." He pointed to the peaks in the distance. "Most of the mining is done in that area. But the ore isn't like that in Leadville. The silver isn't mixed with lead here and there are pockets of almost pure silver. This town is the shipping point for the mines in the area, as well as for livestock ranches farther south. It also used to be an Apache camp. In fact this all used to be Apache land, and they still think it is.''

"We're not in danger, are we?" Shenandoah asked in alarm.

"There's always danger from the Apache. Geronimo still hasn't been caught. Frankly, I doubt if he ever will be. But Fort Bayard is nearby.''

"Good," Shenandoah said in relief.

"That doesn't always help. The road between here and the fort is one of the Apache's favorite raiding areas, but we should be safe.''

"I hope so.''

"Let's get a room and a good night's rest. I want us out of here at dawn.''

"Not until I find Arabella.''

"That shouldn't be hard to do, but leave it for later.'' Rogue picked up their baggage, then started down the boardwalk, his steps long and determined.

Shenandoah hurried to catch up with him. He was back in his own territory now, and there had been a marked change in him the closer they had come to Silver City. She didn't quite understand the difference, but he seemed to have withdrawn from her, perhaps preparing for the job he had to do. She didn't much like the change, but reminded herself that she had Arabella to think about. Rogue was well enough to take care of himself now, and her sister would still need her.

For the past month, Rogue had consumed almost

all her thoughts. He had healed, but it had been slow and he had been impatient. She had tried to learn more about her uncle's killer, but neither she, nor Kate, nor Tom had found out anything new. It had been frustrating, and she had worried about Arabella. But her main thoughts had been for Rogue. She had helped nurse him back to health, and now she had a bargain to keep.

She glanced up at the sharp planes of his face. He was not completely well. He was not as strong as he had been, and the wound in his stomach sometimes pained him. They had tried to get him to rest longer, but he had refused to wait. The trip to New Mexico Territory had been long and hard, but she could see that Rogue had forgotten all that now. He had only one thing on his mind and that was getting to his silver.

She thought of Tom and Kate for a moment. She had never seen a happier couple, and marriage had even been mentioned between them, though they were both so independent they hadn't reached a decision on that. Yet they were joined in a partnership at the Silver Star and were delighted that the silver was assaying out even better than expected. True to his word, all of Tom's kittens were named after Fast Ed, even the females, and there had been no more accidents at the mine.

Shenandoah had left her friends happy but worried about herself and Rogue. When she had promised to send for them if she and Rogue needed help, they had relaxed and wished them good luck. She would miss Kate and Tom, just as she missed her uncle, but she had to think about her future now, and the people who still needed her.

Rogue took them to the best hotel in town, then got keys to the largest room. Upstairs, the bedroom was unexpectedly luxurious. The large bed was covered with a dark blue damask spread. Drapes of the same fabric covered the window that overlooked the street, and when Shenandoah pulled them open she discovered sheer lace curtains covering the lower half of the window. A fine oval mirror hung over the dark wooden washstand that held a china pitcher and bowl. A small rocker stood in one corner, and beside it was a round table with a hand-painted china lamp on top.

Rogue checked the room to make sure it was safe, then turned to Shenandoah. "You should rest this afternoon. It'll be a long ride tomorrow."

"What are you going to do?"

"I've got business."

"Maybe I could help—"

"No. You'd be in the way. I've got to go out and get the lay of the land. It's been a while since I was here. I also want to buy some supplies to take out to the house. No telling what shape it's in. I need to hire some men, but that can wait. I want to see what my cousin Blackie's doing first."

"Do you want me to help you buy supplies for the house?"

"No. I'll just order the staples. After we've seen what it's like, you can get some other things. You go ahead and rest. When I come back later we can have dinner, then look up Arabella. And, Shenandoah, don't go searching for your sister alone. I don't want you running into Spike Cameron.''

"Is that an order?"

He hesitated, looked deep into her green eyes, then said, "Yes, if it needs to be."

"So you're to be my lord and master here? Is that part of the bargain?"

Rogue hesitated again. "If that's what it takes to keep you safe, yes."

She frowned.

He grasped her chin in long, strong fingers. "Would it be so bad for me to be your lord and master?"

She jerked her chin out of his grasp and walked to the window. "Uncle Ed raised me to be independent. I've never answered to anyone until—"

"Now?"

She looked back at him with cold green eyes.

"You made the deal, Shenandoah. You're the one who offered herself to me if I would rescue your sister. Well, I've taken you up on the bargain and now you belong to me. When the agreement ends, you can go your own way."

She said nothing, merely shrugging a shoulder in response.

"Tell me you won't go anywhere while I'm gone, Shenandoah."

"If you have such total power over me, then why do you need me to agree?"

"Damn!" Rogue was by her side in several long strides. He swung her around to face him. "That's just it, as you very well know. I'm not sure of you. I wish to hell I was. I wish you felt such a strong sense of . . . of duty that you would take care of yourself for me."

"I'll stay here, Rogue," she said firmly. "I'm not anxious to confront Spike Cameron alone."

"Well, why didn't you say so?"

She smiled, but there was no warmth in the movement. She didn't like being ordered around. "You didn't give me a chance."

"I know what you need. What we both need." He glanced at the bed. "I was sick too damn long."

Her smile turned even colder.

"But it'll have to wait." He touched the richness of her auburn hair thoughtfully, then said, "I'm beginning to wonder if everything you do for me isn't out of a sense of duty."

"But you just said that—"

"Never mind. I'll be back for you later." He turned from her and stomped to the door. There he stopped, then looked back. "Tonight we'll settle some things between us. I'm not weak any longer."

After he shut the door behind him and turned the key in the lock, Shenandoah walked back across the room. Things weren't going as she had imagined. Rogue was beginning to upset her, and she didn't like that. She wanted to be in control at all times, but she was the stranger here and Rogue was the boss. That worried her. She didn't like being in debt to anyone, especially Rogue, but she did owe him and she had given him her word. He had rescued her sister, and she paid her debts.

She looked in the oval mirror and began to remove the pins from her hair. She didn't mind staying in the room. Every bone in her body ached from the long ride on the stage. She would be glad to rinse her face and lie down. Arabella would probably be asleep right now anyway, so a few more hours wouldn't make much difference.

There really hadn't been any need for Rogue to order her to stay in the room, but he had. She didn't like the way that made her feel. Nevertheless, she would try to remember that he was feeling pressured and worried about his silver. They were finally in New Mexico and he was going to make every moment count. She had better plan to stay out of his way, except when he needed her.

That thought made her feel the heaviness of the debt. Would she never be anything to Rogue but someone to be used? She quickly pushed that thought from her mind because she didn't need him to want her. She only needed to pay off her debt, then go back to her gambling and help her sister. She forced coldness deep into her heart. She must remember to play this game as well as possible, for she was beginning to think that a great deal rode on its outcome.

That evening Rogue and Shenandoah dined downstairs in the hotel. It was an enjoyable meal, except for the growing tension between them. Rogue said little about what he had done in the afternoon, and Shenandoah didn't ask him. The longer they were in

New Mexico, the more reticent Rogue became, pulling away to concentrate on his own problems. And so Shenandoah also retreated, reminding herself that she had problems of her own to solve, the most important of which was finding Arabella and making sure her sister was all right.

As the sun set in the west, they strolled down Bullard Street, looking for a silver exchange called the Rooster's Nest, since Rogue had learned earlier that Spike Cameron had bought it and moved upstairs, along with a woman named Bella. The Rooster's Nest was purported to be luxurious and popular in Silver City and it was not long before they had followed the sound of music, laughter, and gambling to its front doors.

They pushed open the swinging doors and stepped inside a room very reminiscent of the Postmortem, only this silver exchange was not as large or luxurious. But in Silver City it was one of the very best. They paused just inside the doors to look around. Arabella was sitting on the bar, wearing the red satin gown in which they had last seen her. Spike was nowhere in sight. It was a good opportunity to confront Shenandoah's sister.

Arabella was smiling gaily at the activity in the room and did not see them approach.

They stopped beside her and Shenandoah said, "Arabella, how are you?"

Startled, Arabella jerked her head around, surprise and alarm filling her wide blue eyes as they focused on her sister. Shakily she set down her shot glass of whiskey. "What are you doing here? How did you find me?"

"It wasn't hard," Shenandoah responded. Arabella looked tired behind the rouge and powder. There was strain in her face. Perhaps she would soon realize this life was not for her.

"Well, now that you're here, what do you want?"

"Arabella," Shenandoah replied, "you're my sister. I'm concerned about you."

"I'm fine. You can see that. Spike's taking good care of me." She glanced at Rogue. "What made you leave your mine?"

"Sold it," Rogue said tersely, not planning to tell her any more than necessary, for anything Arabella knew, Spike would also soon know.

Arabella looked back at Shenandoah. "I thought that mine was very important."

"It was," Shenandoah answered, "but after Fast Ed died, things changed. Rogue owns land near here. He's going to be mining there. I'm going with him for a while. If you want to contact me, I'll be at Rogan's Range. But before I go, I'd like to talk to you about—"

"Well, speaking of the dead," a smooth male voice interrupted them.

They turned to face Spike Cameron. He was stroking his long waxed mustache while his eyes roamed over Shenandoah. "How's Fast Ed's prodigy?"

"Hello, Spike," Shenandoah said coldly.

Rogue tensed, his hand ready to jerk out the Colt .45 he wore under his vest.

Spike's eyes shifted to Rogue. There was a hint of surprise and anger in the flinty depths. "Hadn't thought to see you here, Rogan."

"No?"

"No. Thought you'd be staying near . . . Fast Ed and the Silver Star."

Rogue's eyes narrowed. "Fast Ed and the Silver Star don't need me anymore."

"I see. Well, welcome to Silver City."

Shenandoah turned to her sister. "Arabella, I'm going to be in the area for a while. If you need me—"

"I don't. I've got my own life. I'm happy."

"I understand. I won't push you. But I'm your sister. I'll stop by again."

"Do that," Spike said, smiling at Shenandoah.

"We'll be on our way then," Rogue said, nodding at Arabella, then turning toward Spike Cameron.

"Come back anytime, Shenandoah," Spike added, his eyes traveling down her body again. "Anytime at all."

Rogue put a proprietary hand around Shenandoah's waist. "We'll be back to see Arabella."

As they turned to leave, Spike said, "By the way, Rogan, if you're going to be doing any traveling around these parts, you'd better watch out for the masked bandit."

"Bandit?" Shenandoah asked, looking back.

Arabella shuddered. "Some lone man in a mask is robbing the stages. Reminds us of Leadville."

"And Tombstone," Shenandoah added.

Arabella's eyes opened wider and focused on Shenandoah a moment before she carefully looked away. "I suppose there are a lot of robbers in the West," she said softly.

"Sure there are," Spike agreed, "but from what I hear, this one's got a lot of style."

"I'd be a little more concerned about the Apache than a lone bandit," Rogue said tersely.

Arabella glanced at him. "Apache?"

"Yes. They've got no love for whiteskins."

"Well, I'm not worried about a pack of desperate savages. I could overcome them any day," Spike boasted proudly.

Rogue raised a brow. "Desperate they may be, and that only makes them more dangerous, but savages? The Apache are honest and honorable. They never break a treaty they make. On the other hand, the U.S. government has broken every single treaty it ever signed with the Apache. Is it any wonder they are desperate and angry? Their motto now is 'Never trust a white man.' I only wish more of our people were as civilized as theirs."

"Ridiculous!" Spike exclaimed, highly affronted. "When they're all dead, we'll be better off."

"At the rate it's going, they may all soon be dead. That seems to be our gift to the Indians. I wish it could have been different."

Spike laughed. "Didn't realize you were so softhearted, Rogan. I'll keep it in mind for later."

"Do that, but remember my concern only extends to those who deserve it. Come, Shenandoah, let's go." He led her quickly from the silver exchange.

Outside, Shenandoah took a deep breath. She was learning more about Rogue all the time. She hadn't known he felt so deeply about the Apache. She was beginning to realize that he was much more than a fast gun, or a man after quick money. As they walked away from the Rooster's Nest, she said, "Arabella still doesn't want my friendship or my help, Rogue."

"No, but now you know she's all right. However, the strain is beginning to show. That life is getting hard on her. She was raised to live very differently. She'll need you, Shenandoah, when she begins to pull away from Spike."

"I hope so, and I hope it's soon."

"Give her time."

They continued to walk toward their hotel, silence stretching between them. The night was cool, stars blazed in the sky, and the scent of piñon wafted down from the mountains. But Shenandoah and Rogue hardly noticed their surroundings, for they were each caught up in their own thoughts. Time was running out for both of them. Rogue had to get things settled with his cousin fast, and Shenandoah was afraid that if she didn't reach Arabella soon, her sister might be lost to her forever.

When they were back in their hotel room, Shenandoah was surprised when Rogue abruptly pulled her to him and began placing hot kisses down her neck.

"You don't know how much I've missed kissing you, holding you. I'm well now, Shenandoah."

His hands searched out the hidden recesses of her body, causing tingling heat to sear her skin. "Rogue," she began, meaning to protest, but stopping as his mouth found hers and his tongue delved deeply, tracing out all the contours and sweet warmth he had for so long missed.

"I've dreamed of holding you like this," he murmured, his mouth finding the cleft of her breasts. His hot breath warmed her bare flesh as his tongue darted into the valley, exciting her, tantalizing her.

"Rogue, I thought—"

"Thought what?" he asked, raising his head. "Thought there wouldn't be time for this?" He kissed her lips, then rained soft kisses over her face. "There will always be time for us." He quickly began to unbutton her gown. "I can't wait any longer, Shenandoah. It's been too long already." In his haste, several buttons popped off, but he didn't seem to notice. His intensity affected Shenandoah and her own long-repressed desire began to flame once more.

When she stood in just her corset and stockings, she said, "Let me help you take off your clothes."

He ignored her words. Instead of answering, he stroked her body, favoring her breasts, but finding equal interest in the hot, hidden depths between her thighs. "Oh," she moaned as his long fingers stroked the sensitive flesh that was heating at his touch. Her body began to burn with desire, demanding that Rogue satisfy her building passion.

Long, slender fingers stole around his neck, then delved deep into his thick golden hair, glorying in the feel of him. His scent enfolded her, just as his arms did, and she pulled him closer, saying, "Rogue, I need you."

"No more than I need you, Doe. No more . . ." He didn't finish his words, but suddenly sat up, shucked off his vest, set his Colt aside, then jerked off his shirt.

As the bare expanse of his hard, tanned flesh was exposed, Shenandoah ran sensitive fingers over the skin, digging in her nails to remind him of where he belonged.

"Damn!" he exclaimed as he unbuttoned his Levi's, then turned to her so quickly that she fell back before the onslaught of his passion. "To hell with the pants," he muttered as his arms came around her, sliding down to her hips. He raised her in one fluid motion, then exposed the heart of his desire and entered her in a quick, hard movement.

Shenandoah's head fell back and she groaned in an agony of delight. As he began to move in her, slowly at first, testing what had been so long denied him, she arched upward, feeling him fill her in a way that could never be forgotten.

"Tight," Rogue muttered, moving harder, faster. "Knew it'd been too damn long. Much longer and—"

She moaned. "Oh, Rogue."

"I know," he said, sweat beginning to bead his forehead, his body shimmering with moisture. "It's going to be—"

Suddenly he pushed hard, his body stiffening, then groaned as his body began to shudder. She responded, moaning as her own body followed his, and they slid over the edge together, merging their bodies, their spirits, their passion.

Then the long moment passed, and Rogue lay down beside her, breathing hard. The tense lines of his face relaxed. He stroked her body, long movements down her slick skin, and she snuggled closer to him, inhaling the smell of passion and power. She was content in a way she would never have thought possible. And, with him, she was happy.

He looked into her bright green eyes and said, "I go a little crazy when I can't have you, Shenandoah."

She smiled softly, touched his broken nose, and replied, "I'm all yours."

His eyes turned dark; then he said, his voice suddenly hard, "As long as I keep you bound by our agreement." He sat up, swung his legs over the edge of the bed, then stood and buttoned his Levi's.

Shenandoah sat up in bed, concern clouding her eyes. "Rogue, what's wrong? I thought you wanted me to keep my part of the bargain. I don't understand."

He shrugged on his shirt, then notched his gun around his chest. Grabbing his vest, he turned on her, his eyes dark and angry. "That's just it. But don't worry, I won't hold you to our bargain forever."

"Rogue, I—"

He stalked to the door, then looked back. "Don't wait up for me."

As the door slammed shut behind him, Shenandoah extended one hand pleadingly, then dropped it to the empty bed. What was wrong with him? He was angry. Tears stung her eyes, but she held them back. Rogue must be feeling stifled with her along. He wanted her in his bed, yes. But he wanted to be free, too. He was back in his own territory. He wanted her in his bed, but not in his life. There was no other answer for his sudden anger. They had been happy. She was looking forward to sleeping in his arms. But now?

She got slowly out of bed and wandered to the washstand. She poured water into the bowl and slowly began to rinse her body. She removed her corset, then her stockings. She felt very, very tired. Rogue was beginning to mean too much to her, and if she weren't careful, she might even fancy herself in love with him.

She looked into the mirror and saw sad, confused eyes. And what of the emotions that she had learned to feel since meeting him? What would she do with the feelings that she could no longer seem to keep in place? Why couldn't he feel something for her? She felt too much like a convenient bargain that he would let go only when he was ready.

By then she feared her heart might not be her own, and even the winning hand of an ace and four kings might not be enough.

She sat down on the bed, feeling terribly alone. Rogue probably wouldn't be back all night and she didn't want to wait for him. She was used to being out at night and she was upset about her earlier meeting with Arabella. Because Rogue and Spike had been there, she and her sister hadn't been able to talk freely.

Hurriedly she threw on clothes. She would go back to the Rooster's Nest and confront Arabella again. Spike would probably be busy, and she could talk with her sister alone. When she was dressed, she slipped from the hotel and began walking quickly down the street, hoping she didn't run into Rogue.

When she reached the alley beside Spike's silver exchange, she hesitated, her back to the dark alley. She took a deep breath to calm herself. She wanted to be poised when she spoke with Arabella.

Suddenly she heard the jingle of spurs behind her. She whirled. A dark shape came toward her out of the darkness. A tall, broad-shouldered man brushed by her, reaching out swiftly to caress her bare shoulder. Then he was gone, lost among the revelers on the crowded boardwalk.

Shenandoah stood still for a long moment staring after him, willing herself to relax. But fear knotted her stomach. And every man who walked by had only one face . . . the cruel features of Tad Brayton. She blinked and the miners wore their own faces again, but she had recognized Tad. She would never forget his arrogant walk, his male scent, or the jingle of his fancy Spanish spurs.

But how could it have been Tad? He was dead. Her mind quickly thought of all the alternatives. If Tad Brayton hadn't died in Mexico, he would have come after them for revenge. He *would* have followed them to Leadville. She shivered remembering that she and Rogue had heard the jingle of spurs in an alley there. Had Tad been that close all along? She suddenly suspected him of killing her uncle and of trying to murder Rogue. Hadn't there been stage robberies by a lone bandit in both Leadville and Silver City? She was very afraid that he was after them all.

She wanted to rush to the hotel and tell Rogue, but he wasn't there. And what if she were wrong? She hadn't gotten a good look at the man. But she felt sure it had been Tad. Suddenly chilled, she hurried into the Rooster's Nest. The bright lights, laughter, and people helped to restore her confidence. But thoughts of Tad still lurked in her mind.

She saw her sister on the dance floor, but didn't see Spike anywhere. Pleased at his absence, she made her way to the dancers. When the tune was over, she pulled Arabella away, saying, "We must talk."

Surprised, Arabella frowned at her, then nodded in agreement and walked to the bar. When Arabella had a drink in her hand, she led them to a vacant spot at the end of the bar.

"Do you think about Tad Brayton?" Shenandoah blurted out, then could have bitten her tongue. She hadn't meant to start out so brusquely.

Arabella raised a brow, then said. "No. I don't allow myself to think of him. But I dream of him."

"You do?"

"Yes. Ever since we left Mexico, I've been having this dream where he comes and takes me away."

Shenandoah swallowed hard, suddenly afraid that her sister's dream might come true.

"Why do you ask?"

"I . . . I just wondered. I sometimes think of him." She realized she couldn't just tell her sister she had seen Tad Brayton. It could have a disastrous effect on her. Fortunately Tad didn't seem to have contacted Arabella.

"He was a strong, fascinating man, but he's dead. Best to let the memories die too."

"Yes, of course. I didn't mean to bring up—"

"It's all right. Why did you come back?"

"I wanted to tell you that Rogue has transferred our eighth of the money from the sale of the Silver Star to a local bank. Half of it's yours. I hadn't planned to spend it yet, since it's Fast Ed's legacy to us. It won't last long if we live off it, but if you want, you can start drawing on it and stop working."

"I appreciate your wanting to give me half, Shenandoah, but Fast Ed wasn't really my blood uncle."

"But he considered you his niece, just like me. He wanted you to have something."

"I'm doing all right. I don't need money now."

"But you could stop working here. I could teach you to gamble."

"Stop it. Sure, the money would come in handy, if you insist on giving me half. But, like you said, it won't go far if I quit working. Besides, I don't want to leave Spike, or my job. I'll never be the same as I was before Mexico. I can't go back."

"That's not true."

"Isn't it? You saw me in Mexico. You've seen me with Spike."

"With Uncle Ed's money we could do something else."

"Two women alone? And what about Rogue?"

Shenandoah hesitated. "I can't leave him yet."

"See. You have your own life. And I've built one for myself."

"It's not what you think. I owe Rogue. We made a bargain, and I'm keeping my end."

"What kind of bargain?"

"Well, when we came after you in Mexico—"

"You mean you—"

"Arabella, I was desperate. I'd have promised anything to get help. You were down there alone. No one would cross the border with me. Uncle Ed was in Leadville. Rogue was there. But he was short of time. He promised to help me if I'd agree to owe him whatever he wanted for however long he wanted."

Arabella leaned heavily against the bar. She turned soft blue eyes on Shenandoah. "I didn't know. I guess I never thanked you for helping me."

"It wasn't necessary. You're family."

"I was hurt and mad and scared. And I didn't want to go back."

"But you're glad you came back."

"No. I wanted Tad Brayton and I wanted to stay with him, no matter what. He was my first man. And I fit in there. I can't thank you for what you did. I can only thank you for trying to help me."

"But, Arabella, those Braytons raped you!"

"I know. I try not to think about it. I am what they made me. And I'm staying with Spike Cameron."

"What happens when he no longer wants you?"

"There'll be somebody else."

"But, Arabella—"

"And you should realize that you don't owe Rogue forever. That was too much of a bargain to begin with. I was desperate after they kidnapped me, but soon I became deadened to the feelings. It's best that way."

"It can't be."

Arabella pushed away from the bar. "You're just not looking at life realistically, Shenandoah. Rogue's not always going to be around. You'd better think about staying here and gambling, not going out to his ranch."

"I owe him. I'm going to pay off my debt, then I'll think about my future . . . *our* future, Arabella."

Arabella simply shook her head sadly, then walked away.

Shenandoah watched her for a moment. Maybe her sister was right. Rogue had never mentioned love or marriage. But she stopped those thoughts. She still owed Rogue. Later, she would think about making a place for herself and Arabella. For now she belonged to Rogue.

24

After a long day's ride, Rogue and Shenandoah turned onto the rich grazing pasture of the old Spanish land grant known as Guarde de Cuguar, or Cougar's Keep.

As they followed the narrow dirt road toward Cougar Kane's hacienda, Rogue thought back to the many times he had visited his friend on this ranch when they were children. Memories of a time that had seemed so far away came closer. His blood seemed to run faster. He sniffed the air. The scent of pine, dust, and buffalo grass filled his nostrils. Cattle grazed quietly in the distance. The Mimbres Mountains cast shadows over the land as the sun began its descent in the west.

Rogue smiled. Home was not far away now, and he suddenly realized how much he had missed this southwestern corner of New Mexico.

Rogue flicked the reins across the backs of the mules pulling the freight wagon loaded down with supplies, then glanced at Shenandoah. The wide-brimmed hat she wore shielded her face from the intense sunlight, but even in shadow she stirred his blood. He was glad he had brought her with him. Then the smile faded, to be replaced by a thoughtful frown. He was beginning to wonder if he would ever warm her cold gambler's heart.

He shouldn't have run out on her the night before, but he had been frustrated and angry that she always seemed just outside his grasp. Now there was a tension between them that hadn't been there before. He looked up. The hacienda was coming into view. There wasn't time now to get things straightened out with Shenandoah, and maybe it wasn't even possible until later. She was extremely stubborn and, besides, he had other matters to attend. He hadn't come this far to let a woman ruin his plans.

He couldn't let her distract him. He would have to be ruthless. He wanted her, needed her, but he would not let her get in his way. There was silver waiting to be dug out of the earth, and he was the man to do it. He had waited a long time for his chance and he wasn't going to lose it when he was this close to success.

Shenandoah Davis would have to keep her bargain a little longer, no matter her personal feelings or concerns. Rogue slanted a hard glance at her, then looked back at the wide expanse of grazing land around them. Yes, she would have to keep her end of their deal until he had his legacy secure. Then they could talk. Then they could make plans.

"Rogue, before we arrive, I want to tell you something. I've been thinking about it all day. I may be wrong, but what if I'm not?"

"What is it?"

"Last night after you left, I went to see Arabella."

"What? I told you not to go to Spike's place by yourself."

"I wanted to talk to Arabella—alone."

"Damn! I wish you'd be more careful. Did something happen?"

"No. Not at Spike's. But, Rogue, before I went in I stopped for a minute by the alley nearby."

"You know better than to—"

"I'm used to taking care of myself. Besides, you left me and—"

"All right. Go on."

"A man brushed by me coming out of the alley, then went on."

"That's all?"

"No. I think the man was Tad Brayton."

Rogue jerked his head around to look directly at her. "Shenandoah! Are you sure? Did you get a good look at him?"

"No. In fact I hardly saw him at all, but I recognized his walk, his scent, and he was wearing those jingling spurs."

"There are a lot of men wearing spurs in Silver City. It's part cow town. A walk? A smell? That's not enough. You were just worried about seeing Arabella, and that made you think of Tad. He's dead. Forget him. We've got a lot of other matters to think about now."

"Rogue, I couldn't forget that arrogant walk, or his distinctive scent."

"A lot of men in the West walk with a swagger, and a lot of them don't bathe often."

"No! It was Tad. I just know it was. Remember, there was a lone bandit in Leadville, and now there's one in Silver City. He's followed us, Rogue. I know he has."

"Shenandoah, it's not like you to fancy things like this."

"I bet he killed Uncle Ed and tried to murder you. He's after us all now, Rogue, and I'm scared."

Rogue squeezed her hand. "I'll take care of you, Doe. Don't worry. And put Tad out of your mind. We may have some problems out here, but they won't come from Tad. My cousin Blackie is the man to watch."

"Rogue, please listen. I really think Tad is stalking us. Who knows what he'll do next? Or whom he may plan to kill? We must do something."

"You're just upset. You've had too much happen too quickly. Now, I want you to relax. I'll take care of you here. We're in my territory and nothing's going to happen to you. I'll handle Blackie if he tries something."

"Rogue, *please* listen to me."

"No. Tad is dead. Blackie is the man to watch."

"I wish you'd—"

"I don't want you to worry. If anybody tries to hurt you, I'll be there. Just put Tad from your mind."

"I'm going to watch for him, even if you won't."

"Damn, Shenandoah! I've got enough problems. I don't need you seeing Tad Brayton behind every bush. Now, forget him!"

Shenandoah didn't reply. Obviously there was no way to reach Rogue. She suddenly felt even more separated from him than she had before. He wasn't going to let anything or anyone distract him from his silver mines and his cousin Blackie. She wouldn't mention Tad again, but she'd be watching for him. She just hoped Arabella would be safe.

"That's Cougar Kane's hacienda ahead," Rogue said, trying to distract her from thoughts of Tad Brayton.

"A hacienda rather than a house?" she asked, letting the topic of Tad Brayton drop.

"Yes. Cougar comes from an old Spanish family."

"Then how did he get the name Kane?"

Rogue laughed low in his throat. "A fast-talking Irishman swept one of Cougar's ancestors off her feet. From what I've heard, it was a stormy, passionate marriage."

"I see."

"Kane's father married an Apache."

"Apache?" Shenandoah asked in surprise.

"Yes. That makes him a very interesting mixture of Spanish, Irish, and Apache."

"You sound close to him."

"At one time we were like brothers. Both of us grew up without sisters or brothers, so we sought out each other."

"I didn't know you didn't have—"

"The main house is very old, although it has been added onto over the years. The other buildings in back are built or destroyed according to the ranch's needs."

"Has this always been a ranch, then?"

"Since Cougar's ancestors received it as a land grant from Spain. As you probably know, the Spanish have been here over two hundred and fifty years. El Camino Real, the Royal Road, was built from Mexico City to Santa Fe, New Mexico, centuries ago and has been used ever since for commerce and travel."

"I didn't know that."

"It's probably better if you know a little of Cougar's background before you meet him."

"Then you've seen him often over the years."

There was a long pause. Finally Rogue replied, "No. I've been gone ten years."

"Ten years," Shenandoah said in surprise, turning to look at Rogue. "But you spoke as if—"

"I know. It's all coming back quickly. I had almost forgotten how much a part of this land I am."

"That's how Uncle Ed felt about the Shenandoah Valley. He never got over leaving it."

Shenandoah turned to look at the hacienda they were fast approaching. The building was large, flat-roofed, and made of stone. Black wrought-iron grill-work covered the windows and the main gate leading into the house. It was an imposing structure, obviously built for protection as well as privacy. There was much activity around the house. People were busy taking care of chores.

As Rogue pulled the wagon to a stop near the front of the hacienda, he and Shenandoah quickly became the center of attention. Most of the work was left behind as people crowded around the wagon, reaching up toward Rogue. Surprised, Shenandoah could only watch as Rogue leapt down and began shaking hands with the people around him. He spoke quickly, calling names, asking questions, and all in a language Shenandoah had never heard him speak before.

"*Qué pasa?*" someone called from behind the iron gates of the hacienda, then a tall, lithe, dark-haired man strode toward them.

Rogue looked up. "*Mi hermano, buenas tardes.*"

Shenandoah simply sat in stunned surprise as she listened to Rogue speak Spanish as easily as he did English. He and the tall, dark-haired man embraced, spoke several more words of greeting in Spanish, then stepped apart. The newcomer turned to the people around them, spoke several quick words, and they scattered back to their work. Then he looked up at Shenandoah with quick appreciation in his eyes.

Rogue followed the man's glance and said, "This is Shenandoah Davis. Doe, meet Cougar Kane."

Cougar grinned, pleasure lighting his dark eyes as his white teeth gleamed against his tanned skin. "My pleasure, *señorita,*" he said, his English accented, as he looked at Rogue for a moment to make sure *señorita* rather than *señora* was correct.

Rogue nodded. "Miss Shenandoah Davis."

"Mi casa es su casa, Señorita Davis," Cougar said gallantly. "You are most welcome to make Cougar's Keep your home."

"Thanks, Cougar," Rogue said dryly, "but she's going to make Rogan Range her home."

"Until my duty is done and I can leave," Shenandoah added sweetly, then turned to step down.

Rogue was by her side immediately, lifting her down, letting her body trail down the length of him as he hissed, "There's no need to involve Cougar in our bargain. It's between you and me."

She smiled innocently at him and whispered, "And just how do you explain my unchaperoned presence with you?"

Rogue grimaced, then turned back toward Cougar as he led Shenandoah around the wagon. "Shenandoah's uncle was a partner in my mine in Silver City. He was killed. She agreed to come with me and help me get my house in order."

Cougar nodded, watching Rogue closely a moment before turning to Shenandoah. "How kind of you, *señorita.* That house has needed a woman's touch for a long time. But, please, let us not stand out in the sun. There are cool drinks in the hacienda. Perhaps you are tired. Would you like to refresh yourself?" Cougar motioned for Shenandoah to precede him.

She stepped from the bright light of the sun into the dim, cool interior of the house, marveling that there could be such a change in temperature. The large house was built around a courtyard, reminding Shenandoah briefly of the Braytons' hideout, but this house was beautifully appointed with heavy, dark furniture, rich velvets, and Navajo blankets, Pueblo pottery, and Apache weapons. It was a house rich in tradition and its age had served only to mellow the colors and smooth the rough edges.

Soon Shenandoah was sitting in a small parlor, drinking cool lemonade, and feeling the tension and pain ease out of her tired body. Cougar Kane knew how to make a person feel welcome and his household staff were amazingly efficient.

Rogue took a shot glass of whiskey in one swallow, then accepted a refill. He lounged easily on the arm of a worn leather chair, as if he were perfectly at ease in this home.

Cougar held a glass of whiskey, eyeing Rogue through dark, veiled eyes. "You came home none to soon, *mi hermano*."

Rogue finished the whiskey and set the glass aside. "How bad is it?"

"It could be worse, much worse, if I hadn't sent a few boys over from time to time to cause some problems."

Rogue chuckled, then said sternly, "You shouldn't have taken the chance."

"For a brother, I would have done much more."

"Thanks. Now that I'm here, I can get it in hand. Did he find the mother lode yet?"

"No. But now that you're here, he will try even harder."

"Damn! Blackie and I can work together. We both own it all now. There's no point in keeping up this stupid feud our fathers started."

"You can try to change his mind, but he's stubborn," Cougar responded, then glanced at Shenandoah. "But we should not bore the young lady. She must be tired. I will send—"

"Thank you, but I'm all right."

"You look exhausted, Shenandoah," Rogue said. "We could both use a bath and a change of clothes."

"How was the trip?" Cougar asked, his eyes intent on Rogue.

"Fine. No trouble at all."

"Good. I sent word you were coming through."

"Thanks."

"Sent word?" Shenandoah asked, confused. "To the fort?"

Cougar chuckled. "No, not the fort. The Apache."

Shenandoah's eyes widened.

"Rogue may not have told you, but I am half Apache. Although I do not keep close ties with my clan since my mother died, the owners of Cougar Keep signed a treaty with the Apache nation many, many years ago. We have kept our end of the agreement, as have they. As long as I keep the treaty, Cougar's Keep will not be bothered by the Apache."

"I see," Shenandoah said.

"Rogan Range also has a treaty with the Apache, but Blackie has been violating it." Cougar stopped, looked at Rogue, and added, "You'll have to do something about it, or you could have trouble."

Rogue nodded. "I will. We were always on good terms with the Apache."

"Only because of the treaty. Break it or do not renew it, and you will find your life at stake."

"I'll take care of it soon, Cougar."

"Good. When it is done, my mind will be at rest."

"Come on, Shenandoah," Rogue said, changing the subject. "Let's clean up before we're served one of the finest meals in the West. Cougar has one of the best cooks around."

Cougar smiled. "And I've never known you not to be hungry, *amigo*."

Rogue grinned, then put a strong, warm hand on Shenandoah's arm and led her from the room.

Later, Shenandoah was treated to more luxury and pampering than she had ever encountered. Small, dark-haired, dark-eyed women who spoke only Spanish brought her a hot bath, filled it with fragrant oil, then insisted on bathing her and putting her to bed. She was surprised that she went to sleep so quickly and easily, but when she awoke her room was dark and the house was still.

Confused for a moment, she let her location sink in, then swung her legs over the bed. She felt better after her nap. She should dress and find Rogue. They had been given separate rooms. Rogue's mouth had tensed when Cougar had told them the accommodations, but for propriety's sake he had said nothing. They would be together again soon enough.

Before Shenandoah stood up, the room was suddenly filled with women lighting lamps, carrying in clothing they had pressed, and beginning to dress

Shenandoah as they pulled her to the center of the room. She could understand nothing they said, but they sounded happy and excited. They probably had few women visitors.

When Shenandoah was suitably clothed in a soft silk gown of blue, her hair coiled and curled in an elaborate coiffure, one of the women handed her the shawl Rogue had given her in Mexico. She hesitated, but perhaps time and distance had helped to heal some of the pain of dealing with the Braytons. She put the shawl around her shoulders, remembering Rogue and nothing more.

Shenandoah was led to another parlor, where Rogue and Cougar awaited her. She stopped in the entrance, surprised at Rogue's appearance. He was dressed in black, silver conchos down the sides of his pants, a short jacket with white designs embroidered on it. He wore a wide black belt with a huge silver buckle. The shirt he wore was full-sleeved, soft, and open at the neck. He looked very handsome, his blond hair in such contrast to the darkness of his clothes, but it was more than that. There was a dangerous quality to him, as if in donning a Spanish grandee's clothes he had taken on the qualities of a man ready to battle, and pay any price, to hold what was his.

That feeling was intensified as Rogue looked up and saw her, his eyes possessively running over her figure, before their fiery depths returned to burn into her wide green eyes. "Welcome, Shenandoah," Rogue said, his voice deep, husky. "I'm glad to see you wearing that shawl. It looks good on you."

"Thank you. It was a very special gift."

Cougar moved, a quick, lithe movement, and bowed slightly. "Your beauty graces my humble home, *señorita*."

Shenandoah smiled. "Thank you." She stepped farther into the room, noting that Cougar wore clothes very similar to Rogue's. Cougar moved with the quality of his namesake and offered her a small glass of sherry.

When Shenandoah was seated, sipping wine from fine crystal, Rogue asked, "Did you sleep well?"

"Yes, thank you. Did you?"

"No time." For a moment he looked preoccupied, then added, "Cougar had much to tell me about his ranch and the area. I've been gone a long time."

"Too long, Rogue," Cougar said, slanting a dark glance at his friend.

"I wouldn't have come back at all if—"

"Perhaps. Perhaps not. It is hard to stay away from the call of the land." Cougar then turned to Shenandoah. "Rogue tells me you're a gambler."

Shenandoah nodded.

"You'll probably miss that life out here."

"I don't know. A change might be nice."

Cougar looked at her a moment longer, then said, "A woman could get used to the bright lights and fast life of a city. Ranch life might not suit her."

"For some women, perhaps," Shenandoah replied, feeling as if he were talking of another woman.

Cougar might have said more, but dinner was announced and they entered a large room with a massive dining table. A silver candelabrum stood in the center, shedding soft yellow light over the long table. The three of them sat at one end. Shenandoah could not hide her pleasure in the rich design of the silverware, the gilded china, and the fine crystal. The tablecloth was of delicate lace. It had been a long time since she had dined in such sumptuous surroundings.

The meal progressed slowly, course by delicious course, and it was a mixture of Spanish, Mexican, Irish, and some Apache food. Shenandoah appreciated the wide variety and excellently prepared food. She had gotten used to eating whatever was served her, and now she realized it had been far from the best.

After several glasses of wine, Cougar began to talk of a young woman he had met in Silver City. "She is of a pure and radiant beauty. You know how I have long wanted a woman at my side, Rogue, but never could I be satisfied. I had hoped to marry a Spanish lady, or from my mother's Apache clan, but my heart was never engaged, so I waited."

"And now?" Rogue asked, obviously surprised at his friend's speech.

"And now that I have found her, she is not interested."

"Not interested?" Rogue asked, disbelief evident in his voice. "What woman wouldn't want to marry the master of Cougar's Keep? Not that you wouldn't attract them on your own. There were damned plenty when we were younger."

"Perhaps that makes me all the more intrigued. However, she is besotted with another man."

"What other man could compare to you?" Rogue asked, defending his friend.

"Thank you, *amigo*, but she wants the gay lights and laughter of Silver City. Perhaps I am too dull for her."

"You, dull?" Rogue asked in disbelief, remembering some of their early escapades.

"All she sees is a man who runs a ranch, and, worst of all, I'm respectable."

"Respectable? You're not making sense, *mi hermano*."

"It's a good thing my father is dead, Rogue," Cougar said. "I've fallen for a dance-hall woman and I'm determined to marry her."

Rogue choked on his wine.

Shenandoah quickly glanced around their sumptuous surroundings, unable to imagine a boisterous, rowdy woman as the lady of Cougar's Keep.

Cougar continued, as if suddenly letting out emotions and thoughts he had long held in check. "I'll have to be careful with her, treat her gently, because someone at some time has hurt her greatly. Nevertheless, I will win the lady's heart and make her my own *señora*."

"Damn, Cougar," Rogue said, "I've never heard you talk like this before. There were women, yes, but—"

"She's captured my heart with her sad blue eyes, that luxurious blond hair, and her perfect small body.

But more than that, it's something about her that I can't explain. She's a lady, raised carefully, gently bred, but something happened. I wish I knew what, wish I could change all that. She isn't like the others. She hurts inside, but she is brave. I don't know. I—''

"What," Shenandoah said quietly, a sudden understanding beginning to build in her, "is this woman's name?"

Cougar paused, then said, "Bella."

"You're right about her," Shenandoah replied, smiling softly.

"What do you mean?" Cougar looked at Shenandoah in surprise.

"Bella. You're correct about her background. Only her real name is Arabella White."

"You know her?"

Rogue clapped a hand on Cougar's shoulder. "You're in luck, my friend. She's Shenandoah's sister."

Amazement flooded Cougar's features. He turned to Shenandoah. "Your sister?"

"Yes. We were separated six years ago when our parents died. I came West with my uncle. She stayed in Philadelphia with her aunt. She came to meet me in Tombstone, but was kidnapped by the Brayton brothers, outlaws who had a hideout across the border."

"We freed her," Rogue continued, "but not before the brothers had—"

"I understand," Cougar said quietly, his dark eyes

beginning to gleam. "I understand only too well. That is why she thinks so lowly of herself. I would gladly kill them."

"We took care of them in Mexico," Rogue responded.

"Thank you for telling me," Cougar said. "It explains a lot. And this Spike Cameron?"

"Ran a silver exchange in Leadville. Arabella got hooked up with him there," Rogue answered.

"We tried to stop her, but she won't listen to us anymore. I'm hoping she'll leave him soon," Shenandoah added.

Cougar nodded. "Then you are her only living relative?"

"Yes."

"Then may I ask for the honor of courting your sister?"

" 'The honor of,' " Shenandoah said, hesitated, amazed at the formality of his words.

"Cougar can be damned honorable when he wants to," Rogue inserted, humor in his voice. "On the other hand—"

"This is important, Rogue," Cougar interrupted. "Arabella White shall be treated with the greatest of respect, the respect and adoration reserved for a great and loved lady. I think it is the only thing that will remind her of what she really is."

"Of course, I would be most pleased if you would see my sister, Cougar, but I must warn you that—"

"I know. Leave her to me. I will see that she is safe. She is too good for Spike Cameron."

"Be careful," Shenandoah insisted.

"I will not push Arabella, nor this Cameron, but I will be there for her."

Shenandoah nodded.

Cougar grinned suddenly, his black eyes lighting up with mischief and determination. "However, I will do everything in my power to foster discontent. And I think she feels something for me, if she would but let herself."

"We'll help you any way we can, Cougar," Shenandoah said, "but it must be Arabella's choice."

"Of course. That is my wish." Then Cougar turned to Rogue. "But enough of my problems. There is much to discuss, Rogue."

Rogue nodded in agreement, then glanced at Shenandoah. "Do you mind going on to your room while we go to the study? Most of this won't interest you."

Shenandoah hesitated. Everything about Rogue interested her, but he wanted to talk with Cougar alone. She felt very left out suddenly, but there was not much she could do about it. She stood up. "No, of course not. You two go ahead. I'll see you in the morning," she said, then left the room.

25

The Rio Grande River cut its rugged, winding path through New Mexico on its way to the Gulf of Mexico. The Mimbres Mountains rose high into the sky east of Silver City. And in between, a wide expanse of land supporting thick buffalo grass was called the Rogan Range. Although the grazing land could have supported large herds of cattle, only a few wild longhorns could be seen taking advantage of the grass and water. Bleached bones glinted white in the sunlight. And a few gnarled trees offered shade along the riverbank.

Rogue Rogan called a halt by the river. Men with tanned skin and hard eyes wearing wide-brimmed hats dismounted and allowed their horses to drink. But the men did not relax, nor did they stop watching the horizon.

Shenandoah accepted Rogue's hand as he helped her down from the supply wagon. It was hot and she took off her hat to fan her face. She too looked into the distance, but saw only acres of vast, open land. A few birds could be seen flying low in the sky.

While the mules drank deeply of the cool river water, Rogue consulted with the six armed escorts Cougar Kane had sent with them. Shenandoah watched as Rogue easily and naturally assumed his former leadership position in the area. The men would not hesitate to obey him. She only hoped there would be no call to use the deadly weapons they all wore on their hips and carried on their horses.

However, the farther they had traveled from Cougar's Keep, the more alert and cautious Rogue and the men had become. Shenandoah didn't know what they expected, but their tension had communicated to her until she was watching the horizon for movement. But so far all had been still.

While the horses and men drank from the river, Rogue turned to Shenandoah and offered her water from a canteen. She was grateful for the cool liquid and smiled her thanks. When they were all refreshed, the party moved on, heading west now, toward the Mimbres Mountains.

That afternoon they reached the foothills. In the distance, built among rocky crags and evergreen trees, were two white houses, set apart but facing each other over a wide chasm. Sunlight glinted off the steep roofs of the two-story houses and highlighted the many wooden buildings that were scattered up from the homes and nestled on the rocky mountain. The small structures obviously covered the entrances to mines, but by their appearance, many had been abandoned long ago.

Shenandoah turned to Rogue. "Is that—"

"There stands proof of the folly of two brothers," Rogue said, his eyes hard, his jaw tense.

"I mean, is that your home?"

"House, not home. The one on the left was built by my father. The one on the right belongs to Blackie now."

"They look well-built, Rogue," she said, trying to be encouraging and not knowing quite what to say.

Rogue laughed a harsh sound. "Yes, they're soundly constructed. My father and uncle did everything with a vengeance."

"There seem to be a lot of mines."

Again Rogue made a harsh sound deep in his throat. "I suppose you could call them that, but as far as I'm concerned, there's not a real mine in the bunch."

"What? But I thought—"

"Oh, they dug out enough silver to do well, following one stringer after another, but they never found the mother lode. *Never*. And they died trying."

"Stringer? I don't understand."

"The silver's pure here. You can follow a line of silver, several inches or feet in diameter, hoping to reach the source, the huge center, the mother lode. That's what they did all their lives. Follow stringers."

"But they built these homes."

"Yes. They were determined to get rich quick. When they found the first stringer, they thought they had made it. Taking what they found, they were able to build the houses, along with running some cattle. They thought they were rich. Maybe they were. The brothers wanted to marry. But they were jealous of each other, and both wanted the same wife. My father got her. Between her and not finding the mother lode, they started feuding.''

''And?''

''What you see ahead is the total of their lives.''

''I see. What happened to your mother?''

''Died. I was too young to remember. And don't ask me how. I'll never know. Those two old men took it with them to their graves.''

''And Blackie's mother?''

''My uncle found her in a bordello. Married her. She ran off as soon as Blackie was born.''

''I'm sorry.''

''Don't be. She was probably better off.''

Shenandoah hated to hear the harshness in Rogue's voice. She knew how hard it could be to lose a parent, but this was much more than that. She wanted to help Rogue, reach out to him, but he was closed, remembering the past. And Rogue's past sounded very hard, especially for a child.

''It's over now, Shenandoah,'' Rogue said, his voice less strained. ''I don't want to keep feuding with Blackie. I'm willing to share with him. We can make the mining a joint venture, if he'll agree. Part of our parents' problem was that they were always undermining each other, trying to discover the mother lode first and keep it from the other. There's no need for that now. I'm willing to work with Blackie.''

"If he hasn't already found the mother lode," Shenandoah added, realizing how much time Rogue had lost helping her.

"He might have, but I can see that he's been mining in the same area our fathers did. He doesn't really have a feel for silver, not any more than our parents did. But he could get lucky. I can't tell from here.''

"Do you know where the mother lode is, Rogue?''

"No one knows for sure, but when I was eighteen I found a stringer I thought would lead to it. I wanted to follow that stringer. I went to my father with the idea. He disagreed, to put it mildly. I never told him the exact location, and I left the next day.''

"And you haven't been back in ten years?''

"No. But I'll find that mother lode and prove I'm right, and I don't even think it'll take long.''

"I'll help you, Rogue.''

He glanced over at her. A slight smile curved his lips. "Thanks," he said, looking back at the mountain. "I know I'm right. I've got to be. I didn't really know what I was doing then, but I do now and I still think I'm right.''

Shenandoah remained silent, knowing she would help him any way she could.

"We're getting close, Shenandoah. Now's the time to be careful. No telling what Blackie has planned. Maybe nothing, but we'll be on guard all the same.''

Cougar Kane's men closed in around the wagon as

they neared Rogue's house. They moved cautiously up the rutted road. Shenandoah clung to her seat as the freight wagon lumbered up the steep incline. She felt the tension of the men around her. But all was quiet as they rolled up to the front of the large white house.

One man was left to guard Shenandoah while Rogue and the others circled the building, then rushed inside. While she waited, Shenandoah looked at Rogue's house.

The structure was more massive than she had originally thought. The long front of the two-story house was shaded by two deep verandas, one on each level. Four doors, plus central double doors, extending from floor to ceiling, opened onto both verandas. Five boxed windows were set across the front of the roof, along with two chimneys. Narrow wooden pillars held up the veranda on each level, although the highest floor was guarded by a railing and the top of the columns was scalloped. Unfortunately, there were no trees, bushes, or grass of any kind around the house. Alone, it clung tenaciously to dry, barren earth.

Across the gorge sat a house almost identical in appearance. It looked as shuttered and closed as Rogue's did, but Shenandoah knew that Blackie Rogan lived there and she wondered if he watched them from behind closed doors.

"Shenandoah," Rogue said, coming to her side.

She turned to look at him.

"The house is safe. Cougar's men are going to

unload at the back of the house. We can go in the front door and I'll show you the place.''

"All right. I'm anxious to see inside.''

Rogue helped her down from the high wagon. As they walked up to the front doors, the freight wagon was driven to the back of the house.

Rogue had a little trouble unlocking the front door. It hadn't been used in a while and the keys Cougar had saved for him were rusty. But finally the doors creaked open and Rogue pushed them wide. Diffused light from the veranda streamed into the foyer.

Shenandoah entered first, coughed slightly at the stale air, then glanced at Rogue. He threw open a door on the right, strode through the entrance, then stopped. She followed him, watching as he opened the door from that room onto the veranda. More light flooded the house.

The room was a parlor. Soft velvet-covered furniture was set in stiff, formal arrangements. It had not been used in a long time and dust covered everything. It would take a lot of cleaning before it could be used. A fine imported carpet covered most of the hardwood floor.

Rogue gestured at the furnishings. "Never used this much. Must have been something my mother wanted.''

He threw open the door to the next room. Heavy, dusty air greeted them. He opened the door to the veranda and more light entered, showing a long oak table with matching chairs and an elaborate sideboard.

"The dining room," Rogue said dryly. "We never used it much either."

Like the parlor, it was covered in years of dust and neglect, but with a good cleaning it would be a fine room, just like the parlor. Rogue's mother had furnished the house well. It was a shame she had not lived long enough to enjoy it.

Rogue turned away from the veranda, crossed the room, and opened a door leading to the back of the house. "The kitchen," he proclaimed, gesturing toward a large airy room that ran across half of the back of the house. Part of the room was devoted to a small dining nook, and the rest to an extensive cooking area. Windows lined the outside wall, and as Rogue began opening them, fresh air poured into the musty room.

"This is a lovely home, Rogue," Shenandoah said softly when he stopped beside her. "All it needs is a good cleaning. The furnishings look in good shape."

"You think it's lovely?" He glanced around. "I never noticed. It was just a place to sleep. Come on, there's more to see." He pointed to a closed door on the far side of the kitchen. "That leads to the storeroom. It's a huge room, as big as the kitchen. My father wanted all his possessions under one roof, so he saved that part of the house for supplies. That's where Cougar's men are putting what I brought."

He led her into the hall that ran down the center of the house. From there a wide staircase led upward. They passed it and returned to the front doors. This time he turned the other direction and threw open the door. Stepping quickly through the doorway, he opened the door onto the veranda. Light entered the room.

"This is the dayroom. Probably used to be a parlor, but the old man used it for a little of everything. Looks like he even had a single bed moved in here."

The room was filled with worn, comfortable-looking furniture. Old newspapers, a few items of clothing, dirty dishes, and discarded books littered the room. Rogue hardly gave it a glance before striding to the next door. He flung that open and entered.

While he opened the door to the veranda in this room, Shenandoah glanced around. It had obviously been the elder Rogan's office and study. A large oak desk covered with papers, journals, and records dominated the room. Behind it was a massive wooden chair padded with cracking leather. There were two other leather chairs, a small bookcase, and again a collected debris of discarded objects.

Rogue hesitated, glanced around the room, then quickly stepped out on the veranda.

Shenandoah joined him. "Upstairs?"

"Bedrooms. Four on the front." He stepped off the veranda, then looked up and pointed. "The one on the left corner was my father's bedroom. The room next to his was the guest room. The one on the right corner was mine. I'll have our baggage put there."

"And the other rooms?"

"I guess my mother didn't get around to furnishing the other bedroom. It's empty. The small rooms across the back used to be for servants. I guess they're mostly empty now."

"You don't need to show me up there."

"Good. Don't have time anyway. There are a few buildings in back I want to check before it gets dark. Cougar's men are going to stay and guard the place. There's a bunkhouse in back they can probably use. Don't worry about food. Cougar sent plenty with them, just like he sent with us."

"All right. What do you want me to do?"

Rogue glanced back at the house. "I don't want you to do any heavy cleaning. Cougar's sending some women over soon. I suppose you ought to just fix us up a place to sleep. Unpack, too."

"Fine. I'll do that. And, Rogue, be careful."

"Sure. You need anything, let me know."

She watched him stride away. When he was out of sight, she turned back to the house. She would leave all the doors open until it was dark. The place had a musty, closed-in feeling that she wanted to remove, but she knew it would take more than fresh air and cleaning to restore the house. It would take love. Perhaps something it had never known.

Later, when night was beginning to enclose the house, Shenandoah heard Rogue shutting and locking the front doors on the lower floor that opened onto the patio. She hurried to finish putting fresh linens on the bed so that she could join him.

The time since he had left her had passed quickly. She had found the linen closet, and although the contents were musty, they were clean. She had unpacked a few of her own clothes, but had left much of what she owned in her trunk. She didn't know how long she would be staying and she felt strange making herself too much at home.

She had glanced into the bedroom Rogue's father had once occupied, but it had obviously been a long time since that room had been used, or the one next to it. Both bedrooms were decorated with fading wallpaper, heavy furniture, and a layer of dust. Rogue's room had improved much with just fresh air from the opened window and veranda door. She had dusted the smooth oak furniture and shaken out the dark blue damask spread. She had avoided doing anything to the blue rug or the curtains, for fear of sending dust flying over the room. Those could be done when there was more time.

She was pleased that the room was at least habitable, and left a small lamp burning in the bedroom as she made her way downstairs. Carrying the basket of food Cougar had had packed for them, she walked to the front of the building, carrying a candle to light her way. Rogue was not in the parlor or the dayroom. She found him in his father's study.

Rogue looked up at the sound of her step. He frowned, lifted the half-full bottle of whiskey to his lips, and took several long swallows.

Surprised, Shenandoah hesitated in the doorway. "I thought we might eat now, Rogue."

"Don't want any food. Can't you see I'm getting drunk?" His words were slightly slurred.

"I don't understand," she said, cautiously entering the room. "I thought you were anxious to get here."

"Well, I'm here."

"Yes, and you have lots to do, don't you?"

Rogue took another long drink, then set the bottle down heavily on the desk. "Look at this, Shenandoah," he said, gesturing to the contents of the room. "This was his domain for as long as I can remember. Now he's gone and it's just a room full of nothing."

Shenandoah carefully sat down in one of the leather chairs in front of the desk. She set the candle on top of the desk, placing the basket on her lap.

"A whole life gone and what is there to show for it? A damn hulking house and some holes in the ground."

"You. He has you to show for it, Rogue."

"Hell! You would say that. No. I'll thank my mother for my birth, and myself for my upbringing. That old man had two emotions: love and hate. And they applied to only two things in his life. Hate went to his brother. Love was reserved strictly for silver. Well, he never found the mother lode. The Earth kept back her love. But I'm going to find it. I'm going to get the one thing he never could have."

Shenandoah felt a shiver run up her spine. Was Rogue like his father without realizing it? Could he love only silver, the mother lode? Could he feel nothing for a real flesh-and-blood woman? Very determinedly she said, "I think we should eat dinner, Rogue."

"Cougar told me those two cantankerous old fools died within hours of each other. I'm not even surprised. Hate was all that was keeping them alive. That and their search for the mother lode.''

"They're gone now, Rogue. You can go on with your own life.''

"Wonder how Blackie put up with it all this time? 'Course, I never knew how he felt about anything. He was always quiet, like a snake waiting to strike. I suppose he's still that way, but I'm willing to work with him.'' Rogue put the bottle to his lips, took a long drink, then grimaced as it burned to his stomach.

Shenandoah was getting worried. She had never seen Rogue like this. She wished Cougar was with them. He would know what to do, and how to bring Rogue out of his drinking.

As if reading her mind, Rogue said, "Hadn't been for Cougar and his family, I wouldn't have had a friend on Earth, or much of an education. I owe Cougar Kane, and I intend to repay him.''

"I'm sure he doesn't want to be repaid, Rogue. You were friends.''

"Still are.'' Rogue leaned heavily back in the chair. It creaked in protest. "I want him to be happy. If he wants Arabella, he's going to get her.''

Shenandoah's breath caught in her throat. She sat up straight. "How can you say that? My sister is not going to be used again.''

"Cougar'd be good for her.''

"That's not the point. She is going to get a chance to make her own decisions, choose her own life. I can't believe you'd say—''

"Cougar wants her. Cougar gets her.''

Shenandoah stood up. She set the basket down on the desk with a snap. "You can eat alone. You can sleep down here, too. I'm going to bed."

She turned to leave the room, but Rogue was fast. He pinned her arm with a hard grip. He jerked her back against him. His body was hot. He smelled like whiskey. "I get what I want, too, Shenandoah, and tonight I want you."

She pushed against him. "You're drunk."

"Not as drunk as I want to be."

"Leave me alone."

"Not tonight." He suddenly swung her up into his arms, knocking over the bottle of whiskey. He watched a moment as its contents ran across papers on the table, then shrugged and took a firmer grip on Shenandoah.

She struggled against him.

"Be still," Rogue grumbled as he strode from the room and down the hall.

As he ascended the staircase, she continued to fight, pushing at him with her fists. "Rogue, put me down. You don't know what you're doing."

"I know exactly what I'm doing," he replied, pulling her closer as he reached the top of the stairs.

In his bedroom, he kicked the door shut and tossed her on the bed. He glanced around. "Been gone a long time." He looked down at her. "You'd have been just as welcome in my bed when I was eighteen as you are now."

Anger was beginning to course through Shenandoah. She didn't like anything that was happening in this house. It had turned Rogue into a stranger. She was determined to resist him until he was once more the man she knew.

But the layers formed by the years of exile were falling away and Rogue was not to be changed. He began to jerk off his clothes, taking no notice of where he flung them. His eyes saw only Shenandoah, where she sat in the center of his bed, light from the small lamp highlighting her auburn hair and turning her eyes into fathomless green pools.

She took a deep breath when she once more saw his body unclothed, the muscles rippling, his eyes filled with desire. She forced down the ready response forming in her body and said, "I'm going to leave. I'll sleep downstairs. We can talk in the morning."

But she got no farther than the edge of the bed before Rogue snared her. He began pulling open her clothes. Buttons flew in all directions. Shenandoah gasped. She pushed at him. He noticed nothing except the welcome exposure of her pale skin. She struggled to keep her clothes, but in the end they were pulled and ripped from her body. She lay naked beneath him.

A cool breeze blew in through the open veranda door and ruffled the curtains as it came in through the window. Moonlight turned her skin silvery as Rogue ran strong, brazen hands down her warm flesh.

"Rogue," she moaned, grabbing his wrists and trying to hold him back.

He tossed her hands away, then secured them above

her head. He grinned. His teeth glinted white in the silvery light. But there was no warmth in the movement. She tried to kick him, but he quickly imprisoned her legs. Immobile, she could only glare up at him.

"Now," he said softly, "I have you where I want you." He bent and slowly began nibbling along her face, his breath hot and whiskey-strong. His teeth nipped at her earlobe. She tossed her head. He chuckled deep in his throat. A fiery tongue teased her lips, tormenting her sensitive flesh until she gave way under his onslaught, opening her mouth to him. He plunged inside, delving deep, asserting his control, his mastery over her senses.

When he at last raised his head, she moaned, "Rogue," and her body moved restlessly under his.

He roved lower. His teeth taught her nipples the splendor of arousal as one hand cupped the fullness of her breasts and stroked her navel, delved deep, then hurried on, his own body beginning to crave fulfillment. At the center of their desire, he stopped, then stroked her with sensitive fingers, plying her heating flesh. "Doe," he murmured, then caught her with his mouth, teasing her to new heights of rapture. She arched upward, her body begging for release.

"Rogue. Oh, Rogue," she said, flinging her head back and forth, trying to free her hands from his steely grasp.

"No. I'll not free you this time, Shenandoah," Rogue rasped. "I've played your games too many times before. I've got you in my territory now. You play my games here."

He suddenly spread her legs and pushed his throbbing manhood against her center. Freed, her legs wound around him, pulling him toward her core. Rogue made a harsh sound in his throat, then plunged into her depths. She cried out, aching with her need, and felt him thrust deeper, filling her completely. Then he moved hard and swift, as if he could no longer wait, no longer cared if he pleased her, just wanted his own satisfaction fulfilled.

Her head rolled back and forth as he staked out his claim, building and building the intensity until they both moaned, their bodies arching toward each other in a final plunge of release. Then they soared together into a time of endless pleasure.

Finally, passion spent, they slowly floated back, their bodies damp, their breath fast. Rogue dropped to the bed beside Shenandoah, releasing her wrists.

She turned to him, wanting to be held, but he was already asleep. She could not help pushing back a damp curl of hair that had fallen on his face. Whatever happened, she could not leave him yet. She was bound to him by more than their bargain.

26

Shenandoah was aroused the next morning by the strong smell of coffee. She looked up and saw Rogue grinning down at her. He held a mug with steam rising from its top.

"Lots to do today, Shenandoah," he said, handing her the coffee.

As she reached for it, the covers fell down around her waist, revealing rose-tipped breasts.

"Are you trying to keep me from working?" Rogue asked, reaching out to stroke one tip into hardness.

She pushed his hand away. "You're going to make me spill the coffee."

"Then give it back."

"Oh no." She evaded his hand and tucked the covers up under her arms. "Now, what was that about work?"

"Shenandoah, I need your help." He sat down on the edge of the bed, suddenly serious. "But I suppose I should apologize first."

She raised a brow.

"Didn't mean to get drunk on you last night. Fine host I was."

"As it turned out—"

"I didn't hurt you, did I?"

She shook her head in denial.

"Good. The sight of you always fires me."

"What kind of help do you need?" She was glad to see he had put the melancholy of the night before behind him, and was eager to help him any way she could.

"I've told you about Blackie and the stringers."

"Yes."

"You know I can't trust him."

"Yes, you told me."

"Cougar's men are going to help dig until I can get into town and hire some others. However, I don't want anyone to know about that special stringer I told you about. Blackie will have spies on Cougar's men. That's fine as long as my other digging takes place in secret."

"You're going to keep the mother lode all to yourself if you find it?"

"No. *When* I find it, I want the opportunity to get the silver assayed and recorded before Blackie knows about it. Then I'll tell him. Otherwise—"

"He might try to take it all for himself."

"And kill anybody in his way to get it."

"I see. Then how can I help?"

"Remember, I've seen you in action."

Shenandoah thought back to Mexico and rescuing her sister. She nodded.

"I'm going to dig for that mother lode myself, but I need someone on guard. I need someone I can trust. We'll do it in secret. I'll put Cougar's men to work, then say that we're searching for more silver in the foothills."

"Will we be safe?"

"We haven't been safe in a long time, Shenandoah. Blackie will stop at nothing to have it all. I'll feel better if you're with me, anyway."

"All right. Let's get on with this, then. I want you to find this mother lode and settle this with Blackie, so—"

"So you can go back to your sister, then to Leadville and find your uncle's killer."

"Yes, I want to do those things, but I also—"

"Gambling. Don't tell me." Rogue got up and walked to the door. "Go ahead and get dressed. I'll be downstairs getting the men to work."

By the time Shenandoah got downstairs, the house was humming with activity. Rogue was giving instructions, checking equipment, and marking maps. Cougar's men had excited gleams in their eyes and looked anxious to get on with their work.

The house had not miraculously changed overnight, but the fresh air blowing in through open doors and windows was already making it more livable. As Shenandoah grabbed a quick breakfast from a basket Cougar had sent, she heard a wagon pull up outside. She hurried out front to find several dark-haired, dark-eyed women laughing and gesturing toward the house.

Rogue joined her and they walked to meet the new arrivals. It was not long before Rogue had the women in the house, explaining in Spanish what Shenandoah wanted done to make the place habitable. The women were soon busily engaged with buckets, mops, and dust rags, their excited speech swelling as they exclaimed over the condition of the house.

Not long after that, the men went out to mine at an old digging, leaving Rogue free to join Shenandoah. He carefully packed two horses with food, supplies, picks, and shovels; then they mounted.

As they rode away, she looked back and Rogue said, "Don't worry about them. They've always worked well for Cougar and I'm sure they will for us. They don't need us there to explain what to do."

"But I had thought you wanted me to—"

"You decided what needed to be done. They'll do the actual work. I need you with me."

That matter settled, they rode on, urging their mounts higher into the foothills of the Mimbres Mountains. A cool breeze blew around them. The horses picked their way over uneven ground, their hooves clicking on rocks and stone. Insects buzzed. The sun was warm on their backs. They rode in silence awhile, Rogue continually watching the land around them.

After riding for some time, they disappeared into a stand of piñon trees, a strong pungent scent enclosing them. Guiding their horses over the needle-softened ground, they could see no farther than the trees ahead. They wound in and out of trees until they arrived at an outcropping of rock. Rogue stopped his horse and got off. Shenandoah joined him, and he led her to an old gnarled tree.

She looked down over the edge of the rock. Land stretched out far into the distance. A thin, snaking line running north to south was the Rio Grande River. Dark places in the tall grass of the plain indicated cattle herds. And below were two white houses, separated by a chasm. A deep, quiet calm settled over them. The wind whispered in their ears.

"You can watch from here, Shenandoah."

"You mean this is the place?"

"Yes. Back there, on the other side of the trees, I found the stringer in the face of a cliff. Looks like solid earth, but it's got a stringer."

"Let's go see if it's still there."

Rogue chuckled. "That silver's been there a lot of years. It's not going anywhere until I move it."

"Nevertheless, someone might have found your diggings."

"I don't think so. Nothing looks disturbed up here. Besides, it's got good cover. Behind a large tree."

"What if someone has found another stringer leading in from another direction?"

"Not likely. Fortunately, most of the digging's been done lower, nearer the houses. I'm glad to see Blackie hasn't been looking up here yet. But I want to make sure it hasn't been discovered. He could possibly be digging in secret."

"I'll come with you."

"No. I want to make sure it's all safe first. You

can watch from this old tree. You'll blend in with it so no one will notice you from a distance. I'll tie our horses in the trees.'' He slipped a rifle from his saddle and handed it to her. "You may need this," was all he said before leading the horses away.

When he was out of sight, Shenandoah leaned back against the tree and looked out across the wide expanse of land. She would see anyone who came up from the valley in plenty of time to warn Rogue.

A little later Rogue slipped to Shenandoah's side. "Everything's fine. Blackie didn't find it."

"That's great, Rogue."

"Sure is. Come on back with me. I want you to see what I've got."

She glanced around, made sure nothing moved on the horizon, then joined him. They had to push their way past a scratch piñon tree, but behind it was just enough room to stand and work. Rogue took a good grip on a pick, then swung, digging deeply. A few hard hits and dirt crumbled away, revealing a narrow, solid wall of silver about a foot in diameter.

"Rogue," Shenandoah exclaimed in awe, reaching forward to run fingers over the smooth surface.

"Wait a minute," he warned. When she withdrew her fingers, he sank the pick into the silver several times, extracting a large piece. He handed it to her.

The chunk of silver was heavy. She turned it over and over in her hands, then gripped it hard. Solid silver. She could hardly believe it had been that easy to take out of the earth.

She looked up at Rogue. "It's beautiful."

His eyes gleamed. He gouged out another chunk, rolled it around in his own hands, smelled it, then set it down. "I tell you, Shenandoah, the mother lode is back in there someplace. I can feel it."

Shenandoah looked at the sheer cliff rising around them. She could feel nothing. She shook her head. "I don't know, Rogue. If it were a game of poker, maybe I could feel it too, but this is a game I don't understand."

He grinned, grasped her shoulders. "No matter. I know it's there. I've known for ten years. What I've got to do is dig this silver out, following the stringer. It won't be that hard. I'll store it in burlap bags I've brought, then hide it around here. I don't know how long it'll take, but the mother lode must be close."

Shenandoah hoped he was right. She didn't want to see him disappointed. But how could he tell? It all just looked like a hunk of earth to her. "Do you want me to help you dig?"

"No. I think you should guard. I can't take a chance on anyone sneaking up on us."

"All right, then. You want me to go back?"

"Yes. And, Shenandoah, thanks."

She smiled. "I'm glad to help, Rogue. You helped me before."

As she walked away, she heard the pick begin to hit hard surface in a soft, muted cadence.

After she had been watching the valley for several hours, Rogue joined her. He sat down near her, looking hot and dusty.

"Seen anything?" he asked.

"Just the activity down around the diggings below. How's it going?"

"Easy. Almost too easy."

"I know what you mean. I've had games like that. You keep winning and you begin to wonder when you're going to lose. The streak can't go on forever."

"I know, but I want this streak to continue until I hit the mother lode. Then it can go."

"How long are you going to work?"

Rogue looked at the sky. "We'll eat, then I'll work until the sun is low. We've got to get back a little early so we can get cleaned up. We're going over to Blackie's tonight."

"What?"

"I sent a message, wanting to meet with him. I'm going to try to establish a friendly basis for our working relationship at least."

"Why do you need me there?"

"I'd also like to make it a social occasion and try to stop this feud. Bringing you shows my good intentions. Wear something pretty."

"All right," Shenandoah agreed, knowing what Rogue must have felt like when she got him to go into Mexico. This could be just as dangerous, but he needed her and she owed him.

Rogue looked out over the valley, assured himself that all was normal, then went to get their lunch. When they had eaten, he went back to the silver, and she continued her watch.

Late that afternoon he returned hot, sweaty, but

satisfied. "I've got the bags stashed away. Nothing but a cougar could ferret those out."

She stretched, trying to relieve her cramped muscles. She was tired, but not from hard work. The strain of being on guard, watching, waiting, had been exhausting. But on seeing Rogue she felt energy begin to flow through her once more.

They mounted restless horses, then returned to the house from a different direction, taking the long way around. Rogue did not want anyone getting suspicious or knowing their exact movements. He also used the time to look over the land again.

The men were just returning from mining, and Rogue hailed them, asking about their day's work in Spanish and then continuing the conversation as they arrived at the house. Soon women spilled from inside, joining the group congregated in front. They added their voices to the dialogue.

After a while the conversation died away. Rogue and Shenandoah dismounted, then sent their horses with the men and women as they made their way to the bunkhouse in back.

As they walked to the house, Rogue explained the conversation Shenandoah had been unable to understand. "Those men and women are married and excited about staying here for a while. They'll be doing new things and they like it."

"How did it go for them today?" she asked as they walked into the foyer.

"Well, I think the house should speak for itself."

Shenandoah smiled in delight as she entered the

parlor, then continued into the dining room. The dirt and dust of years had been removed, revealing fine furniture in pleasant surroundings. Even though the wallpaper was stained and the draperies faded, the rooms were very nice.

"Looks good," Rogue said, stopping beside her in the dining room.

"Yes. They've done a great job."

"The other rooms will have to wait, but they can work here as long as we need them, or until I can find others to take their place."

"That's good."

"I agree, but for now let's get cleaned up. Don't forget, Blackie is expecting us."

"I couldn't forget. Do you think it'll be safe, Rogue?"

"Some of the men will ride along. I want us to present a solid front and a show of strength."

"We will."

And that was exactly what they presented as they rode along the steep trail between the houses. In a green satin gown trimmed with lace, and warmed by her white shawl, Shenandoah rode sidesaddle following Rogue. Two men rode in front and two behind.

When they arrived at Blackie's house, the double front doors were thrown open and light blazed a trail into the darkness. Shenandoah stiffened when she saw a dark figure silhouetted in the open doors, and was glad she had worn her derringer strapped to her thigh. Rogue helped her from her horse and she took comfort in the strength of his arms. Then she was being led toward the house, Rogue's hand warm on her waist. Their armed escort was left behind as Rogue swept them into the foyer.

"Welcome, *cousin*," a deep, caustic voice said. "Come into my parlor."

As Shenandoah's eyes adjusted to the light, Rogue steered her into a room almost identical to the one they had at home. She sat down on a settee, its upholstery a worn rose velvet. She glanced around and discovered that the room looked in about the same condition as the parlor in Rogue's house, but perhaps not as clean. She suddenly felt eyes burning into her, and glanced up.

Rogue's cousin Blackie was looking at her with ill-concealed intensity. She could understand where he got his name. He had a thick pelt of black hair, and small close-set black eyes dominated a face otherwise unremarkable. He was slight of build, but a wiry strength emanated from him. He was dressed formally in black, but even indoors he wore a six-shooter strapped to his left thigh.

"And this lovely lady is—"

"Shenandoah Davis," Rogue answered his cousin. "Her uncle was in business with me before he died. She graciously agreed to accompany me and see to the ordering of my house."

"Gracious, indeed. Such a big job for such a little lady."

Shenandoah didn't know if Blackie's remark was meant as a compliment or insult, so she smiled sweetly and said, "A big job, yes, but one I'm sure I can handle."

"No doubt," Blackie replied, moving closer to her. "I'm sure you handle any job well."

Shenandoah glanced at Rogue. She didn't like the intensity in Blackie, especially when aimed at her.

Rogue's blue eyes encouraged her, and he took a seat nearby. "How've you been, Blackie?"

Blackie's eyes darted to Rogue, then returned to rest on Shenandoah again. He sat down on the settee.

Shenandoah shrank back.

Rogue stiffened.

"Very well," Blackie responded, his eyes roving over Shenandoah's face, then moving lower to take in the wide expanse of soft white flesh exposed by the décolletage of her gown. "Very well indeed."

"Glad to hear it. Sorry to learn about your father."

Blackie's head jerked around, his black eyes slitted as they glared at Rogue. "Are you?"

"Well, you were fond of the old man, weren't you?"

Blackie nodded slowly. "We're all fond of our fathers, aren't we?"

Rogue's eyes narrowed. "Wanted you to know that I see no need to carry on their stupid feud. I'm willing to work with you. Maybe we can finally find the mother lode."

"I've been getting good silver from the stringers."

"Yes, but finding the mother lode would set us up for all time."

"Certainly, but if our fathers couldn't find it, what chance have we?"

"Plenty."

Blackie looked back at Shenandoah. He picked up her hand and brought it toward his lips. He stopped, examined it closely, then said, "You have the hands of a lady . . . or a gambler."

Shenandoah stiffened, but forced herself not to remove her hand. "Perhaps I could have a drink."

"Of course. How thoughtless of me. And I was determined to be the perfect host." He reluctantly let go of Shenandoah's hand. Standing, he turned hard eyes on Rogue. "I'm afraid I've never been one for sharing anything, Rogue. You should know that."

As Blackie stepped from the room, Shenandoah tried to relax her tense muscles. A clock ticked in the background. Muted sounds came from the kitchen. A slight breeze entered through the open door.

"Did you notice the similarity in the two houses, Shenandoah?" Rogue asked to cover the uneasy atmosphere.

"Yes, it's quite remarkable."

"Not really," Blackie said, quietly entering. He carried a silver tray holding three glasses and a bottle of wine. He set the tray on a low table, poured the dark red liquid, then offered a glass to each. "Our fathers were very sensible men. If they had built different houses, one would always have thought the other's house was better. This way they avoided that particular jealousy."

"I see," Shenandoah said, then took a quick drink of wine. It was a very fine vintage. She nodded her pleasure at Blackie.

"There is little enough to enjoy in life," Blackie told her. "Fortunately fine wine is a pleasure I can indulge in this remote country."

"I've set some men to digging at that old stringer of my father's, but I'm going into Silver City soon and hire some miners. If you like, we can go in together on a new dig."

"As I said earlier, I really care little for sharing anything, especially what is important to me. I suggest we continue to work as our fathers did. Whatever you find, you keep, as will I."

Blackie abruptly sat down beside Shenandoah. "You're very beautiful."

She looked in alarm at Rogue.

"Did you know that Rogue's father and my own loved the same woman?"

"I've told her, Blackie."

"You see, they always wanted the same thing."

"That's very interesting," Shenandoah said, leaning back from the man's heat and intensity.

"Yes, isn't it? But Rogue's father got her."

Shenandoah took a quick sip of wine.

"Perhaps justice will be done in this generation," Blackie said, then stood up.

Rogue also stood. "There's no justice involved here, Blackie. My mother made her choice. I've offered to work with you, and—"

"And I've turned you down. When you offer me something in which I'm more interested"—Blackie glanced at Shenandoah—"I'll let you know."

Rogue's brows shot together. He set down his

glass sharply. "We can work together, Blackie. Let me know when you change your mind. Shenandoah, let's go."

She quickly joined Rogue.

At the door, Blackie took Shenandoah's hand again. He raised it to his lips, but before he could kiss it, Rogue pulled her away, leading her to their horses. A black scowl twisted Blackie's face as he watched them ride away; then he went inside and slammed the doors.

27

Two weeks later Shenandoah was in Silver City. While Rogue bought supplies and hired miners, she set out determinedly for the Rooster's Nest. Rogue's house was cleaned. They had made good progress on his secret silver mine. Blackie hadn't caused them any problems. And now she thought it was time for her sister to come for a visit. On Rogan's Range, far from a town or Spike Cameron, Arabella might see herself differently. Shenandoah was not going to take no for an answer. It was time she and her sister spent some time together.

Shenandoah pushed open the swinging doors to Spike Cameron's silver exchange. Since it was late afternoon, only a few customers sat quietly drinking or playing cards at tables scattered over the room. She barely noticed their presence as she walked to the back room. She pushed open the door, knowing that was where most owners spent their afternoons, counting their profits.

Spike Cameron was no exception. At her entry, he glanced up, a frown on his face. But upon seeing her, a smile replaced the frown. He stood up. "Welcome, my dear. I see you've already gotten tired of country life. I thought it wouldn't take long."

"You're wrong. I'm here to get some supplies, and—"

"And wanted to see me." He stepped around the desk. His breath was warm on her face. "I haven't changed. I still want you." Strong hands went around her shoulders, pulling her close.

"No." She pushed at his chest.

"I'm getting tired of your refusals, Shenandoah. Let's go upstairs to my room. I can satisfy you."

She pushed harder. "Let me go."

He squeezed hard, making her wince. "I've been gentle with you so far, Shenandoah, but if you want a brute, I can oblige."

"You don't understand. I—"

"Of course I do. You're like all women. You have to be shown what you want." He pulled her hard against his body, one hand clasping the back of her head so she couldn't refuse the lips that covered hers, then ground harshly against her unwilling flesh. After a long moment he raised his head, anger glittering in his eyes. "I don't like to be rejected, Shenandoah. I suggest you try to make me happy. That was like kissing a statue."

Again she pushed at his chest. He didn't budge. "I didn't come here to ease your passions, Spike. There are plenty of women who would be happy to do that."

"But you aroused them, so you should ease them."

"No. I came here for Arabella."

A closed look came over his face. "That is not open for discussion."

"Spike, I want her to come out to Rogan's Range for a while. She needs some time away from the city."

"You mean away from me. I haven't tired of her yet."

Shenandoah let out a heavy sigh. "Spike, I want to spend some time with my sister."

He looked at her for a moment. "What will you give me if I let her go with you?" His hands traveled meaningfully down her shoulders, over her back, to clasp her hips, pulling her against the rising heat of him.

Shenandoah hesitated, tried to pull back, then stopped. "I don't have to give you anything. She's my sister."

"Yes, but she's my mistress. She won't even want to go with you, especially if I don't want her to go."

She knew he was right. "I'm not going to your bed."

He laughed and released her. "You are amazingly stubborn, Shenandoah. Just like your uncle."

"What do you know of my uncle?"

Spike leaned back against his desk, drew a thin cigar from a case, then lit it. He blew smoke high into the room. He shrugged. "Everyone knew Fast Ed was stubborn."

"Only when he was right."

"You want your sister. I want you. Why don't we trade?"

"Nobody's trading anything," Rogue announced as he entered the room, his blue eyes hard and narrowed.

Surprised, Shenandoah whirled to look at him.

Spike took a long draw on his cigar, exhaled, then said, "This is none of your business, Rogan."

"Everything about Shenandoah is my business, and I'm warning you now, if you ever touch her, you'll have to answer to me."

Spike shrugged. "Shenandoah's a free woman. She makes her own choices. Isn't that right, my dear?"

Before she could answer, Rogue captured her arm and began pulling her from the room. As they stepped into the main room, he hissed, "I thought I told you to stay away from Cameron."

She tried to jerk her arm free, but his hand was like an iron band around her.

Spike followed them to his door, leaned against the frame, and said, "Leaving so soon? Arabella will be sorry she missed you."

"Where is she?" Shenandoah called back as Rogue continued to hurry her across the silver exchange.

But before Spike could reply, Arabella suddenly pushed open the swinging doors and stepped inside, several packages filling her arms. Upon seeing Shenandoah and Rogue, she stopped, her eyes wide.

"Arabella," Shenandoah said, halting near her sister. "I was looking for you."

"I was out shopping." Arabella struggled to look happy and carefree, but succeeded only in looking exhausted.

"Rogue and I want to invite you out to his place. We're going back soon, and you could ride with us."

Arabella looked from one to the other, the blue eyes in her rogued and powdered face trying to appear uninterested. But a light had been struck in the depths and would not be extinguished. She hesitated, glanced back where Spike watched them. "I'm not sure."

Shenandoah was delighted that Arabella didn't refuse outright. Perhaps she was beginning to change. "There's plenty of room. And it's beautiful country. I'm sure you would enjoy seeing it. Why don't—"

"There's my work to do." Arabella's eyes darted back to Spike, but she was obviously torn by indecision.

"We'd like to have you visit," Rogue encouraged. "And we have some nice neighbors. Cougar Kane visits us frequently."

"Cougar?" Arabella looked surprised, but interested. "I've met him."

"He's a good man, one of the best."

"We could go riding," Shenandoah pushed, beginning to have hope.

"I don't know about Spike," Arabella replied hesitantly.

"Go upstairs and pack a few things," Rogue ordered, his mind made up. "I'll tell Cameron."

"Oh no. I might like to go, but I don't want Spike to get angry. Later he would—"

"Feel free to come with us. If Cameron dared to try to hurt you, Cougar and I would tear him apart," Rogue said, deciding that if he had his way there would be no later. Arabella wouldn't come back to Cameron.

"I'll help you pack," Shenandoah urged.

But Arabella didn't seem to hear Shenandoah's words. She was staring at Rogue. "Why would Cougar Kane help me?"

Rogue hesitated. "Come on out to the Range and find out."

Arabella's eyes widened, then quickly firmed with decision. "Are you sure you want me? I'm not considered the best of company anymore."

"Of course we want you to visit," Shenandoah insisted. "We'll all have a good time. Just tell Spike you're going."

Arabella hesitated a moment longer, taking a long look into their eyes. Satisfied with what she saw there, she said, "All right. I'll ask Spike." Straightening her shoulders, she walked away.

Shenandoah took a step after her, but Rogue stopped her. "She has to do this on her own."

"But I'm afraid he won't agree."

"If he doesn't, I'll break his arms."

Surprised, Shenandoah glanced up at Rogue. But he was obviously quite serious. His eyes were trained on Spike, willing the man to agree or suffer the consequences. She looked at Spike and Arabella. As they spoke, anger suddenly flared in Spike; then he had it under control. He nodded, put a proprietary hand on Arabella, leaned down and kissed her thoroughly, then slapped her bottom as she turned for the stairs.

Spike walked straight to Rogue. His words were clipped when he said, "I could keep her here, Rogan. My bouncers would see to that. But I won't. I'll let her get it out of her system. But she gets a week. One week only. She'll be bored in no time out there anyway. I know Bella. She wants lots of good times." He looked at Shenandoah. "Just like her sister. And don't forget, my dear, now you owe *me*. And I always collect my debts."

Before anything more could be said, Spike motioned to his bouncers. As they moved into place near Rogue and Shenandoah, the owner of the Rooster's Nest disappeared in the back room.

"He'd be surprised how little those bouncers would help if I decided to go after him," Rogue said.

"And I don't owe him anything," Shenandoah added.

"No. I wouldn't let you owe another man."

She glared at him. "Well, you certainly have collected *your* debt."

"Yes, but I wouldn't let another man. If Spike pushes just a little harder, I'm going to take care of him. I don't like him, and I sure as hell don't like the way he looks at you."

"He just wants to use me."

"And I know how." Rogue pulled her a little closer. "But he'll never get the chance. I'd kill him first."

Surprised at the intensity of his words, she looked up at his face. His eyes were narrow and hard. He meant exactly what he said. She felt a little breathless. Rogue could be very possessive at times, but he was probably just concerned about getting the full value of their bargain.

"And don't think I've forgotten the little matter of your disobeying me, Shenandoah. I told you not to come here alone. I know what Cameron wants, and so do you. Were you trying to lure him into—"

"No! How dare you suggest such a thing?"

"It would have worked. I heard his suggestion."

"I came because you were busy. There was time and I didn't want to wait. Anyway, I don't have to explain myself to you."

"Are you going back on our deal?"

"No, of course not."

"Then you belong to me and must do as I say."

She clenched her fists, totally frustrated. "All right. You've made your point."

"I hope so. If there's a next time, I'll have to explain it a little more firmly."

"You're just trying to ruin Arabella's visit."

"No, I'm not," he said more gently. "I'm trying to keep you safe. You don't realize how dangerous men like Spike Cameron are. I don't even think you realize how desirable you are to men."

"I don't care about all that. I just want Arabella to be well and happy."

Rogue stroked her arm. "She will be, and this is the first step."

Arabella came hurrying down the staircase carrying two carpetbags. She looked anxiously where she had last seen Spike, but he was gone and his door was closed. She lifted her chin, then walked straight toward Rogue and Shenandoah.

After a day of traveling, Shenandoah, Rogue, and Arabella arrived back at Rogan's Range. They were surprised to be met on the veranda by Cougar Kane.

"Welcome home," Cougar greeted them, although his eyes were only for Arabella.

"How'd you know we'd be back today?" Rogue asked as he climbed down from the wagon, then lifted Shenandoah to the ground.

"You know there are no secrets from me in this country," Cougar replied, extending his arms to help Arabella from the wagon. He set her gently to the ground. "I'm glad you came for a visit, *querida*. Especially since I'll be spending a few days here too."

Arabella glanced questioningly at Shenandoah.

"I didn't know he was coming, but he's very welcome," she answered her sister's unspoken question.

"Already made yourself at home, Cougar?" Rogue asked, smiling at his friend's familiarity with the Range.

"I didn't come empty-handed. After you sent all your workers back to the Keep, I found a married couple who have come to take care of your house."

"Thanks. And you're going to stay awhile?"

"Absolutely. I've already moved into a spare bedroom."

"Great," Rogue replied.

"Which of this baggage is yours?" Cougar asked Arabella. When she indicated her carpetbags, he lifted them and started toward the house. When she didn't follow him, he stopped and looked back.

"Come on, Arabella, I'll show you to the guest room," Shenandoah said, leading her sister into the house.

Rogue followed with their baggage, stopping in the foyer to meet the wiry man and plump woman of Mexican descent who would be working for him. After he had indicated that they should unload the wagon in back, he followed his guests up the stairs.

Arabella was quiet, almost shy, and quite unlike the gay, gregarious woman who worked in Spike's silver exchange. Everyone noticed the change, but said nothing as she was shown to her bedroom. Cougar had taken the one next to it. They were on one end of the house, while Shenandoah and Rogue shared a bedroom on the other end. While the women refreshed themselves in their rooms, Rogue and Cougar went downstairs for a drink.

"Did you hire some miners?" Cougar asked as Rogue handed him a shot glass of whiskey.

"Yes. I was lucky. Hired six. They'll be arriving in a few days."

"You were equally lucky to return with the lovely Arabella."

"I think she is finally beginning to recover. If we

can keep her away from Cameron, maybe she can overcome the pain.''

"We will give it a good try, *mi hermano*, but remember to be gentle. We must not push. It could undo all our plans.''

"That's more up to you, Cougar. I got her here. Now—''

"I will see to her.'' Cougar tossed his drink down in one swallow. "Give me plenty of time alone with her.''

"Suits me. Shenandoah and I have been riding over the land, checking the old diggings, sniffing out anything new. We'll just continue that.''

"Good. And Blackie?''

"I wish I knew what he was up to. He's got plenty of men roaming around. But he's been too quiet.''

"No trouble?''

"No. He turned down my offer to work together, but I left it open. I'm hoping—''

"He's like his father. Forget it.''

"I know. I'm keeping an eye on him.''

"Smart.''

"He's probably planning something.''

"You can handle him.''

"Yes, and I'll find that mother lode yet.''

Cougar nodded, his eyes suddenly drawn to the entrance of the parlor.

Arabella and Shenandoah had changed clothes. They each wore pale gowns of soft cotton, buttoned high under the neck. Long sleeves covered their arms, and pale lace accented the bodices, sleeves, and bustles.

Their hair had been demurely caught in chignons at the back of their necks. They smiled.

Cougar and Rogue stood up. Rogue stared at Shenandoah. For the first time he did not see a gambler standing there. He saw a well-bred young lady. A tightness formed in his chest. He had somehow never thought of Shenandoah as she might have been if she had not moved West with her uncle. Now he saw her as the great lady of an estate. It altered something in him, but he didn't know what.

Cougar strode to Arabella's side, lifted her hand, and kissed it tenderly. "Please come in, *querida*. You are looking unusually lovely tonight."

As Arabella stepped into the room, Rogue no longer saw the wanton woman of the Braytons', or the dance-hall darling of Spike Cameron's establishments. She too could easily grace the home of a great plantation or estate.

Rogue stood uneasily as Shenandoah entered the room and smiled at him.

"Have I suddenly turned green or something?"

Rogue laughed. "I've just never seen you look quite like that, Shenandoah."

She looked down and smoothed the skirt of her gown. "Arabella has hauled this all over the West. It's a gift she brought me from Philadelphia."

"It's very nice."

"Both the gowns are lovely," Cougar agreed.

"I made them," Arabella said shyly.

"You are truly a treasure," Cougar said.

"I wish I could sew this well," Shenandoah added. "But Uncle Ed knew how to gamble, not sew."

Arabella laughed, a small tinkling sound. "Maybe I could help you sometime."

"Thanks. I'd like that."

"What's that I smell?" Rogue asked. "Don't tell me I've hired a cook as good as yours, Cougar?"

"I found you the best I could," Cougar replied. "They should be ready to serve dinner soon."

"I couldn't be more delighted," Shenandoah said, looking at Arabella. "That's not one of the things Uncle Ed taught me either."

Arabella laughed again, the happy, tinkling sound making her look younger. "Aunt Edna made sure I learned all the household arts, and sometimes I'd think of you in the West doing exciting things and I'd wish I wasn't stuck there sewing or cooking. Then when I came West, I . . ." She stopped, looked stricken, took a few steps toward the veranda, and stopped.

Concerned, Cougar took her hand and pulled her back, saying, "It must be time for dinner, Arabella. The night grows dark. Let's light the candles in the dining room, then check with the cook."

She quietly followed him from the room.

Shenandoah turned to Rogue, worry in her eyes. "Do you suppose she'll be all right?"

"Yes. Give her time. Cougar will help."

"Yes. He's good for her. I'm glad he came."

"So am I. While they spend time together, we can go back to our search. I think we're going to hit the mother lode soon."

"I hope so. And I hope Arabella is happy here."

Soon they were called to dinner. Silver, china, and crystal had been found and cleaned. The table setting was as beautiful as Cougar's had been. The food was delicious, the wine light and refreshing. The couples toasted the changes in Rogue's house, and wished him fortune in finding the mother lode.

Eventually they returned to the parlor, feeling relaxed and happy. A cool, fragrant breeze blew in from the veranda and they followed it outside. They could see far into the distance. Stars twinkled in the sky and a bright Moon cast soft light over the Earth.

The only flaw in their happiness was the brooding house across the chasm.

28

A week later, Shenandoah and Arabella sat on the veranda outside the dining room. A cool early-morning breeze stirred the air. Steam rose from the mugs of coffee they held. They were both dressed to go riding, and were awaiting Rogue and Cougar.

As they rocked, sipping the strong brew, Arabella said, "It's so peaceful here. The country is so vast, so beautiful. I could never have imagined anything like this when I was in Philadelphia."

"It took me a while to get used to the wide-open spaces of the West."

"But I like it, especially now that I'm . . . well, now that . . ."

"I understand. I'm just glad you're safe."

"I think I needed a little rest. And I've enjoyed my visit here. Cougar has been so kind to show me the countryside. He even took me to his home yesterday. It was lovely. I couldn't help but like it."

"And Cougar?"

"Yes, I like him too. How could I not?"

A board creaked on the veranda, then a hard male voice said, "I could tell you things about Cougar Kane that might change your mind about him."

The women jerked their heads in the direction of the voice.

Blackie Rogan stood on the veranda not far from them. He was dressed in dark clothing, a pistol slung low on his left hip. His boots clicked on the veranda as he walked to their side. " 'Morning, ladies." He tipped his hat.

Shenandoah nodded, tightening the grip on her mug. "Hello, Mr. Rogan," she replied coldly. "I don't think we want to hear your stories about Cougar."

"No? Too bad. I see my cousin's doing all right by himself." Blackie's hard dark eyes inspected Arabella.

"This is my sister, Arabella White. Arabella, this is Rogue's cousin Blackie Rogan."

"Pleased to meet you, ma'am. Seems Rogue knows how to liven up the old place."

"My sister is here visitng *me*," Shenandoah said firmly.

"Sure she is."

"Why are you here, Mr. Rogan?" Shenandoah asked.

"Same reason as your sister. I wanted to see you. No law against that."

Shenandoah stiffened. "Rogue and Cougar will be here any moment."

"Will they now?"

"Yes."

"Too bad. That'll spoil our little party, won't it?"

"What party is that?" Rogue asked, coming around the house, Cougar at his side.

"These lovely ladies on your veranda remind me of parties. Perhaps I should give one in their honor soon."

"We're a little busy for that right now, Blackie," Rogue replied, his eyes running over Shenandoah to make sure she was all right.

Cougar went to Arabella's side and held out his hand. "Come, *querida*. The day awaits us."

As she put her hand in his, Cougar said, "Rogue, we're going down to the Rio Grande. See you this evening."

"Have a good day," Rogue called as Arabella and Cougar left the veranda, pointedly ignoring Blackie.

"Like I said, I could tell you a lot of stories about that half-breed," Blackie continued.

Rogue stiffened. "Have you come over to work with me, Blackie?"

"No. How's it going?" He sat down in the empty chair by Shenandoah, his eyes roaming over her body.

"Nothing new. Still following stringers. Why don't you throw in with me? We could get more done."

"She looks as good in daylight as she did by candlelight," Blackie said, continuing to observe Shenandoah greedily.

"That's just because you've lived alone too long, Mr. Rogan," Shenandoah replied.

"Spirit, too. I like her, Rogue. She'd do very well in my house."

"But she's in *my* house," Rogue replied, his hand hovering near the Colt .45 on his hip.

"Only for the moment," Blackie retorted, then stood up. "Well, must be on my way. You'll tell me if you find the mother lode, won't you?"

"You'll know," Rogue replied through gritted teeth. "And you know what I'll do to you if I catch you sniffing around Shenandoah again."

"Just to be neighborly, I'll let you know when I lay claim to *my* mother lode." Blackie's eyes rested on Shenandoah long enough to let Rogue know what he meant; then he stepped off the veranda and disappeared around the house.

Rogue took a step after him, but Shenandoah stopped him, clinging to his arm. "No, Rogue. Let him go. He was just trying to make you mad. He's jealous, and he's afraid you'll find the mother lode before him."

Rogue turned angry eyes on her. "*His mother lode*! He'd better never lay a hand on you." Rogue swept her into his arms and pressed his lips to hers, kissing her with a passion and possessiveness that took her breath away. When at last he ended the kiss, she leaned weakly against him, all thoughts of Blackie swept from her mind.

"Come on," Rogue said gruffly. "Let's see if we can find our mother lode today."

They mounted horses and rode up into the foot-hills. The day was clear and cool, with a touch of autumn in the air. Birds flew gracefully through the sky. Small animals scurried out of sight when they tethered their horses among the piñon grove. They made sure their mine had not been discovered, then set to work.

For several days Shenandoah had been helping Rogue in the shaft he had dug into the cliff. While he dug, she pushed the silver into burlap bags, then carried them outside to their hiding place. Loose earth also had to be removed. It was dirty, grueling work, but Shenandoah found it preferable to standing watch for long hours. In all the time they had worked, no one had even come close to their hidden mine, so Rogue had finally decided that it was safe enough for her to help him.

By late afternoon they were tired and dirty, but the work had been going twice as fast since Shenandoah had been helping. They both felt a great deal of satisfaction and accomplishment as they paused for a break. Dark, moist earth loomed around them. Shadows from their candles flickered on the walls. A deep quiet surrounded them. And they sat close to each other in companionable silence.

"You can almost hear the Earth speak to you like this," Rogue said, glancing around them.

"What do you hear?"

"I think we're close, really close." He reached out and touched the silver end of their tunnel. He pressed. Stopped. Looked surprised. Then pressed again. "Shenandoah," he said, his voice hushed. "Come here."

She moved closer to him.

"Here, feel this."

She reached out and put her hand beside his. The silver felt smooth and cool. But that was normal. She looked questioningly into his face.

"Push."

She did. The wall of silver gave. She pushed again. The silver felt thin. "Is this the end of the stringer? Have we missed the mother lode again?"

"No," Rogue replied, his voice edged with excitement. "Hand me my pick."

When he had it in his hands, she moved back. He swung. The silver crumbled. A dark hole yawned beyond them. "Quick, Shenandoah, bring a candle."

She knelt by his side, holding two candles. She handed him one, then watched as he extended it into the darkness beyond them. Its light was brilliantly reflected over and over, the light cascading off walls of pure silver.

Rogue grabbed Shenandoah's hand and pulled her through the opening. They held up their candles. They stood in the center of a huge silver room. They turned round and round, holding their candles up and down, seeking some flaw in the silver, but it was perfect. Pure silver. They ran their hands over the smooth, slick sides of the cavern, feeling the cool texture of the silver, then turned to each other. Their faces were full of awe.

Then Rogue threw down his candle and grabbed Shenandoah. He swung her around, chanting, "The mother lode!"

When he finally set her down, she caught her breath and exclaimed, "Rogue, it's beautiful!"

"I knew I was right," he said, pacing the room. "I knew it ten years ago. And I've proved it. I found the mother lode."

He stepped back to her. "This makes me very, very rich, and Blackie too."

"Can you trust him to—"

"No. I'll get this claim recorded first. My cousin would try to steal it all if he knew it existed. I'll tell him only after I know it's secured."

"You'll have to go to Silver City."

"Yes, but I don't want to rush off. That would make Blackie suspicious. And I'll need to get some samples to take to the assay office. Now I'll have to be more careful than ever."

"I can't wait to tell Cougar and Arabella."

"No. We can't tell them yet. They'll be safer and so will the mine if no one knows except us until I can get it registered."

"I see. All right. You'll have a lot to do here now, won't you?"

"Yes. And I don't want you here anymore. It's too dangerous. You'll be safer at the house."

"But, Rogue—"

"No. Don't argue. We found the mother lode. And I want you safe."

"I can shoot."

"You don't know Blackie."

"But, Rogue—"

"Damn!" he exclaimed, taking her arm and pulling her to the entrance. "This is what I've spent my life searching for. Now that I've found it I'm not going to let Blackie steal it away, and I'm not going to let you get hurt."

Shenandoah was silent as Rogue pushed her into the tunnel, then followed. "I'm going to make sure this entrance is well hidden, then we'll go ride around the Range awhile. If Blackie's watching, I want him thrown off the track. He'll just think we're still looking for stringers."

After Rogue was satisfied that the mother lode was well hidden, they rode down, checked on the miners he had working on a stringer, investigated some of the older diggings, then dug around in a few promising areas.

By the time they returned to the house, the sun was setting and Shenandoah was feeling completely left out of Rogue's life. He didn't need her anymore. His house was in order. A couple would take care of it now. And he had found his mother lode. He had all he had ever wanted. That meant she would soon be free. Her debt paid. She only wished the thought made her feel better.

After dinner that evening, Shenandoah went up to Arabella's room. Her sister was packing. Spike had given her a week, and that week was up. She was following his orders and getting ready to leave. The visit had done Arabella a lot of good. She looked very relaxed and even happy. Shenandoah hated to see her leave.

"Arabella, why don't you just stay here? You could extend your visit indefinitely."

Arabella hesitated, then carefully folded a petticoat before placing it in an open carpetbag. "This has been nice, Shenandoah. I'm glad I came, but there's no place for me here. You know I don't belong anymore."

"That's not true. You'd be happy and safe here."

"Like you?"

Shenandoah hesitated. "Well . . . yes."

Arabella turned sharp blue eyes on her sister. "That's not true and you know it. What are you going to do when Rogue gets tired of you?"

"What are you going to do when Spike tires of you?"

Arabella shrugged. "I'm prepared for that. I know how it feels. I expect it. But you?"

"I don't plan to stay here forever."

"Then why invite me to stay? Sooner or later, I'd have to go. I'll leave now while it's my choice, and before it's too late for me in Silver City."

"But you should have a different life."

"Shenandoah, you're being stubborn and blind," Arabella said impatiently.

"No, I'm not. What about Cougar?"

There was a long pause. "Cougar and Rogue are two of a kind, Shenandoah. They have their great houses. Soon they'll want to marry nice ladies. Do you think we really qualify?"

Shenandoah hesitated. "But I've only worked as a gambler, never in a brothel."

"I've only worked in silver exchanges, not in a Tiger Alley. But what's the difference? We've both worked, and in places where nice ladies would not even be seen. We no longer qualify for great ladies."

"I don't want to be a great lady."

"Perhaps not, but you want Rogue, don't you?"

"No more than you want Cougar."

"They're not for us, Shenandoah. Not like we are now. You'd better think about getting back to gambling. I'm going back to a job I do well. Besides, I like the miners. I like making them happy. And Spike has been good to me."

"But, Arabella, you could stay here longer."

"Just how long do you plan to stay?"

"I don't know. But I wish you'd stay."

"I can't. And, Shenandoah, if you'd stop and think, you'd see that you're not much better off than a woman in Tiger Alley."

Shocked, Shenandoah could only look at her sister. "That's not true."

"You're living here alone with Rogue. That makes you his mistress. You're dependent on him, but you're not his wife. I know losing Uncle Ed hit you hard, but what do you think he would say? He left you a little money and raised you to take care of yourself, to be independent. Well, are you?"

"I hadn't thought about it that way. I had a debt to pay, and I always pay my debts."

"Well, surely you've paid off this debt by now. Think about going back to gambling. Make a place for yourself again. You'd be good at the Rooster's Nest, as long as you stay away from Spike."

"I don't want him."

"That means nothing to Spike. He takes what he wants. On second thought, you'd better gamble somewhere else."

"But, Arabella—"

"No, I'm not going to let you make me soft. I know where my station in life is. I've got no place here, and I've got no place with Cougar Kane. I'm going back tomorrow, and you'd better think about doing the same."

"Arabella, I wish I could change your mind."

"You can't, but you'd better think about what I've said."

"I will, only—"

"Please, Shenandoah, let it go. I need to get a good night's rest. We'll be leaving at first light, so just leave me in peace for now."

Shenandoah stood up. "All right. I'm glad you came."

"So am I. Thank you. Maybe I'll see you in Silver City soon."

"Good night."

Shenandoah slipped from the room, her heart heavy. She was glad Rogue and Cougar were talking in the parlor. They would probably be down there for a long time. She hurried into her bedroom. She needed some time to think. Some time alone. Arabella had made a lot of sense, even if Shenandoah didn't want to believe her.

29

Shenandoah sat at a poker table in the Lucky Lady gambling hall in Silver City. She had been gambling all night and she was tired. She had ridden into Silver City late in the afternoon, then gotten a job at the Lucky Lady. After a few hours' sleep in her hotel room, she had started gambling.

Although her concentration wasn't as good as usual, she had needed the game to occupy her thoughts. She hadn't wanted to think about Rogue Rogan, or the Range, or the mother lode. That part of her life was ended. She had heeded Arabella's words well. Soon after her sister had left with Cougar, planning a detour by his ranch, she had left Rogue a note and borrowed a horse. A long day's ride later, she was in Silver City.

But for a person who had made the right decision, she felt terrible. Her concentration kept slipping and she was having trouble maintaining the calm coolness a gambler needed to win. And she had lost this evening more often than she liked. She supposed that in time she would be back to her old self.

That is, if Rogue didn't follow her. She didn't think he would. He had a lot to do on the Range. And he had Blackie watching him. But Rogue didn't like to lose any more than she did. He might be angry enough to come looking for her, or he might just get on with his life. In either case, she didn't expect he could make it to Silver City for another day, unless he rode all night, which would be dangerous.

But she didn't want to think about Rogue. She twisted her mind back to the game. She was holding two jacks and three small cards. She discarded those and dealt herself three more. Another jack. She had something to work with, and with a little bluffing she might turn the hand into a winner. Pushing several more chips into the center of the table, she laid down her hand. She won, but it didn't give her the elation it once had.

As she cut, shuffled, and dealt again, she realized that her hands were not as soft as they had been. Working on the mine with Rogue had roughened them. She would have to soak them in soapy water, then rub lotion into them. Her fingers had to be very sensitive to play her best, and she was on her own now so she would need to be a better gambler than she had been tonight.

She would sleep all day, then see Arabella in the afternoon. At least her sister was now in the same town with her. She would have felt very alone otherwise.

Her mind wandered too far this time and she lost the game. The winner was elated. Shenandoah smiled, then dealt the next hand. She concentrated better this time and soon won. Pleased, she continued to hold her concentration firm like her uncle had taught her, and after a time she was beginning to play more like her old self. She was just starting to feel confident when a hand clasped her shoulder.

Annoyed that someone would touch her, she tried to shrug off the hand, but couldn't. She looked up. Rogue stood glaring down at her, his face a grim, tired mask. His clothes were dusty, his pistol was still on his hip, and his grip on her shoulder was like iron.

"Finish the game. I'll be at the bar." Then he turned and was gone.

A coldness invaded her. He must have ridden all night. She didn't want to confront him. She just wanted to be left alone. Perhaps he would go away. She carefully concentrated and won the game. She was just about to deal another round when her shoulder was grasped again. She looked up to find Rogue towering over her.

He downed the shot glass of whiskey he held, then said, "Your game's over for the night, Shenandoah. It's almost dawn anyway."

She hesitated.

"I'm not going to take no for an answer. We're

going to talk. We can do it easy, or we can do it hard.''

He meant what he said. She didn't want to be embarrassed in her new job. She stood up. "Gentlemen, I'll arrange for another dealer." As she stepped away, she hissed, "I'll meet you outside."

Rogue nodded once, then walked away.

After making excuses, she left the gambling hall, not at all pleased to have left early.

Rogue waited for her on the boardwalk, holding a bottle of whiskey and two shot glasses.

"Now, what did you want?" she asked, appearing cool and calm.

Rogue shook his head. "Reminds me of when I first met you in Tombstone. You know what I want. Come on."

"We can talk here."

"No. I'm tired. You've led me quite a chase. Where's your room?"

"There's no need to go there."

"The longer I stand here, the meaner I get."

"There's nothing to talk about. I left you a note."

"I'm starting to get real mean."

"There's no need—"

He grasped her arm, then started pulling her down the street. "Don't you think you owe me an explanation for running out on me?"

She hurried to stay up with him. "I'm willing to talk, Rogue, but—"

"You want this broadcast all over town, or do you want to go to your room?"

She gave in. "I'm staying where we stayed before."

Rogue crossed the street, heading for the hotel.

"There's no need to be so rough," she complained, her arm starting to hurt from his grip.

"I'm not letting you go until I get you behind a locked door. You have a way of disappearing that I don't like."

Once they were inside her hotel room, he set the bottle of whiskey and two glasses on the washstand, then poured two drinks. He handed her one, then downed his and poured another. He looked around. "Same room, isn't it?"

She nodded.

"Drink up."

"You know I don't drink much."

"Drink."

She took a small sip. "What do you want?"

He frowned. "You know damned well what I want. What the hell are you doing here?"

She suddenly realized that he was keeping a boiling temper under tight control. She sat down in the small rocker, sipped the whiskey, felt it burn all the way down. She didn't want to say anything.

"You could have been hurt on that road alone. Do you realize that? There are Apache. Not to mention Blackie or who knows what. Just what are you trying to prove?"

She took a deep breath. "I left you a note."

"You sure as hell did." He pulled a crumpled piece of paper out of his pocket and flung it at her. "There. Explain it."

The note fell short of her. She let it lie on the rug. "I told you in the note. I've done everything you wanted me to do. You don't need my help anymore. I thought I should get on with my life."

Rogue slammed the glass down on the washstand and sloshed more whiskey into it. "I thought you already had a life."

"Uncle Ed is dead. Arabella is making a place for herself. It's time I—"

"Damn! What are you talking about?"

"I think I've paid off my bargain, Rogue."

Rogue stopped, looked surprised, then tossed down another drink. "The bargain. That's what this is all about, isn't it?" His anger cooled. He glanced at the wide bed, then back at her. "All right, Shenandoah. You want out of the deal. I guess you've given more than you ever thought you'd have to. I got more than I ever thought I would. Problem is, the more I got of you, the more I wanted. I suppose a man can only take so much."

"I was glad to help you, Rogue. Without you, Arabella might still be in Mexico. You helped me, and—"

"I don't want to hear any more about help or bargains."

"But, Rogue—"

"The deal's over. You've paid your debt. You don't owe me anything else." He poured another drink, then swallowed hard, setting the glass down with a clink.

"Over? You mean you've set me free?"

"The debt is paid."

She smiled, feeling a strong rush of joy, then one of apprehension. There was nothing to hold them together now. "Thank you, Rogue."

"Don't thank me. I got my money's worth."

"You came all this way to set me free?"

"The hell I did." He was beside her in two long strides. He took the drink from her hand, set it aside, then pulled her to his chest. Gazing deep into her eyes, he said, his voice husky, "I'm done taking, Shenandoah. I want you to give."

"Give?"

"And the last thing I want is to set you free." He covered her mouth with his, kissing her with a hard urgency that made her want to lose herself in him forever. But something nagged at her. She broke the kiss.

"I thought you'd set me free."

"Damn! Then it's all been a bargain for you." He turned from her, took several strides to the door, then stalked back. "Good intentions be damned. I'll never let you go."

He lifted her in his arms and carried her to the bed. He set her in the center, his blue eyes fierce as he began to undress her. "Don't say anything. Don't tell me to stop. I can't. I want you too much."

"Don't stop."

"What?" He stopped in surprise.

She pulled his hands back, placing them against her warm, inviting breasts. "I want you. Must I tell you how much?"

"But I thought . . . Show me how much," Rogue said as he stripped off the rest of her clothing, then ran hot, hard hands over her naked flesh. She writhed up toward him, offering herself to him. Rogue groaned, pulled off his own clothing, then joined her in the bed.

"Shenandoah, I can't get enough of you," he said, pressing moist kisses over her face, stopping to tease her lips, his tongue tormenting her until she opened her mouth to him. He pushed inside, delving deep into her inner warmth, and her tongue returned his fire, inflaming him further.

"Rogue . . . Rogue," she murmured, arching up against his hard body as she ran her fingers through his thick hair. "I didn't want to leave you, but—"

"The bargain. It's over. Everything you give me now is because you want to. Give, Shenandoah. Give me all of you."

She pressed fiery kisses over his face, tasting him, smelling him, reveling in him. Her body melted against him. Fire replaced ice. All the control she had exerted for so long dissolved. There was no need now to fight him. He wanted her for herself, not for what she could do for him. Warmth cascaded over her. She wanted to give. Yes, she wanted to give him all of herself. She burned kisses into his neck, down to his shoulders, then nipped along his collarbones.

Rogue groaned and rolled to his side, pulling her to face him, letting the tips of her breasts lightly touch his chest as he pushed his hard staff slightly against the heart of her. She moaned, ran hands down his broad chest to the hot, hard flesh that teased her. She stroked him. Rogue groaned and pushed toward her. She intensified her movements and he rolled over on her, pushing in between her thighs.

As he moved, sliding back and forth against the most sensitive part of her body, she ran nails down the straining muscles of his back. In retaliation, he lowered his head and nipped the taut peaks of her breasts. Taking a nipple in his mouth, he made her moan with delight, arching up against him. His hands drew fiery patterns over her flesh, molding to the creamy skin of her breasts, then moving lower to enter the dark inner depth between her thighs.

She writhed against him, his hand causing fire to shoot through her. As he continued to excite her, moisture beaded her body. She clung to him, her body begging him for release. But she was not to have it yet. When his hand was done, his mouth followed, and she groaned in mounting tension, her body moving in sharp, restless motions. As his tongue delved into her, she dug fingers deep into his hair, pulling, silently begging him to finish what he had started.

Finally, when she was hot and ready, he moved over her, gliding up her sweat-slick body. She grasped his shoulders, her green eyes wild with desire. He pressed the tip of his passion against her softness, then stopped.

"Tell me."

"What?" she asked, tossing her head back and forth as she felt him press harder.

"You're giving yourself to me freely. No bargain. No debts."

"Rogue!" How could he have such control? She squirmed against him, trying to force him inside her.

"Tell me."

"Yes! Oh yes. I've always wanted you, Rogue. That was never part of the bargain."

"What?" His body tensed, shuddered briefly, then stilled as he held himself back.

"This was always just between us, Rogue. I would never have used my body to pay off a debt. I wanted you. I still want you. And if you don't—"

Rogue pushed inside her.

She gasped, then pressed her lips to his, saying, "Kiss me, Rogue. Give me all of you."

He needed no words to reply. His tongue moved deep into her mouth just as he staked out his claim in her body. They moved together, clinging to each other, worshiping, giving, taking as Rogue sharpened their desire with fast, hard strokes, bringing them closer and closer together, paving their way to bliss.

As Rogue filled her completely, she arched up against him, dug her nails into his back, then shuddered as waves of pleasure began to pour over her. Feeling her movement, Rogue thrust hard, then let the passion take him as long shudders passed through his body, welding him with Shenandoah as they reached completion together and spiraled into esctasy as one.

Rogue did not move for a long time afterward. Even when his breathing had slowed and the sweat on his body had begun to dry, he waited, drinking in all that she had to give, unwilling to separate them. Finally, when Shenandoah stirred under his weight, he rolled over and pulled her close.

She snuggled against his body and smiled.

"I never wanted your body to be part of the bargain, Shenandoah. I wanted you for yourself from the first moment I ever saw you."

She placed light kisses over his chest.

"But you were so damned cold and arrogant. I had to keep you with me somehow. I figured the bargain was the best way."

"It worked."

"Yes, but I soon wanted more than that."

"What more?"

"You. All of you."

"You have me, Rogue."

"At last," he said, then added, "You'll come back with me tomorrow."

"You're leaving so soon?" she stalled, waiting to hear words of love or marriage. Wanting, she suddenly realized, was not enough.

"You know I've got to. I'm going to register the claim, then get back. Who knows what Blackie may try to do in my absence."

"I understand you have to go back."

"Good. We'll go back as soon as we can tomorrow."

"And take up where we left off?"

"Sure. We've got the mother lode now, Shenandoah, and if we can keep Blackie in line, everything will be fine. But I've got to be there."

Shenandoah moved slightly away from him, then quickly stood up.

"What is it?"

"I won't be going back with you, Rogue."

"Hell! Now what is it?"

"I . . ."

"You what?"

She couldn't beg him to love her and marry her. She had too much pride. If he wanted that, he would have to ask. She needed to be left alone. She needed time to put the pieces of her life together. But Rogue would not give her that time, not knowing how much she wanted him. She decided to lie. "I'll be safer here, Rogue."

He swung his legs over the side of the bed and stared at her. "Safer?"

"Blackie. And then, Arabella's here. I can spend some time with her."

Rogue slowly nodded. "All right. I see. I've rushed you. You want me, but you don't want to commit yourself by moving out to the Range."

"Well, I . . ."

"Now that you're out of the bargain, you want to gamble again. Look into your old life. It's not going to work, Shenandoah." He started pulling on his clothes. "That's behind you now. And I'm not going to let you get away."

"It's not that, Rogue."

He buckled on his Colt .45. "I understand you better than you think. If I didn't have to get back to the Range, I'd stay and make you see this clearly. You're right about one thing, though. You're probably safer here. Until it's all settled out there, I can't even offer you anything but my desire."

"That's no small thing, Rogue."

He laughed, a harsh sound. "You're right about that, too. Okay, stay. But I'm warning you now. When I've got the mother lode producing and Blackie in control, I'll be back. Then we can make some plans."

Shenandoah nodded, unable to speak. Rogue was going to walk out the door and she didn't know if she could stand losing him again. Did pride really matter anymore?

He touched her face gently, and noted the tears glistening in her eyes. He placed a soft, warm kiss on her lips. "Don't worry, *querida*, I'll be safe. Just remember, the only thing these men in Silver City get from you is a game of poker."

"Rogue, I—"

He kissed her again. "You're mine, Shenandoah. I'll come for you as soon as I can."

He was gone before she could recall him. And perhaps it was for the best. After all, Uncle Ed had said that you don't always win in life.

She lay down wanting Rogue, missing him already. But she had done what was best. She snuggled against the pillow where his head had lain, inhaling his scent. Relaxed, she began to drift into sleep. Then she heard the jingle of spurs nearby.

She was instantly wide-awake. Her heart pounded fast. She glanced around the room in alarm, then at the window. Rogue had left the draperies open and the window raised for a breeze. A movement caught her eye. A dark, broad-shouldered shadow hovered there for a moment, then disappeared.

"Rogue?" she said hesitantly, fighting a growing panic.

She forced herself to get up and walk over to the window. She looked out, dreading to see another shape. But there was nothing to see. She jerked the window down, pulled the draperies closed with a snap, then rushed back to bed. When the covers were drawn up over her chilled body, she let her mind roam.

Her first thought was of Tad Brayton. The jingle of spurs. The powerful shoulders. He *was* still stalking them. She had been right. Then she stopped her thoughts. Of course, it might not have been Tad. She hadn't seen his face. But deep down she knew it was Tad Brayton.

She wanted to be free from her fear of this powerful man and she wanted revenge for the murder of her uncle. But she knew she would need help in dealing with the outlaw. Rogue had helped her before, and she needed him again. Once his mine was under control, he had promised to help get Fast Ed's killer. She would convince him of Tad's menace and hold him to that promise. When the time was right, they would go after Tad Brayton.

She drifted into an uneasy sleep.

❦ 30 ❧

Shenandoah walked down Bullard Street tapping a folded note against her left hand. The late-afternoon sun warmed her, highlighting the color in her muted green cotton dress. The note she held confused her. All week she had been meeting Arabella for coffee before they both dressed for work in the evenings. They had enjoyed talking about old times and telling anecdotes about their lives the six years they were apart. However, they had carefully not talked about the present. She couldn't say they were friends yet, but at least they were speaking.

The scented note had been delivered outside the door of the small café where they usually met. A small boy had handed her the note, then scampered away. There had been no chance to question him. The note asked her to meet Arabella at the Rooster's Nest. It really didn't make any sense because Arabella had been careful to keep her away from Spike Cameron. Arabella did not trust her where men were concerned, and especially didn't trust Spike's interest in her. She was happy to stay away from Spike, but the note instructed her to come to Spike's domain, the Rooster's Nest. She didn't understand it, but she was going. There wasn't much else she could do, if she didn't want to antagonize Arabella.

Cautiously she pushed open the swinging doors to the silver exchange and entered. The place was totally quiet. There was no bartender, no gamblers, no one stirred in the place. A shiver ran up her spine. Arabella was nowhere to be seen. She walked farther into the large room, looking left and right. No sounds. No people. Nothing.

She headed for the back room. Perhaps Arabella awaited her there with Spike. She gently pushed open the door. The room was dark and empty. She shut the door, then looked up the stairs. She didn't want to go up there, but she was beginning to become alarmed. What if something had happened to Arabella?

As she mounted the stairs, she called, "Arabella . . . I'm here."

Absolute quiet reigned over the Rooster's Nest. It was eerie. A silver exchange was always noisy, even in the off-hours. Had Arabella moved away without telling her? Then why the note? She continued up the stairs with dragging feet, feeling a coldness settle over her. Something was wrong, very wrong. But what?

At the top of the stairs, she called again, "Arabella? Are you there?"

A muffled voice replied, "Here. Shenandoah, I'm in the room on the left."

She thought about leaving, but she had been looking after her sister for too long to consider that for long. Arabella was here and wanted to see her. Perhaps she had some problem to discuss. She had to help her, if she could. Uneasily she pushed open the door and entered. It slammed shut behind her and a lock clicked into place.

She whirled around. Spike Cameron stood triumphantly behind her, his back against the door. She turned away, looking for her sister. Arabella was reclining on a massive bed, dressed in only corset, chemise, and stockings. Her face was caked with powder, red color covered her cheeks and lips. Shenandoah hardly recognized her as the woman she met for coffee every day.

"Arabella . . ." Shenandoah said hesitantly, completely confused.

"Spike wanted to see you," Arabella said coldly.

Shenandoah turned back.

Spike advanced on her, his eyes raking her body. "That dress doesn't become you. Take it off."

"Don't be ridiculous. I came to see Arabella. I wouldn't be here if she hadn't sent me a note."

"That is *my* note. Arabella wrote it for me. I gave you time to decide to come to me on your own. Whatever your game was, it didn't work."

"I'm not playing any games with you."

"Too bad you didn't find me as interesting as your sister does. Isn't that right, Bella?"

Arabella didn't reply.

"Bella!"

"Yes, too bad," Arabella agreed softly.

"I decided a long time ago that I would have both of you. You have proved difficult, Shenandoah, but no more. The cards have been dealt in my favor."

"Stacked, more likely," Shenandoah said angrily. "I'm leaving, Spike. You can't hold me."

"The door's locked. No one is around to hear you call. You are completely alone with me and Bella. There is no one to rescue you."

Shenandoah tried the door, then looked back. "I'm not going to play keys with you again, Spike. Open this door."

He chuckled. "You are beautiful when you're angry. Bella, help her change her gown. I want her looking good for our little meeting tonight."

"What meeting?" Shenandoah asked suspiciously.

"Nothing to concern yourself with, my dear. But soon, not only will I have you two lovely sisters, but I will also have a fortune to keep you in style."

"What is he talking about, Arabella?"

Arabella shrugged. "I have no idea, but I suggest you do as he says."

"How can you say that?"

"I know Spike. You should have stayed away from me and Spike."

"One of the things I like best about you, Bella, is that you obey me without question. Someone must have trained you well."

Arabella flushed a dull red.

"Now I will have the pleasure of teaching you to obey my every command, Shenandoah. I will take my time and train you well, until you will accept no master but me."

"That is utter nonsense!" Shenandoah exclaimed.

"Not in the least. Look at your sister. Was she always so?"

Shenandoah felt a chill touch her heart. "You won't get away with this, Spike."

"By tomorrow we will be on our way far from New Mexico. With a fortune at my command, and Bella to obey my every wish, you will soon know the pleasure of succumbing to my will."

"Arabella, help me. We can overpower him."

Spike chuckled. "She will listen only to me, isn't that right, Bella sweet?"

Arabella nodded in agreement. "You might as well do as he says, Shenandoah. You will have to anyway."

"No. I won't."

"Take off your dress, Shenandoah," Spike ordered. "Bella will help you."

"No."

"Do as I say and I'll tell you a little story about your uncle."

"Uncle Ed?"

"Yes. You've been looking for his killer, haven't you?"

"Of course."

"Well, remove your dress. I have a prettier one I want you to wear tonight. Then I'll tell you about—"

"Tell me now, if you know anything."

"Oh, I know plenty. I rarely lie. Isn't that right, Bella?"

"Yes," Arabella agreed, then added, "Come on, Shenandoah. Change dresses."

Shenandoah hesitated, but more than anything she wanted to learn about her uncle. Also, she must stall for time until she could persuade Arabella to help her. She slowly began to unbutton her gown.

Spike nodded in approval. "You know, I don't like to force people. I like for them to do my bidding on their own. It's so much more pleasurable."

"Tell me about my uncle."

"First the dress."

Shenandoah frowned, but went ahead and slipped the dress up over her head. Arabella took it from her. Spike greedily examined Shenandoah's exposed body, nodding in approval.

As Arabella helped Shenandoah into the red gown Spike had chosen for her, she thought of the derringer she wore on her thigh. Fortunately, Spike wasn't making her change petticoats. This way he wouldn't see the gun and she had a way out. But the derringer had only one shot. It would have to be carefully used if it were to do her any good.

Spike pulled Shenandoah in front of a full-length mirror and said, "While Arabella transforms you into a lady of the night, I will tell you what you want to know, but first—"

Before Shenandoah could realize his intentions, Spike had grabbed her arms and wrenched them behind her back. She struggled against him, but he overpowered her, tying her wrists together with a leather thong. When she was bound, he let her go and stepped back.

Furious, she whirled on him. "You tricked me! You were never going to tell me about Uncle Ed." She launched herself at him.

He grabbed her, squeezed her shoulders painfully, and said, "Oh yes, I'm going to tell you all about Fast Ed Davis. It's a lesson you need to learn. Your first from me. I don't think you have quite the respect you need. After my story, I think you will."

He pushed her back in front of the mirror. She stood there, her breasts heaving, as Arabella straightened the red satin gown, adjusting the bodice so that her swelling breasts were almost pushed out of the tight fabric.

"This dress is terrible," Shenandoah complained.

"It's perfect on you," Spike responded. "Now, take care of her face and hair, Bella."

Shenandoah was set in a chair. Arabella began to apply powder and rouge to her sister's ashen face. That done, she curled the long auburn tresses into sensuous swirls on Shenandoah's head.

"Your uncle insulted me, Shenandoah," Spike said, stroking his long mustache as he watched the transformation. "No man gets away with that. Besides, he was in the way and causing trouble."

"Are you saying—"

"I killed Fast Ed Davis."

Shenandoah's head snapped up. She looked squarely

into Spike's eyes. "I don't believe you. I suppose you'd like me to believe that you're the masked bandit who robs stagecoaches in Leadville and Silver City."

"Not at all. I would never expend so much energy on something so risky. I don't take chances. I always play to win."

"I simply don't believe you," Shenandoah repeated.

But Arabella had stepped back, her blue eyes wide with surprise and horror, belief firmly etched on her face. The other two didn't notice her reaction. Spike and Shenandoah were totally concentrated on each other.

"He was ambushed out by the Silver Star," Spike said.

"Everyone in Leadville knew that."

"Yes, but only I knew that he was tramping around in the woods. Looking for a mother cat and her kittens, wasn't he? Found them, too, didn't he?"

"No one knew that except—"

"You, Rogan, Tom, and probably Kate."

Shenandoah cried out and threw herself at Spike, but he forcefully subdued her, then slapped her across the face. An angry red welt rose on her right cheek.

"Now, look what you've made me do. Bella, fix that. I want her looking especially beautiful tonight."

Spike thrust Shenandoah back into the chair. Arabella applied more powder to Shenandoah, but her hand shook slightly. Then Arabella started to repair the hair. Shenandoah sat tensely in the chair, anger coursing through her. She would have revenge, sooner or later. Spike Cameron had just sealed his fate.

But fear also coursed through her. She had not truly considered Spike a threat. Now she knew better. He was a man to be feared, and she would have to do as he said to escape alive. She had him as well as Tad Brayton to worry about. Even if Tad hadn't killed her uncle, he was still out there just waiting his chance to get them.

"I'm glad to see you believe me. You know I mean business now. If you don't do exactly as I say, things could get very rough for you . . . and Bella."

Shenandoah glanced in concern at her sister. She would have to be careful, very careful.

"There's something else you might like to know. I shot Rogue Rogan, too."

Shenandoah jerked out of the chair. Spike put a restraining arm on her shoulder and pushed her back down. Arabella continued curling her sister's hair, but her hands were suddenly clumsy.

"He should have been dead, then I wouldn't have had to wait so long for my fortune. You'd have still been in Leadville, and we could have picked up right where we left off there. That's a fine town, big enough for a man to keep his actions concealed."

Shenandoah took a deep breath, remembering how Rogue had struggled to live with a hole blown in his stomach. This man had killed her uncle and tried to kill Rogue. He was trying to ruin her sister, as well as herself. He *must* be stopped.

"You are unbelievably despicable, Spike Cameron," Shenandoah finally said, then took a deep breath, forcing the icy calm of a gambler to take over. She must not let Spike scare her or make her weak. Since he held the trump card, she would have to bluff him to win. And to do that, she needed a cool head and a cold heart. For the sake of Uncle Ed and all he had taught her, she would not let anger and fear overcome her.

Spike chuckled. "You are absolutely beautiful. Like a cold, hard diamond sheathed in fire. Look."

Shenandoah glanced in the mirror. She did not let the surprise she felt reach her features. But Spike was right. Her skin was like alabaster, her features set in cold, haughty lines, but her auburn hair had picked up the color of her red gown and now shimmered like a pulsing, burnished halo around her head. The red gown glowed warm around her body, beckoning, just as her cold, pale skin and hard expression repelled.

At last Shenandoah understood how her sister could be so transformed. The new appearance seemed to dominate, making the wearer want to change into the imposed image. Shenandoah resisted the urge, remembering Uncle Ed's teachings. Cool, calm all the way through. In order to win, she must bluff her way to freedom and safety.

"Surprised, aren't you?" Spike continued. "You did a good job, Bella. Now, you dress. But first . . ." He pulled Arabella into his arms, then kissed her long and deep, while letting a hand run down Shenandoah's shoulder to the deep cleavage of her breasts. Shenandoah did not try to stop him as he squeezed one breast, then the other. She didn't want Arabella to know that he was touching both sisters at once. Besides, she must bluff Spike by making him think she had succumbed to his threats.

Finally Spike released them both, a satisfied smile curving his lips. "You two are going to give me a great deal of pleasure. Go ahead and dress, Bella. Shenandoah, come with me." He led her to the bed, then sat down beside her on the soft velvet-covered mattress.

While Arabella pulled on a red satin gown, Spike continued, "I'm glad to see you've taken my little story to heart, Shenandoah dear. Although I would hate to mar your beauty in any way, I can be quite deadly."

"I realize that now, Spike," Shenandoah said quietly, feeling the derringer against her thigh. If she could get Arabella to untie her hands, she might be able to win their freedom.

"Good. I thought you would." He leaned down and nibbled her bare shoulder. "Such beautiful pale flesh." He ran a hand down the curve of one breast, then cupped it to feel the weight in his palm. He smiled. "You aren't fighting now. Perhaps you wanted me all along?"

She shrugged, forcing down the temptation to bite off his ear, but she wanted him lulled into security. Once he felt in control, she could try to escape. "I thought you belonged to my sister, Spike."

"I belong to no one, my dear, but now *both* you lovely sisters belong to me. Isn't that right, Bella?"

"Yes. Yes, of course."

"See?" His hand moved lower, tracing her flat stomach to her thighs. "I hate to disappoint you, but I don't like to rush things. And we have another appointment tonight. We must not be late."

"What appointment?"

He chuckled, then leaned forward and pressed hot lips to hers. His mustache scratched her. She started to lean away, then stopped. She felt his wet tongue trying to force entry. She pressed her lips together. She could stand his touch only so far.

But she was spared any further demonstration of his desire by Arabella. "I'm ready, Spike. How do I look?"

Spike reluctantly ended the kiss. "Later, my dear Shenandoah. There will be plenty of time later." He turned to Arabella. She wore a red gown identical to Shenandoah's. Spike stood up to straighten it, then slid long fingers down to cup her breast, weighing it as he had earlier done Shenandoah's. "Almost of the same size," he said thoughtfully.

Shenandoah shuddered, tried to pull her hands from the thong, but couldn't. She tried to catch Arabella's eyes, but her sister turned from her.

"We're going to take a long drive, Shenandoah," Spike said, reaching for a hooded crimson cape. "You'll need this." He pulled her to her feet, slipped the cape around her shoulders, tied it under her chin, then twirled her around. Before she realized what he was doing, she was gagged with a black silk scarf. When she turned angry eyes on him, he said, "I never leave anything to chance, my dear,'' and pulled the hood down to conceal her face and cover her eyes.

Arabella slipped into a similar cape, then stepped to Shenandoah's side. Spike looked them over, then picked up a long black coat. "The night will be cool, but we'll be warm together, ladies. Come, my carriage awaits us in back. Soon I will be rich, and you will be my beautiful, willing toys."

∽ 31 ∾

Bound, sitting between Spike and Arabella, Shenandoah was taken on a long, wild ride. When the carriage finally came to a halt, she knew dawn could not be far away. She had no idea where they were, and she was given no chance to find out. Spike lifted her into his arms, making sure the hood of the cape still covered her eyes. She struggled against him, but he merely tightened his grip and began walking rapidly away. Arabella followed him.

After a short time, Spike bent down and carried Shenandoah in a crouch. She suddenly felt a difference in the air. The smell of earth filled her nostrils. A heavy silence hung over them. In the distance she heard the slow drip of water.

Spike abruptly stopped and set Shenandoah on her feet. Then he threw back her hood.

Blackie Rogan stood before her, his black eyes alight with triumph. Amazed, she looked farther around, then groaned. They stood in the mother lode.

Silver gleamed all around them. Shenandoah felt weak all over. How had Blackie found it? Did Rogue know?

"Welcome, Shenandoah," Blackie said, untying her gag, then removing her cape. "You can scream, but it won't do you any good." Then he gestured around them. "How do you like *my* mother lode?"

"It's not all yours. Rogue found it."

"With your help, I understand."

"You won't get away with this. Rogue won't let you steal this mine."

"*Steal?* This mine, and Rogan Range, will soon belong only to me."

"Rogue will never give up what's his."

"Such loyalty. I like that in a woman. Don't you, Spike?"

"Yes. And if it doesn't come naturally, she can be taught."

"Of course. I see you brought the charming Arabella. Did you have to teach her?"

Spike chuckled, reaching out to draw Arabella's soft warm body against him. "She was well on her way to learning her lessons before she met me."

Shenandoah glanced from one man to the other. "Whatever you've planned, you won't get away with it."

"You're wrong, Shenandoah," Blackie said. "I'll have everything my way. I have so far. Why should I stop now?"

"What do you mean?" she asked suspiciously, wondering how she could get untied and reach her derringer. She was afraid she could not count on Arabella's help.

"In a moment. Arabella, there is champagne over there. Spike will open it for you; then you can pour and serve. We have much to celebrate."

"I'm not celebrating!" Shenandoah exclaimed, stepping away from Blackie to stalk the mine, looking for help or escape. For the first time she noticed the second entrance. Somehow Spike had learned about Rogue's discovery, then dug in from the opposite side. She felt a shiver of horror run through her. Rogue would not know about this. She must get free and tell him.

"Stop pacing, Shenandoah," Blackie ordered in annoyance. "You can't escape." He pushed her to the ground near a silver wall. "Stay there. Arabella, where's the champagne?"

Arabella quickly handed brimming glasses of bubbly liquid to Blackie and Spike. Then she took one herself, carefully avoiding Shenandoah's eyes.

Blackie held his glass up high. Light from lanterns and shimmering silver gleamed in the crystal. "Let's drink to our wealth and our women."

He and Spike eagerly drained their glasses. Arabella sipped from hers. Then Blackie took champagne to Shenandoah.

"Drink to my success, Shenandoah."

"No."

He dug hard fingers into her hair, tilted her head back, then pressed the glass against her mouth. Champagne dripped down her chin to her breasts, staining the bright red of her gown. He dug fingers into her jaws, forced open her mouth, then poured champagne down her throat. She choked, swallowed, gagged, but drank.

Blackie let her go, then refilled his glass. Sipping the champagne, he said, "A second toast. Arabella, see to Spike's needs."

While Arabella refilled Spike's glass, Blackie continued, "Now to our main toast. Shenandoah, I want to thank you first for making our party possible."

"Me?"

"Yes. You will prove to be my cousin's downfall."

"That's impossible."

Blackie swirled champagne in his glass while regarding Shenandoah with dark eyes. "I suppose you do deserve to know it all now. You can't stop anything that's going to happen."

"What are you talking about?" Shenandoah was beginning to feel confused, as well as desperate. She glanced at her sister for help, but Arabella was slowly drinking champagne and watching Blackie.

"Spike has been working for me. He tried to stop Rogue in Leadville. I didn't want my cousin coming back here. I was digging into more and more stringers. Sooner or later I would have found the mother lode myself. In the meantime, I was getting rich anyway."

"You had Spike cause the accidents at the Silver Star?" she asked, her eyes darting from Blackie to Spike, then back again.

"That's right. And when those didn't stop Rogue, I had Spike kill your uncle."

Shenandoah tried to get up, but couldn't. She twisted her hands cruelly in the leather thong to get free. But she was helpless. Wild, furious green eyes bore into Blackie. "You! But why? Why?"

"I didn't want to kill a blood relative unless absolutely necessary. I thought if Rogue's partner died, the mine would be closed. Then Rogue wouldn't have the money to return here and work his inheritance."

"But that didn't happen, did it?" Shenandoah hissed.

"No. Rogue sold the mine and came anyway."

"You won't get away with killing my uncle."

"I've already gotten away with it. And you aren't going to do anything about it."

"Yes, I will."

"I like your spirit, but don't push me. Of course, Rogue wouldn't have gotten here at all if you hadn't saved his life in Leadville."

"So you had Spike shoot him too," Shenandoah said, beginning to understand that Blackie had been behind all their troubles.

"It finally seemed the only way to stop him."

"But you didn't stop him, did you? And you won't now," she said triumphantly.

"You're wrong. You will be his downfall, just as I said."

"Never!"

Blackie took a sip of champagne, drinking in the sight of her furious beauty.

"I would never hurt Rogue," she continued, struggling to get free. "And there was no reason for you to. He would have given you half of everything. He still would."

"But I don't want half of everything. I want it all. I'm not a man who likes to share, just like my father. I will take it all . . . because I can."

"Rogue won't let you."

"He would try to stop me, of course, but he won't get the chance."

"What do you mean?"

Blackie chuckled with pleasure, then sent an amused glance at Spike. "There's going to be an unfortunate accident here at the mother lode. While working, Rogue is going to accidentally set off some dynamite. His friend Cougar Kane will probably be with him."

"Rogue would never be careless with dynamite."

"No, he probably wouldn't, but he will die all the same."

"Die!"

"That's right—then the silver, the Range, and you will all be mine."

"I didn't know you were going to keep Shenandoah," Spike said, a frown furrowing his brow.

Blackie glanced at him. "Isn't one of them enough for you?"

"I just thought—"

"You can't do this!" Shenandoah cried.

"Anytime now, you should hear the explosion." Blackie lifted his glass in a salute, then drained it. "Arabella, more champagne for everyone."

Arabella's hands shook slightly as she poured the pale liquid. "Cougar Kane is at his ranch, isn't he?"

Blackie laughed. "That's right. You spent quite a bit of time with him, didn't you?"

Arabella flushed, but stood her ground.

"No, I imagine Cougar will be joining Rogue when they come busting in through the front entrance to rescue Shenandoah."

"What do you mean?" Arabella backed away from him.

"I sent Rogue a note telling him that he must come to the mother lode tonight if he wanted to see Shenandoah alive again. His price, of course, would be signing over his half of everything. Since he was at Cougar's Keep when the message was delivered, I imagine his old friend will be joining him, even though I told him to come alone."

Arabella's face paled. "It's a trick, then. Even if he signed—"

"Of course it's a trick. I have no choice but to kill Rogue, and whoever's with him."

Arabella quickly turned away.

"Rogue doesn't know about the back entrance. He'll come through the front, and when he does, the dynamite that's hidden there will be triggered. He'll be blown to bits, along with anyone who's with him."

"It'll soon be light," Spike said, opening another bottle of champagne as he took a hard look at Blackie. "Shouldn't they be here soon?"

"Any moment, I'd calculate."

Shenandoah turned pleading eyes on Arabella. Her sister looked desperate a moment, then suddenly pushed Spike aside, knocking him against a wall. She ran from the mother lode and rushed down the tunnel toward the entrance to warn Rogue and Cougar.

Spike pushed away from the wall and started after Arabella, fury contorting his features.

"Let her go. She's too late," Blackie said.

Spike reluctantly stopped, but continued to watch the tunnel entrance.

Shenandoah closed grateful eyes. It wasn't too late. Arabella would warn them. Her sister had not deserted her after all. Rogue and Cougar would be saved. She would be rescued.

Suddenly a loud explosion rocked the silver chamber, and dust and debris blew back into the mother lode. Shenandoah screamed, jerked forward, struggling to stand.

Blackie pushed her back down again, then said as the noise abated, "Nobody could have come out of that alive. Now we can really celebrate."

Shenandoah could not move for a moment. Not only Rogue and Cougar, but Arabella had been killed. Tears stung her eyes, sobs caught in her throat. All her family was dead. Even Rogue. In that moment she realized just how much she had loved Rogue. How foolish she had been to let pride stand between them. If he were there now, she would throw herself into his arms and never let him go, no matter what. But he was gone. It was too late. What more was there for her?

Then she lifted her head, green eyes bright with unshed tears. Revenge remained. These two men would not get away with what they had done. She would see her loved ones avenged.

Her thoughts were suddenly cut short by the sound of clinking glasses. She looked toward the sound. Blackie and Spike were saluting themselves with champagne. Then they turned greedy eyes on her. She shrank back from what she saw in their faces.

"Since you have lost your woman, Spike," Blackie said, "and since you have been such a big help to me, I'll share mine. I can afford to be generous."

"We're both rich now," Spike said, his eyes feasting on Shenandoah. "We can have all the women we want."

"Yes. Tomorrow I'll deposit money in a Silver City bank for you, but tonight we begin our celebration with this proud beauty before us. After such a victory, I feel a strong need to—"

"So do I," Spike agreed, advancing on Shenandoah.

A new horror was upon her. For the first time she realized what Arabella must have felt when the Braytons kidnapped her, then used her. These men would have no mercy. They were drunk on champagne and drunk on victory. She represented part of that victory, one that could be claimed immediately. "Stay back!" she commanded, determined to fight them.

"She's needed this for a long time," Spike said, reaching toward Shenandoah. "She needs to learn some respect."

Blackie glanced sidelong at Spike, then added, "I want her to drink to our victory first." Blackie held a glass to her lips, then forced her as before, more sparkling liquid running down her breasts than entering her mouth. But Blackie persisted. When he was satisfied, he let her go. "You'd better start trying to please. You couldn't be more helpless."

Spike leaned forward and ran a hand down the smooth bare skin exposed by the low décolletage of her gown, then squeezed one breast. "There's plenty for us both."

Blackie stroked her other breast, his dark eyes glowing with hunger.

Spike leaned forward and placed hot wet lips to Shenandoah's mouth.

She squirmed, trying to get away, feeling fear and hatred and anger wash over her. It would be easy to give in, accept defeat, but she couldn't. There were too many she must avenge. She kicked out at Blackie. He grabbed her legs, holding them down as he chuckled at her helplessness.

Suddenly a hard voice from the back entrance to the mine commanded, "Stop!"

Shenandoah recognized Rogue's voice. Stunned disbelief, then happiness rushed through her.

Blackie whirled around, going for his gun. He pumped several shots at the entrance, as Shenandoah threw herself against Spike, causing him to lose his balance. The sound of gunshots filled the mine. Suddenly a slug caught Blackie. He spun backward, blood spurting from his chest. He struck the floor hard, and his gun slid across the cavern.

As Spike pushed Shenandoah from him and fumbled for his gun, Rogue rushed into the room. One hard punch in the jaw and Spike collapsed unconscious to the ground. Rogue pulled the pistol from Spike's holster, shoved it into his Levi's, then turned to Shenandoah.

He quickly cut her loose, then pulled her gently against his chest.

"I thought you were dead," she said.

He looked down at her, strain showing in his face. "No. Blackie wasn't as smart as he thought. I knew about the back entrance. Cougar was supposed to come in through the front. Together we'd have gotten them. After the explosion I waited to see if Cougar came around to the back. He didn't."

"Arabella tried to warn you. She was caught in the explosion too."

"Damn! Shenandoah, I'm sorry. That's terrible. Fast Ed, and now Arabella. Even Cougar. None of this was worth their lives."

"There was no way you could have known Blackie's plans."

"I should have guessed."

"Don't blame yourself. We're lucky to be alive."

"Yes, but at what a price. You're safe? When I saw them on you, I went mad. If they've harmed you in any way, I'll—"

"No. I'm safe. If I'd been here with you where I should have been, maybe none of this would have happened."

"Blackie would have tried something else then." Rogue paused. "Did you say—?"

"I belong with you, Rogue. I don't care how you feel about me. Just let me stay with you. I'll—"

"Don't you know how I feel about you? I love you."

Stunned, Shenandoah stood speechless in his arms, her face turned up to his.

"And you're right. I shouldn't have left you alone in Silver City. I'm going to claim you right now. Will you marry me?"

"Rogue, I—"

"You don't have to love me. Just stay with me. I'll take good care of you from now on."

"Oh, Rogue. I do love you. I love you with all my heart. I—"

Rogue pulled her to him, his face filled with emotion, then gently kissed her, his lips warm and tender. When he lifted his head, he said, "I'm going to marry you so fast you won't know what happened."

"Tomorrow won't be too soon."

"Rogue," a voice called from the back entrance.

Rogue spun around, pushing Shenandoah behind him. He went for his gun.

Cougar Kane entered the mother lode, dirt clinging to his clothes.

"Cougar," Rogue exclaimed, dropping his hand from his Colt. "We thought—"

"I'm well. It's good to see you're the same. Your enemies are vanquished. That, too, is good."

"Cougar," Shenandoah said softly. "Arabella . . . She—"

"I'm here." Seeing it was safe, Arabella stepped

forward. She was dusty, her blond hair hung in a riotous mass to her hips, and her gown was torn. But she was safe.

Shenandoah joyfully pulled Arabella into her arms, then spun them around. Shenandoah ended up with her back to the rear entrance, facing her three friends. Then she set Arabella from her, looked her over, and said, "I can hardly believe it! I'm so glad to see you're all right!"

"What happened?" Rogue asked Cougar, who now stood beside him.

"I didn't trust Blackie. I threw a timber into the mine entrance to see what happened. It exploded. Arabella hadn't reached it yet. I heard her cry out, then dug her out of the rubble. She was unhurt. We had to walk around back. Couldn't use the front."

"Glad you made it, *amigo*."

"So am I," Shenandoah said, then stopped. The next words never reached her lips.

Spike Cameron had recovered from Rogue's punch and had crawled quietly to Blackie's fallen pistol. He was just raising it when Shenandoah saw him. All the others had their backs to Spike. There was no time to warn them. She had to act fast. She jerked her derringer from under her skirt. As Spike leveled his Colt, she took careful aim and shot him in the chest.

Surprise marred his face for a long moment; then he crumpled forward, blood spilling from his body.

Rogue and Cougar whirled, drawing their guns, but the danger was over. They turned back to Shenandoah.

It had taken only a second, but it had seemed like forever. She didn't think she would ever forget the shocked look in Spike's face. He hadn't known she was wearing a derringer. Uncle Ed was finally avenged. Blackie and Spike were both dead, but Shenandoah did not feel elated. She wished it all could have been different. She wanted her uncle to still be alive. Blackie and Spike had cost her too much for her to be able to rejoice at their deaths, but she was glad they could never hurt anyone else.

Then something seemed to break in her. Tears swam in her eyes. She did not hold them back. There was no more need to control her emotions. Tears began to roll down her cheeks. Her body shook with released tension. All that she had repressed for so long suddenly emerged. The weight of it overwhelmed her. She felt terribly alone and vulnerable for a moment; then Rogue took her in his arms.

She melted against him and listened to the soft, comforting words he whispered in her ear. She clung to him, feeling his strength and support surrounding her. She was no longer alone. She no longer had to suppress her emotions. She had someone to share her dreams and feelings and hopes. The weight of the past lifted from her. She raised her head, her green eyes filled with love and happiness. "Hold me closer, Rogue, and never let me go."

He tightened his embrace and whispered, "I'll love you forever."

After a long moment, he dried the tears on her face, then led her from the mother lode.

Arabella and Cougar followed, their arms entwined.

Outside, the sun was just rising in the east, casting long fingers of light over the countryside. The air was cool and clean. The couples turned their faces to the rising sun, feeling its warmth flow over them.

"Don't move," a voice rang out.

They stiffened.

"Don't touch those guns if you want the ladies to live."

Rogue and Cougar hesitated.

"Bella baby, take their guns, then bring them to me."

Arabella glanced around, a look of confusion and surprise darkening her eyes.

"Do as I say, quick!"

"T—Tad?" Her voice quivered.

"Glad you remember me, Bella honey," Tad Brayton said, rising from behind a rock, a rifle pointed at them.

"But, Tad, you're dead!"

"I don't look dead, do I? Took me a while to recover, but I did. Got a score to settle. Now, get their guns and get over here." He took several steps toward them, spurs jingling.

She hesitated. "Where have you been?"

"Right behind you. I was in Leadville. I was in Silver City. I've been watching you all along, Bella baby. Your sister too. But couldn't do anything till I had money. Knew something was brewing with your fancy man. Just waited around, robbing a few stagecoaches. Now I've got you, and Baby Doe, and the silver. My brothers would be right proud of me. Now, get the guns."

Arabella's hands were shaking as she pulled Rogue's gun from his holster. Then she turned to Cougar.

"You can't go with that man. He's the one who—"

"He was my first. I belong with him."

"Don't talk!" Tad commanded. "She knows she belongs to me. I don't care what she's told you. Bella's my woman. Baby Doe too. Take his gun, Bella."

Arabella took Cougar's gun, then started toward Tad Brayton, reluctance in every step. Halfway to him, she turned back, her eyes on Shenandoah. "I told you to leave me in Mexico. I belong with Tad. We're two of a kind."

"That's not true," Shenandoah said, desperate to stop her sister. "He's using you, just like he did from the first. Break free of him, Arabella. You can—"

"Shut up, Baby Doe! I'll deal with you later. Come on, Bella. Let's get this over with. We've got a lot of living ahead of us."

Arabella took several more steps toward Tad. When she was close, he smiled, then aimed at Cougar, his finger ready to squeeze the trigger.

"No, don't kill them!" she cried, suddenly realizing his intent. "Let them go."

"Are you crazy? Dirk there lost his life the minute he killed my brothers. That other one goes first. I didn't like his hands on you."

"No, please. I'll go with you."

" 'Course you'll go with me. We won't leave no trail and no witnesses."

Tad set his sight on Cougar. "Those men are dead."

"No! You can't shoot them. I won't let you," Arabella said, her voice suddenly calm. She dropped one of the pistols. The other she aimed at Tad, holding it with both hands.

He looked at her in surprise. "Whatever your game is, I don't like it. Drop the gun."

"No. I see it all now. My mind's clear. You wronged me, Tad. You made me hate myself. You tried to make me like you. But it didn't work."

"You're trying my patience, Bella. Drop the gun. You couldn't shoot me."

"You hurt me. You used me."

"You just got what you're made for. Now, shut up, drop that gun, and get out of my way. It'll just take a second. Those two'll be dead and we can go on our way."

Arabella's hands began to shake from the weight of the gun in her outstretched arms.

Tad glanced at her, chuckled, then fixed his sight back on Cougar. "You *couldn't* shoot anybody."

Arabella took a deep breath. As she exhaled, she said, "You're wrong. Dead wrong," and pulled the trigger. The recoil knocked her backward and she hit the ground hard.

Tad Brayton slowly crumpled, dead the moment the bullet went through his left eye.

Cougar rushed to Arabella's side, took the gun

from her clenched hands, and helped her to her feet. Shenandoah and Rogue hurried to her too, but she pushed them all away and walked to Tad Brayton.

She looked down at him and said, "He deserved to die. I'm glad I shot him." She looked back over her shoulder as if daring someone to refute her words. But they were silent, noticing the glittering tears in her eyes.

Cougar put an arm around her shoulders and began to lead her away. "I'll take you home now, *querida*. You were very brave. You saved our lives."

"I did what I had to do."

Shenandoah watched them walk away, then turned to Rogue. "You know, I always thought she was the weak one."

"She was strong. She had to be to endure all she did." Rogue picked up his Colt .45 and slipped it into his holster. He glanced at Tad's body. "She almost missed."

"I don't think she had ever fired a gun before."

"Lucky for us her first shot was a good one."

"Yes, we're very lucky."

Arabella and Cougar, mounted on horses, waved good-bye as they rode away.

Watching them, Shenandoah said, "I think maybe we should plan a double wedding."

"Looks like Cougar finally won his lady, or perhaps she won him."

Shenandoah smiled at Rogue. "Let's make the wedding all satin and silver."

"Whatever you want. Let's just make it soon."

ABOUT THE AUTHOR

Jane Archer was raised in Texas, but has lived and traveled throughout the United States. She has a B.A. in art and has worked as a graphic designer. For the past eight years she has been writing novels. She is an avid collector of Wonder Woman memorabilia, and currently lives in Dallas where she is at work on her next book.